THE JUDAS SPOON

MAIREAD ROBINSON

The Judas Spoon

KDP ISBN: 9781983306068

For Nuala Fagan

PROLOGUE

The Magpie

You've seen me. Gun-cocked head and bead eye looking down at you from a tree branch, a fence pole, a window ledge. I stink. My feathers entrap dust, skin flake, sand, biting mites and jumping fleas, smashed shellac of dried blood. I preen, peck with pincer beak to swallow or spit; spider's leg, beetle wing, the dross and froth of survival. I disgust you, but are you any different? Do you not crawl with secrets and lies and dark rememberings?

You know me. Sing-a-sing-song-song for me. One for sorrow, two for joy - nothing but a thief and vagabond, ol' Maggoty-pie. I chatterchatterchack and hop hop for your pleasure, wait till your back's turned and flashgrabbitquick, it's gone; the gilt wrapped sweet you pocketed home for your child. The wedding band unscrewed from a finger before your lover called round. The dull shine of an earring hooked on the pillowslip - you should thank me for that one, but no, damn magpie; you'd shoot me but I'm off in a clatter and green shine flap to my twig nest, lined with mud and grass and yolk and all the pretty things I've found; milk bottle lid and rivet, eyelet and tinsel bit, pen nib and silver chain link.

I've seen it all. I'm ancient as the stones standing silent on the hill above this raggle-tag gobbet of houses. I know each brick and chimneystack, each gutter and gable. It's me pecks at the ripening apples, me who shits on the fresh laundered sheets, me who raided the nesting box and broke the pretty chicks' necks – well, a bird's got to eat, right? Fright me off - there are places I can go. I know where the best pickings are.

There's an old man lives in the wood. He tries to scare me from his berry bushes with spoons. They hang from every branch, glittering pivots of light, tiny moons prickled in stars. I jab to hear them ring, stab at them like eyes, then feast on the berries; redcurrant and gooseberry, damson and sloe, 'til the old man dashes at me with a broomstick - *take that, Magpie!* And I'm up and off and away elsewhere. Lifting o'er the wood and down to where the thick of the village thins, to the farthest edge, to the house where our story begins.

Off the beaten track it is. Gated and overgrown. A dark garden, all bramble and nettle patch, all rhododendron tangle and long lost things. All safe for Maggoty-pie though, for she never comes out, the woman, not to the garden. I see her sometimes, staring from the window to watch the boy as he plays. I watch him too, the boy. He has hiding places in the undergrowth, a network of beaten paths, a tree house in the sycamore. I grub about for worms. Fish fish-heads from the bin. Flap to a window and peer through the pane.

I see them. The mother. The father. She murmurs soft bafflement. He casts words, which fall perfectly formed, cold as eggs.

Three for a girl and four for a boy - where's the boy? Let's begin with the boy. Another window, slatted across but I scritch scritch on the frame. Put an eye to a chink. See misty landscapes hanging in frames. Dustless ornaments in tall glass towers. I cling, flap for balance, dig a talon tip in the wood and hold steady, still, watch, for there the boy stands at the open door.

Neither too tall nor too short. Brown hair, badly cut, neatly combed. He has cloth grey eyes (his mother's) and a manner of furrowing his brow, which leaves no room for doubt as to his paternity. Just a boy, but there's a touch of the magpie in him for he's eyeing a certain something in the room, and the way he tilts his head, listening, tells he has no permission to enter and take it. Should he chance it? Five for silver, six for gold - what's he looking at?

A box.
Containing what?
Let's see

CHAPTER 1

Edward

The box sits on the uppermost shelf of three that straddle the wall above his father's desk. Elsewhere in the house, his mother maintains a certain order, but his father's study is an Aladdin's cave of intrigue. He could twist the key in one of those cabinets and hear it unlock with an oiled thunk to reveal nuggets of glittering rock. He likes the craggy strangeness of their names; aragonite, malachite, pyrites. Or he could tip out that jar of coins on the desk, watch them slither over each other in a mound, and examine the dates, the countries, the heads of dead kings, while his fingers absorb their cold, coppery taint.

This room fascinates him, always has, with its shelves crammed full of books and old catalogues. Not lined up in neat rows like the ones in the village library, but piled in untidy stacks with their corners jutting out. On the surface of the desk there are more books, one of them splayed face down like a drunk man he saw in the street once. There are other things too; an old fashioned telephone, a lamp, a rusting typewriter with its black and red ribbon wrenched out.

There's a chair tucked in under the desk with a raincoat draped over the back. The floor is bare wood and the edges of the boards curl up slightly in long, straight ripples. He looks again at the top shelf, and the box.

Prick up your ears, Edward. Miss Pilcher said that to him once, and he thought she meant to prick his ears with a fork the way his mother does with pastry, but he's older now and he knows what it means. He listens. From another part of the house he can hear the ebbing drift of voices; his father's, deep and low; his mother's, softly rustling, lifting and falling like a magpie in flight. Edward bends down and unlaces his new, stiff shoes. He takes them off and places them neatly by the door. Then he pulls his socks up. Pull your socks up, Edward. That's another thing Miss Pilcher often says. Lightly, he steps into the room. A board squeaks and he freezes with one grey socked foot in front of the other, listening. The murmur of voices continues as he breathes in the air smell of wax and polish. He lifts his back foot in an exaggerated arc, as though pedaling a bicycle, and places it tiptoe down. Hunching his shoulders, he creeps across the room. A strip of shadow from the closed blind falls over his eyes, masking them. He makes his way to the desk and pulls himself up, scraping his shins as he does so, but on standing up straight, his eyes are level with the box.

The sides are of a deeply polished walnut and the bevelled glass lid is frosted, making the contents seem as murky and distant as minnows on a river bed. Twelve spoons, all in a row, with a gap at the end for the missing thirteenth. 'Find that one and I've got myself a fortune,' his father once told him. They lie on a bed of soft purple cloth and each one is different, with handles carved into the shapes of little men. One holds a cup. Another, a key.

Apostle spoons, they're called. Hundreds of years old and very nearly a full set, though where the last one could be is anyone's guess. Family heirlooms, made for the christening of a forgotten ancestor. Edward's father showed them to him one night, turning them gently in his hands and naming the parts; the bowl of beaten silver, the elegant stele, the knop in the likeness of a saint; Peter, Andrew, Bartholomew, John. Each apostle is tinily capped with a nimbus that bears the initials - MH - painstakingly pricked out by hand.

But the spoons were sold off at different times. Pawned to redeem debts, bartered and swapped, or simply mislaid. Edward's father has collected them together again over years, starting with just three and travelling the breadth of the country in search of the others. He found them at auction houses or in private collections. One turned up in a kitchen drawer somewhere in Suffolk. A further two at a museum in Denmark.

But the final spoon, the Judas spoon, evades him still. Edward reaches out and edges the box towards himself.

He should place the box carefully on the desk before climbing down and opening it. But he doesn't. Instead, he awkwardly manoeuvres the box so that it balances, tray like, on one outstretched palm. He tries to lever the lid up with his thumb, but the lid's heavy and despite his clumsy effort to catch it, the box falls. It hits the edge of the desk in a shrill explosion of glass, then drops to the floor, splintering on impact and violently ejecting its contents. The spoons land with a tuneful silvery clatter. He stares at them, numb.

'What the hell have you done?' His father's voice booms furious and Edward can't look at him. He keeps his eyes fixed on the mangled mess of wood and glass and feels his face scorch. 'Of all the things, of all the things!' His father kneels, extracting the spoons from the shattered glass with a finger and thumb held like crab claws. His mother hovers in the doorway, a wilting rose of tissue paper hangs from her hand and her eyes look glassy and tired. I, attempts Edward, but Damn it, says his father as he slices his thumb on a piece of glass. He sucks at the wound, glaring at Edward before examining the cut. Glass needles cling to his trousers and glitter in the shafts of yellow light that slot through the blinds. Edward wants to say sorry, but the sorriness sticks his chest, flapping against his ribcage like a fish in a net. His face burns. His mother steps into the room and his father turns to look at her.

He looks at her for a long time.

And then, his father's arms fall loosely to his sides and his hand opens to release the spoons he has gathered. They drop to the floor with a metallic clang.

'I'm leaving,' says Edward's father quietly, and he lifts the raincoat from the back of the chair and walks past Edward's mother, out of the room.

A year later, and he still won't have come back.

CHAPTER 2

Skylark

The alarm jolts me awake with a high, sonic wail that seems to come direct from the centre of my head, making me cold and goose bumped. I wait a bit. Maybe it's only a drill. Everyone ignores drills, don't they? I've been stuck inside my office all morning, catching up on a stack of late paperwork and I swear I've only been asleep for five minutes, but my eyes are so jammed with gunk that it splinters as I open them, and this alarm is screaming, ripping through brain tissue. I stumble outside thinking some fresh air might stop me from throwing up in the wastepaper bin, and that's when I see the smoke.

The fire is in the canteen; I can see bright yellow flames illuminating the interior. 'Faulty fryer,' says Mick, the caretaker, as I join him on the driveway to watch the fire brigade swing into action. 'Nothing a damp dish towel couldn't have sorted out.' The kids clap and cheer from the safety of the tennis courts, while the kitchen staff huddle tearfully on the tarmac, hugging each other and dabbing at their eyes. Mick gives me a cigarette and cracks a joke about smoke inhalation as great clouds of the stuff bilge from the canteen windows. They spread out into gauzy sheets. Warm and bitter and reeking of scorched fat.

The fire crew won't let anyone back inside the main building for a while, so the students are herded off to the playing fields to mill about on the grass. The teaching staff stand loosely at the edges, chatting amongst themselves and squinting into the May sunshine, while groups of girls string daisies together and wind them around each other's necks. Brearley's in his element, of course, striding about with a megaphone, exhorting everyone to remain calm, but even he can't dispel the carnival atmosphere.

I hover on the fringe of a group of teachers for a while, but I feel too hot and listless to bother with small talk. The teachers view me as a bit of an oddity anyway. I only deal with the problem kids, those Brearley terms as 'our more intractable incumbents'; teenage girls, just fleshing into womanhood, arming themselves against the world with an arsenal of hard stares and thick applications of eyeliner. And the boys, all gangling limbs and erratic spurts of facial hair, muttering, 'I don't give a shit,' in newly gravelled voices. I chat to them about their worries, help them catch up on schoolwork, and talk them out of being the pains in the arses that most of the teaching staff think they are. On my office door there's a sign saying, 'Ms S Riley - Learning Mentor'. It's a job I often feel unqualified to do. 'Of course, you don't

14

really know what it's like to be in a classroom,' one of the French teachers said to me recently. She was combing me with her eyes, from my tangle of reddish hair to my thick soled leather boots. I'd gone to negotiate with her on behalf of a Year 10 girl who had told her to go fuck herself, as no one else ever would. The teacher was livid, but what she didn't know was that the kid had got into a fight with her alcoholic mother the night before, and had wandered the streets 'til dawn before coming to school as normal. She'd had nowhere else to go, and had slumped untidily at her desk rather than write a letter outlining her daily routine for an imaginary French pen pal. 'I'm quite within my rights to refuse to teach her,' the woman told me. Her eyes hardened as she spoke, reminding me of nails hammered into place. I was inclined to wonder if the girl hadn't been right. Would anyone fuck her? Had she ever been fucked? My thoughts, I confess, aren't always charitable.

Anyway, it's a hot day and my head feels like wet cake. I'm hung over from a three day binge on red wine and daytime TV, and from life dealing me yet another shitty hand. The sunshine's a palpable, weighty force, pressing on my skull and clutching at my eyeballs, so I slip from the playing fields and head back to my office. That's when I see him. The boy.

He's in the quad. It's the oldest part of the school, the only place you won't see any concrete or tubular steel. The stone built classrooms enclose a garden. It's really quite pretty, with a stretch of soft grass, and all sorts of flowering plants and shrubs. Some are just coming into bud, erupting into dark red knots, and the magnolia tree's in full bloom, with loose explosions of pink socketed onto each stick and twig. The boy's lying beneath it, flat on his back, with his arms outstretched.

There's something about it, the whole scene. It's like turning a corner and finding yourself inside a painting or something. One of those Victorian scenes, full of light and stillness, but with that slight uneasiness that comes from feeling you shouldn't be looking, as though you've stepped in on a private moment and need to back out of there. There's a breeze, and loose petals peel away to fall on him, brushing his face as they drift to the ground.

I'm supposed to act like a teacher when I see the school rules being broken, and students aren't allowed on the grass, so I call to him, 'Hey you,' and he lifts his head to look at me before propping himself up on his elbows. 'Come over here,' I say.

It's his clothes that strike me then, as he's carefully stepping between the flowerbeds. He's wearing the school uniform, but there's a neatness about it at odds with how the kids generally wear it. His shirt's very white, and tucked into a pair of long grey shorts that end at his knees. Shorts are allowed for the summer months, but I've never seen a kid wearing a pair before. His school tie is tightly knotted at the neck, bucking the current trend for big lazy knots that hang over the chest like some kind of cattle halter. He's wearing grey woollen socks and heavy leather shoes. I think of those black and white photos of evacuee children in the war, dwarfed by their over sized suitcases, luggage tags pinned to their lapels. He has something in his hand. Something shiny and small. 'What're you doing here?' I say, 'you're meant to be on the playing field.'

His face is blank. An unsurprised expression, like when you're staring into space and thinking about nothing in particular. I take it for surliness, something I see a lot of in my job, but my head hurts and I don't want to deal with it right now. He uses his fingers to brush hair away from his forehead and watches me patiently, waiting for what I might say next. It's fucking irritating. 'What's your name?' I ask, 'Who's your form tutor? Why aren't you with everyone else?' He answers in logical succession. 'Edward. I don't know my form tutor's name, but he has a beard. I don't know where everyone is.' He looks around, as though the everyone in question might jump out from behind the bushes. 'I'm new,' he says. That explains it. 'Well, go down to the playing fields,' I say, 'you should've gone with everyone else when the fire alarm went. Didn't you hear it?' That blank look again. A sudden emptying of expression, like a plate rinsed clean.

'I heard something,' he says, before pausing and looking beyond me at some spot in the air. 'There's a boy. My friend,' he falters, 'I mean, the boy who's supposed to be looking after me. I waited for him, but he didn't come, so,' he gestures, using the silvery object in his hand to indicate the quadrangle garden, the magnolia tree. Despite my headache, I'm curious. 'Is that a spoon?' I ask.

He looks at it before holding it out to me. 'It's St Bartholomew,' he says, 'I brought him for luck.' The sunlight flashes off its concave bowl as I take it from him. The tiny figure on the handle holds a knife. 'It represents his death,' Edward explains, 'he was flayed alive.'

'Flayed?' I say. It's funny to hear such an antique word in so young a mouth, but he thinks I'm asking what it means, so he tells me. 'Beaten,' he says, 'till his skin was hacked off.' The way he says it, with a troubled frown, chills me.

'Doesn't sound very lucky,' I say, handing the spoon back. 'C'mon, get off to the playing fields,' and I watch him walk away from me before I carry on towards my office. Odd kid, I'm thinking. The spoon had felt heavy in my hand, and I think about Xav turning up on my doorstep at the weekend, tall and slim hipped in the doorframe, dishevelled in his old biking jacket and with a flimsy half smile hovering about his mouth. His bike was propped on the kerb behind him, emitting tiny mechanical clicks as it cooled. I hadn't seen him in six months, so I let him in and made him coffee in the kitchen, keeping up a nervous babble of small talk as I scooped granules and sugar into a mug. He stood close to me and his shirt smelled of motor oil and open roads. When I hand him the mug he lifted the teaspoon from it and pressed the still hot metal bowl of it to my lips, to quieten me, before kissing them.

The sex was urgent at first. A mindless collision of limbs and flesh and need. Afterwards, when he wanted to talk, I chose not to listen. I've changed, he tried, I'm getting my life back on track. Phrases more worn than the tread on his bike tires. Just leave it, I'd said, and he didn't persist. It was the sex that mattered, that's all. He was like a tall glass of cool water, and I felt slaked. I didn't want to feel anything more than that. Strange though, how bodies have a way of remembering each other. How they align and realign into something at once familiar, yet new, like a rucked bed sheet smoothed back into place. By Sunday, I was admitting to myself that I liked having him around. I skipped work on Monday, ringing in sick before falling back against pillows that now bore his faint, petrol tang. I listened to his moving around sounds in the kitchen below; the opening and closing of cupboards to find bread, teabags, milk, and I must have drifted back to sleep because when I woke up it was midday and he'd gone. He had taken the bank card and money from my bag. He hadn't left a note.

I sit at my desk for a while, staring at the darkened computer screen and willing myself to switch it on. My shadowy face stares back at me from a frame of nebulous hair. The eyes are dark smears. With an hour of the school day left I could clear my email backlog and start working through the tilting pile of paperwork on my desk, but from outside, I hear the burble of students' voices as they're released from the playing fields back to the classrooms. The phone rings and I pick it up, regretting it immediately as it's the school receptionist asking if I can supervise a class this afternoon. I get asked to do that sometimes when one of the teachers goes home sick or whatever. In this case, the dizzying combination of the fire and an hour in the sunshine has struck one of the History teachers down with a migraine. At least history is something I know a few things about, so I say okay and head for the classroom.

When I get there the kids are arriving in excited gaggles, gabbling about the fire. It's a Year 7 class, all fresh faced and clear eyed, and I recognise the boy from earlier. He's trailing behind one of the other boys, who tells me, 'He's new Miss, he's shadowing me for the day.' This responsibility discharged, Edward's companion slouches to his seat, leaving his shadow standing awkwardly in the doorway, unsure of what to do.

'We meet again, Edward,' I say, and I direct him to a spare desk at the back of the room.

The students are too wired to settle to anything useful, so I tell an anecdote about the Great Fire of London. About Pepys burying his best cheese in the back garden before fleeing on one of the river boats that plied up and down the Thames. It's a scene I've always imagined taking place at night for some reason. Pepys in his silk frock coat, pushing his long wig out of his eyes as his softly slippered foot presses the lug of a spade into the turf. The cheeses are wrapped in cloth. The London sky crackles and flares behind him.

I ask the children what they'd save if their houses caught fire. People and pets aside, what object do they value enough to dash back through the flames and retrieve, though their skins blister and their soft lungs clog with soot? My phone, someone says (nods of agreement), a family photograph (more nodding, less vehement), my teddy bear (laughter). 'What about you, Edward?' He's been silent throughout the chatter, running a thumbnail down the laminate rim of his desk and looking around the walls at hand drawn sketches of Roman Villas and complicated family trees. 'What would you rescue?' The question throws him into thoughtful consideration. By the time he answers the eyes of the entire class are upon him and a susurrus of impatience is spreading through the room.

'I have some spoons,' he finally says, and the room erupts into laughter, 'Spoons? Who rescues spoons?' He lowers his head as scarlet washes up from beneath his shirt collar. I rescue him. 'Don't laugh,' I say, 'personal possessions make important historical artefacts, and we can learn more about how people lived from looking at their household items than we'll ever learn from remembering what battle happened where, or when.' But switching to teacher mode is losing them. A boy flicks a pen lid at another boy's head, a girl rummages noisily through her pencil case. My voice rises an octave, 'Your phones and teddy bears are a lot like the Romans' pottery and jewellery.'

Did Romans have phones, Miss?

My teddy bear got ripped up by our dog.

Did the Romans have spoons?

Adam's nicked my rubber, Miss.

I never, retard.

Adam, don't use language like that.

What? Retard? It's a proper word, Miss, it's in the dictionary.

What would you save Miss?

Fuck's in the dictionary too.

That's enough.

And bastard, my Dad showed me.

I won't have this language. It's inappropriate.

What would you save, Miss? What would you save from the fire?

Fucking retard bastard.

Adam!

He started it.

For fuck's sake, stop it!

I've lunged between the two boys, who have risen from their seats ready to launch into each other, and all eyes are on me now. From the back of the room, Edward watches, suddenly intrigued, and my outburst hangs in the air like a mosquito buzz in the thin silence. Teachers don't use words like that. 'I'm sorry,' I say, 'I shouldn't have said that.' Someone giggles, and the tension clatters apart. 'Naaah, don't worry about it, Miss,' says another voice and the lesson descends into noise again. 'What would you save from the fire, Miss?'

'I'd save your exercise books,' I say, and they groan.

I spend the rest of the lesson trying to dispel the rumours that've already sprung up about the fire. An arsonist torched the kitchen, they tell me, it was an ex-student seeking revenge for his recent expulsion. The chief dinner lady caught fire and ran shrieking from the kitchens with her hair ablaze. Brearley did it, for the insurance money.

When the final bell sounds, they rush out in a disorderly mass and Edward trails uncertainly in their wake, blinking as he steps outside. I tidy up the classroom a little, tucking chairs beneath tables and wiping the board clean before heading back to my office. I keep replaying the moment when I swore at a bunch of 11 year olds. Shit. If it gets back to Brearley, I'll probably be waving goodbye to my job.

The day's losing some of its heat and when I get to my office the quad's drowsy with bumblebees in a honeyed, liquid light. I glance at the magnolia tree and think of Edward as I first saw him, stretched out on his back, his face upturned, his eyes closed. I want to walk over the grass in bare feet and do the same, feel the quiet touch of petals on my eyelids and breath in their warm vanilla scent. Instead, I grab my bag from the office and walk to my car.

A History of Stonemoor
by Pauline Pilcher

On a bright April morning in 1972, conservationists working on an irrigation project near Stonemoor saw what appeared to be a human hand reaching out from a peat bog. Shaken by this most gothic of sights, they alerted the local police, who sprang into action immediately and sent a fleet of panda cars to the scene, only to find that the moorland track leading to the bog in question was impassable by car. Undaunted, the Chief Inspector requisitioned a tractor and led his team of brave bobbies to the potential scene of the area's first murder since that of a Mr James Frobisher, some 20 years earlier. (~~This unfortunate soul had been killed by a hot poker, administered sharply to the head by his wife when he complained about the ampleness of her posterior blocking the heat from the fire.~~)

Having exhumed the body from the bog, and subjecting it to a battery of tests, the Police were disappointed to discover that their murder victim's time of death appeared to be some 3000 years earlier. The body was handed over to the Royal Archeological Society and the police returned to their usual duties ~~of doling out parking fines and discovering the whereabouts of lost cats~~.

For the budding local historian, however, the discovery of Dartmoor Boy (as he came to be known, along with the more waggish soubriquet of Doug Upp) was an occasion of great fascination. The boy was estimated to be about 14 years old at the time of his death, ~~the same age as myself at the time,~~

and I eagerly observed his story
unfolding in the South Dartmoor
Gazette each day. As the
archeologists got to work, the
assumption that the boy had simply
tripped and fallen in the bog while
out hunting was quite undermined. He
had a wound to the cranium,
suggesting that his death had been
caused (like poor Mr Frobisher's) by
a sharp, heavy object. A puncture
wound to the stomach bag (still
filled with his final meal of
charred bread) showed he had almost
certainly been stabbed, but most
sinister of all was the length of
twine pulled taut about his neck, a
garrote! He was naked when found, a
statement that sent a small shiver
through my schoolgirl frame, except
for a strip of fox fur, which
covered his eyes.

The village became a Mecca of
sorts. While the Henge that
dominates the skyline of the village
has always attracted walkers and
history buffs, now this little
village became a magnet for all
manner of ghoulish daytrippers
interested parties. Archeologists
appeared first of all. Armed with
their trowels and complicated
looking equipment, they surveyed the
whole area, but found nothing of

further interest. The Henge, and the burial mounds that lie beyond it, had already been excavated years before and yielded no further secrets. Next came a party of druids, ~~middle-aged crackpots with a fondness for pointy hats~~, who held a fire lit ceremony by the light of the moon and chanted as the sun rose over the Henge. They cleared out once the weather turned bad, as did the Pagan Folk Festival crowd who set up tents near the stones and sang plaintive ballads about the murdered boy. The local shop did a roaring trade in metal detectors for a while, and anorak clad forms could be found at the site most days, generally finding nothing more exciting than old ring pulls left behind from the folk festival. An Historical Re-enactment society staged an entertaining battle one day; Celts versus Anglo Saxons. They showed up in full regalia, the Anglo Saxons in sackcloth cloaks and cross gartered leggings, shaking their spears at the woad painted Celts, who set up a convincing display of grimacing and howling. At a given signal they charged at each other, wailing and gnashing their teeth, only to meet and give a rather tame display of hand-to-hand combat, full *of rather limp sword thrusts and dainty taps on each others' heads with replica battle axes. After a great many melodramatic deaths, (some had even brought fake blood) and the odd verbal exchange along the lines of 'oops, sorry Geoffrey, didn't mean to hit you quite that firmly' they all sauntered to the village pub to engage in some good natured wassailing, before taking the train back to their usual lives as insurance clerks, dentists and librarians.*

With the discovery of a further bog body in Wiltshire about a year later, interest in Dartmoor Boy began to wane. For me though, a permanent resident of Stonemoor and possessed of an imagination which had been captured by the sad tale of the boy's demise, the events of that year sparked what has become a life long interest in the history of this seemingly modest and uninteresting village. Approaching my sixties, and having never known the joy of marriage and children, I have sunk myself into the study of other lives that shit! Shittshitshitshitshuiirt sdhgrtioh a giu aiueg

Pauline Pilcher's fingers flail at the typewriter keys for a little longer before she rips the sheet of paper from the feed roll, scrunches it into a ball and tosses it out through the open window to join others, which have blown up against the compost heap in a drift of origami snowballs. The type levers have jammed and in prising them loose, Pauline Pilcher's fingertips graze the inky letters. She rubs a finger along her upper lip to dismiss a small but irritating itch, and crushes the jumbled vowels and consonants into a black smudge. As the levers settle back into place she licks her lips, blackening her tongue with the foul tasting ink and indulging in a great deal of genteel spitting and wiping with the soft cloth usually reserved for cleaning her eye glasses. 'Shitty shit,' says Pauline Pilcher.

She slumps back in her chair and surveys the scene of her endeavours. The typewriter and the history books; she has read them all, fastidiously bookmarking relevant sections with torn strips of yellow post-it notes. They stick out from the pages like jaunty little flags. Inside, key information is highlighted with florescent marker pens bought especially for the purpose. Particularly useful sections glow pink. Less useable (but still interesting) areas bedazzle in a startling lime green. Pinned to the wall above the table is a large hand drawn map of the village, and a collection of aerial photographs in which the shadowy lines of old land boundaries have become as familiar as the frown lines of her own face. But what's the use?

29

The book has existed in her head for years, but has only begun evolving into words since the day Eleanor Parry informed her that her services as a private tutor were no longer required, and that Edward would shortly be attending school, just like a normal boy! Eleanor's Pinocchio eyes had gleamed as she said it. Take something, she said, take anything! Pauline took the typewriter.

Since then, each night, she has taken her books to bed and jots marginalia by the puddle of light cast from a clip-on reading lamp. Sometimes she nods off and dreams beneath her floral coverlet, of farthingales and ruffs, of fallow fields and famine. But months have passed and she hasn't yet got beyond the introduction. She hasn't yet managed to strike the academic yet accessible tone she craves and her attempts at cool, accurate description have slid down a mud bank of self-referential nostalgia, unsubstantiated anecdote and fatuous bigotry. Middle-aged crackpots with a fondness for pointy hats, she murmurs. When did she become so judgmental and intolerant? How did she become so cynical? At what point did she become so old?

She remembers the folk festival. Creeping from the shared bedroom that shook with her mother's snores, to steal through moonlight to the Henge. How strange and exciting it had been, to hear the murmuration of voices spangled with laughter, to see faces lit pale by firelight, while the stones' wavering shadows were cast outward in a dark coronet. Oh how she longed to be amongst them when a tall, skinny man with a drooping moustache lifted his guitar and plucked at its belly. The notes rose like birds, like bubbles, like shards of pure gold into the cool air.

Secretarial College, her mother said, a good job so as you can start paying your way. She was scrubbing the stone step outside the shop as she spoke, her rump thumping the air aside as her thick soaped brush bristled in a lather of grime. Pauline stood at the shop counter, leafing through the University brochure that had arrived in the post that morning. You're not bright enough for yoonifersity, her mother said, sitting back on her haunches to dip the brush into a bucket of silted water. Some of the girls at the festival had worn flowing kaftans, purple and turquoise and green, and they'd woven glass beads through their hair. They smoked slender cigarettes and spoke together in soft, musical voices. When one wandered into the shop to buy bread and coffee, Pauline had taken her money and dropped coins back into a palm that was as pale and smooth as the inside of a wrist. She remembers the herbal scent the girl left behind, how it meandered through the shop like a cat, curling around the pyramid display of corned beef tins, rubbing its soft head against the Fridgidaire, and nestling beneath the vegetable crates. Hussey, her mother muttered, slamming the till drawer shut.

Pauline Pilcher takes a fresh sheet of paper and inserts it into the feed roll. She watches her own hands as they twist the side knobs and hover over the keys. Thick fingers, spatulate at the tips. Bulbous, baggy skinned knuckles. Square nails severed straight across. Liver spots seeping through the skin like grease stains. Her mother's hands. She decides to make a cup of tea and some toast.

As the kettle boils, she imagines herself sitting before a long queue of shoppers at the Waterstones in Exeter; 'And to whom shall I dedicate this copy?' she asks, peering over her spectacles at an adoring fan. She cuts two slices of bread and puts them under the grill. Possibly, the book could become available in a special coffee table edition with glossy photographs and thick creamy pages. She closes her eyes and sees a hand gently and respectfully lifting a page (swish) and pausing before letting it drop (floop). She breathes in, searching for that intoxicating, slightly chemical smell, but finds instead the stench of charring toast. Shit! She yanks the grill pan out from under the flames and throws it into the sink, opens a window to release the smoke and disturbs a magpie who is grubbing through some peelings in the compost heap outside. He kerfuffles his feathers and skrarks at her, before dipping his head down to retrieve a fat white grub. Its stumps waggle helplessly as the bird crushes it in its beak.

Pauline gives her head a shake, a habit of hers, to make the fanciful clutter drop away. It makes sense to begin with the bog boy, she thinks. That's when it all began. The day his beseeching fingers curved from the dark innards of the bog, she fell for history and its mysteries, its secrets. It opened the portal to academic study in cloistered halls rather than a life spent tending the counter of a village grocery. She shudders at the thought of her father in his wheelchair, hacking the outer leaves from cauliflowers with a broad kitchen knife, while her mother emptied sacks of cheap flour into the scoop-your-own kegs down the side of the shop, coughing as soft clouds rose to powder her eyebrows and coat her hair. Her father grunted and scratched the groin left magically intact by that well-aimed grenade on Sword Beach. 'Make the girl do it,' he growled. Her mother dusted herself off, and snorted a nostril of floured residue into the balled handkerchief she kept up her sleeve. 'Girl's good for nothing,' she said, 'she'll spill it.' Pauline considers her conception from the loins of these two; fleetingly sees an expanse of dimpled buttock above a pair of reddened stumps, then shakes her head again, vigorously.

The boy, she thinks, but it's Edward who wanders unbidden to mind, standing beside her in the museum at Plymouth where the bog boy lay on a bed of earth. When was that? Not too long before his father walked out and everything came together for a while, before falling apart. The bog boy had been part of a temporary touring exhibition and together they had stared at the folded moon of his skull, the leathery curve of his body, his tucked in, foetal legs. 'See how the humic acid in the bog has preserved the skin so perfectly,' she said, turning to Edward to check he was making notes in the spiral bound notebook she'd given him. 'Edward? What's the matter?' He was resting his forehead against the glass case, his face level with the bog boy's closed eyes, and he was trembling. 'Edward?' she said. He was usually interested in their museum visits. Full of questions and curiosity and never squeamish, but now he was pale, and when she took his hand to lead him gently away it felt clammy.

Born with a silver spoon in his mouth, that one, her mother would have said. She remembers him as a five year old. A quiet boy even then, eyeing her from behind the door while his father looked through her credentials; her degree certificate, and the teaching reference from the private boarding school she'd worked at from the start of her teaching career until her retirement three years previously. You will find, in Miss Pilcher, a stalwart enthusiast for traditional teaching methods, the reference said. Her decision to take early retirement leaves the school bereft of a fine academician and a much loved and respected teacher. She'd spent so long formulating those phrases, she'd come to believe them. And it wasn't much of a lie. Surely a real reference would have said as much. Wouldn't it? Despite what had happened – the passionate letters she'd exchanged with one of her older students, the scandal when the girl's parents had found them, even though there'd been no harm done, none at all. 'Early retirement seems like the best option,' the headmistress said. Pauline's mouth goes dry as she remembers it.

Mr Parry seemed satisfied though. 'My wife and I are keen that Edward be educated to a higher standard than the local schools can offer,' he said, 'home tuition seems to be the way forward in that respect.' He was a handsome man, though a little short, with a short man's air of bullish confidence. He didn't look at Pauline as he spoke, but maintained his attention on the bogus reference. He worked with art and antiques, she knew, some kind of dealer, who spent much time away. In London, she supposed, or travelling the world in search of treasures, while Eleanor Parry was old money and had grown up in this house. The room they were in was low ceilinged and dimly lit, the original medieval wing, whereas the rest of the house, added during the Edwardian era, consisted of wide, lofty rooms with tall windows and elegantly faded furniture. 'My wife will discuss the day to day arrangements with you,' Parry continued. 'She's unwell at the moment.' He hesitated. 'She gets headaches. She'll telephone you, I'm sure. Come in here, Edward. Meet Miss Pilcher, your new tutor.'

The boy sidled into the room and stood beside his father, blinking up at her. She smiled, and he stepped back behind Parry's legs. 'I should explain to you, Miss Pilcher,' said Parry, 'that Edward isn't used to strangers.' He touched the boy's head, a little awkwardly she thought. Even then, there'd been something not quite right about the way Edward flinched away from his father's hand, though he allowed it to rest lightly on his shoulder instead. Parry coughed. 'You should also know that my wife, Edward's mother,' he said. Pauline nodded encouragingly. 'She doesn't go out,' he said. 'Rarely, anyway.'

'I see,' said Pauline. She didn't see.

'Agoraphobia,' said Parry.

'Ah,' said Pauline.

'It's a Greek word,' said Edward.

'Yes, it is,' agreed Pauline.

Edward smiled. She smiled back. A nice looking boy, she thought. Slightly built and solemn faced, with intelligently lit grey eyes.

'By the way,' said Parry. 'I've already checked your reference. I spoke to the principal himself last week.'

'Ah,' said Pauline, meeting his eyes for the first time. He held her gaze. 'It all seems in order,' he said, and he smiled from the corner of his mouth. She smiled back. Something not right about him. She knew it, even then.

Back to the book, back to the book, a shake of the head and back to the book. Her tea has gone cold and she sluices the cup and leaves it in the sink with the grill pan before returning to her study.

'Edward seems distracted,' Eleanor Parry said a few days after the museum visit. Pauline closes her eyes and tries to remember the exact timbre of her voice. Since leaving the Parry house with the typewriter in her arms, she has not seen Eleanor, and this sudden gift of recollection astonishes her. 'Edward seems distracted.' Was it accusatory? Or confiding? She evokes Eleanor. Sees her standing at the kitchen window, light flooding through and making a nimbus of her fine blonde hair. She was wearing something loose and diaphanous, and was fumbling with the beads around her neck.

Ackackack! Pauline starts at the magpie, which has alighted on her windowsill. Shoo, she cries, shoo. It retreats to the fence and unfurls one wing like a fan, a coquette picking fleas from an armpit. Pauline looks at the typewriter, then opens her desk drawer and retrieves the other object taken from the house that day. A silk scarf, purloined from a coat pocket while Eleanor Parry counted ten pound notes into an envelope. Severance pay. The scarf is a hazy blue and delicately scented. Pauline Pilcher buries her head in its folds. *Ackackack*, says the magpie.

Eleanor, says Pauline Pilcher.

CHAPTER 3

Skylark

My mother's balanced on a stepladder, stripping paper from the living room wall. She's decked out in a canary yellow boiler suit and a pair of marigold gloves. 'Mum, I don't need this right now,' I say, as I wade through the ankle deep twists of soggy paper accumulating on the floor. She's spraying water from a bottle with one hand and attacking the dampened patches with a stripping knife held in the other.

'Oh, but Skylark, you can't live with this.' She holds out a newly peeled scrap and lets it dangle in front of my nose. 'It's just so brown.'

'This is a rented house, Mum. Rented as in not mine. The landlord should do this sort of thing.'

'He won't mind,' Mum says calmly as she turns back to the wall, 'this place needs a good spruce up. He hasn't done anything in here since about 1972 by the looks of things.'

I flop onto the sofa, feeling sulky. 'I like 1972,' I say.

'Well, I can't stick it back on, can I?' says Mum.

I've had the cottage a couple of months now, ever since taking the job at the school. It stands in a row of weaver's terraces and is pretty basic. It has a tiny porch, which opens into a square living room. An open tread staircase runs up one wall to the bedroom and bathroom. Other than that there's a tiny kitchen, featuring a cooker, a fridge and a small, round dining table with mismatched chairs. The only heating comes from a rusting wood stove in the living room. I made the mistake of giving Mum a spare key in case mine ever gets lost and since then, she has turned up regularly to rearrange the furniture or look disparagingly into the kitchen cupboards. 'Look at the new wallpaper I've bought,' she says cheerfully, 'it's Laura Ashley.' She says Laura Ashley in the same tone of hushed reverence she uses when talking about George Clooney, or members of the Royal family. I glance cursorily at the paper carrier bag she has stowed under the staircase, from which the new wallpaper sticks out in thick creamy rolls. Some kind of blue green pattern, chosen to match the curtains I've already had no say in.

'You could help me,' Mum suggests, wheedling.

'I don't have another stripping knife,' I reply.

She sighs. A long, heavy, exaggerated sigh. 'You know, Skylark, I'm going to start on the other wall after this one. Couldn't you just move those boxes you've got stacked there?' She attacks the wall with renewed savagery, 'And, if you can't bear to sit there watching me destroy your life through the medium of home decoration, perhaps you could actually unpack them rather than living like some kind of,' she pauses, searching for just the right expression of derision. 'Hobo,' she decides.

'Hobo? Have you been reading Steinbeck again?'

'Just move the boxes.'

There are three in total. Cardboard crates containing the vestiges of my shared life with Xav. Books and CDs mainly, and a few pots and pans I didn't bother to unpack as I've mainly been living on Pot Noodles since moving in. I heave them into the kitchen, but carry the third one upstairs as I know it contains the clutter scraped from my dressing table in the Exeter flat.

While Mum sprays and scrapes in the living room, I tip the crate out onto my bed. Make-up and perfume bottles, some deodorant cans and a couple of framed photographs. Xav smiling woozily into the camera at some party, and an old faded picture of my father with three year old me perched on his shoulders. I'm grinning in the picture, clinging onto his hair while he winces in pain. It's not the best picture, but it's the only one I have of him. Mum burned the others. There's some jewellery too. Costume stuff mainly, and a tangle of necklaces, and a soft velvet bag drawn tight with string at the top. What would you save from the fire, Miss? Of course. I'd save this.

I loosen the drawstring and let the contents fall into my open palm. A plain silver cross. It's quite chunky and heavy, with a thin leather strip threaded through the top loop. I fasten it about my neck and glance in the mirror to admire it. I love its simplicity and the cool weight of it against my skin. I love the imperfections in it too - the slightly rough edges and the pitted surface, which traps tarnish and gives it a mottled look. It adds some character and charm, and that reminds me of the person who gave it to me for my fifteenth birthday, a decade ago now. My father. It'll piss Mum off to see me wearing it. I smile at her as I walk downstairs.

'I didn't think you still had that ugly old thing,' she says.

'What? A mother?'

'Put the kettle on, Skylark.'

She leaves eventually and I wave goodbye from the doorstep as she drives away through the evening. The sky's fading to pale lilac as the sun sinks behind the Henge, and the street is soft with shadows as I close the door and return inside. I found the cottage through a handwritten postcard in a shop window on the same day I was offered the job at the school. All it took was a phone call, and within an hour the landlord was there with the keys. A tiny, wizened man with white hair standing up from his head like a hedge. 'I am Peter Lempel. I used to live here myself, but I live outside the village now,' he told me in a slow, vowel heavy accent, one I couldn't quite place. 'I have a bigger garden there. These things,' he added, gesturing to a box left on a shelf, 'you can throw out. I don't need these things. You pay the rent on time, I leave you alone.' As contracts go, it was a hard offer to beat. Mum lent me money for the deposit. 'No room to swing a cat,' she sniffed when she helped me move in. 'No room for you to come and stay either,' I said. She didn't reply to that.

She was pleased about the job though, mainly because I'd been camping out at her place since the split with Xav. 'Oh Skylark, I'm sure you'll be wonderful at it, they'd be mad not to keep you on next year.' She spoke with too much enthusiasm to convince me she didn't think otherwise. Understandable I suppose. After all, I'd messed up my History degree, quickly becoming bored with the dusty exertions of military commanders and dead politicians. I skipped lectures and seminars, and I tired of the student scene too. Instead, I sought out the local pubs on the outskirts of town and found dingy basement bars fogged with cannabis reek and sweat. Beer came in cans and men wore elaborate tattoos. We swayed to the thump of ska punk and reggae, grinning, unable to hear a thought through the noise. Men came and went from my tiny student room. Quick, drunken couplings. They thought my quietness came from an inner mystique when really, I just had nothing to say.

After failing my second year, I used the last of my student loan to rent a grubby one-bed flat, and got a job in one of the late night dives I habitually frequented. That's when I met Xav again, an old school friend from way back. He showed up at the bar one night, drunk and looking to score some weed, and it was easy to fall in with him. Within a few weeks he'd moved into my basement flat and was dividing his time between getting stoned, and working on his motor bike, which for several months lay dismantled in our poky kitchen. He's a waste of space, Mum grumbled. But it was Xav who encouraged me to train as a counsellor, and it was Xav who listened to me whining about the workload and the other people on the course, and it was Xav who went out to get drunk one night and ended up in another woman's bed. He's half French, said my mother, what did you expect?

She disliked him, of course, seeing in him shades of my errant father, dead now. (He had it coming, is her darkly uttered verdict on that score). He died, my father, a few days after giving me the necklace.

He was murdered.

It's something I don't really talk about, especially not with my mother. It's easier that way. He and mum divorced when I was about four or five. I liked him though; he was always nice to me. His murderer was never found. I touch the silver cross at my throat.

The living room feels hollow and echoey with its stripped back walls. Mum has promised to return another day to do the papering, and has repaired the crumbling plaster with filler that runs like seams of quartz through the yellowing surface. I stuff the old paper into black bin bags and put them outside in the long, thin garden that runs from the back door to a cluster of gnarled fruit trees at the bottom. Weed infested vegetable beds run alongside a narrow path and there's a dilapidated shed, a windowless greenhouse, some rose bushes. I come back inside to unpack the boxes of books and CDs and arrange them in a low cupboard that stands beneath the mullioned window. I've never gotten around to throwing the landlord's stuff away and unpack that box too. There's an old biscuit tin inside, containing outdated invoices and a few photographs, and a bundle of hand written letters stuffed into a brown envelope. I consider taking one out and reading it, but it feels wrong to do that, so I close the tin and tuck it into the cupboard beneath the kitchen sink, resolving to return it to the landlord when he comes to collect the rent. It's cold, so I light a fire in the wood stove and go into the kitchen to heat a tin of soup in one of my newly released pans. As it bubbles, night clouds roll in from the moor, dark blue and umbrous against a fingernail moon.

Christ knows what I'm doing here. Stonemoor. An eclectic collection of quaint cottages, Victorian terraces, and newer brick-built houses. The whole place looks like it's been blown down the hill rather than built with any design in mind. It's named after the Bronze Age ring of stones that crown the moor to the West, a poor man's Stonehenge if you will, and local businesses do their best to trade on it. The corner shop sells Henge tea towels and Henge snow globes, and the village library, which doubles as a tea shop, sells framed photographs of the stones standing moodily against a backdrop of wild furze and purple heather, or dramatically silhouetted by the setting sun; the sky's charcoal streaks shot through with a deep blood red. It's not the sort of village people live in though. Not real people anyway. I mean, people live here, of course, but it's too off the beaten track to work as a commuter village for Exeter or Plymouth. Mum lives in one of the villages near Exeter, full of trendy artisan shops selling over priced furniture and quirky gifts. If you need a handcrafted stuffed owl to prop your door open, then Mum's village is the place to go. But if you want bleak, windswept moorland, and long evenings with absolutely nowhere to go and nothing to do, then Stonemoor could be for you. I thought, when I took the cottage, that I did want that. Now, I'm not so sure.

Henge School is on the outskirts of the village, but the kids bus in from every nook and cranny of the moor. Farm kids, many of them, but also the children of dentists and lawyers and accountants who crave a simple country life when they're not out earning wads of cash in the city centres. I was drafted in to work there when my male predecessor got a girl of 15 pregnant. Apparently, there was an ugly scene when the girl's father marched into morning assembly to punch the guy in the mouth. He was left on the floor, spluttering his front teeth out in a flood of bloodied drool, while the gathered students filmed him on their camera phones. He resigned, of course. 'It's a delicate subject, and one we're keen to move on from,' the head teacher, Brearley, said briskly at my interview. It was late in the school year and I was the only applicant for the job. I'd completed the first stage of the counseling course before leaving Xav, which was enough for Brearley at the time. 'Temporary for now, and we'll readvertise in the summer when we have a stronger field to choose from,' he told me, before hesitantly adding, 'you'll be welcome to reapply, of course.' I accepted the job. I needed the cash.

I take the bowl of soup back into the living room and pull the sofa nearer the stove, then sit and watch firelight dancing over the bare walls, painting them ochre, umber and gold. I fall asleep at some point and dream I'm in a giant cave, daubing prehistoric figures on the walls with fingers dipped in pigment. A group of people are huddled near the fire, sleeping beneath rough furs and stirring gently in their sleep. One figure is awake, and watches me at my work. When I turn around to face him he stares at me with pale blue eyes and the pigment on my fingertips drips a dark blood red.

I wake up then, starting, in the way you do when you dream of falling. The fire has gone out and the room's pitch black. I pick my way to the stairs and go to bed.

Peter

Stonemoor

Dear Anna,

Spring comes to the moor at last. Today, as I worked in the garden, the sun broke from behind a cloud and warmth touched my back with the tenderness of an old friend. I have dug over the vegetable patch and have already set potatoes out on a tray to chit. If I get them into the ground early enough, I may have two or even three crops this year. I'm planning onions, carrots, green beans and peas. The berry bushes and fruit trees are pruned back and should flower in the next month or two. I shall have jam to see me through the winter and still enough for a pie or a jelly now and then. Crab apples and cherries, Anna, and bright yellow plums by autumn. Such plenty.

I'm retired now, Anna. I sold the business some years ago to a young, hungry conglomerate, who aim to see only their shoes on every woman's foot, and their handbags hanging off every woman's arm. My little factory made shoes and bags, belts and schoolboys' satchels, and I was sorry to see it go but, ah Anna, what does an old man like me know about the whims of fashion? The factory was failing at the last, and selling it meant the workers could keep their jobs and enjoy a new production line of fashionable heels and fancy clutch purses. I was weary, Anna, so I came here, to this little village, where I have a cottage quite sufficient for my needs, and a garden to potter about in from morning till sunset. You would like it, I think. I'm a wealthy man, and have invested my money in houses, which I rent out to people here in the village. I keep their homes in good order, and my life is not complicated.

Every so often, I receive a catalogue from the factory - a mere gesture from its new owners - thin pages adorned with beautiful women in their stylish shoes. One arrived this morning, and as I gazed at a slim, elegant girl in heels and evening gown, I remembered an afternoon from our childhood. I was studying in my room, as usual, and you burst in through the door, in a long flowing dress from our mother's wardrobe. You tottered on her heels and you'd looped her beads about your neck, and how you laughed at my astonished face. 'Dance with me, Peter,' you cried, 'don't be dull.' And that's how our parents found us on their return from wherever they'd been, dancing in the living room to one of our father's gramophone records, you berating my stumbling feet and clumsy turns. 'Shall we show them how it's done?' our father said, taking our mother's hand. We watched them twirl about the floor, incredulous at their effortless grace. Ah, Anna. Is it wrong to remember such times? For so long, I have chosen to forget.

I live quiet days; tending my garden, reading my books, walking through the wood which crowds the valley bottom, and taking pleasure in the rise of a hill that leads from there to an old stone circle, the Henge, they call it here. You'd call me a dull fool again, I think, but you'd like it up there, amongst those stone monoliths. Some rise twice as high as the tallest man. Such ancient magnitude; they seem to mock the fickle proliferation of houses that make up the village below. Beyond them, lie the wide purple spaces of open moorland and standing on the hill, with the evening sun at my back, I like to watch my own shadow stretching ahead of me. I imagine myself a standing stone. Like them, I am grey and slightly stooped. My bones are succumbing to the weary fragmentation of age, but I'm comforted by those mottled giants. Like me, they're chipped and worn and pitted by time. Witness to so much, yet remembrancers of nothing.

But memories have a way of creeping in. Broken memories. Shards of times past.

Walking out into the garden, one day last year, my face brushed against a cobweb that some industrious arachnid had seen fit to weave over the span of the back door, and I was startled at the unexpected softness of it. Not from any fear of spiders, but because it recalled a moment, long ago, when a curl of damp hair brushed my cheek. Quick as a spider, it was gone, and the flimsy web gone too, as though it were never there. But here was I, caught in it just the same, and beating my frantic wings to be free.

The warp and weft of a web, so like memory, don't you agree? Bound together with such intricacy. Such terrible beauty. And as much a destroyer, as it is easily destroyed. That something so perfectly engineered, so deadly, can be torn into ephemera by the touch of human skin. These were my thoughts, anyway, as I took some tools from the shed. My intention, that morning, was to turn the compost I have rotting down in a far corner of the plot, and there it happened again, as I dug in my fork to break up the clumps. The scent of it, like something at once animal and human, and for the slimmest thread of time I was there again, in that darkness, where my only comfort was, well, I won't say it. As I told you, I have chosen to forget.

But today. The girl in the catalogue, and the sunshine, and the promise of spring remembered you to me. Not as we were at the end, but as we were before, and my darling Anna, I found myself weeping for the first time in years.

My dearest, how I wish you could see the garden.

Love as always,

Your brother,

Peter

CHAPTER 4

Skylark

My phone's already ringing when I arrive at work, with that shrill, hysterical top note some phones have. I hate the insistence of phones - that sense of the imperative built into their ringtones. I pick it up, and it's Brearley's secretary asking me to report to his office as soon as I can.

Strange. What could he want?

As a rule, I'm beneath his notice, but I grab my notebook and a pen and set off for the main building. The kids are just arriving for the day and a girl from the History lesson I covered grins at me and waves. Then I remember. I swore in front of the class, and now Brearley wants to see me. Shit.

His office is an expanse of soft carpeted orderliness on the top floor of the main building. Brearley's standing by the large plate glass window from which he can survey the whole school site, and he's talking on the phone. I've been waved to a large leatherette chair and am waiting for him to put down the phone. His words are clipped and precise, snipping like scissors.

He's facing away from me, and I study his back. Ramrod straight, and clad in a well fitting suit of dark cloth. He's an ex-military man. An officer. Decorated twice for conspicuous bravery in the Falklands, before turning to education and rapidly rising through the ranks to head teacher. He believes in hard work and decency, and approves of those students who display a firm commitment to running around on a rugby pitch, preferably in the rain. Most of the kids I work with think he's a dick head.

I push myself more upright in the chair, but end up slumping further down the shiny upholstery. For the first time, I notice the clothes I hurriedly dressed in this morning after sleeping too late. There's a five rung ladder in the knee of my tights and my boots are scuffed and mud encrusted from a walk I took up to the Henge last week. My skirt's too short, and there's a faint wine stain on my tie dyed shirt, though it's hopefully not too noticeable against the grape purple swirl of the pattern. I slip a little further down the expanse of chair. Who am I trying to kid? I know why I'm here. In a moment, Brearley will end his phone call, sit down at his desk and, calmly and professionally, tell me I'm fired.

I look around the room. At the neat shelves of box files, at the clean line furniture, at the desk in-tray containing just a few type written documents, and a plain manilla folder. Brearley's life is orderly and efficient. His days are neatly segmented into hourly slots, regulated by precisely timed bells and governed by clear rules and expectations, which don't include some unwashed hippy coming in and using the word fuck in front of his students. I run a hand through my hair, and my ring gets tangled in a knot. I'm trying to free it when Brearley hooks the phone in its cradle and looks at me. 'Skylark,' he says, then hesitates as I sharply yank my hand down and wrench a few hairs from my head, making my eyes water, 'Sorry to keep you waiting,' he says.

Get on with it then. 'That's okay,' I murmur.

He sits at his desk, leaning forward slightly with his hands loosely clasped, and smiles at me. A ray of sunlight from the window winks off his gold cufflink and sends a laser beam ray of it into my right eye. 'So,' he says, 'how are things going?'

'Fine,' I say, squirming in the shiny seat. What is this? He seems almost friendly. 'You've been with us a while now,' he says, and he pulls a sheet of paper from his in-tray and picks up a ballpoint pen. The paper looks like a questionnaire, with a series of statements and little square tick boxes beside each one, and as Brearley's thumb clicks the top of the pen, I click too. 'Interim employment review,' he says, 'just a formality.' I'm not here to be sacked. Relief gushes through me and loosens my tongue. 'OH,' I say, and I'm reeling off the things I've been doing; meeting kids for anti-bullying workshops, setting up peer friendship groups and an after school homework club, finding work placements for a couple of Year 11s. Brearley's eyes are developing a dull sheen. 'I've been talking to parents, I say, 'and talking to teachers.' The manicured nails of his left hand are quietly drumming the desk. My own nails are chewed to the quick. I stop talking, and he smiles again with neat, white teeth, and runs down the review checklist, ticking each box.

'Well, that all sounds splendid,' he says, spinning the document around and handing me the pen, 'sign in the box and you're done.' His signature is already there in big, flourishing letters. I squash my own in beneath it, cramped and illegible. 'Before you go,' he says, 'there's one more thing.' He lifts the manilla folder from his in-tray and places it in front of me. 'New boy for your caseload,' he says. 'He's been home schooled until now and seems to be having trouble fitting in.' There's a passport style photograph clipped to the folder, along with a name, Edward Parry, and I recognise him at once. Staring into the camera with blank grey eyes, his dark hair neatly combed to one side. 'Being a bit awkward in lessons, apparently,' says Brearley, 'asking questions and such, bit of an irritant.' I can't help but raise my eyebrows at that, isn't asking questions what kids are supposed to do? But Brearley doesn't read my eyebrows. 'Not quite Henge,' he says. Henge, presumably, meaning kids who answer questions, rather than ask them.

'I've already met him,' I say.

'You have?' That's quick work, well done. You'll know what I mean then,' and he taps the folder with his pen, 'it's all in there,' he says, 'read it at your leisure.'

I don't look at the folder straight away, because when I get back to my office one of my more familiar clients is there, waiting for me. 'Hello Kayleigh,' I say, and she glares at me from beneath thick, pink eyelids. 'Got kicked outta Maths,' is all she says.

Strictly speaking, I'm not supposed to deal with discipline issues. My main job is to support students; helping them cope with their workload, or teaching them basic social skills so they can better handle the school environment. But a lot of my time gets taken up with kids like Kayleigh, who see me as a sort of retreat when they're thrown out of class. Rather than go where they've been sent, to be disciplined, they turn up at my office door in the hope I'll be free to listen to them rant about the injustice of it all, about how Miss so-and-so is a bitch, or Mr so-and-so is a wanker. In theory, I can send them away, but sometimes it's easier to just let them get their frustrations out and calm down a bit. Then I talk to them about the teacher's point of view, and how he or she doesn't necessarily know about the student's break up with boyfriend/parents' divorce/fall out with best friend, and really just wants them to understand photosynthesis or whatever. So, I listen to Kayleigh, and then meet with some of my regular appointments; a semi-literate Year 11 boy, who brings me his coursework so I can correct the spelling and punch full stops in the right places; a Year 8 boy who struggles to concentrate in lessons and is therefore always in trouble; and Melissa, who has missed two months of school because of some mysterious illness and has just recently returned. I meet with her twice a week and talk her through the work she needs to catch up on. She's monosyllabic, and listens in silence, occasionally glancing at me with unconcealed dislike, but then she gets on with whatever she has to do and leaves me with a precious hour to catch up on paperwork.

It's near the end of the day when I pick up Edward's folder. Unusually, for a child on my caseload, it's very thin. The other kids tend to have files bulging with documentation; test data, school reports, detention slips, copies of letters home, that sort of thing. To tell the truth, I rarely read half the stuff I receive. I prefer to meet the child and draw my own conclusions about them, but Edward's file contains only one typed sheet. It details his date of birth, and his address, but no telephone number. A few lines sum up his background. He lives with his mother and has been home tutored since the age of five, by a local woman called Pauline Pilcher. He has been enrolled at the school because Miss Pilcher is no longer employed to teach him, though there's no explanation as to why not. He has no known learning disabilities or medical problems. That's it. I write a post-it note to myself, reminding me to meet with him tomorrow, and stick it on my computer screen. Then I pick up my empty coffee mug and set off towards the staffroom to refill it.

There's an art class going on outside. Kids are dotted around the space between the quad and the main building with sketchpads on their knees. I spot Edward sitting on a plastic chair facing the smoke damaged canteen. It has been cordoned off with traffic cones and yards of yellow tape. The school caretakers have been landed with the job of cleaning it up before the building contractors arrive, and they're standing beside the entrance, surveying it with much chin scratching and shaking of heads. I veer towards Edward and pause behind him, but he's so lost in concentration that he doesn't notice me. I'd assumed he was sketching the blackened building, but the sketchpad is covered in portraits of the two caretakers. He has captured them perfectly, their jowled cheeks and clenched brows so skillfully delineated that I stifle a laugh. His hand moves over the page in quick, confident strokes, pausing only when his eyes flick up to watch them for a few moments, before setting them down again. I cough, and he stops drawing and looks back over his shoulder at me. I nod at the page. 'Very good,' I say. He studies his own work for a moment.

'They have interesting faces,' he says, before continuing to sketch.

Colin Ford, the art teacher, is standing in the kitchen area of the staffroom eating a packet of chocolate digestives. 'Caricatures?' he says, when I mention Edward's sketches, 'Why the bloody hell is he drawing those? He's supposed to be drawing a view.' He's a tall, sandy haired man with a long, thin nose and large, protuberant eyes. He bites into a biscuit and his jaw moves up and down. He reminds me of a camel. 'Mind you,' he says, 'that boy's not really the full shilling.'

'Do you think so?' I say, 'Why d'you say that?'

He offers me a biscuit. 'Well, the work they're doing, it's about perspective. I told the kids to bring in a picture of a view, a landscape of some sort, cut from a magazine or off the internet. Easy enough, but what does Edward bring?'

I shrug. What does Edward bring?

'Guernica,' he says, as though that explains all.

'Guernica as in Picasso?'

'Yup.' Biscuit crumbs fly from his mouth on the plosive. 'Great painting, of course, but hardly a landscape.'

I try to configure Guernica in my mind, come up with broken limbs, sightless eyes. 'It's a landscape of sorts,' I try.

Colin twists the digestive packet closed and takes a slurp from his coffee mug. 'You could argue that,' he agrees, 'but that's not the point of the lesson. The point of the lesson is to look at how perspective exists in a landscape picture, and then apply that by choosing a view and sketching it. Not dick about drawing cartoons.'

'They're very good cartoons though,' I say.

He smiles. The weary smile of the teacher who can't be bothered to explain what I clearly don't understand about art, or about teaching, or about teaching art. 'Thing is,' he says, 'the boy doesn't follow simple instructions. And he comes across as a bit, y'know,' he taps a forefinger on the side of his head, 'abnormal.'

I fill the kettle at the sink. He hadn't struck me as abnormal exactly. A little odd, maybe, but Colin hasn't finished. 'He knows what landscape means, all right,' he continues. 'He reeled off the names of half a dozen artists he's familiar with, and even told me his father owns an original landscape by Gainsborough.' He laughs.

'What's funny about that?'

'Oh c'mon Skylark. An original Gainsborough? That'd be worth thousands, if not more, even you should know that.'

'Yes, even I should know that,' I say flatly, and give him what I hope is a piercing look. He has the decency to look sheepish, and grins. 'What I'm saying is, a man who's got a Gainsborough on his living room wall doesn't send his kid to a comprehensive school.'

'No, I suppose not,' I say, but Colin's already heading for the door. 'Best get back to the rabble,' he says. I flick the on switch on the kettle and wait for it to boil. Edward's file hadn't mentioned a father. But home schooling with a private tutor probably doesn't come cheap. Divorce? I speculate. Dad's run off with another woman and taken all the cash? And suddenly, as the water begins to fizz and churn in the kettle, Xav's in my head again. Does he know how angry and hurt I am? Does he even care?

I arrange my first appointment with Edward the following day, but I'm late and he's already in my office when I get there, standing at the far side of the room with his forehead pressed against the window glass. It's something I do myself at the end of a difficult day. 'Hello Edward,' I say, 'sit down.'

The weather has turned cold, and he's buttoned into a navy blue duffle coat that's way too big for him. He still wears shorts beneath it though, and one of his grey socks has fallen down. It slumps baggily around his ankle, which is milk white and bony and strangely touching. When he sits down the duffle coat rucks up around his neck and over his chin. He peers out of it like a turtle.

'I'm Miss Riley,' I say, 'but some students call me Skylark, because I'm not a teacher.' I always begin with that when I first meet a student. It disarms them a little. Creates a tiny chink in their armour, but Edward interrupts before I give him the spiel about what I do.

'I know,' he replies, 'I looked you up on the school website.' And he repeats the bio about me from the webpage; 'Miss Riley provides support and advice to students who, for various reasons, have difficulty engaging with the curriculum.' He says it in the bright voice of a radio announcer, and it's me who's disarmed. We regard each other silently for a moment. I can't read him. Was that sarcasm? Or an honest attempt at humour?

'Right,' I say, 'well, okay. You've been here just over a week. How are you settling in?'

His shoulders shift beneath his coat. I wait. 'It can be boring. School,' he says, eventually.

'Sorry to hear that, I say. 'In what way is it boring?'

The shoulders shift again, and he fidgets with the overlong sleeve of his coat.

'It's just,' he says, 'it's just, when I started here I was excited. I thought there'd be more to learn, more to know.'

'And isn't there?'

'I know everything already,' he says, 'and when I ask about other things the teachers get annoyed.'

I give my best psychiatrist's nod. 'So what you mean is, you don't feel challenged?'

He shrugs.

'So, if I said to your teachers, Edward needs to be challenged?'

'I don't think they can.' He looks at me levelly. 'Like the other day, when you told that story about Samuel Pepys escaping from the fire of London.'

'Yes?'

'You were wrong. Pepys didn't dig a hole, another man did that to bury his wine and Pepys just put his things in the same hole.'

'Oh, well,' I start, but he hasn't finished.

'And he didn't escape from the fire on a boat. He didn't escape at all. He stayed put, and the fire never reached him.'

He folds his arms and leans back on his chair, disappearing further inside his coat as he does so. 'Ah, well, the thing is Edward, that story was just off the cuff, I mean, I'm not a History teacher, and I didn't research it beforehand or anything. It was just because we'd had a fire and,' I trail off. 'I mean…it's a good story.'

'But history,' he says, leaning forward in his chair and emerging from his coat, 'is about learning the truth, isn't it?'

He regards me earnestly, with those solemn grey eyes that look too old to be in his young face. I can see how other teachers find him irritating, though. I change the subject.

I ask him if he's made any friends. 'No, no one seems to like me,' he says. Why does he think that might be? 'They think I'm weird,' he replies, 'and I'm not used to being around kids.' He says kids like he isn't one. Wouldn't he like to make a friend? Someone to hang out with and chat to? 'I suppose so,' he says. He looks out of the window and is silent for a moment. 'I wanted to make friends,' he says quietly. 'When I first came here, I thought it'd be easy and that I'd make some friends and be able to invite them round for tea and things.' He looks extremely, pathetically, sad, and I instinctively reach out a hand to touch him, but he flinches away.

'Making friends can take time, Edward.'

He doesn't reply.

'What about other friends?' I say. 'Old friends who don't come to this school. Family friends, or relatives, you've still got those.'

He continues to stare outside, but for a moment I see a struggle in his face. A slight buckling of the chin as he presses his lips together, and then, a blankness. Like in the quad that day, a slackening of the features and an emptying of the eyes. 'No,' he says casually, almost brightly, 'I don't have any of those.' He's like one of those fast motion films of clouds rolling across the sky, emotions shifting and unfurling and shrinking to nothing. I'm not sure what to say to him.

'Well,' I say, fidgeting with a stapler on my desk and tidying some papers, 'I'm sure you'll make some friends eventually. Have you thought about joining a club perhaps? One of the after school clubs? Do you like sports?'

'Not really,' he says, 'why do you wear all those bracelets?'

I look at my wrist, on which I wear a variety of silver bangles and bracelets. I have a habit of fiddling with them when I'm nervous, and I've collected them over years. I tell him this while stretching my arm out over the desk so he can look at them more closely. 'I collect things too,' he says mildly. I'm about to ask him what things, but he suddenly says, 'where did you get that?' and he stands up, tipping his chair over behind him.

He's staring at my necklace, the silver cross I put on to annoy my mother and which I haven't bothered to remove. It'd been covered by my shirt, but on leaning forward to show off the bracelets, it's swung loose. 'What? This?' I say, holding it up, foolishly conscious that I must look like Peter Cushing warding off Christopher Lee. Edward's staring at it intently, that empty expression replaced by one of pure wonder. This kid really likes jewellery, I'm thinking. 'Would you like to look at it?' I ask, unclasping the fastener and holding the crucifix out to him. It dangles from my hand, catching light from the window and reflecting a glimmering pool back onto the desk. He reaches out, pausing, as though about to grasp a nettle, but then he takes it and gazes at it in his palm. His eyes flicker over every part of it, turning it this way and that and he runs his fingers over the rough edges. Then, he puts it in his mouth.

'Hey!'

'He looks up, startled, the cross held between his teeth. 'Sorry,' he says, letting it fall back into his hand. 'It's just that, I know this necklace. I've seen it before.'

I take the cross from him and wipe it with a tissue from the box on my desk. Perhaps Colin Ford was right about this kid. Abnormal. 'You mean you've seen a necklace like it,' I say.

'No,' he says. He watches as I clasp the necklace back in place around my neck. What he says next comes in a whisper, as though speaking to himself. 'That's the one. The one that was mine, before it all happened.'

'All what happened?'

He looks at me then, steadily, the same look as when he'd put me right about Samuel Pepys, but denser somehow, more direct and challenging. When he speaks, it's calmly and slowly, as though each word is a playing card in a fragile pyramid, to be placed with infinite precision.

'Before I died,' he says. 'That necklace was mine. Before I died.' He stoops to pick up the fallen chair, and sits back down on it, his face again sinking into the folds of his ridiculous coat. 'I used to be dead,' he explains, 'and then I was reincarnated.'

Edward

He keeps his feet square on the slabs. Running, he mustn't hit the cracks. Sometimes, he forgets himself and when he looks down, there's his foot on a crack, and then the only way to keep going is cracks all the way home, or he'll jinx it. If he jinxes it, he cups his thumb in the spoon bowl in his pocket, and counts to ten. Cracks in slabs don't count, just cracks between slabs. If he sees a black cat it cancels the slabs out, and the cracks. Black cats are lucky, except on ships. Leave new shoes on the floor and never spill salt. If he sees a magpie, he says aye aye captain and salutes. Two magpies together don't jinx, but one alone'll pinch your luck to line its nest.

Things have changed.

The first thing that happened was his mother going to bed. She said, 'I'm going to lie down, Edward.' He was sweeping up the mess of broken glass in the study and checking the spoons weren't damaged, and he mumbled, 'okay' and off she went upstairs, and she didn't come down again for five days.

He didn't know then, that his father leaving was his father leaving. For good. He didn't know that until he found red bills stuffed in the kitchen bin and thought, 'uh oh,' and his mother explained about the money and how they'd be tightening their belts from now on. 'Your father dealt with all that,' she said, and Edward said,

'Dealt? That's past tense,' and she said, 'Yes, he's past tense too.' Edward wondered if he was dead. 'No,' she said, 'but he may as well be.'

That was later though, long after she'd come downstairs again. He's reached the main road and slows himself before stopping altogether. After she came downstairs, but before Miss Pilcher left. He squints his eyes, pinpointing the moment. There's a low brick wall running beside the pavement and he steps up onto it and walks its length, one foot in front of the other, as though on a tightrope. When he reaches the end, he jumps flat onto the pavement before continuing towards the village. Miss Pilcher doesn't come anymore. His mother let her go, and that's why Edward attends Henge School now. He wishes she hadn't been let go. Letting her go makes him think of an astronaut floating away through space, getting smaller and smaller and smaller until there's just a speck. Edward would like to float in space.

Miss Pilcher wasn't there when his mother went to lie down. She'd gone away on a week's walking holiday, and that first day, Edward passed the time by making a model of the Hubble Space Telescope, using toilet rolls and margarine tub lids covered in tinfoil. But there was no one to show it to, so he went into his mother's room to show her.

It was dark in there, and the smell reminded Edward of clothes left damp for too long. He stood beside the bed and coughed, but she didn't move, so he went to the window and drew the curtains back a little. In the dim light his mother's face looked grey and one of her arms was flung out to the side. He reached out to touch her, but stopped himself. She looked cold, and his heart jittered in his chest. Then she moved. Just slightly. She turned her head on the pillow and Edward asked, 'Are you getting up today?' in a voice that came out whispery and thin. Her eyes opened, just for a moment, but she didn't look at him. 'Not today,' she said. Her voice sounded foggy. He waited a little longer, watching her, waiting in case she said something else. But she didn't.

He worked on the telescope for the rest of the day; dismantling it, and putting it back together with moving parts made from drinking straws and paper clips. He cooked himself a baked potato with cheese, and did some sketching for a while. You have natural ability, Miss Pilcher once told him. Edward took his sketchpad into his mother's room and drew a picture of her sleeping face. He spent some time staring at her eyelids to see if there was movement beneath them, a sign she might be dreaming, but they remained still. When it got dark, he carried a pillow and quilt from his own room to her room, and made a bed on the floor.

That night, huddled at the foot of his mother's bed, he had the dream again. Always the same one. He's walking between some low buildings, and people are standing at the entrances and staring at something. He's looking up at their faces, and then he feels something cold on his mouth, and he's being crushed, and the ground falls away, and everything goes black. He didn't understand the dream until Miss Pilcher took him to see the bog boy, and then it all made sense.

It's not a dream. It's a memory.

Edward knows that he's the bog boy.

He knows he was murdered.

Seeing the dead body in its museum case made him remember. Not just the bits from the dream, but the bits in between the dream. The solid undreamlike stuff. Like the smell, and the weird language the people were speaking, and the tangy, metal taste. And the man's face. He can recall the face of the man who took him to be killed. Though he saw him for just a second before the blackness came, it's clear in his head, clearer than anything else. The man's face, and a feeling of terror. In the museum, Edward remembered the terror. A feeling like that stays with you. For centuries.

He has reached the outer fringe of the village, and the road branches here. The upper limb winds through the village itself, past rows of cottages and clusters of red brick houses and bungalows. Miss Pilcher lives in one, but he doesn't know which one. She always tutored him in his own house. The lower road leads to the woods below the village, petering out into little more than a track that loops between trees and alongside a stream, before rising again to join the main road leading out from the village and toward his own house. This is the one he takes. He's in no hurry to be home.

On the third day of his mother not getting out of bed, the phone rang. Edward stared at it. His mother dislikes the phone. It's connected to an answer machine that kicks in after the tenth ring. Sales people call sometimes to talk about windows or burglar alarms, but his mother never calls them back. On the ninth ring, Edward lifted the receiver and held it to his ear.

'Hello,' a voice said.

Edward didn't reply.

'Hello?' said the voice, 'Can I speak to the householder?' A woman's voice. Edward opened his mouth, but no sound came out.

'Helloooooo?' said the voice again, as though the woman were wandering around a big, empty house. He wanted to say hello back to her, and tell her about his mother being in bed, and ask what he should do about it, but his voice didn't work and the woman hung up.

After that, Edward roamed around the house for a little while, from room to room. It's a big house. A house you could easily hide in, with many rooms and corners and secret places. When he was much younger, Edward used to play at hiding in cupboards and behind doors, but no one ever came to find him. He learned that it's easier to just hide inside himself.

On the fourth day, he used a big roll of tape to repair the box his father kept the spoons in. He replaced the glass with a sheet of cardboard and arranged the spoons neatly inside, then put it under his bed for safekeeping. He made a plate of cheese sandwiches, and replaced the ones he'd left on his mother's bedside table the day before. He saw they'd been nibbled at, and a little later he heard the toilet flushing in her bathroom. She's all right really, he told himself.

Miss Pilcher came back from her holiday the following day. Edward watched from the window as she wobbled up the driveway on her tall black bicycle. The wire basket at the front was weighted with new books, making it troublesome to steer across the blistered tarmac. He opened the front door for her and she burst in, smiling, chattering about good weather. Then she stopped very abruptly and looked at him. 'Whatever's the matter, Edward?' she asked. So he told her, and she went upstairs.

After about an hour, he went upstairs too, and pushed the door of his mother's room open just a crack so he could look inside. His mother was sitting on the edge of the bed, with her back to the door. Her pale hair was knotted and dull looking, and she seemed even thinner than usual. Miss Pilcher was kneeling in front of her. They weren't speaking, but Miss Pilcher was holding his mother's hand in both of hers. One thumb moved slowly, backwards and forwards, stroking his mother's skin.

The track through the woods is stippled with light slanting through the canopy. Edward walks with his head flung back, staring up at the green. He stretches his arms out and spins around, watching how the trunks close in on him, bending to him as though he were the whirling centre of a vortex. Above him, the green brightens and blurs until he feels dizzy and when he stops spinning the trees continue to turn about him. He steadies himself against a pine and as the world slows and stills, he sees an old man watching him from the far side of the stream. Edward walks on, embarrassed, but turns to glance back at the spot where the man stood, and sees that it's empty.

Do people in dreams have dreams about us? Are we shadowy like them? When the blackness comes, Edward wakes up, and the blackness he opens his eyes to is the same as the blackness in his dream, the same blackness as the bog boy sees. In that moment of waking, is it Edward lying in the dark, or the bog boy? This is what he wonders as he holds his breath in the night. He and the bog boy, not breathing. The bog boy and him. Same person, slipped through time. Maybe that's what reincarnation is, Edward thinks. A slip through time to another place.

The school woman has the necklace. He knows it's the same one. In the dream the cross is around his neck, on a long piece of leather, and he's holding it in his mouth. He likes the tangy, metal taste of it. The school woman says it can't be the same necklace. She's had it for years, she told him.

'Three thousand years?' he asked.

'It can't be that old,' she said, 'and anyway, why would an iron age boy have a silver cross? For a start off, it's the iron age, not the silver age, and a cross is a religious symbol, a christian symbol. Your bog boy lived way before Christianity.' She sat back with her arms folded. Point proven.

'Are you a Christian?' asked Edward.

'Well, not really,' she said.

'But you're wearing a cross.'

'Not as a symbol though, it's just jewellery to me.'

'Iron age people wore jewellery too,' he told her, 'for decoration. So why not a cross?'

She'd taken the necklace off from around her neck and was studying it, stroking it gently with her thumb the way Miss Pilcher stroked his mother's hand that day. 'How do you explain a young village boy owning a piece of silver jewellery?' she asked him, and he answered straight away, because he's thought about that a lot. 'It's stolen,' he said, 'that's what I think happened. I stole it from someone important in the tribe, and that's why I was killed. As punishment.'

She laid the cross on the desk and frowned at it. For the first time, he wondered where she'd got it from, and asked her. When she answered, he noticed that her voice seemed a little thinner, as though it were passing through a sieve. 'My father gave it to me,' she said. She didn't look at him, and he got a feeling she was hiding inside herself, which made him feel a bit queasy. He reached into his coat pocket and closed his fingers around the spoon he'd brought that day. Simon Zealotes (beheaded and sawn into pieces). 'Do you know where he got it from?' he asked. She looked up and smiled at him, a crooked smile. 'I think he might have stolen it too,' she said.

So far, she's the only person Edward has liked at Henge School. She's tall and thin, like his mother, but without his mother's way of quietly gliding around. Miss Riley is gawkier, with sticky out elbows and a long thin nose. She jangles and clatters when she moves, and her office is cluttered up with half dead pot plants and papers everywhere. She seems kind though, and unlike the teachers, she listens without smirking. The children smirk at Edward too, like they're sharing a joke and not letting him in on it.

'Have you made any friends?' Miss Riley asked him. It amazes him now that he thought he might make some friends. Before starting at the school he'd wanted to make friends, and asked his mother if he could perhaps invite some of his new friends to tea, which she looked a little unsure about, before walking up and down the stairs six multiples of four, which alarmed Edward as it was a lot, even for her. But then she came into the kitchen where Edward was frying an egg and said it would probably be fine for an hour or so, that she'd cope all right with that, and she wasn't scratching the backs of her hands when she said it, so he really did think it might happen.

But it hasn't.

On his first day he was shown around by his new form tutor, Mr Balham, and he was introduced to a thin, freckled boy with a close cropped red hair. 'This is David,' said Mr Balham, smiling through his beard, 'He'll be your buddy for a few days, eh Davey? You'll show him the ropes, won't you Dave?' To which the boy called David, or Davey, or Dave, said, 'Yes sir,' and Mr Balham said, 'Good man, off you go then lads, have a great day.'

There seemed to be endless miles of corridors and classrooms, which made Edward think of the word labyrinthine. He pointed this out to David, and said he hoped they wouldn't meet a minotaur. David looked at him blankly. 'From Greek mythology,' said Edward, 'you must know the story.' But David shrugged and continued to walk, so Edward filled him in as best he could until they eventually arrived at a plain wooden door with 'Room 12' written on a little plaque. 'And like Theseus, we reach our destination,' Edward said triumphantly, because they got to the door just as he'd reached the end of the story. David had his hand on the door handle and he turned and stared at Edward. He stared for such a long time that the broad smile on Edward's face began to ache and slip. 'You can sit next to me today,' said David, 'but tomorrow you'll have to sit on your own.'

There must be some rule about seating arrangements, Edward thought, though he couldn't remember reading about any in the glossy school prospectus, which had arrived in the post a few weeks earlier. He'd virtually memorized the page on school rules. *Keep left on the corridors* (though lots of people didn't, he'd noticed). *Chewing gum is banned throughout the school.* Edward had never even licked a piece of gum, never mind chewed one. He raised his hand to answer questions in the different classes, even though other students tended to call out. At lunchtime he kept to the 'recreation area', which turned out to be a patch of concrete near the canteen. David disappeared at lunchtime, so he sat by himself on a bench and ate his butter and beetroot sandwiches. Then he didn't know what else to do so he opened his new French textbook and practiced saying, 'Je m'appelle Edward, j'ai onze ans'. Some girls were standing nearby and they looked over at him and giggled, which made him feel embarrassed so he stopped and pretended to look for something in his satchel instead. A bell rang for the end of lunchtime and he knew he should go to a science lesson, but he didn't know where the classroom was. The recreation area was emptying out, but two of the giggling girls were still there, chatting, so he walked up to them and said, 'Excusez-moi jeune les dames, pouvez-vous m'aider à trouver ma classe?' The French he'd been practising was pretty basic, and he wanted to set the record straight, because he was proud of his French speaking ability; Miss Pilcher had once told him that he spoke it like a native. One of the girls said, 'Oh my God, he's actually French!' and started giggling again, while the other one said, 'We speak English in this country,' and they ran away, laughing. Edward returned to his bench and waited for David to come and collect him for the science lesson. He was looking forward to it. In the prospectus, there'd been a picture of a science lesson in which a boy had placed his hand on a metal dome, making his hair stand up in an electrified fuzz. In the picture, the boy was grinning, and so was the teacher. Edward waited until he was the only person left in the recreation area. Just him and a few fat gulls. He threw them his leftover sandwich crust and watched them squabble over it, until a magpie swooped down and snapped it from right under their beaks. Then he picked up his satchel and walked to the main building.

By the time he found the right classroom, the lesson was in full swing. The teacher cut him off before he could explain why he was late, and how David was supposed to be showing him the ropes. 'Go and work with Dave as he's your buddy for the day,' she said. The class were doing an experiment with torches and mirrors, and he'd already done that experiment with Miss Pilcher at home, so he knew it was about how light behaves and he told David about wave theory. 'Light behaves like waves in some situations,' he said, 'and particles in others, which was very confusing for scientists until Einstein suggested the possibility of photons, which explains everything perfectly.' David kept shining his torch beam directly into Edward's eyes while he was speaking, which Edward found very off putting, and when the teacher wasn't looking he shone it onto his middle finger so it cast a giant shadow on the whiteboard and everyone who noticed laughed and started doing the same, until the teacher saw what was happening and made everyone switch their torches off. The rest of the lesson was spent in copying some diagrams from a textbook, and no one was allowed to talk to anyone else. When the bell went the teacher made everyone stand up straight behind their desks before saying, 'Class dismissed,' and everyone ran for the door at the same time and got stuck in a big bundle of bodies and bags, so no one could get through. It all looked a bit unsafe to Edward. He loitered in the classroom until the teacher noticed him. 'When will we study electricity?' he asked her, 'I'd like to do the experiment with the metal dome, the one that makes your hair stand on end.'

'You mean a Van de Graaff machine,' said the teacher. She was packing books into a carrier bag. 'We don't have one. We just hire it in for open evening,' she said.

He tried to find David when he got outside. Some boys he recognised from the science class were hanging around the bike racks so he asked them if they'd seen him, and one of them said, 'Why? Is he your boyfriend?' and the others all went whooooo and made kissing noises, and Edward felt his face going red, so he walked away. He saw David outside the school gates, and he waved and started to walk towards him, thinking this might be a good time to ask him to tea, but David turned away when he saw Edward. He said something to a boy standing beside him, which made the boy laugh, and there was a note of cruelty in the laugh that made Edward stop and change direction. He carried on walking with his head down, watching where his feet landed, between the cracks.

Emerging from the trees, Edward rejoins the road and follows it until the main body of the village is at his back. A narrow side road leads downhill and he walks along its edge until it curves and dips towards his own house. The tall gates are almost obscured by rogue rhododendrons, the wrought metal is entwined with bindweed and ivy. Perhaps he should ask Miss Riley to tea, he thinks.

He wants to study the necklace again, or even try it on. Maybe she'll let him borrow it for a while, so he can be the bog boy in this time as well as that time. He tugs at the gate and threads himself through the gap before pulling it closed behind himself. It frightens him, being the bog boy. He told Miss Riley that, but he also told her that in the dream, he feels more himself than he does in his present life. He looks up at the house before entering. At the grey walls and blank windows. 'This life doesn't fit,' he told her. Like his new coat, it's too big and awkward. He feels stupid in it.

CHAPTER 5

Skylark

Not for the first time, I relive the night of my fifteenth birthday. I should have been asleep, but something had woken me. It was a hot London night, suffused with street glow and the drone of distant traffic. The moon was far off and pale yellow, the bedroom curtains were shifting in a listless breeze, and a figure was sitting on the windowsill. Not sitting, crouching. Poised and alert and listening. I could hear its breath. I waited, watching, as it slipped from the sill with an easy grace, like a fall of water, and unfolded to stand full height and smoothly silhouetted. As my eyes adjusted, I made out a profile. Long straight nose and pointed chin. There was something in its mouth, a small, square package clamped between its teeth. It lifted a hand and removed it, then twisted its head. 'Skylark?' it said.

'Dad,' I murmured, and sat up to point at the curled heap of Xavier, cocooned in a sleeping bag on the bedroom floor. Only his hair was visible, and the soft rise and fall of his breathing. Dad hesitated, before stepping over him and picking his way towards the bed. 'I have something for you,' he said, and he handed me the package before sitting on the edge of the bed. In the dim light from the window his face was illumined, revealing a dark growth of stubble. He smelled of tobacco smoke and something else, a sweetish, sickly scent. Whiskey? The parcel fitted into my hand and I could feel the curve of his teeth marks wetly imprinted on one corner. 'I can't stay,' he whispered, and he leaned in and kissed me on the forehead.

He'd been out of prison a few years, but had only tried to resume contact with me a few months earlier. This was the second time he'd shinned the drainpipe at the back of the first floor apartment. Mum had refused visitation rights, leading to surreptitious meetings after school in a greasy spoon cafe on the high street. I wonder what we talked about. School, I suppose, and Mum. It took him a while to adapt to my age; I was nine when he was imprisoned and had long outgrown Barbie dolls and trips to the park. 'You drink coffee now?' I recall him saying, disapprovingly, tapping ash from his cigarette into a squat glass cylinder on the formica table top. 'Whatever next? Boyfriends?'

I smiled. Enigmatically, I hoped. No boyfriends, only Xav, my confidante in these liaisons dangereuses. I relished the thrill of Dad's secret texts arriving on my new phone, and lying to Mum about where I'd been, and with whom. We'd meet, but he'd ask me nothing more adventurous than if I was keeping up with homework, or what I liked to do in my spare time. I wanted to ask about prison, and about his crimes. 'Ah, that's all behind me now, Skylark.' He'd drum his fingers and hum a little tune. 'How's your mother? Is she seeing anyone?'

She wasn't. She was too busy spying on me. Reading the texts on my phone and following me home from school. She saw us together in the cafe, and confiscated the phone. The first time Dad climbed in the bedroom window it was to bring me a new one. The second time, it was to give me the birthday gift.

Through the gauzy dark, I peered at the package. I could feel the sharp square edges of a box, and there was dim lettering on the surface. 'What is it?' I asked. He took a breath and started to say something, but then there was a sharp click and a flood of white light. Mum, standing in the doorway in her magenta dressing gown and gold Gucci slippers. 'What the hell is going on?' she barked, each word diamond tipped. I was staring at the box in my hands.

It was a packet of cigarettes.

Dad was remonstrating, holding his hands aloft, as though she had a gun leveled at his chest. 'Ah now Jeannie, calm down.' Conciliatory, but anxious too. In the glare he was ashen skinned and his shirt was rumpled, grimy at the cuffs. His eyes darted from Mum, to me, to the window.

'I will not calm down,' she said. Xavier's head protruded from his sleeping bag, his eyes clamped shut against the brightness. 'What's going on?' he mumbled.

'Skylark's father is just leaving,' said Mum.

'Jeannie, c'mon, let me explain.'

'I'm calling the police,' she said. She had her mobile phone in one hand and she was punching the numbers in.

'Okay, I'll go, I'm going. Jesus Jeannie, Skylark, I was never here. I'll call you'

'Cigarettes?' she said, spotting the packet, 'You gave her cigarettes?'

But he was already sidling down the stairs. 'Skylark,' he called, 'keep safe, you hear?' and the front door clicked and clunked behind him.

'How dare he? How dare he?' Mum raged, pacing to the still open window and slamming it closed. 'Whatever did I see in that man? I wish I'd never met him!'

'And not had me, I suppose.'

She span on her heel to stare at me. Ran manicured fingers through her hair. 'You know that's not what I mean. I mean, he's a common criminal, in and out of prison like a jack-in-the-box and then he turns up here and,' she paused, narrowed her eyes. The air turned unnervingly chilly. 'Just how, Skylark, did he get this address?' Xavier retreated into his sleeping bag and I followed his example, shrinking beneath the bed covers, but she was off, a nine force gale of fury and resentment. 'I didn't ask him to break in,' I complained, but she wasn't listening. I'd betrayed her trust and placed him above her. 'Your own mother!' she exclaimed, slapping a hand to her bosom. A dull thumping from the other side of the wall told us the neighbours had had enough of this late night soap opera. 'We'll talk about this in the morning,' she said, striding towards the door. 'And get rid of those disgusting cigarettes.' She flicked the light switch and plunged us into darkness. 'Good night Xavier,' she added, as she closed the door behind her.

'Wow,' said Xav.

There was a reading lamp on my nightstand and I switched it on. Xavier was grinning at me from the floor. 'Never a dull moment round here,' he said. I raised the cigarette packet. 'Fancy a smoke?' I said, and tossed the packet across the room to him. He caught it deftly in one hand. 'Thanks but,' he shook the box and it rattled. 'Should cigarettes do that?' he asked. He knelt up in the sleeping bag and shuffled over to the bed to hand me the box. 'Open it,' he said. His eyes shone with excitement as I flipped open the lid and emptied the contents onto my palm. A silver crucifix. Heavy and mottled, a thin leather strap threaded through the top loop. Xavier gave a low whistle. 'Must have cost him a packet,' he said. 'More likely he stole it,' I replied.

We stayed awake and talked for a while. Xavier drifted back to sleep before I did, and I turned off the reading lamp. I'd slipped the crucifix under my pillow, and reached in to rest my fingertips against the cold, pitted metal. It was a good gift and I resolved to show it to Mum when she'd calmed down, as evidence of Dad's thoughtfulness. Despite her resistance to him seeing me, I felt sure she'd relent eventually. Okay, he was a disappointment and an embarrassment, but he'd never done me any harm. I knew Mum. Her anger tended to be short lived, blazing and fading like a flare, but she'd come round when she saw the birthday gift. It was a sign of his goodness. He wasn't all bad. I'd give her a few days.

But I never got a chance to show her the necklace, because a couple of days later two police men turned up at the door and told us that a body had been dragged from the Thames.

'There's no point raking over old ground,' my mother says. We're sitting at a table in Renaldo's, and she's pouring cream from a little silver jug over the back of a spoon, so that it puddles into an oily float on top of her coffee. Every so often we meet for dinner at this little Italian place that sits above the dry cleaning store beside her shop. My mother is the proprietor of Voluptua; a small fashion boutique for large ladies. She herself is completely devoid of excess fat, and can only be described as petite, but her clientele is made up of women ranging from plump to morbidly obese. Many of them have become firm friends in the years since she opened the shop. 'Having a slower metabolism doesn't exclude you from looking sexy,' she tells them as they squash themselves into imitation designer dresses, cut on the bias to disguise thunderous thighs. She does a brisk line in bottom skimming jackets, and she buys in knee length boots, which have cunning folds of stretchy elastic in the leather - no calf can remain unconcealed. The ladies love her for it, and if they resent the fact that she is able to eat generous slices of cheesecake with no perceptible impact on her waistline, they don't show it. She's doing very well for herself. 'It's history, Skylark,' she says. 'I moved on a long time ago, why can't you?'

We're talking about Dad, of course, but it has taken a starter of Bruschetta Rustica, a main course of Linguine Marinière, and a bottle of Sauvignon Blanc to venture into the topic. Mum hates talking about my father, and his death is generally a no go area, but it's amazing what a few glasses of wine can achieve in cranking open the floodgates. I'm wearing the crucifix, and I've told her about Edward and his reincarnation story - I mean, it's crazy - but he's so certain about the necklace, so sure he's seen it before, where did it come from? Mum shakes her head. She doesn't know how Dad came by it. I stir my own coffee moodily. 'Don't you ever at least wonder about what happened?' I say, 'you were married to him once, and he was my father,' but she cuts me off.

'We were married far too quickly, Skylark. I barely knew him, and I was already pregnant with you before I found out how he earned his living.' She takes a sip of her coffee, and it leaves a thin white line on her lip. 'He told me he was an art dealer,' she adds wistfully. I've heard it all before, of course. How Mum went to London to study fashion design, and was charmed by a tall, emerald eyed stranger in a pub one night. He looked good in his expensive suit, and he made her laugh with corny jokes told in his lilting Irish accent. He invited her back to a swanky apartment, where they sipped chilled champagne on a narrow balcony, above a picture perfect view of the Thames. 'I thought I'd found Mr Right,' she says. The story of that first night ends with him gallantly giving up his sumptuous double bed to sleep on the sofa, though I've never really believed that part. (My mother's parenting skills may be flawed, but she won't be faulted on her dedication to safeguarding my morals.) So, no first date sex for her then, and the subsequent whirlwind romance, unexpected pregnancy, and resultant elopement to Gretna Green, all serve to illustrate the dangers of choosing the wrong man. There's no greater calamity in my mother's book. In her case, the wrong man turned out to be a crook. The swanky London flat was on loan to him while its equally crooked owner lay low somewhere near Marbella. Dad's job was to live there, pretend he'd never heard of the owner should the police or anyone else come calling, and feed the tropical fish that lived in an enormous tank built into a dividing wall. As Mum's abdomen swelled, Dad earned his living as a safecracker and art thief. 'He used to tell me he had to attend gallery openings in the evenings,' she tells me. 'He even brought me along to a few genuine ones, just so I'd believe him.'

The restaurant is busy, and Renaldo himself is gliding between the tables with incredible grace for his bulky frame. 'And for my favourite ladies,' he says, planting two complimentary balloons of brandy on the chequered tablecloth. His black moustache lifts like a bird's wings as his face widens into a grin. He likes my mother. She flirts with him, and she recommends his restaurant to her customers. After all, they like to eat, and he's always careful to flatter them on their new outfits. It's a profitable reciprocation of interests, and a legal one.

While Mum's waters were breaking in the back of an ambulance, Dad was being caught red handed in the home of a Tory MP, lifting a Matisse from the wall. She endured the 18 hour labour alone. He was released on bail, and later sentenced to 2 years imprisonment. In the interim, soft eyed and awash with new fatherhood, he apologised for everything, promised to go straight, and moved us to a cheap, but honestly rented flat in Tottenham. Mum forgave him that first time (though not before adding a bottle of bleach to the tropical aquarium). She dutifully remained faithful while he served his prison sentence, and on his release, she welcomed him home to the domestic bliss of a loving wife and a beautiful baby daughter.

It wasn't to last.

'He just couldn't resist it,' she says, sipping at the brandy. 'Of course, he wasn't any kind of master criminal, he wasn't clever enough for that. He stole for someone else and they paid for his work.' She shrugs. 'When he was eventually arrested again I divorced him, and as far as I'm concerned Skylark, that was the end of our relationship. You were four years old, and whatever he got up to in the next ten years, before he died, is of no interest to me.'

I swirl the brandy in my glass and stare into its depths as though into a crystal ball. 'Before he was killed,' I say. 'Not before he died. Before he was killed.' I take a swig, and feel the warmth plummet into a mushroom cloud somewhere beneath my lungs, like an inverted nuclear explosion. The restaurant buzzes and hums around us, but my mother's stillness encapsulates us both for a moment, as clear and smooth as my emptied glass. At least she doesn't sigh. 'You don't know that for sure,' she says gently. 'There's no way of knowing what really happened, and it's no good asking me. The only contact we had was when he came to see you, and God knows,' the kindness bubble pops and drips into her habitually scornful tones, 'those times were few and far between.'

I can't blame her really. My childhood memories are punctuated by my father's erratic attempts at paternal bonding. Days out at the zoo. Fairground trips, where I was thoughtlessly allowed to eat my fill of candy floss and drink buckets of lemonade before being hurled around on the crazy waltzer to the point of throwing up. He was charming and kind and easy going. He made me laugh, and when I was with him, he made me feel that the entire universe rotated about the still point of me. But he never had a fixed address, and was utterly unreliable. He'd call and arrange to take me out, then simply not show up. I'd put on my favourite clothes and wait for him, gazing from my bedroom window for hours and staring hard at each car as it drove past, willing it to be his, though in reality, I'm not even sure he ever owned a car. He drove a different one each time. Borrowed for the occasion.

I think of what Edward has told me about his father. The lengthy wait for his father's return from London each month, just one weekend in four to break the monotony of lonely days in that big house. I was a little younger Edward when my own father landed himself back in prison again. There was a fuss surrounding the trial, I remember. He stayed with us for a couple of weeks, sleeping on the sofa, and for the first time ever, he behaved like other people's fathers. He walked me to school each morning and picked me up in the afternoon. Mum told me once that, despite everything, she didn't want her daughter's father in prison again and agreed to stand trial as a character witness in the hope it would alleviate the severity of the sentence. He was to plead guilty, and she was willing to pretend he'd returned to the bosom of his family, for a short time at least. They maintained an uneasy truce. Sharing tea and toast in the morning, watching TV together in the evenings. I spied on them once. Creeping out of bed and peering through a crack in the living room door. They sat together on the sofa, legs stretched out and parallel, arms folded, silently gazing at the flickering screen. Just like normal parents. I hugged myself.

Despite Mum's efforts, something went wrong at the trial and he was sentenced to four years. I stopped talking for a while. Mum went along with it at first, accepting written responses to questions without batting an eyelid. 'How was school?' she'd ask. Fine, I'd scrawl on the pocket exercise book she gave me. 'Would you like pasta for tea?' I'd shake my head. 'Pizza?' I'd nod. At school, I'd never been an outgoing child, and my withdrawal from playground games was shrugged off by other kids. My teacher arranged an appointment with a psychologist, who asked me to draw a picture of my family. Naturally, I put Dad behind bars. 'Shock,' was the verdict, 'she's finding the imprisonment hard to deal with.'

'That's very insightful of you,' my mother deadpanned.

One day, the teacher brought a clutch of speckled hen's eggs to class, and kept them in an incubator in a corner of the room. I was given the job of gently turning the eggs every so often, reaching in beneath the heat lamp to renestle them into a bed of warm, fragrant straw. Once, I saw a movement deep within a shell, a dark flicker, more a suggestion of motion than the real thing. The eggs were due to hatch any day and I held one to the heat lamp and peered at it, willing another sudden pulse to appear. Within the shell, the chick's outline breathed and I tried to make out the beak, scrabbling clawed feet, clamped wings, but saw only a darkness shaped by what I knew a chick to look like rather than recognisable in itself. When I think back to that period of silence, the pocket I dropped myself into and refused to leave, I remember the chick in its shell. Why did I refuse to speak? I must have had questions about the trial. I must have wanted to display anger and upset, and to seek comfort. But I did none of those things. I breathed inside my shell, my hot heart beating, and peering back to the day of the trial itself, I recall nothing. Where was I when my parents went to court? I know they didn't take me. I remember my mother coming home through the front door and shaking her head at me. Who else was there? What did I do next? I look back and see shadow. Shapeless, utterly enclosed; faceless as the eggs in the incubator, even though I know there are wings, a beak, clawed feet. 'A neighbour looked after you,' says my mother, 'an elderly lady. She lived upstairs.'

'What was her name?'

'Mrs Craigie? No, Creedy? I can't remember Skylark, it was a long time ago.'

We moved to a new apartment during the summer, and I started at my new secondary school. Tired of silence perhaps, I started speaking again on the first day there, and made a few friends, including Xav. He'd lived alone with his father since the death of his French mother a few years earlier. Children have an inbuilt radar for finding each other, and while neither of us spoke in any kind of serious terms about things that had happened to us, we gravitated towards each other. Xavier had been raised speaking French, but the language had withered inside him in the years since his mother had died. Perhaps, after my months of silence, I recognised what it was to lose words, and was drawn to the boy who, like me, was reconstructing himself in a new tongue. Navigating its slipperiness, its knots, its obstacles.

My mother is waving at Renaldo and miming a scribbling action on the palm of her hand. The alcohol has flushed her cheeks a pretty pink, to match her lipstick. 'I want to find him,' I blurt, 'the killer.' This time, she does sigh, before leaning in over the table and lowering her voice. 'Skylark. There's no definite proof he was murdered. He was drunk. The injuries on his body could have come from the fall when he slipped, the police had nothing to go on.'

Renaldo is nimbly edging towards us, the dinner bill in his hand. I touch the silver cross at my throat. Dad's body was badly bruised, more damaged than a tumble from a bridge into water could have caused. There were broken ribs and fingers. A cut to his head. Mum once admitted that she'd suspected suicide, but she couldn't equate that with the man she knew. He wasn't the suicide type. 'An accident,' she reckoned, 'a drunken fall in the dark.' The police thought differently. He was down on his luck, an ex con, with an estranged ex-wife and daughter. A typical suicide case. They stamped the file and closed it, and Mum accepted it. Let's move on, she said, make a fresh start, and that's what she did. Within a couple of months we were living in the South West and she'd rented the empty shop space that was to become Voluptua. I stumbled in her wake, punch drunk with loss and confusion, the silver cross dangling heavy around my neck. 'Where on earth did you get that monstrosity?' she said one day, so I told her and she stared at it for a while. Silent and inscrutable. 'It doesn't suit you,' she said, finally.

Renaldo flourishes the bill. 'Delicious as always,' Mum simpers. He beams and bows, black eyes twinkling. Mum pats at her hair, all smiles. They enact the familiar pantomime of her handing him money and him taking only a fraction of it.

'Oh really, Renaldo, you mustn't.'

'It is my pleasure Jeannie, you light up my evening with your smile.'

I gaze at my own reflection in the restaurant window, and beyond it to the rain stained street and the broad backed hills beyond. The Henge isn't visible from here, but I find myself thinking about it standing motionless in the moorland winds. The bog boy stole a necklace, and was murdered beneath its impassive stones. Did Dad steal it too? Is it old and valuable? His punishment, to be beaten, and cast into the sluggish depths of the river. I picture the bog boy sinking through pure blackness. My father, lying on the silt bed, limbs lifting gently with the current and catching on discarded London junk; car tyres and shopping trollies, rusting iron hulks. The reflected crucifix twinkles in the light from the restaurant candle. Iron age, I think. No crucifixes in the iron age.

Renaldo has returned to his kitchen and Mum has put on her coat and is standing behind her chair, waiting, and looking at me. When I meet her gaze she looks away, as though distracted by a sudden noise, and her eyes skim the room restlessly as I slip into my jacket and fish around under the table for my bag. When I'm ready to go, I stand, but she doesn't move. Her amber freckled eyes have returned to me, or not to me, it's the necklace she's looking at.

'In all the time I knew him,' she says, 'he never remembered your birthday.'

A History of Stonemoor
by Pauline Pilcher

While the bog boy is undoubtedly the most well known erstwhile resident of the (then, embryonic) Stonemoor, the village can boast another celebrated son. Tom Watkins was born here; parish records indicate him to be the son of an illiterate tenant farmer, who was carried off by the ubiquitous 'sweat' in an epidemic of 1562, along with Tom's mother and siblings. Little is known of his childhood beyond these facts. In the normal course of events, such an inauspicious start to life should have been followed by an equally inauspicious future; raised on the charity of others, possibly through being employed as a field hand or

99

labourer, and a thoroughly miserable existence of backbreaking hard work, poverty, and early death. Bucking the trend, however, Watkins left Stonemoor at some point to become a sailor, and somehow managed to clamber up through the ranks to achieve the captaincy of his own ship, The Magpie. He fought alongside Sir Francis Drake, against the mighty Armada, and returned to Stonemoor in later life as a wealthy man. He built a fine house in the village, married, and fathered six children. But why is he celebrated? Why is his grave mentioned as one of 'special interest' in several regional tourist guides? The answer, ~~dear reader~~, lies not in historical fact, but historical hearsay; Tom Watkins was probably a pirate! And that makes him a whole lot more interesting than a simple 'local boy done good'.

But where does the pirate myth come from? Galling though it is to the true historian like myself, for whom the reality of the past must be firmly rooted in evidence, it appears that the myth arose from the ~~enthusiastic ramblings~~ creative leanings of an Anglican vicar named Kingsley Swarthmore, who presided over services at Stonemoor's pretty

16th Century church during the first half of the second world war. Not content with administering to the needs of his village flock, Reverend Swarthmore indulged himself in writing a weekly adventure serial for the South Dartmoor Gazette, in which Tom Watkins was reincarnated as a dashing English pirate, fond of swashbuckling his way around the Caribbean to rescue fair maidens, while simultaneously doing battle with gangs of distinctly teutonic Spaniards. 'This one's for Blighty,' growls Tom, to the unimaginatively named El Capitan Adolpho Hitela. What Swarthmore lacked in subtlety, he made up for in prolificacy, and by the time he was ~~obliterated~~ tragically killed by a wayward bomb in the Plymouth blitz of 1941, his stories had been picked up by the war office to be more widely published in the national press, no doubt as a subliminal tool in encouraging recruitment. ~~The stories are available in book form, though the title escapes me~~. In such ways, is spurious history created. The basis for Swarthmore's adoption of Tom as his piratical hero is a single line in a single letter of 1573, from Francis Drake to his then wife, Mary Newman. In the letter he expends some time on describing the attributes of his crew members, and refers to a young deck swabber called Thomas Watkins as 'a stout hearted and sureful young fellow'. Sureful indeed if he was secretly pocketing a portion of Drake's ill-gotten loot, for at this time, Drake was famously engaged in pirate raids upon gold laden Spanish ships, and if the Watkins of Drake's letter is the same Watkins who is buried in Stonemoor's churchyard, then it is likely he was involved in Drake's lucrative missions. No doubt this is the basis for Swarthmore's stories, but from a genuine historian's point of view, it is an execrably shoddy basis on which to build a career as an historical fiction writer. For the past is like the salt encrusted sailing charts that Captain Watkins no doubt studied in the creaking chambers of The Magpie; the known parts are so intricately drawn, so meticulously labelled, but beyond them, loitering at the edges, the unknown, the undiscovered, and here may be dragons indeed, especially when a talentless vicar decides to twist them to his own ends for the sake of his own vanity!

Good God, she thinks. Where's her self control? She's jealous, she knows, of Swarthmore's reputation as Stonemoor's chief literary figure. He lived to a ripe old age, the acknowledged expert on anything to do with Watkins. She made up the bit about the bomb. Wishful thinking. Anyone can fill a book with imaginary exploits. She entertains a thought for a moment, one she has had many times since beginning to write her own history book, that she could, possibly, attempt a more literary project – a collection of stories, or even a novel? She gives her head a shake – no, things must be rooted in fact.

She had let Edward read Swarthmore's book, however, crammed with tales about Watkins' privateering, and his audacious feats of thievery from gold laden Spanish ships. Filled with overblown descriptions of his death defying tactic of balancing on the shafts of firing cannons and leaping aboard ships, armed with his trademark flintlock and cutlass.

'He mustn't have cared about dying,' said Edward. They were in the churchyard at the time, having researched Watkins' origins in the parish register. She'd set Edward the task of rubbing over his gravestone with a sheet of paper and charcoal, while she sat on a tartan blanket, peeling hard boiled eggs for a picnic lunch. She'd been trying to explode Swarthmore's mythology; it seemed unlikely a man could balance on a firing cannon, or leap the distance to the targeted galleon. The flintlock was decidedly anachronistic too, but Edward loved the stories so she'd acquiesced in the face of his enthusiasm by admitting that yes, perhaps pirates did those things. 'Perhaps he was just brave,' she said. Edward traced the epitaph with coal black fingers. 'Maybe being brave is just that,' he said. 'Not being scared of dying.' He leaned back from the charcoal rubbing, eyeing his work critically. 'Or maybe he even wanted to die. Maybe he wanted to begin again.'

Pauline gives her head a quick shake. Edward had become interested in all kinds of New Age theories before she left her job at the Parry House, reincarnation especially. Starting the history project on Tom Watkins hadn't done the trick of distracting him. She ponders. Would Edward dig deeper? Would he look beyond the flimsy fabric of memory to locate hard, historical evidence? Might he discover the truth? She glances upwards, to a small hatch above her head, which opens into the loft space of her small bungalow. Surely not. Even if he tried, he couldn't possibly get as far as herself in piecing his own history together. She's been solving the jigsaw of Edward for years now, and has come so very close she can almost smell the truth. But still, uncertainties remain. She dislikes uncertainties.

She's restless. She leaves the typewriter, the scattered notes, the books, and paces the house. From the small living room, along the narrow hallway to the kitchen, and back again. 'Edward's not himself,' Eleanor Parry had said, 'he's having strange thoughts about his past. Memories.' It was those words which reignited the dormant speculations she'd often entertained about Edward. Memories. Why would Eleanor use that word? They were in the kitchen of the house at the time; a wide, sunlit room, quite unlike Pauline's own poky space of fitted cupboards and cheap linoleum. She misses the house. It's faded charm. More than that she misses those cosy periods of intimacy when she and Eleanor sat together at the long oak table, drinking tea from white cups of thin, pellucid porcelain. Eleanor, pale hair framing her face in wisps and tendrils, frowning into the teacup. Once, Pauline had reached out a hand to smooth a strand of loose hair from Eleanor's face and Eleanor had spoiled the moment by standing hurriedly and upsetting the cup, so the contents spilled out and dripped from the edges of the table. 'Oh now, let me,' Pauline had said, fetching a cloth. Eleanor remained standing, clutching the back of a chair. 'It's all right,' smiled Pauline, 'you mustn't upset yourself, Eleanor.' She relished using her name. Hitherto, it had always been Mrs Parry, but with Edward's father gone and Pauline increasingly being given a place as chief comforter, the name had been proffered as a gift. A sign of friendship. A soft parcel of vowels that said, thank you Pauline. I need you.

And then, she no longer needed her.

It's evening, and rain hangs in a drizzle over the village streets. Pauline puts on her coat and steps outside. She pulls the hood about her head and breathes in the thinly wetted air. As she walks, tiny drops cling to her face, her eyebrows, her clothes, until she feels her outline must be blurred, like TV static, invisible and crackling. She walks along the side of the main road that trundles through the village centre. A few cars pass, but it's unlikely anyone notices her silent progress towards the houses that lie out at the village's edge. There's a spur off the road behind some trees, and she takes it, descending downhill towards a faint square of light in the distance. She has taken this walk frequently in the six months since leaving the Parry house. Always at night, and for no reason exactly, other than to set herself at ease. She likes to stand near the gated entrance to the grounds, hidden by the tumultuous overgrowth that springs around it, watching the lighted windows and knowing that Eleanor is moving about the interior. This pilgrimage brings a certain peace to Pauline Pilcher. A quietude born from the knowledge that soon, when enough time has passed, and when the last pieces of the puzzle have been set into place, she can reclaim her place in the elegant house. Not as Edward's tutor, but as Eleanor's one true friend. She, Pauline Pilcher, will take care of her.

Approaching the iron gates, Pauline stops walking, startled by a sudden movement in the darkness. The house lights burn as usual, and the gates are shut, but beneath a spreading rhododendron, the place where Pauline herself likes to stand, there's a figure. She steps off the road, holding her breath, and stares intently. It's too dark to make out any details. The figure is tall and thin, wearing a long coat, and it's peering in through the gate towards the house. Every so often, a single red ember brightens as the stranger draws on a cigarette. Pauline takes a step further into the greenery, hides herself behind a tree, and watches as the stranger walks out from beneath the rhododendrons, towards a car that stands further back from the gates. Only when the car has purred away up the hill into silence, does she step onto the road again. She hurries to the spot where the person stood and scuffs at the ground with one toe of her shoe, until she locates the discarded cigarette end and slips it into her pocket.

In the house, Edward sleeps. Eleanor rarely goes to bed before the early hours of the morning. She prowls soundlessly, in bare feet, in and out of rooms. She tidies Edward's school books into a neat pile. She corrects the positions of ornaments on the mantlepiece. She washes her hands. Sometimes, she stands at an upstairs window and looks out at the garden behind the house, thoughts flapping in her head. She walks into Edward's room and looks at his face, before returning downstairs to make tea, to complete a crossword, to stare at the walls.

Pauline Pilcher returns home, up the hill, and back along the main road to the village. On the way, she passes a row of cottages. Inside one of them, a young woman sits by the fire, holding a pendent crucifix in her hand. She's remembering something. A conversation from long ago, when she wasn't much older than a child. 'Keep safe,' her father called, his final words to her, 'Keep safe, d'you hear?' She has drawn the curtains across the window, and doesn't see Pauline Pilcher as she scurries past towards the modern bungalows that squat in a cluster off the main road.

The village sleeps, for the most part. The moon shines behind clouds, birds roost in trees. In his house in the woods, an old man mutters through troubled dreams. On the hill, the Henge stands as it has for thousands of years. A still witness to history.

The Magpie

Ancient I am. I saw it. The boy dragged to the bog, fur strapped on his eyes, still clammy with fox. We're all there; raven and rook, hooded crow. And buzzard spiraling high, tracing the Henge. Not every day there's a killing.

Afternoon sky's soft as doves. Up the hill they come, beating a drum of bent wood and leather and chanting in their curlew voices. Boy's stumbling, thin legged, sobbing. Hands bound back to back. His fingers scrabble like upturned beetles. They reach the stones and step within, push him to his knees. We settle at the edges, scratch scritch on the granite, and fold our wings. A respectful parliament. Who's to say what crime was done? Who's to say if there were crime at all? Men give thanks in mysterious ways, or plead. Maggoty-pie got no opinion, Maggoty-pie follows the hot reek of blood to get at the pickings.

He's naked. Shivering on the trodden grass as words are said. An incantation rolls from the throat of the elder. It lulls him, but still he shivers as the drum thumps like a slow heart. We watch. Heads sunk into ruffs, pods for eyes.

They lower a loop about his neck. It's thin as hair twine, and cruel edged. The elder raises a hand, his vowels gather and spin and there's a rustling as we shift our feet and skrark into the wind. The hand drops. The loop yanks back and twists tight. The boy gutters as a long pike punches his belly, and a rock smithereens the egg of his skull.

He falls.

We hop about.

Pickings.

But they raise him. Soft body. And there's a tenderness as they gather him and cradle him away, out of the circle, over the moor, to the murk. They cast him into the black and watch as

109

he sinks. Who's to say the pool doesn't carry him to the centre of the Earth?

The men carry their silences to the village below, where babes squall in huts and women cook on open hearths, and we gaze into depths darker than wing beats. Bereft.

Beautiful droplets jewel the grass.

CHAPTER 6

Skylark

The bog boy's on tour. I catch an item at the end of the local news as I spoon cold, slippery noodles into my mouth from a foil container. *From Ancient Times*, they're calling it. *A fascinating experience for the whole family!* The perky eyed presenter burbles from the wide atrium of what I recognise to be the Central City museum in Exeter. In the background, men in hi-vis vests are piecing together what will be an Iron Age walkway, complete with round, low roofed dwellings and gated animal pens, to be stocked with papier-mâché geese and sheep.

Visitors will be able to experience the sounds, sights and even smells of an Iron Age settlement, the presenter enthuses, before cutting to an interview with the museum's director, who proudly shows her the revolutionary 'smell box' - a small, square device through which the authentic stench of the unwashed Iron Age will be channelled. 'Why go to the bother,' sniffs my mother, who has begun work on repapering the living room walls. 'The Iron Age couldn't smell any worse than here,' and she glances pointedly at the leftover Chinese takeaway I'm eating, before letting her eyes wander to an overflowing bag of dirty washing beside the door. 'I haven't had time to go to the launderette yet,' I murmur. The camera's panning around the exhibition space to show scrag bearded mannikins in cloth tunics, display cases of wrought metal, rough clay bowls, rusting axeheads, and finally, Dartmoor Boy himself, encased like a macabre interpretation of Snow White in a dimly lit glass coffin.

'They should lay that boy to rest,' says my mother. She's unfurling a length of the blue flowered wallpaper over a rickety pasting table. 'Bury him,' she adds, with such finality that I study her face for a moment. Compassion?

'You're good at that, I say. 'Burying things.' She looks up at me, perplexed for a moment, before rolling her eyes in a familiar not that again way. 'This pattern'll be the devil to match up,' she says, marking out a cutting line with a pencil, 'how about you make yourself useful and mix up the gloop.'

I do as I'm told, and take a bag of wallpaper paste into the kitchen. Since our talk about Dad's death, we've again reached stalemate on any discussion of how I might find out more. Changing the subject is her usual tactic, but she couples this with regular deployment of pithy aphorisms; 'Live in the present, Skylark,' and 'what's past is past.' I add water to the wallpaper paste in a plastic bucket and watch it thicken to murk. Past is past, I mutter to myself, paste is paste. I picture the disinterred bog boy rising from his glass case to wander the museum's unlit corridors. Lost. A waif.

I suggest the museum trip to Edward the following day. 'I don't need to see him again,' he says, 'I am him,' but all the same, he's pleased at the idea and allows a faint smile to accompany the thin shrug of his shoulders. 'Will we go tomorrow?' he asks, but I explain that it's not quite so simple.

'We'll need your mother's permission,' I say, 'she'll need to sign a form. And I have to check with Mr Brearley that I'm allowed to take you out of school for the day.'

'The whole day?' he asks, his voice catching slightly. He's been tense since he walked into my office, his skinny muscles taut as violin strings. I nod, and he slackens into his chair. Unfolds. 'A whole day,' he repeats, wonderingly.

Edward hates school.

I've watched him, the way he moves around the campus, eyes down and skinny legs moving quickly, like scissors. He's always alone. That morning, I'd glanced through my office window to see a familiar brown satchel gliding high into the air, twisting inexorably, papers and books flung outward to flutter and fall. A group of kids stood around Edward; their eyes shining, as though they'd launched a firework rather than a schoolbag. I rapped at the window and they ran for it, leaving Edward to gather his scattered belongings, methodically stooping and lifting.

'The boys in my class like to lark about with my things,' he says when I ask him about it.

'Lark about?' I repeat. That anachronistic diction usually makes me smile, but today it angers me on his behalf. 'How does this larking about make you feel, Edward?' Again, the slight struggle in his face, before he assumes his customary blankness. 'I suppose it's how boys are,' he says. 'Up to high jinks all the time.'

I mention the 'high jinks' to Brearley when I call into his office at the end of the day. 'It'll be good for him to have a day out,' I argue. 'Give him some headspace.' But Brearley thinks otherwise.

'Normal for boys to indulge in a little horseplay now and again,' he says. 'Might do him some good. Toughen him up.' He regards me from beneath raised eyebrows. 'Can't see that a museum outing'll help him fit in any better. Other boys might see it as, y'know, a bit sissy.' I gaze back at Brearley. Am I the only person in the school who doesn't speak like it's 1957? His eyebrows remain raised. 'And how does this outing tie in with the curriculum?' he asks. I'm lost for a reply, and incredibly, the eyebrows are nudged even further up his forehead. 'Learning objectives?' he asks.

'Do I need any? It's just that he's interested in that sort of thing, and,' but Brearley is shaking his head and muttering, 'Skylark, Skylark, Skylark,' while pulling open a filing cabinet and flicking through layers of meticulously ordered documents. 'Trips Protocol,' he says, pulling out a sheaf of papers and setting them before me, before reciting the first line of an extensive opening paragraph; 'Any trip that takes place must be fully risk assessed, and have clear learning objectives, which aim to support and develop the curriculum.' He watches me leaf through the document, a bureaucratic tangle of questions and tick boxes; *Fully explain how the excursion will develop and extend the knowledge and/or skills of students. How will the learning outcomes of the excursion be evidenced?* God, how should I know? By a smiling child?

'Mind you,' says Brearley, who has returned to his chair, and is steepling his fingers in a thoughtful, headmasterly pose; he must have been watching Goodbye Mr Chips. 'If you were to run a trip like this, say, for a group of students rather than just one, we could pass it off as a team building exercise. Probably get some brownie points from Ofsted on the pastoral side of things. How many students do you mentor? Ten or so? Enough for a minibus?

'I don't have a minibus license,' I tell him, 'I was thinking I could take Edward in my car.'

'Ah, but I have a minibus license. And d'you know? I rather fancy seeing this exhibition. Let's go ahead.' He grins. 'You do the organising, and I'll drive.'

Most of my evening is spent filling out the trip document, formulating phrases that I hope look convincing. *Reflecting upon societal structures of the past will aid students in recognising possibilities for their own future roles in society*, I type. *Group discussion of these will strengthen bonds between students, and help them to form social and team-building skills.*

I take off the necklace and loop it on the corner of my laptop. And why do I want to see the bog boy? What do I hope to see? My father's necklace dangles from the laptop, tapping gently against the side of the screen as I type, a meaningless Morse code.

The kids are uninterested in learning objectives and outcomes, but delighted to hear they can have a day off school. 'We get to see a real dead body? Cool!' says 13 year old Jakey (fostered, dyspraxic, recently caught shoplifting when he fumbled the loot and dropped it on his way through the exit). Even moody Melissa looks vaguely enthused; 'We can go shopping too, right?' They all manage to return their signed consent forms within days.

All of them, that is, except for Edward.

'I've lost it,' he tells me, so I hand him a replacement. He looks at the form. The toe of one shoe moves in tiny circles, stirring up a mini-maelstrom of acrylic tufting on the carpet. 'My mother doesn't want me to go,' he says.

'Why not?' I ask.

'She didn't say.'

He's not looking at me. Keeps his eyes fixed, instead, on the sheet of paper in his hand.

'I'll write to her,' I say. 'I'll explain why you should come. Go to class. Come pick the letter up at the end of the day.'

I write the letter. I emphasize Edward's interest in Iron Age history, and the opportunity he'll have to share this with others in the group - his peers, his could-be friends. Edward doesn't come to collect the finished letter, so I post it instead. She doesn't respond.

'I don't mind, really,' mumbles Edward.

I ask Edward for his phone number, but he claims not to know what it is

'She doesn't like answering the phone anyway,' explains Edward.

'Does she like answering the door?' I ask. The evening before the trip's due to take place, I drive to Edward's house.

It's a large, slightly intimidating house. Tall and steeply roofed, with high arched windows and an imposing front door, albeit with peeling paint, and cracks in the stained render of the walls. It has been built onto, though it's hard to tell which bits have been added to which. A squat, sloping section bulges from the left hand side, while at the other side some kind of glass structure clings on, the metal framework rusting away. I park up outside the gates, and slip through them into a dilapidated courtyard area. Dandelions have ruptured the tarmac in places, and foliage encroaches from the edges, the shine of rhododendron against a rough mesh of nettle and bindweed. I walk up three wide steps to the door, and ring the bell.

There's no response initially. I ring the bell three times and it's Edward who eventually opens the door, still in his school uniform of too long shorts and crisp white shirt. I say hello, and smile, warmly I hope, but Edward seems gripped by inertia. His hand, tightening on the doorframe, whitens at the knuckles. 'Can I come in?' I ask. He shuffles his feet, looks at them, and opens the door a little wider. Beyond him, in the dark corridor, a tall slender woman stands with her hands raised to her eyes, shielding them from the light.

'Mrs Parry? I'm Skylark Riley,' I say over Edward's head. She steps back a little, looks uncertainly from me, to Edward, to me again. From where I stand, she's all wisps and shadows. Long flowing dress and thin, anxious face. Her hair floats over her shoulders and her hands move constantly, twisting over each other in a Celtic knot of pale skin and slender fingers. As I move forward and extend my own hand, she stills for a moment before taking it. The handshake is brief and insubstantial, like something composed of air and water - light, and chill.

'Skylark,' she says, as if considering the meaning of the word. She doesn't say anything else, just stands, blinking at me, twisting the gold band on her finger.

'I'm Edward's Learning Mentor,' I start to explain, 'I...'

'I know who you are,' she says, and there's something in the way she says those words. A softness to her voice; a modulated, weightless cadence. I was expecting defensiveness. Irritation at my calling at the house, or anger even. Instead, there's aloofness tinged with resignation. And beneath it, something else.

Fear?

She collects herself. 'Please come in, Miss Riley.'

I follow her down the long hallway, glancing at the paintings on the walls as I pass them. I'm no expert, but they look like the real McCoy to me; darkening oils of landscapes and old, bearded men. I remember Colin Ford telling me about the Gainsborough, though I wouldn't know one if I saw one. There are spaces on the wall too, empty squares of unfaded wallpaper where paintings have been removed. The hallway opens into a large kitchen with homey furniture; a waxed pine table and chairs, an old fashioned cooking range and a wide welsh dresser laden with plates and pans. There's something odd about it though, and I work out what it is as Eleanor Parry fills a kettle at the sink. It's too neat. Too tidy. Every family kitchen I've ever been in has a warm, lived in feel to it; pans in the sink, kids' drawings stuck to the fridge, but this kitchen is spotless. Bare. It doesn't even smell of food. And there are candles, everywhere. It's early evening and still light outside, but the kitchen's only dimly lit from the window, and candles burn on the table and on the sill; some in candlesticks, others melted at the base to stand upright on saucers and tin lids. Mrs Parry sees me looking at them as she brings a teapot and cups to the table. 'We're saving on electricity,' she says, with a forced brightness.

'It's expensive,' adds Edward, who is hovering in the kitchen doorway.

'We do have power,' says his mother, 'but little money to pay for it.'

'The candles look pretty,' I offer.

'Yes,' says Mrs Parry. She stands beside me and pours tea into a cup. I breath in her perfume; floral, syrupy scent that doesn't waft from her so much as peel from her in sheets. Beneath it, I catch something softer, more malodorous, like damp or ripening cheese. 'I think Edward has homework to do in his room,' she says idly, 'don't you Edward?'

'I've done it already,' he says.

'Perhaps some reading then.' She doesn't look at him, but her body stiffens, and though

120

neither says anything, I sense a battle of wills playing out; the air thickens as Edward lingers, resisting, but then he relents and turns to be swallowed up by the hallway.

'How may I help you, Miss Wrigley?'

'It's Riley,' I say.

She pauses to consider this a moment, narrowing her eyes. 'Yes. That's better,' she says. 'Less like worms.'

It sounds like a joke, but there's no trace of a smile on her lips. 'Riley,' she's muttering, 'Riley. Skylark. Like the bird.' She pulls out a chair and sits at the table, opposite me, glancing about the room as she does so. I get the impression that she's checking all is in order before her eyes turn, sharply, to me. 'Why are you here?' she asks.

I tell her why I've come, reiterating the phrases from my letter. She hears me out, even retrieving the letter and blank consent form from a drawer in the dresser. 'So, what do you think?' I ask. She has unfolded the letter, and is smoothing it at the creases, slowly pressing them with the flat of a long fingernail.

'It isn't possible, Miss Riley,' she says.

I let the words hang there for a few seconds, floating out around us. She's still smoothing the letter. 'Why isn't it?' I ask.

Again, she looks around the room, an exasperated roving, as though trying to pinpoint the whereabouts of a buzzing fly. Her eyes settle, eventually on the yellow burn of a candle and she watches it for a moment.

'Dreams, Miss Riley,' she says, smiling the sort of soft brave smile usually seen through tears. 'Edward has dreams. Nightmares, really.' She pauses. 'He's suffered from them since he was,' she frowns, remembering I suppose, 'very young,' she decides. 'His former tutor took him to see the bog boy once, and they became worse for quite some time.' She lifts her teacup and sips from it, eyeing me over the rim. Your move, Miss Riley.

I know about Edward's nightmares. I say. 'I think...well, I'd say,' I don't know what to say. I wonder if I should show her the necklace, which I've stowed in my coat pocket, and tell her how, when Edward talks to me of his life, of his dreams, of her, he likes to hold the necklace in his hand. I know that she never leaves the house. I know that groceries are delivered from a shop in the village once a week, and left at the door. I know that she often disappears to her room for hours, days at a time, leaving Edward to look after himself. She has never taken him to a park, or a fairground. She didn't explain, or apologize, when his tutor, his one guide to the outside world, was dismissed. And because the boy has learned to contain himself, because his entire life has been one of boundaries not to be overstepped, because he loves her and fears her withdrawal, Edward has accepted this loneliness as normal. As routine. As his.

I look at Eleanor Parry. She's pale and interesting, and undeniably beautiful in a timeworn, tragic sort of way. Wide eyes, and wreathed in expensive looking, diaphanous fabric. Shit, who does she think she is? The Lady of fucking Shalott?

I let rip.

'Tell me, Mrs Parry,' I ask. 'Have you ever taken medical advice about Edward's recurrent nightmares?' She blinks at me, slowly. 'If it's such a problem, such a worry, don't you think some help should be sought?'

She's folding the letter. Concentrating on reinstating the folds exactly where they were. 'And don't you think, Mrs Parry, that his nightmares might, just might, be connected to the fact he's spent his whole life caged up in this house. He dreams of suffocating, he's told me. He wakes up breathless. Hardly surprising when he lives with,' I gesture at the candles, 'Miss Havisham.' I regret the comparison even as it escapes my lips. It comes out a bit squeakily.

She's not looking at me. Is, instead, pushing the folded letter back into its envelope, and not making a good job of it either as her hands are trembling. I want to say more, but I'm not sure where to go now I've thrown Havisham into the mix. I remember that Eleanor Parry has been deserted by her husband. I want to glance at her feet beneath the table, check they're both inside shoes.

'Miss Havisham,' she says emptily, 'was abandoned by a man she loved.'

Oh dear.

'As was I, Miss Riley. As was Edward.'

She stands, walks to the window. The light has faded and the candles on the windowsill burn more brightly in the gathering dark. Eleanor Parry's face is reflected in the window. I watch it as she speaks.

'Please believe, Miss Riley, that I love Edward, and want the best for him. I know him. You do not. Not fully. He's not an ordinary boy. He's sensitive, and he has suffered the loss of a father in the last year, as well as changes to his schooling.'

'His father's not dead though,' I say. 'There's a chance he may come back, isn't there? Or at least make contact.'

'No,' she says simply. 'There's no chance of that. Not now.'

I wait. She's staring at her own flickering reflection, or perhaps beyond it, at the overgrown garden beyond the window. She presses her palms on the edge of the sink, steadying them. I watch her mouth moving, an almost imperceptible shifting of the lips. She's counting, slowly, each number granting calm as they're silently shaped. One. Two. Three. Four. Her shoulders begin to slump a little, the arms loosen at the elbows. I wait, until she turns to face me.

'My husband,' she begins, 'married me for my money. The money has now gone, and so has he.' She smiles weakly. 'He won't be back.'

I'm not quite sure what to say to this, so I take a gulp from my almost cold tea. It's weak, bitter edged. Eleanor Parry sits back down at the table, clasping her hands in front of her in a way that, weirdly, reminds me of Brearley in one of his Skylark, Skylark, Skylark moods.

'Edward will not be visiting the Iron Age exhibition because museums are filled with things that will remind him of his father. Collectable things. His father was a collector of things.' One of the candles on the table has begun to gutter, and she reaches out a hand to pinch the flame between two thin fingers. 'I don't want him upset. School provides a distraction, but a museum will unsettle him.' Smoke from the snuffed candle billows between us, an acrid ribbon.

'He's already unsettled,' I say, gently. 'He's struggling to adapt to school, and a day out may do him some good.' I stand to leave. 'Please, Mrs Parry. Consider it.'

'These candles,' she's says, fiddling with the extinguished wick, 'too long. They flicker.' Suddenly her head is moving, as she looks from one candle to another, to another, to another, momentarily studying each flame until satisfied. 'Goodbye,' she says, lightly and pleasantly. I stare at her, fascinated, as she takes a pair of nail scissors from the table drawer and sets about using them to nibble the tip of the candle wick. She seems oblivious to me. A light touch on my elbow makes me jump, but it's just Edward, returned from his banishment upstairs. He leads me away, to the front door. 'You tried,' he says, simply. A statement of fact rather than consolation. He walks outside with me over the courtyard. 'Don't worry,' he says, giving me his old man smile, and I have a sudden compulsion to hug him. Or at least put an arm around his shoulders so I can squeeze them in an *oh well*, sort of way. But he's gone before I touch him, walking back to the house in that quick, straight legged way of his.

I feel a little rattled by the whole thing to tell the truth, and light a cigarette before climbing into my car. The evening has closed in with a chill clamminess, and I stand for a while, breathing it in. That palpable still of a windless night, when if you listen hard enough, you can hear the trees growing. That's what Xav told me once. I listen, and I do hear a slight movement in the leaves that makes me stare for a moment, even if it spooks me a little. But it's just the green dark staring back at me. I get into the car and drive home.

Peter

Dear Anna,

And so I set my inked pen to paper again. Do you recall our father's fountain pen? His pride and joy; a gift from our mother. Silver cased, but gold nibbed. We weren't allowed to write with it, but sometimes he would sit me on his lap and allow me to draw ink from the well into the barrel. I recall the sharp scent of it, the heft of the pen in my hand. The one I write with now is similar, though not so elegant as his. I wonder where our father's pen is now - they took it of course, on the first day they came.

I have always said that I do not want to remember that time, yet increasingly, when I take my daily walk to the stones above this village, my mind curves back to the streets we played in as children. Of course, once the soldiers arrived, the streets were no longer our playground. Rather, a death ground. The tuberculosis had struck that chill winter and we were not permitted outside at all for fear we'd contract the illness. Sometimes, I've considered it would have been better if we'd simply caught the disease ourselves.

Oh Anna. Would things have been different had our father not been a medical man? He stayed, when so many others had already left, quite unable to walk away from the patients he had known all his life, the children he himself had delivered. And it was his status as medical man that gave us our chance, our opportunity. Do you recall the Captain? How he came to us one night, knocking gently at the door rather than smashing it open as his comrades had done on previous occasions. He was pale faced, with shining beads of sweat standing out on his forehead. His teeth were gritted in pain as our mother calmly led him inside and guided him to a chair. He was limping badly, and our mother lifted his injured foot onto a cushioned stool and ordered me to bring him a glass of water before fetching our father. She loosened the stiff collar of his uniform and dabbed his forehead dry.

He had stepped on a nail and the sole of his foot was punctured and infected. The army doctor was an idiot, he told us. He needed a proper surgeon and he'd heard that my father was the best in the city. And so, despite the Nazi insignia on his collar, despite me standing outside the door with fists clenched in fury, my father diligently treated the wound, cutting away the infected flesh, applying powders to soothe the pain and recommending medicines Herr Capitan should take to halt the possibility of blood poisoning.

'A sick man is a sick man,' was all my father said to me after the officer had left. 'I am a doctor, Peter, my purpose is to heal.' No more was said on the matter.

We did not see the captain again until that awful day, the last day we spent with our parents. We had been ordered to the railway station and stood in a line on the platform, awaiting instructions to board the train. Herr Capitan himself was marching up and down the line, noting down names and occupations. When he came to my father, he hesitated, before standing back and loudly reading out my father's name from his notes. "Lempel, Lucien. Married. No children,' he said, before moving on down the line. I was standing with you, behind our mother, when I felt a hand on my shoulder and was shoved backwards away from the line. 'Run you little fools,' hissed the voice of one of our neighbours, 'Both of you, go. Go now, you're not on his list.' I stood dumbstruck, but you grabbed my hand and pulled me back from the line, dragged me in behind one of the station buildings and put your hand over my mouth to stop me from crying out.

The station that day was full of noise and whistles, the clipped stamping of Nazi boots, the barking of their ferocious dogs, the confused chatter of the passengers boarding the carriages through huge sliding doors, orders screeched in German and broken Yiddish, the high yelps of women as they were led away from their husbands, and you, Anna, you. You were always the bossy one. The one who made decisions. 'Let's go, Peter,' you said. And we went, slipping unseen through a gap in the chain link fence and dashing for the fields that lay beyond the station, high with yellow corn and perfect for concealing two children.

We never saw our mother and father again.

Anna, I weep as I write.

Forgive me,

Peter

A History of Stonemoor
by Pauline Pilcher

From whence comes History? I mean, of course, in the tangible sense. Perhaps I mean palpable? Either way, I mean, how does History, those lost and shadowy dramas of the past, become corporeal? Real. Factual. Solid as brick. Certain.

Evidence, dear reader. Evidence.

Take the bog boy. We know of his ritual murder because of his wounds, and the garrote about his neck. We know what he ate on the day of his death because it was found in a half digested mulch in his stomach. His teeth provided his age. Even the colour of his hair is under no dispute. ~~(His eye colour, however, a moot point; the pigment having been leached away by the bog.)~~ *But why was he executed? In what manner was he arrested and charged, if at all? This, we will never know. History has a way of closing over the details,* ~~plugging the orifices, so to speak~~. *Rather like the black quagmire of the bog closing over the murdered boy, shaping itself so perfectly about him that all extraneous detail is blacked out. If we want the whole story, the whole*

truth, we must construct a scaffold;
a framework built from conjecture,
from probability, from likelihood
and possibility rather than (as in
the case of our old friend Kingsley
Swarthmore) pure invention and wild
fantasy.

In writing a history of this
village, I have been careful to
build my castle on the firm bedrock
of hard fact. Verifiable
documentation. Archaeological
findings. Proper and meticulous
research. No piratical Swarthmore
tactics here. Swarthmore - even the
name has something of shifting sands
about it. Rest assured, reader,
Pauline Pilcher is never anything
less than thorough.

She punches that last full stop with a
flourish, and reads back over what she has read,
lifting the edge of the paper so it stands upright in
the feed roll. Evidence. Yes. She pulls the sheet
free and lays it on top of the thin manuscript,
which is gradually rising on her desk, page by
painstaking page. She stares at it, becoming
conscious, in the silence, of tiny noises around her.
The ticking of a clock on her desk, the creak of her
wooden chair, the intermittent flitter and squawk
of birds out in the garden, and the low hum of
something inside her own head; the click and
whirr of electricity, synapses swinging open and

slamming shut like little doors. She remembers the scene; a stranger, standing outside the house where strangers do not go. Where they are never, ever welcomed.

She has placed the cigarette stub she collected from outside the Parry house in a white saucer on her desk. Now, she pushes the typewriter back and lifts the saucer, placing it carefully before her. She has brought a small pair of sugar tongs from the kitchen, and she uses these to prod the stub, so that flecks of black ash fall from the burned end, like fragments of crushed black pepper. She opens a drawer in the desk and withdraws a magnifying glass. Then, she delicately squeezes the tongs around the butt, and lifts it, turning it slightly in the light from the window, while her right eye balloons and recedes behind the thick glass lens. She has a notepad and pen beside her, and laying the butt back on its saucer, she writes a few lines. Now and again she scrutinizes the cigarette stub, sniffs it even, nostrils flare to suck in the redolent stink of cold tar.

She leans back against the rigid chair back, thoughtful, tapping the pen on the pad. She has written;

No lipstick - so a man? Not certain.

Burned down to filter - but letters visible D I A - N?

Heavy blend - tarry - heavy smoker?

It's not a lot to go on, but it's something. A link. A clue. A step in the right direction.

Surveillance is what's needed. Something concrete, like the car registration plate. She's irritated she didn't think of that at the time, it could have led her to a name. And once she has a name, then what? A confrontation? An unwitting confession uncoiling from the very lips that were pursed about this cigarette? The butt is slightly dented, no doubt slicked with saliva that would give a DNA match if she were in any way resourced to discover it. Not to worry. A name will do. One that can be looked into, from which a viable conclusion may be drawn. One that will add substance to the theory she has formulated about Edward over the years. Once she has that, once she can go to Eleanor with that all important thing - evidence - then, things will change.

She has taken to wearing Eleanor's blue silk scarf about her own neck. The scent of it dizzies her.

CHAPTER 7

Skylark

It's a drag, of course. Arriving at work to see Brearley decked out in his golfing casuals; primrose V-neck, pale slacks; on his feet, brown loafers. Do I really have to spend a whole day with him? My heart slumps a little in my chest. He's buzzing around the minibus with a clipboard, ticking off tyre pressures, oil level, fire extinguisher, 'We need to check all indicators are in working order,' he says, in lieu of hello. I stand behind the bus, giving a thumbs up in the wing mirror as they flash on and off.

The kids are hovering at a distance, but gravitate towards the bus when they see me. They're largely different ages and eye each other up, keeping within their own spaces like polarised magnets. I wish Edward was amongst them, giving some kind of point to this whole trip, and then I see him, hurrying in through the school gates as the others board the bus under Brearley's direction. He has a piece of paper in his hand and he presents it to me with a flourish and a formal little bow, which ought really to be accompanied by a smart click of his heels. The consent form, completed and signed. 'Wow,' I say. 'She signed it?' He doesn't answer, but looks me full smack in the eyes and raises his eyebrows. I study the signature; an artful scrawl, but who's to know? 'Welcome aboard,' I grin, and he boards the bus.

The journey to Exeter passes relatively calmly. Brearley, as it turns out, is a stickler for the speed limit, even in the fast lane. We're regularly tailgated and flashed by speedier motorists, leading to surreptitious middle finger showing from the boys on the back seat. 'You're forgetting that the name of the school is on the side of this bus,' says Brearley through gritted teeth, glowering at them in the rearview mirror. For the most part, though, the kids stare at their phones or listen to music for the whole journey. Edward sits towards the front of the bus, alone in his long school shorts and blazer, his leather satchel balanced on bony knees. The others, almost without exception, are in hoodies and trainers and ill fitting skinny jeans. The sort that makes my mother tut when she sees people wearing them. 'Why are you in uniform?' I hear Melissa ask him, herself in a wine colored dress and leggings, and red wedge-heeled boots, of which I'm a little envious. I don't hear his reply, if he even gives one. When I glance back at him he's leaning his head against the window, one eye closed, watching the road lines arrow past. Melissa has plugged herself into her phone, lips moving gently to whatever invisible music it transmits. I wish I could listen to some music myself but Brearley is running through his requirements for the day ahead. Students are to stay together at the museum. Have I prepared some kind of worksheet for them to do? No? Regretable. There should be a clear focus with students like these. Under no circumstances should they be allowed to wander freely, or they'll be chipping the Ming vases and sitting on the Chippendales. I lean my head against the window and, like Edward, close one eye and watch the road markings blur.

There's a kerfuffle in Exeter as Brearley attempts to navigate the one way system and find a car park. 'Surely you thought about where we'd park?' he snaps at me. I point out that, as he himself offered to drive, I'd have thought that was his responsibility, at which the kids whoop and cheer and yell, 'Geddon, Miss!' while their headmaster slams on the brakes before an almost missed turn and virtually launches them out of their seats. But we get parked up eventually, and after Brearley has made a speech about responsibility and behaviour and the reputation of the school, we get out of the minibus and head for the museum. The kids chatter and get in the way of pedestrians as we walk down the street. 'Keep left!' shouts a red faced Brearley as the kids meander and pause, hang back or charge ahead. It's a short walk, but cluttered with distractions;

shop windows and kiosks, a party of Japanese tourists, a bearded busker. 'He's shit,' says Josh loudly (15, recently suspended for coming to school drunk. Has a police record for criminal damage). 'You're shittier,' responds the busker laconically, as Brearley grabs Josh by the shoulder and pulls him along.

When we get to the museum, an official in peaked cap and uniform places himself between us and the revolving doors. 'Have you made a group booking?' he asks. I stare at him blankly. 'If you're here with a school party,' he explains, 'you should've made a group booking.'

'Oh,' I say. I glance at Brearley beside me. His fists are clenched at his sides, and a vein in his right temple is visibly throbbing. 'If you go in, they might be able to offer you a time slot,' says the official. The group of Japanese tourists we passed earlier are ascending the museum steps, waving tickets and picking their way through our own group, who have clustered on the steps and are blocking the way. 'Eeeee-aaaah kuuung foooo,' I hear from one of the younger kids. He's stretching the corners of his eyes into matching slants with his fingers and wobbling his head from side to side. The Japanese people gaze at him inscrutably. 'Sort. It. Out,' mutters Brearley dangerously as I slip through the revolving door.

The only time slot they can give us is for 2pm, two hours away. There are already three school parties booked in to view the exhibition, and another group would make the whole space too crowded, the receptionist explains. I take the print out admission slip and head back outside, where the kids have slumped on the steps, much to the annoyance of Brearley, who is exhorting them to stand up and move to the side. 'Ah, Miss Riley,' he says loudly as he sees me emerge, clapping his hands together and twisting his face into something resembling a grin, perhaps to detract from the fact the kids have largely ignored his requests; only Edward stands to the side, while the others lounge in various poses of insouciance. I notice that Josh is rolling a cigarette. I tell Brearley the bad news, that we have two hours to kill before we can enter the structured confines of the museum. Brearley's face crumples. 'But where can we take them?' he asks desperately, 'is there a children's playground or something?' It's hard not to smile at the image this conjures of Josh, fag dangling from his bottom lip, on a seesaw with Melissa scowling at him from the other end. I turn to the group. 'Look everyone,' I say, 'we can't see the exhibition until 2 o'clock. So what we're going to do is let you have a look around the town and the shops for a bit, and meet back here at quarter to two.'

'Awesome!' cries Liam (recently excluded for having a swastika shaved into the back of his head) as he punches the air and leaps to his feet. Josh has already slipped from the group and is heading down the street. 'Stay in pairs or small groups,' I call, as they vacate the steps and head for the town centre, 'and don't let me down.' One or two lift a hand in acknowledgement as they disappear. Brearley is staring at me agog. 'What are you doing?' he says, his voice strangely high pitched, 'they'll run amok.' I turn to Edward, who has remained, alone and awkward. 'Now, what would you like to do?' I ask.

'He can come with me,' says a familiar, quiet voice. Melissa stands at the bottom of the steps. 'I don't want to hang out with that lot.' I hesitate, as does Edward, but then his brow furrows into a sudden decision and he moves towards her. The two set off wordlessly, with Melissa in front and Edward trailing behind like a recalcitrant little brother.

I have to say to you, Skylark,' Brearley is saying, in his favoured officious tone, 'that I'm highly disappointed in the way you're conducting this expedition. Not thinking to book in advance, letting them wander off unsupervised, it's highly unprofessional. Why, that tall boy was lighting a...a... a reefer as he walked away.'

'More likely it was just a roll up,' I reply. 'I'm sorry I didn't book in advance, I had no idea I'd have to, but as it is, I don't see the harm...'

'You'll see the harm when we're back at school and I conduct a review of your role at Henge,' he says. 'For now, we'll just have to see what this ridiculous situation brings.'

'It's not ridiculous to put your trust in them,' I say, losing the calm I've been trying hard to maintain. 'The whole way here you've done nothing but put them down with school reputation this and standards of behaviour that, you've not even mentioned what they might gain from being here. You judge them entirely on what you're afraid they might do, never on anything they actually do, or what they're interested in.' Brearley's face is reddening again and he's wagging a long finger in my face while hissing, 'Keep your voice down, Miss Riley.' The uniformed doorman is smirking at us from his post as Brearley regains his composure and runs a hand across his balding head. 'We'll discuss this back at school,' he says finally. 'For now, we have two hours to kill together. Any suggestions?' And I realise with dismay that in sending the kids away, I've unwittingly submitted myself to the company of Brearley. But then, from behind me, a voice that stops my thoughts entirely. 'Skylark?' it says. Cautious. Uncertain. I turn around and see Xav standing on the pavement.

Edward

He must keep up with the girl, but he doesn't feel comfortable walking beside her. She wanders rather than walks, pauses to look in shop windows, speeds up and slows down. He calculates five paces behind as being about the right distance and he puts all his energy into maintaining it, but it's difficult - she's too erratic - he has to stare at her back, concentrating hard, unable to watch his own feet and check where they're landing in case she stops, suddenly, like now. He grips the spoon in his pocket (St Thomas - speared to death) and feels the thin edged bowl bite into the fleshy mound of his palm. Again she stops and he stumbles - careening forward at just the moment she turns around. Instinctively, she puts out her hands and catches him under his armpits. 'Fucking hell,' she says, 'will you stop it?'

'What?' he says.

'This,' she says, righting him like an overturned vase. 'you nearly totalled me - boom, crash!' He blinks at her and she studies him. 'Tit,' she adds. Then, 'I'm hungry, got any cash?'

He hasn't. 'I didn't know we'd need any,' he says.

'Shame,' she says. 'I was hoping to bully some out of you.' He stares at her, and closes his hand around the spoon in his pocket, but her face creases into a faint smile. 'Just kidding,' she says, 'I've got money, and I fancy a burger. C'mon.'

He has never been into a burger bar before. Miss Pilcher had a preference for tea shops with cakes on the counter. She would always let him choose which one they should take a slice from; tall sponge sandwiches kept beneath plastic bell jars, or crumbly wedges of tiffin bursting with fat glace cherries. The burger bar doesn't have any food on display and is all shining surfaces and bright plastic chairs. Melissa hands him a paper bag and he opens it to find a cardboard carton and a small bag of french fries. She shows him how to open the carton and tip the yellow fries into the lid. Salt glitters on them. The burger bun is soft, the burger thick and greasy, and the cheese a melting slab that sticks to his tongue. It's the most delicious thing he has ever tasted. Melissa looks bemused, 'Nice, yeah?' He nods and closes his eyes before taking another bite. 'Wow, you really don't get out much,' she says, 'anyone'd think you've never had a burger before.'

'I haven't,' says Edward. He wipes his mouth on the sleeve of his blazer and peels the lid off the paper cup of coke Melissa has brought him. He has tasted coke before and remembers the shock of it - the sweet cold fizz. He brings his face close to the rim of the cup and watches the bubbles pop. 'Why did you say you'd stay with me?' he asks. Melissa swallows a mouthful of food before answering. 'They wouldn't have let us go wandering round the town alone,' she says, 'had to pair up with someone.' Edward sips at the coke. 'What about the others? Aren't you friends with them?' She shakes her head. 'Truth is, I'm a loner Ed. You and me are two of a kind.' He feels his

143

forehead puckering into a frown. 'I'm not really old enough to be your boyfriend,' he says. 'Wow,' says Melissa, 'don't sweat it Ed, I'm not after a toy boy.' He feels himself reddening; he's said something wrong again, but when he glances up, Melissa is grinning at him. It changes her face, he notices, makes her eyes light up. 'C'mon Ed, she says, drink up. There's a street near here with the coolest vintage clothes shop and I need to get there before we have to meet up for this shitty museum trip.'

'I like museums,' he says.

'You're a weirdo,' she says, 'but so am I, so we'll be ok.'

Edward drains the coke cup. He feels fine.

Skylark

He's less crumpled than usual, Xav. I watch him ordering coffees from the counter of the cafe we've found, you know the sort of place - all trendy wholefoods and long wooden tables and benches, so people can share elbow space with strangers and pretend to be open and un-english. Luckily, there are small bistro tables on the pavement outside and I grab one of those - the day is damp, but warm enough to sit out. Xav's wearing a dark overcoat and his haircut looks

144

recent; his brown hair has been clipped close to his scalp and looks soft, vulnerable even. I want to touch it. When he turns from the counter I realise I've been gazing at the back of his head with my mouth hanging slightly open, only just short of drooling. I compose my features and sit more upright and cross-legged. The bastard stole from me, he's not going to have an easy time, I'm a woman scorned.

'So,' he says as he pulls out the metal chair with a scraping noise that makes me wince. Composure, I think. 'So,' I reply, cooly. We regard each other. He's wearing a tie, which is at odds with his flannel checked shirt. The man could never properly dress himself. 'Nice tie,' I say, 'court appearance?' He grins, 'Just had a job interview actually,' and then as he clocks my surprise, 'I know, I know...wonders never cease, eh?'

'I'd hardly call you a wonder.'

'No?' And he puts on a corny American accent, 'We've had some wunnerful times though. You and me.'

'Oh, fuck off Xav.' I fumble in my bag for my cigarettes and can't look at him until I've lit one. When I do, he's staring at me with a mixture of amusement and disbelief. 'What did I do to deserve that?' he asks.

'Oh, what the hell, Xav? You turn up at my house, sleep with me, and leave with the contents of my bag in your pocket.

'What the hell yourself, Skylark. I borrowed a twenty to put some petrol in the bike and I tried to ring you later that day, but you must've blocked me on your phone or whatever 'cause I couldn't get through. Plus, you'd made your feelings about us perfectly clear so I didn't think I could rock up and see you again any time soon.'

'And my bank card? You borrowed that too?

'What bank card? I didn't take your bank card.'

'You did.'

'I didn't.'

'Piss off Xav, you did.'

'No I fucking didn't. How many bank cards did you lose when we were together, Skylark? Did you check your jacket pockets? That's where they normally are.' He shakes a cigarette loose from my packet and picks up my lighter. I notice that his hand trembles slightly as he sparks the flame. 'Damn it. I've given up,' he says, throwing the cigarette down.

I stub out my own cigarette as the waitress appears with our coffees and places them on the table. I find myself surreptitiously placing a hand on my jacket pocket. It's true - I have a habit of using cards and then just putting them in my pocket rather than back in my purse or bag, and I own a lot of jackets. There's something else he said though, that's bothering me more.

'What do you mean,' I say, 'with what you said...that I made my feelings perfectly clear?'

He doesn't look at me as he replies, 'That there was no 'us' anymore. Your words, Skylark. Your words.'

I think back to that last weekend together. The bike cooling on the pavement outside, the hot spoon against my lips. I can't remember saying anything. I sip the hot coffee; it scalds my throat as I swallow. 'Even if I had taken your card,' Xav says carefully, 'which I didn't, what about the cash you took when you emptied our joint account, yeah?'

I feel my face redden and I lift the cup to my lips again. Okay, it's true, I did take all of our shared money when I left the Exeter flat, but there were reasons for that - I was angry. 'You slept with someone else,' I say, 'I was angry, Xav. I wanted to, I don't know, hurt you, I suppose.'

'Wasn't I hurt enough, before?' he says softly, so very softly, that I hate him for it. 'I've got to go,' I say, 'we're taking the kids to the museum soon.' I stand abruptly, nudging the table so my remaining coffee slops onto the surface and I automatically say sorry as I grab serviettes from a dispenser to mop up the mess, 'I'm sorry,' I say again. He takes my hand by the wrist but I wrest it free. I don't want to talk to him, I just can't. 'Sorry,' I say, and there's something welling in my chest, a wave rising and gathering force - before - I can't think about before, I have to get away, now, right now, and here's my chance because I see Brearley striding down the street towards me, and not just Brearley, but Melissa, and not just Melissa, but a short, apple cheeked man with a scrub of beard on his face, and he has a hand on Melissa's shoulder as though guiding her, or making sure she can't get away. Brearley's face is... no, not red exactly, but a kind of mottled burgundy, veering towards purple in places. Florid, that's the word. 'This is Miss Riley,' he is saying as they approach, in that unusually high voice he has used a lot today, 'she's the team leader, she's responsible.' I'm amazed his words are even audible through such tightly clenched teeth. 'What's happened?' I ask.

'What's happened?' Brearley starts, but he is interrupted by his companion.

'You then,' says the man, who, beneath his scrappy beard is just as florid and angry as Brearley, 'unless we can sort this out I'm phoning the police.' I look from one face to the other, baffled.

'It's Edward,' says Melissa calmly, 'he nicked something from a shop and then ran off, and now we can't find him.'

Edward

He runs. Phillip holds a staff. Simon, a saw. They fill his head, jostling for space and shouting, their metal robes swishing into life and clattering as each brandishes the object of his death – Matthew with an axe, chop-chop-chopping and Andrew, a cross, like an X, clasped to his chest, while Edward's own chest aches ready to burst as he runs. There's yelling behind him and the apostles yell back from his head. He dodges people - they seem to part for him - clearing a path like the Red Sea for Moses, and a voice calls out, *stop*! But he runs. St Thomas jumps in his pocket and beside St Thomas, the one. The spoon. The one he's been missing. People, cars, buses, scream of brakes, pedestrian lights, a siren somewhere, and suddenly, salvation - a swing door, people, families, no - better - a tourist group just heading in, so he tags along, mingles, then down the stone steps, through a door, and down down down behind them. The route is lit with a string of pale lights but Edward takes a left into the dark and walks down down down again and another left - a right - a left - and there's a crawl space smelling of cold rock and wet soil, so he pulls himself through on his belly, through into a dark pocket, and he waits.

The chatter of tourists fades to far off and distant, and there's just quiet and cold and his own hot breathing, slowing now. He can't see in this dark, but he can feel with his fingertips and runs them over the spoon, the spoon he found and took and ran with; the missing spoon. His father's missing spoon. The bowl feels a little dented, but it's the one. He knows. The missing apostle spoon;

St Judas with his tiny hands clasping a fat bag of money. The Judas spoon, and Edward is holding it in his own two hands.

Skylark

'Tell me exactly what happened?' I say to Melissa, but Brearley can't contain himself.

'Have you any idea how bad this will look if the police get involved,' he hisses, 'if the press get hold of it?'

I turn to him. 'Anyone'd think you're more concerned about the school's reputation than you are about Edward's safety.' Xav, who is hovering nearby, smiles. He has always accused me of possessing a sharp tongue, but to tell the truth, I don't feel good about silencing Brearley with a neat reply - I'm too anxious about Edward.

'We were browsing in an old shop,' Melissa tells me, 'you know, one of the old junk shops on that little side street,' she points vaguely back at the direction she arrived from, 'loads of them have vintage clothes and old jewellery, so I was looking through some stuff on a clothes rail, and Edward was just mooching about - I wasn't paying any attention to him to tell the truth - then suddenly that bloke,' she nods at Beard, who has retreated to a little distance with Brearley, 'the shopman, he says, 'where are you going with that, young man?' and I glance up and there's Edward, like,' she laughs, 'little Edward, yeah? And he just barges past him and out the door and he legs it.'

'Go on,' I say.

'Well, that's it really,' she replies. 'The guy set off after him, and I'm like, woah - did that just happen? And I was about to go after them but there was a woman there too and she basically told me to stay put - she'd seen us come in together - so I stayed, and the man comes back all outta puff, and he threatens to ring the police but I managed to convince him to come with me to see you instead. Problem is, 'she rolls her eyes and lowers her voice, 'just Brearley was there outside the museum so he got all arsey about it and brought us to find you, and here we are.'

'And here we are,' I say. I've never heard Melissa string so many sentences together. 'What the hell did he steal?'

She shrugs. 'He had something in his hand but I couldn't really see what it was, it was all so quick.'

I can hear Brearley making all kinds of promises to the shop owner; he'll get to the bottom of this, he'll deal with the boy himself, very severely, and of course his parents will be involved, and really, there's no need for police involvement at this stage. I join them, and point out that as an 11 year old boy is missing in an unfamiliar city, then perhaps police involvement may be just the thing we need.

'Well then, Miss,' says Beard, 'shall I ring them or shall you? Because believe me, that lad's gonna wish he was still missing when I get my hands on him.'

'Are you making threats against a child, sir?' I ask

Over the man's shoulder, Brearley is glaring at me, and, rather bizarrely, running a finger across his throat.

'I think you should call the police, Skylark,' says Xav, who has appeared at my elbow, 'a missing child is a serious matter; they've got a better chance of finding him than we have.'

'How would they find him though?' I ask innocently. 'I suppose it would involve a lot of manpower, a lot of fuss?

'In a lot of cases, they use a helicopter,' says Xav.

'Or a TV appeal?' I add.

'Probably,' says Xav.

Brearley looks like he might faint any minute, so I put him out of his misery. 'But I don't think we can say he's missing until he misses our rendezvous at the museum,' I say, 'and that's still an hour away.'

We agree to wait and see, and while Brearley waits at the meeting point, I walk Melissa and Beard to the shop. Xav tags along too. Melissa leans in towards me as we walk. 'Is he your boyfriend?' she asks.

'Ex,' I reply, curtly. She glances back at him over her shoulder.

'Not behaving like one,' she says.

The shop is one of a parade that's tucked into a narrow side alley not too far from the main High Street. It has a traditional olde worlde theme going on; a Penny Farthing is suspended from the ceiling, and tin replicas of old 20's and 30's ads for Pears Soap and Cadbury's chocolate adorn the window. The sign outside reads, Mr Boyle's Emporium of Antiques, Curios and Retro, in a suitably curly font. Mr Boyle himself is represented in a garish painting as a monocled and moustachioed gent, complete with top hat and cane. A far cry from Beard, who is in fact Mr Boyle, and who has calmed down a little during the walk back to the shop.

'Trouble is,' he explains, 'teenagers come in and lift stuff all the time. If I don't call the police every now and then, then they'll see me as a soft touch and keep coming back for more.' The shop is dark and dingy, and packed to the hilt with all manner of what my mother would call car boot nonsense. One wall is invisible behind a teetering stack of dressing tables, bedside cabinets and dark oak wardrobes with heavily carved facades. Dusty table lamps jostle for space with tinted glass vases, tea sets and candlesticks. A tangle of moth eaten dolls stare, blank eyed and cherub mouthed, from faded velvet dresses and beribboned shoes. A whole glass cabinet is given up to the art of taxidermy; an otter's sinuous body curls around a mounted collection of songbirds, a fox snarls at a sleeping cat. There are unstrung guitars, horsehair cushions and elaborately feathered hats, mannikins resplendent in ball gowns, rack after rack of jackets and coats, shirts and waistcoats, dresses and high heeled shoes. 'Just look at this place,' I say, 'how can you tell when anyone's stolen anything?'

'Oh, I can tell,' says Boyle, tapping the side of his own head with a stubby finger, 'I've got it all logged, y'see.'

'And Edward?' I ask. 'What did he steal?'

'Something from here,' he says, pulling out a large wooden tray, which is filled with mismatched metal cutlery. 'I peer at the contents of the tray, and work it out a whole lot quicker than Boyle takes to tell me.

'A spoon,' I say, more to myself than to him, but he nods.

'That's right, a spoon. How did you know?'

'He collects them. Tell me, was it a special kind of spoon, an apostle spoon?'

'Well, sort of,' he says. 'A replica, silver. I had it priced at a fiver.'

'Five pounds? You're making this much fuss over five pounds?'

'Hey listen love, I'm a businessman, not Dr Barnardo.'

Xav steps in. 'Can I pay for it,' he says. He pulls out his wallet. 'If it's paid for, then it's all square.'

'Well I don't know, I'm sick of kids coming in here and thinking they can just...'

'Ten pounds then,' says Xav, searching in his wallet, 'Oh, look at that, I've only got a twenty - will you accept that?'

The shopkeeper hesitates, then gives a gruff nod and the deal is done.

'Thank you,' I whisper to Xav.

'We're quits on that twenty now,' he replies stonily, 'So, you ran after the boy, did you Mr Boyle? How far did you get?'

As the shopkeeper regales Xav with details of the chase – apparently, Edward can run like a whippet and is a proper Houdini in the art of escapology - I aimlessly prod apart a cluster of costume jewellery that adorns a stand on the counter. Glitzy trash mainly, but I'm a sucker for pretty stones and I find myself holding a fake emerald pendant against my dress. 'Goes with your eyes,' says Boyle, whose own eyes appear to be so fixed on my breasts that I spontaneously bring my hand up to draw the collar of my shirt more fully closed. I glare at him, but he's licking his lips and continuing to stare, 'That's a nice one. Antique?'

'What? This?' My silver necklace, the cross, has caught his attention. 'Unusual, that,' he says, 'I'm trying to place it. Pre - Victorian, definitely.'

Xav is looking too, now. 'That's the one your Dad gave you that time?' He reaches out and lifts it gently from my throat, his fingers momentarily brushing my skin.

'Yes,' I say, plucking it back and tucking it inside my shirt. 'We really need to get to the museum, the kids will be rocking up soon and Edward...'

'Might even be Georgian,' says Boyle, 'I'd need a closer look but...'

'Would that make it expensive? Valuable like?' says Melissa.

'Original Georgian jewellery? In good nick?' He gives a low whistle, 'You're talking four figures sweetheart. If it is Georgian - might be even older judging from the shape of it, and the wear. A bit small for Elizabethan though, can I take another look, love?'

'It's not old,' I say. 'My father had it made for me a few years ago, it's not worth much at all. And please don't call me love. I'm not anyone's love. I catch Xav's eye for the tiniest second before he looks away.

'Sorry darling,' says Boyle. There's a silence, which Melissa fills by humming a nervous little tune. 'Thanks for your time, Mr Boyle' says Xav as he heads out of the shop. I follow him, but as he strides away from me I say his name, and he stops and waits for me to speak. I can't think what to say, and so we stand there until he glances at his watch, 'I've got to be going, Skylark.'

'Right,' I say. But we continue to stand there, on the pavement. Me looking vacantly at cars as they trundle past. Xav, looking intently at the sky, in the way of someone trying to pinpoint what the weather might do. The bell from the shop chimes as Melissa steps out and stands between us, looking from his face to mine. 'Are you going to help us find Edward?' she asks earnestly. Xav nods his head, slowly. 'Edward needs to be found,' he agrees.

'He'll probably turn up at the museum,' I offer, 'he wants to see the exhibition.'

'Right,' says Xav, 'you're probably right. I'll head off then.'

'But he might not,' says Melissa, an ominous note to her tone. 'He might be scared of being in trouble. Anything could happen to him.'

I hesitate, but then, 'Xav,' I say, 'we could do with your help.'

'Right,' says Xav. 'I'll hang around for a while.'

'Cool,' says Melissa.

'Thank you,' I say.

We head off towards the museum, but as Melissa and I take a right, Xav takes a left and leaves us hesitating on the street corner. In the distance, I can see the kids lounging on the museum steps, two of them astride the recumbent stone lions that flank the entrance, while Brearley strides back and forth on the pavement, stabbing at his mobile phone with one finger - to reach me, as it turns out. I can feel my phone buzzing in my pocket, and am about to reach in and answer it when I hear my name being called and turn to see Xav standing at the far end of the street, beckoning me. I reach into my other pocket, and pull out the museum tickets. 'Melissa, you're in charge,' I say. She stares back at me, wide eyed, but I don't fall for it. 'You're the oldest and the most sensible. They'll listen to you. Just tell them to shut up and behave - a guide will be showing you around anyway. I'll join you as soon as I can.' I walk away before she can argue and, glancing over my shoulder, I see her joining the rest of the group at the steps, brandishing the tickets as she does so. 'Let's go see a corpse,' I hear someone shout as I approach Xav standing where the road curves around a busy pedestrianized area.

'See that?' he asks as I pull up beside him. I don't see. He's pointing across the wide precinct, through the shoppers and the office workers, and seemingly at a large branch of Next, which dominates the street from behind huge plate glass windows and loud red and yellow sale signs.

'What? Do you need a new pair of slacks?' I ask, at which he smiles.

'Who says slacks? That's your mother talking - no, there.' I follow the line of his finger to the narrow glass door he's indicating. 'Do you remember how Boyle reckoned he'd just disappeared?' he says. 'Well, suppose he'd just ducked in somewhere, out of harm's way for a moment. From what I've gathered, I think that's an Edward sort of place right there.'

I find myself nodding. It's absolutely an Edward kind of place. Exeter's medieval underground passages, quietly running beneath the city for the last 600 years, and entered by the narrowest doorway imaginable, are very much an Edward sort of place.

'C'mon then,' says Xav.

Edward

The bog boy lay in the dark, and Edward lies in the dark. He breathes in and out until the earth smells begin to separate; he smells water, and stones crushed by time; tinctured air, metals. There's a stink, a reeking miasma that floats over and beneath, but between it, a purity; he wonders if that's the way light might smell.

From above, he can hear the rumble of tyres on tarmac, dulled and grumbling, and he feels pressed in, so he tries to imagine clouds bulging with rain and bumping over the ground, over himself, down here, far below.

Other noises too - the guides with their trailing lines of tourists. There are two guides he works out - they take turns at bringing the tourists through. He tries to imagine what they look like from their voices - he can't make out words, just intonation. The woman's voice is flat, with curled edges. The man's more slow and deliberate. He looks at his watch, pressing the tiny button on the side that lights up the face and he uses it to time the tours - 15 minutes each. He knows he can't stay, but it feels nice here. Safe.

And he has the spoon in his hands.

Edward's eyes close, but only for a moment. The voices fade and all's quiet so he pulls himself to his feet and walks out into the passageway. He looks left and right. The lights used to illuminate the tourist routes have dimmed a little. He follows them back the way he came in, but something is different because when he reaches the place where he remembered the main entrance to be, there's no door, just more tunnel. He keeps walking, following the bend round to the right for what seems like a very long way. 'Who's in the Labyrinth now?' he hears, and he spins around, but there's no one there.

He walks back the way he has come and sees a spur of tunnel branching to the left, it must be the turn, he must have missed it, so he follows it, and the lights are growing dimmer, but it must be the right way, it must. He feels for the spoon in his pocket, the new spoon, and to his surprise, his hand closes over all of the spoons at once. He must have brought them all here without realising, and they now lie in his pocket, neatly stacked and pressed together by his squeezing hand. He lifts them out to look at them and hears a voice - his father's voice, angry - *what the hell have you done?* And he drops them, drops them onto the soft earth, where they start to sink into the mud. He scrabbles for them, but the lights flicker and fail so he can't see - he can't see the spoons sinking into the mud - and he must cry out because a voice says, *don't worry, don't worry, come with me,* and he feels his body go cold as someone puts an arm around him, because it's him. It's the man who took him before, when he was the bog boy, and he's lifting Edward up, and he can taste the metal taste in his mouth again and smell the weird stink of hands as they cover his mouth and he already knows what will happen next. He knows the dark will come, and the nothingness, but he needs the spoons. He needs to gather them before they sink away completely, so he fights. He fights and struggles and flails his arms and calls out. He calls out, but the arms hold him so tightly that he screams, and he screams himself awake because in the next second he opens his eyes to see lights and a face close to his own and it's saying his name. Saying, *Edward, it's me, it's Skylark,* and he knows the face and the voice, but still he cries out because it's not the face he wants to see, and it's not the voice he needs to hear. He cries it out again and again, a word he has never heard himself use before. And Skylark folds her long arms around him and tells him that it's all right. That everything will be all right. He presses his face into her shoulder and sobs, unstoppable. *It's all right*, she says.

He doesn't believe her.

Skylark

Once we've entered the foyer to the tunnels and explained ourselves, we are led down a series of stone steps by a short, dumpy woman with a head of platinum silver curls. 'I s'pose it could happen,' she says, 'but it never has happened. Not that I knows of anyways.' She hands us torches and tells us about the tunnels as we shuffle through. Built to carry water into the city, the tunnels are lined with ancient brick and just wide and tall enough for a man to pass through. 'We take the tourists just along the main pathways,' she tells us, 'but if your boy's down here he's likely to have crept through into these side passages,' she bends down and shines her torch through an opening barely bigger than that to a badger set. 'Little lad, is he?' she asks.

We find him eventually, in one of the slightly wider passages that spur off from the main circuit, though I have to crawl through, sliding on my front to where he's curled like a cat - asleep.

162

The shock of waking makes him scream, but there's no room to manoeuver in there so all I can do is put my arms around him and rock him gently, to and fro, until his sobbing subsides. 'Mama,' he chokes at one point. Like a toddler, 'Mama.' He buries his head into my neck and weeps while I rub his back and breathe in the smell of his damp hair.

And like him, I feel my face wet with tears.

Things are pretty uneventful after that. The staff are mortified that an 11 year old boy has managed to creep into the unlit passages, and they allow him to use the staff shower to clean himself up and wipe the grime off his knees and clothes. They're bending over backwards to be helpful, offering us tea and biscuits from a large tin while we wait. Xav explains how he thought of the tunnels. 'A combination of listening to Mr Boyle's description of which way he went, and from what I could gather about Edward from you and Melissa talking about him,' he says. 'You seem kinda fond of him, Skylark. Who knew you could get to like kids, eh?' and he smiles wryly at me, before standing to leave. 'I've got to go,' he says, 'and my work here is done. Good luck back at the museum – I'll call you soon, yeah?' I nod, and as I watch him go I start to feel a familiar emptiness opening in the pit of my stomach; an emptiness that I haven't felt since that day, so long ago it seems now, when I told Xav what I'd done.

The thing I did. Before.

There's no easy way to admit it. I got pregnant, and couldn't handle it, so I had an abortion. I didn't tell Xav until afterwards, and he was...well, furious, I guess, and angry, and upset. So upset that he went out and shagged another woman a few days later. Not the most grown up response, but sort of understandable under the circumstances because I just refused to admit he might have had a right to know I was carrying his kid. It was my body, I told him, and my choice, and no way were we set up to have a baby. Even so, that hurt look in his eyes, when I told him. That has stayed with me. Edward emerges from his shower, and I close the feeling down. 'Ready to go?' I say.

We're too late for the museum tour; it has ended by the time we're able to join everyone else, and Brearley won't hear of me taking Edward through on his own, preferring to subject Edward to a full scale spleen-vent in all its apopleptic splendor. 'Have you any idea the trouble you've caused, young man? Do you? Do you!?' Edward receives it silently, his eyes downcast, shoulders slumped, a picture of misery, though I suspect he isn't hearing a word of the lecture. I have confiscated the stolen spoon, and Edward thinks I intend to send it back to the shop he stole it from. I fidget with it in my own pocket, waiting for Brearley's rant to end. 'His eyes'll pop out in a minute,' remarks one of the older kids.

When Brearley finally boards the minibus to sit glaring through the windscreen, the other kids skulk toward Edward with renewed interest, like a pack of hounds circling their master's feet? 'What did you nick? You should've seen that guy from the shop - lucky you didn't get chinned.' Edward glances warily from face to face, his body visibly shrinking in on itself. I hurry them all on to the bus, hoping they'd lose interest in him, but as Edward clambers the step one of the older boys slaps him convivially on the back. 'Ed mate, you're solid,' he says.

Brearley is in so much of a hurry to be off that most of the kids don't even have time to buckle their seat belts before we're careering round a tight corner and onto the main drag out of the city. They have a lot to say about the tour, though most of it is centered on the disappointing appearance of the bog boy. 'It was minging, its face was all squashed up and like, totally, rank.' By and large, they've been reasonably well behaved (save two lads sloping off for a crafty fag in the toilets, and the disgrace of one boy smearing a chocolate brownie on one of the tables in the museum cafe and claiming that the bog boy must have had a crap there). 'I made him apologize to the waitress,' Melissa says, 'and she was fine about it, really. I told her he was retarded.' Out of the corner of my eye, I see Brearley's leather driving gloves crinkle as he tightly grips the wheel.

The traffic's pretty heavy on the dual carriageway, and a diversion near the turn off to Stonemoor means we get back to school too late for the connecting school buses, so have to hang around with some of the kids until their parents can pick them up. It's getting pretty late in the day by the time they've all gone, and Brearley has made Edward stay with us because he wants to tell Mrs Parry about his unacceptable behaviour. I try and explain that she's unlikely to come and collect Edward, and that it's pointless to phone her as she simply won't answer the phone. Well, no wonder his behaviour is intolerable, hisses Brearley, no boundaries at home. I think of Eleanor Parry, alone and agoraphobic - the whole house a boundary where she's concerned. I tell Brearley that I'll drive Edward home and report matters to his mother in person, which mollifies him a bit. 'Well, good night, Skylark,' he says. Then, more officiously, 'Don't forget that I wish to see you in my office in the morning.'

Great.

Edward

He cannot comprehend the mistake he has made. Comprehend; Miss Pilcher once used that word. *I just can't comprehend it, Edward*, when he told her about the bog boy dream. After the anxieties of the day; quick grab from the shop, dash through the streets, dark of underground tunnels; after failing to see the bog boy again when he had so wanted to, after Skylark taking the spoon from him and driving him home through the grey shift of late afternoon, not speaking to him, making him feel alone despite being in the car beside him. He knows she's angry with him for stealing the spoon, but it doesn't feel like an angry silence, not really. More like a sad silence. And while he doesn't want her to feel that way because of him, more than that, he wants her to give him the spoon back.

She stops the car outside the gates to his house, yanks the handbrake up, and turns to him. 'Edward,' she says carefully, 'I have to come inside with you to explain what happened today to your mother. It's my job to do that. But here,' and she fumbles in her jacket pocket, extricating the Judas spoon with her thumb and forefinger, and hands it to him. And he looks at it, lying flat across his palm, and he turns it, to locate the tell tale initials - MH - that should be there on the tiny cap the Judas figure wears, and he cannot comprehend it.

There are no initials.

It's the wrong spoon.

He's still staring at it when Skylark jerks open the passenger door to let him out of the car. When he doesn't move she squats beside him and asks him what the matter is. He tells her, but the words come out small and cramped and barely audible. 'Let's go inside and look at it properly,' she says, and her voice is warm, and he feels like crying.

Edward has a key to the house and he uses it to open the front door. The hallway is dark, and there's no light spilling from the other rooms. Skylark loiters as Edward walks from room to room. He feels a ball of sickness gathering in the pit of his stomach as each room reveals itself to be empty. 'I'll look upstairs,' he tells Skylark, who nods. He finds his mother in her bedroom, asleep, her mouth slightly open. He waits a moment - sometimes she wakes immediately, as though sensing his quiet presence - but this time her breathing is deep and regular. He leaves the room, gently shunting the door so it closes with a quiet click. From the top of the darkened stairwell he watches as Skylark, unaware of his eyes on her, cranes her neck to peer through the slightly open door to his father's old study. He knows his mother won't wake for several hours; he has grown used to the circadian patterns of her days, but even so, he'd rather not take the risk of her waking to find Skylark in the house. He silently slips down the stairs, on cat paws, and Skylark startles as he touches her elbow to turn her away from the dark study. 'She's asleep,' says Edward, 'perhaps you should go home now.' Skylark looks thoughtful, as though considering the suggestion carefully. 'No Edward,' she says, eventually. 'I'll wait a little while in case she wakes up'

'Sometimes she sleeps for days,' says Edward.

'Even so. I'll stay,' she replies. They stand for a few moments, regarding each other. Grey eyed boy and green eyed woman. 'C'mon,' she says, 'show me your spoons.'

Skylark

His room is stupidly neat and tidy for an 11 year old, but then, this is Edward so that shouldn't really surprise me. His narrow bed is against one wall. There's an old pine wardrobe with matching drawers, and a tall bookshelf topped with home made models of things; aeroplanes and spacecraft and so on. The other shelves contain neat lines of books, his school folders, and a tray of drawing materials; pencils and charcoal crayons. I don't notice any toys or games anywhere, and the walls are devoid of posters other than a large world map of the sort found in Geography classrooms, complete with garish colouring and curled corners. Edward kneels on the rug in the middle of the room and reaches a hand under the bed to retrieve a long, narrow box. It has been taped at one corner with a length of gaffer tape, securing a splintery looking crack in the wood. What must have been a glass inset in the lid has been replaced with a sheet of corrugated cardboard. It is dented and bent out of shape, but Edward handles the box reverentially, laying it carefully on the floor in front of where I perch on the edge of his bed. 'Here,' he says, lifting the lid and carefully lowering it back on its hinges.

I must admit, arranged in a line as they are on a plush velvet backcloth, they look impressive. Two are missing; but the first space is immediately filled by the St Thomas spoon, which Edward has been carrying with him all day. The second space, at the end of the row, remains agonizingly bereft. I'm holding the stolen spoon and in comparison to the others it is only marginally shorter, though perhaps the bowl is a little less deep, and the silver is tarnished whereas the originals gleam as though new minted. It's not hugely dissimilar though, and I can see why Edward, in the dim interior of the shop, mistook it so readily. I lay the spoon in the end space. 'There!' I say brightly, 'That doesn't look so bad - if you polish it up you'll,' but I'm cut short by Edward's expression; what could it be called? Advanced contempt? Distilled scorn? 'You'll...never tell the difference,' I try, regardless. He doesn't respond.

'Okay. Maybe you will.'

I remove the spoon and Edward closes the lid. 'They're beautiful Edward.' He pushes the box back beneath the bed and gets to his feet.
'I think you should leave now,' he says.

'Actually, I think I'll just go and tap on your mother's door.'

'No. That's not a good idea'

'Which door is it?'

'It's better if you go home now please.'

'She'll want to know what happened,' I say, 'And I have to tell her. Edward, it's my job, you can't just steal things from shops.' He moves his feet, his shoulders, his head shakes in exasperation, 'But she doesn't know,' he says.

'Know what?'

'That I was there. That we were in Exeter. About the bog boy.'

I remember, in that moment, the flourished permission slip, the dubiously scrawled signature, my own blind eye turned full on it. 'But why is it such a big deal, Edward? We didn't even get to see him.'

'You don't know,' he says, 'what she's like about it, about my reincarnation.'

'She doesn't like the bad dreams, you mean?' I recall the conversation in the candlelit kitchen, when Eleanor Parry's thin hands had fluttered like birds, folding the permission slip, her face crumpling and her voice faltering on her words; *Dreams, Miss Riley.* I gaze at Edward, who is still standing on the rug, twitching with desperation that I just get the hell out of his house. 'Edward,' I say, patting the crisp white of his bedspread beside me, 'Sit here. Tell me what she's like about the dream.'

There's a stand off. A minute's silence, maybe.

Then, he relents.

'When I first told her,' Edward tells me, his voice dropping to a whisper, 'it was after Miss Pilcher took me to see the bog boy. She started to walk around too much.'

'Walk around?'

'Around the house, and she started counting things, like the stairs, and the cups in the kitchen, and the candlesticks. Whatever she could count, she counted, over and over and over again. She does that a lot anyway, but after I told her about the dream, she did it more than usual. And she kept scratching her hands,' he adds. 'She scratched them until they bled.'

'But Edward...'

'Even though I bandaged them for her, she just kept scratching through the fabric, until it all snagged and unravelled, and the blood stained through.'

'It's all right, Edward,' I say. He's trembling, his words tumbling and his own hands echoing the action of his mother's until I close my own hands over them. My own hands on his, stilling them, until he calms and his body softens. I want him to talk about something else, so I reach in under the bed to pull out the box of spoons again and I ask him to tell me about them. And he does, one by one, lifting each from the cloth and turning the apostle figures towards me, explaining who each figure is, and what they carry in their hands; the Christ spoon holds a cross and orb, and St John, a cup of sorrow.

Evening light fades outside the window. The day's grey cloud breaks pinkly and drifts away as a crescent moon sharpens its point above the dim outline of the Henge. Quiet stars appear as Edward talks, and as I listen. He tells me about the day his father left. Of how, before that day, on the rare occasions of his father's visits, they would sometimes sit together in his study and look at the things his father liked to collect. 'Most days, he didn't seem to like me,' Edward tells me, 'but when he showed me the spoons, or other things, he'd be a lot nicer.' Finding the missing Judas spoon, he explains, would mean the full collection could be sold for lots of money to help pay the bills and then maybe Miss Pilcher could tutor him again. Then he wouldn't have to go to school every day and feel stupid and strange.

'Lots of children feel stupid and strange, Edward,' I tell him. 'Actually, most adults feel like that too sometimes. I know I do.'

He looks at me. 'I don't think that about you,' he says, donning his familiar old-man-on-young-shoulders' face, 'Actually, I think you'd make a very good mother.' It throws me off balance, just for a moment, but I shake it off, and even laugh, and glance at my watch. It's surprisingly late, and I tell him I'm heading home.

And that's when it happens.

Whenever I think about it, the thing that happened next, I see it in slow motion. Even now, when I rewind the tape in my head and arrive at those moments, everything sharpens, each frame pin bright and bathed in an impossible light because the room was dim, lit only by a small shaded reading lamp, which Edward had flicked on as the day faded. I'd just told him I was heading home, and I'd promised that I wouldn't be returning to report the theft to his mother. I stood, while Edward slid the box of spoons back beneath the bed, but as he did so, something blocked the box, and he reached beneath the bed to remove the offending obstacle, pulling it out of the way so it lay beside him on the rug. It was a sketchbook, bound in blue card, and I stooped to pick it up. 'Can I look?' I asked, and he shrugged as I flicked through pages of his exquisite drawings; deft pencil drawings of objects in the room, of a magpie sitting on a fence, of his own mother's sleeping face. And on several pages, repeated perhaps 50 times, line drawings of a man's face. A man with long, thin features and a slender nose. Thin lips, thickly stubbled chin, quizzically arched brows over intelligent eyes. I opened my mouth to speak, but no sound came out, and I could hear a rushing in my ears as the sketchpad slipped from my grasp and fell to the floor. Edward, oblivious, picked it up and handed it back to me, and I sat on the bed again, the pad in my lap, feeling my heart subside.

I turned to the pages again to where the man's face was delineated over and over again. In profile, angled, and the largest, most detailed sketch, full face, staring out from the page.

'Edward,' I say carefully. 'Who is this man?'

'That's him,' he says casually. 'The man from the dream. The man who took me to be killed.'

'I see.' I say. And I do very well, considering. I smile brightly at Edward, and say good night. He walks me downstairs to the door and opens it for me, releasing me to a rush of cold night air, to the scent of damp green, and the sensation of being punched in the gut while simultaneously spinning.

The man in the drawings?

My father.

CHAPTER 8

Skylark

The cottage is freezing when I get home, and all I want to do is stand beneath a hot shower and wash the confusion out of my head. There's a text on my phone from a newly unblocked Xav, and several from my mother, who has spent the day in Ikea and wants to know if I need any tea lights, a lampshade, some bargain cushion covers. I ignore the texts and walk upstairs to the bathroom, shedding my clothes as I go, to step into the tiny bathtub that doubles as a shower. When I turn the dial though, an ominous gurgle rises from the pipes, and cold water spits and splutters over me, before it thins to a miserable trickle.

Bugger.

I dress again, feeling like a tape on rewind as I retrieve my scattered clothing, and call the landlord to discuss the water situation; he doesn't pick up the phone and I find myself leaving an irate message on his answer machine before slamming the receiver down.

Then, I burst into tears.

Even as I'm wrapping a sofa throw around myself and using a corner of it to smear tears and snot around my face, I'm not even sure why I'm crying. The sketches of Dad, for sure, have left me shocked and winded and determined to think them through. What the hell is he doing in Edward's sketchbook? And in Edward's dream? I consider calling my mother and confronting her with what has happened - surely she must know more than she's letting on, but I don't want to deal with her sarcasm right now - *you're telling me your father burgled someone's dream? Typical.*

I replay the day in my head. Edward in the tunnels, and my own wet face as he sobbed into my shoulder. The crushing disappointment on his face as he looked at the wrong spoon in his hand, and the way his thin body leaned into mine as he showed me the battered box and its treasures in his dim, tidy room.

I think you'd make a good mother. Isn't that what he said? And another guttural sob chokes me, so much so, that I almost don't hear the light rapping at my front door. I hold my breath, uncertain if I've imagined it. But it comes again, a tapping at the window this time, and a low voice. 'Skylark?'

He steps straight in when I open the door and he places two hands on each of my shoulders and stares hard into my face, which is blotchy and red and mottled with ruined mascara, and the words, so long contained, spill from my mouth. I tell him I'm sorry, and that I was always sorry,

177

and that I wish I'd trusted him a year ago when, on discovering I was pregnant, I chose to keep it to myself and opt for the termination. He puts his arms around me, and strokes my hair, and is simply there, where, I know now, he would have been all along if only I'd let him.

As we head upstairs, we shed our clothes as we go.

We sleep in the next morning, and I call work to tell them I have a problem with the plumbing and that I'll be late in. The landlord calls almost immediately after I've put the phone down and tells me he'll be over later in the day, so I go back to bed and drape myself over Xav, and fall back to a fitful sleep in which Brearley is standing over me, shouting, and shaking Edward's file in my face, which turns into the sketchbook, and Brearley turns into my father, smiling at me, and winking. In moments of wakefulness, I feel Xav's warm body beside mine, and wrap myself closer to it.

It's Mr Lempel who eventually gets us up. I hear a loud, scraping sound from outside and, as Xav has commandeered the pillows and is holding them over his own head to block out both light and noise, I slip out of bed and peer from behind a curtain to see the old man using a thick jemmy to prize up a paving slab directly in front of my door. The guy must be 80 years old if he's a day, so I open the window and call to him to stop. 'Water pipe,' he calls back, by way of explanation, 'external stopcock,' and bends back to his task. 'He'll kill himself,' I say, shrugging on a dressing gown and hurrying downstairs. Xav only groans in response and huddles himself deeper beneath the muddle of sheets on the bed.

Despite my protestations, Mr Lempel seems quite content to heave the paving slab to one side and twist the water supply off with a giant allen key he has brought along for the task. I have some bottled water in the fridge, so I tip it into the kettle and put it on the hob to boil while Lempel twists taps and grunts at the thin murk that pulses into the sink. 'Blockage somewhere,' he decides, 'old pipes, corrode, fill with dirt.' He shakes his head and sits at my tiny dining table. 'My house has brand new pipes and tank,' he tells me. 'I'm long dead before they rust.'

'You shouldn't talk that way, Mr Lempel,' I say, 'the way you heaved that slab up, like it was made out of cardboard, you'll outlive me.'

'Living. Overrated,' he grunts, as I place a mug of tea in front of him.

The old man's in the process of levering up the wooden floorboards in the living room to further access the pipes when Xav strolls downstairs. His hair is sticking up and his clothes are creased and rumpled, but his smile is broad and roguish as he introduces himself to Lempel as 'a close friend of Skylark,' (Lempel nods, but says nothing) and strolls into the kitchen as though he owns the place; peering into the teapot and opening the fridge to divest me of ham and cheese. I find myself considering him as he sits in the seat vacated by Lempel, a hastily folded sandwich in one hand and a cup of tea in the other.

In bed, we'd talked. He had folded his body over mine like a bird's wing and listened as I explained the way I'd felt on discovering I was pregnant. A boozy weekend together meant the pills hadn't been taken as they should've been. To tell the truth, I'd often forgotten to pop them out of their little blister pack and had gotten away with it for so long that it was a genuine shock to see the blue line swimming into focus on the stick. It didn't seem possible. I was halfway through the counselling course Xav had encouraged me to do, and I felt I was getting on my feet. How could I have a baby? Me? A fucked-up university drop-out with a murdered father and a mostly stoned boyfriend ('Hey, I've cut right down,' Xav had admonished). I kept picturing the foetus; saucer-eyed and fish-like; a floating alien, like the weird creatures I'd seen suspended in glass jars on the shelves of biology labs. Not a baby. It wasn't a child I had inside me.

'It was the not telling that hurt,' Xav confessed. 'I'd have supported your decision, you know. But you didn't give me a chance to think about it, to take it in, to discuss it even.'

And so, we had lain in the warm bed, the occasional passing car sending a swathe of pale light through the window, across the walls, over us; and we had talked, our words reaching and connecting like tendrils in the dark. My body nestled into his. A perfect fit; like a pair of spoons.

I consider Xav, eating his sandwich and sipping his tea. He is observing Lempel through the half open door. I know he wants to help the old man. That he loves to fix things; to tinker and prod and poke. He's just waiting for his moment. When the old man sits back on his haunches, scratching his head in irritation, that's when Xav will spring, 'Let me have a look.' And I consider saying nothing at all. About Edward, I mean. We'd only talked about ourselves, and as far as Xav is concerned, Edward is simply a student of mine; a boy who was lost and now is found and returned to his mother. Xav doesn't know about the sketches in Edward's book; the unmistakeable representations of my father, exact and precise and multitudinous over the pages. Yes, perhaps I should say nothing. Leave it. Continue to exist in this small bubble of untroubled happiness where Xav drinks tea at my breakfast table in a creased flannel shirt.

'Found it,' calls Lempel, 'come see.' Xav enters the living room and peers into the open cavity beneath the floor where a length of pipe has corroded and fallen in on itself and sprung a leak, so the surrounding sub-floor is damp and darkened. 'Rusted through,' Lempel tells him. 'I go to car. Have tools.'

Yes, I could just leave it. Why not? Go to work for the day, report to Brearley's office to receive my bollocking for yesterday, and then do my job. Chat to kids about this and that, dole out advice, come home and have Xav cook dinner and massage my aching feet. I hear my mother's voice in my head. *What's the good of pursuing a dead man?*

Xav returns to the kitchen. 'Pipe just needs replacing. I could've done it.' Xav. The man I should have told about his baby, and didn't. The boy who was there on the last night I saw my father alive. The child who, like me, had no words to speak about his pain.

I tell him about the sketches.

'I just can't figure it out,' I say, as Xav frowns into his teacup. There's some junk mail on the table and he pulls a plain brown envelope towards him and looks around for a pen. I hand him one, and he draws a line on the envelope. 'Timeline,' he says, and speaks as he annotates. 'You lived in London until age of 16. And apart from a few spells in prison, your father did too?'

'As far as I know,' I say.

'And he died...what? Ten years ago?'

'I do a quick calculation, is it really that long?'

182

'Yes,' I say. 'It'll be 10 years this Summer. My birthday,' I falter, recalling that last night. The dark shape of him on the windowsill, Xav's tousled head protruding from the sleeping bag, the sharp brilliance of the light snapping on. 'And Edward's how old?' asks Xav.

'Twelve,' I say, 'no...eleven according to his file.'

Xav sits back on the chair. 'Can kids remember that far back?' he asks. If he ever did see your father, he can only have been a baby.'

I shrug.

Lempel returns with a thick pair of cutters and a length of copper piping. He carries a canvas bag filled with all manner of odds and ends, and sets about rifling through it. Metal connectors, hinges, nails and screws all clatter together.

'Well, Edward's mother is the obvious one to ask,' muses Xav, but on seeing the expression on my face, gives a wry smile. 'Not a good idea then?' I set about explaining my dealings with her so far; her strangeness, her aloof manner. 'To put it mildly,' I say, 'she's barking mad.' From the living room, we hear Lempel pause in his work and I find myself wondering if he knows anything of Eleanor Parry himself - he has lived in the village a long time, after all. 'What about the tutor?' Xav asks. 'She might have a few insights if she worked for the family a long time.

'Yeah, possibly,' I say. But how do I find her? Edward doesn't know where she lives - she always taught him at the Parry house.'

'Phone book?' says Xav. But I don't have one in the house. I glance at my watch. 'I've got to get ready for work,' I say. 'Can you stay until Mr Lempel has finished?' Xav nods, but Lempel is entering the kitchen, wiping his hands on an old rag, and telling me to try turning the tap. I do, and clear water gushes from it.

'I could look up the tutor,' offers Xav, 'what's her name again?'

I tell him, but just as he's writing it down on the back of the envelope, Mr Lempel interrupts. 'Pauline Pilcher?' he says. 'I can tell you address. She is tenant of mine. Odd lady, but very good. Always pays rent on time.' He recites the address, which I recognise from my walks around the village as being pretty close by. We can go there later, when I'm home from work,' I say.

'We?' says Xav. There's a frozen moment, in which Mr Lempel glances from Xav's face to mine, before hurrying back to his bag of tools in the living room. 'Well, no,' I say. 'You've got to get home, I guess.' Xav drains his tea mug in one swallow. 'Not really,' he says, 'I'll come if you want me too.' And I feel something in my chest, a fluttering, as though a humming bird has got in there. 'I'm off to get dressed,' I say. 'Not on my account,' says Xav as I scamper over the floorboards that Lempel is nailing back into place.

184

'Young love,' I hear the old man mumble as I fly upstairs.

A History of Stonemoor
by **Pauline Pilcher**

Evidence, all important.
Research reveals that the cigarette filter could originate in Eastern Europe. Brand = 'ESSE' - matches letters visible on stub. Also, tall, slim figure leads one to believe *could* be Eastern European/Russian/Scandinavian - those nations having a predilection for athleticism, as commonly seen in Olympic Gymnastics competitions.

Newspaper reports from the time. No new stories after initial furore suggests...what? Lack of interest from UK police? No leads? Mother leaves country....note to self...what was Mother's name? East European connection?

Of course, she'll need to investigate. Pauline Pilcher's eyes flick to the small, square hatch above her head, the loft access. She doesn't own a ladder, but a chair will suffice. It's a long time since she has opened the loft hatch to pour over the contents of a cardboard shoe box she keeps up there, but now, with the cigarette butt, there's an inkling of a possibility of a clue. A missing piece in the jigsaw puzzle that will turn conjecture to fact. She has taken precautions, of course. Her notes are buried in the manuscript of her book. No one will find them there if they come seeking the truth, or to hide the truth. And with truth will come - she hardly dares think it - Eleanor. Eleanor's tragic indebtedness. Eleanor weeping at her feet. Pauline allows herself a moment of still reverie as she places a bentwood chair beneath the loft hatch. But Eleanor, she rehearses, my dear Eleanor. Of course your secret's safe with me. She giggles, and a sudden flurry at the window startles her. That wretched magpie again. As she climbs onto the chair, she decides to look into the possibility of poison. Magpies are vermin, after all. From a fencepost beyond the window, the magpie observes her with its black pod of an eye, as she stands slowly upright, brogued feet planted slightly apart on the flat chair seat. She wiggles her broad hips, to test stability, before reaching up to the hatch.

She has to stand on tiptoe. The shoe box is close to the edge of the hatch, it must be coaxed out with mere fingertips once she has shunted the hatch to the side. She unclips two small hooks, which clasp two nail heads in the wooden surround, and she pushes the hatch upwards - it sticks - swelled shut by damp seeping through the eaves, but she pushes more firmly and it pops open, releasing a scent like wet leaves from the space above. She is about to move it to the side, when the doorbell rings.

She freezes, hands in the air.

Her doorbell never rings.

Should she ignore it?

Out in the back garden, the magpie is bobbing his head up and down, sidestepping his way along the wooden fence. His beak is half open and from it, a black tongue protrudes. It chatters, as the doorbell repeats its cheerful polyphonic chime.

Fiddlesticks.

She lowers her hands, allowing the hatch to sink back into its opening with a soft sigh, and she carefully steps down from the chair. Patting the disheveled strands of her grey hair back into place, she hurries towards the door.

There are two people standing outside when she opens it. She has never seen them before. 'May I help you?' she asks.

'Perhaps,' says a tall, thin man. 'Pauline Pilcher?'

There's something unnerving about him. The way he presses towards her. He's smartly dressed in a black suit and long, cashmere overcoat, and he places a shiny, black shoe into the aperture of the open door. 'I think, perhaps, that you are. May we come in?'

Pauline Pilcher wants to say no, that it's terribly inconvenient at the moment thank you very much, and she isn't interested in whatever they may be selling, but the words can't escape her throat. The man has pushed the door wide, and is entering the house, brushing past her as though she isn't even there, and he's followed by the second man - a short, rough looking fellow with a baseball cap pulled low over his eyes. He catches the door with his foot and slams it closed, then turns and locks down the safety catch before turning to Pauline Pilcher and grasping her firmly by the elbow. He propels her back along the hallway and into the large, square living room, where the first man awaits. 'Won't you sit down, Miss Pilcher,' he says. She lowers herself onto the bentwood chair. His teeth are straight, and very white, and his eyes are blue, the blue of willow pattern plates or deep seawater. 'I think, perhaps, you could furnish me with some important information, Miss Pilcher,' he says. The smaller man stands close to her, she can sense the animal tension in his limbs. Slowly, she nods, and the taller man smiles.

'The boy. Edward Parry,' he says. 'Where is he?'

Skylark

I make it to work just in time for the start of the morning break. The car park is already full, so I have to leave my battered little Fiesta out on the main street and walk in through a throng of kids who habitually hang around near the big metal gates at the entrance. 'Yo, Miss Riley,' says Jakey, who is loitering amongst them, and he raises a hand, which I automatically high five as I pass. The teacher who's on duty beside the gate rolls her eyes at me. I know what she's thinking; *Fucking Learning Mentor, no wonder that boy shows no respect*, but I sail past her with a cheery good afternoon and stroll to my office. As I turn towards the quad, I see Edward standing with a small group. He's slightly apart from them, rigid in his stance, but there's the shade of a smile playing about his lips as one of the boys from the museum trip regales the others, gesturing all the time towards Edward. Tales of yesterday's exploits, no doubt. Kudos, I think to myself, as I unlock my office door.

My good mood only lasts until I get a call asking me to report to Brearley's office. 'He's not looking too happy,' his secretary confides over the phone, and when I reach his office she slips me a surreptitious thumbs up before buzzing me through the door.

Look, I could go into the conversation that took place. I could tell you about the handwritten notes he's compiled on an A4 pad, about my incompetence at running the trip. Really, everything from not knowing where we could park, to not booking the tickets in advance, to not producing worksheets for the kids to fill in, to not having a back up plan for when the museum couldn't accommodate us straight away, and even the fact that I had an assignation with a man unconnected to the school. 'How was I to know he'd turn up?' I argue, 'and actually, it was Xav who found Edward, so all in, it was a pretty lucky assignation, wasn't it?'

'Which brings us the main failure of the whole fiasco,' says Brearley drily, as he lays the pad down and removes his gold framed reading glasses to fix me with a myopic stare. 'You lost a child, Skylark.' He's got me there, and I've got no idea how to respond.

And that's it. I'm given a fixed suspension for two weeks, during which time an investigation into what happened will be carried out and a full report prepared and presented to the school governors. I have to collect my things immediately, and vacate the premises. Under no circumstances am I to contact Edward or his mother. 'You'll hear from me shortly,' says Brearley. 'Good day, Ms Riley.'

As I leave, the secretary allows me a sympathetic smile of such warmth that it makes me want to cry. I don't, of course. I keep looking straight ahead, marching out of the main building and across to the quad. I go inside my tiny office, sit at my desk, and look around myself at the four walls, at the paperwork in my in-tray, at the view outside to the garden with its magnolia tree and soft green grass. I catch sight of myself in the blank computer screen; familiar shadow of unkempt hair, the plains of my face converging to a suggestion of my father's bone structure; slim, with a too long nose. I stare at it for what feels like an age, before balling my hand into a fist and punching the screen.

Fuck.

When I get home, there's no sign of Xav and the cottage feels cold. Mr Lempel hasn't tidied up the mess left from levering up the floorboards, and loose splinters are scattered around the living room, along with a damp smell left by the leak. I decide to keep myself busy until Xav shows up, so I sweep the floor and tidy up the kitchen a little. I need to remain positive, I decide. A suspension of two weeks doesn't necessarily mean I've lost my job, after all. And it'll be nice to have a couple of weeks to myself, to get the cottage fully sorted and maybe spend some time exploring the area. I may take a walk up to the stone circle later, or visit the local library to take out a few books - I'll have plenty of time to read over the next fortnight.

As I'm tidying, I find Mr Lempel's bundle of old letters and photographs beneath the sink and curse myself for not remembering to give them to him that morning. I also find an almost full bottle of vodka. It's not quite 12 o'clock, and I text Xav asking him to call me. Then, I pour a few fingers of vodka into a tumbler, top it off with a slug of juice from the fridge, and take it into the living room. It's good to have a drink. The slow hollow burn of it feels cleansing, so I decide to have another one.

By the time Xav arrives, I've finished the bottle. It's late afternoon, and he finds me sprawled across the rug, with Mr Lempel's letters strewn out around me. 'Look,' I cry, 'look at this.' I'm brandishing one of the old photographs. 'Course, his hair's not white,' I giggle, and hiccup, 'he's only a kid in this, but it's him, you can see it.'

Xav has a carrier bag in one hand, and as I stand and lurch towards him he drops it on the floor with a clunk so it slouches over to the side. I've stood up too quickly and the floor shifts beneath me. He catches me awkwardly, but can't keep a hold of me, so I slump to the floor beside the carrier bag and spy the mouth of a bottle of red wine poking from the interior. 'Ooooh, what's this?' I say, peering inside to see two steaks wrapped in cellophane, and a couple of slim wax candles. 'Oh Xav,' I say. I try to stand, but it's not easy. I have to paw my way up his legs and once I'm on my feet, I'm scared to let go of him because his face is moving in and out of focus, rearranging itself like a Picasso portrait, and the room beginning to slope and turn. I cling to his shirt, and he's trying to disengage my hands while saying something, but I've no idea what it is because I can feel bile rising from my stomach in a sudden rush. 'Jesus, Skylark,' I hear, as a wave sweeps up through me and disgorges itself all over him. I stagger away and through to the kitchen just as another wave rises. This time I get to the sink, and throw up in the basin. 'How much did you drink?' asks Xav. He has retrieved the empty bottle and studies it for a moment, before peeling off his wet shirt and throwing it in a ball into the bespattered sink. I'm hanging on to the edge of the ceramic, my body quivering as yet again it's racked by a swell of nausea. Xav puts an arm around my shoulder, and with his free hand, he lifts my hair from where it has stuck to my face. 'Just like old times,' he says, 'you gonna tell me what this is all about?' I'm trembling, and the trauma of being sick has started me off crying. 'There, there,' says Xav, rubbing my back gently. 'I've been sacked,' I tell him, the words emerging in a thick smear, and I heave again.

'I'm putting you to bed,' says Xav.

'Easy Tiger,' I say, attempting a lascivious wink.

'To sleep,' says Xav, firmly.

Edward

He looks for her at the end of the lunch-break, but her office door is locked. He has brought the stolen Judas spoon, misshapen in his pocket - the dent jars against his thumb when he rubs the bowl. He wishes he had left it at home; Simon Zealotes had caught his eye that morning, his jag-toothed saw winking as he held it up to the morning light, but he'd felt the need for penance, self flagellation, and he wants to apologize for the fuss he caused, for running and hiding like that; he betrayed her trust, and so he has brought Judas. There's a window beside her office door, and he stretches up on tiptoe, letting his shoes scuff against the pebble dash, to peer inside at the darkened room, her empty desk.

Edward Parry!

He drops and spins around to see Brearley striding towards him, his pinstripe jacket flapping in the breeze as he bears down on Edward like a steam train. 'My office. Now!' Edward blinks at him. 'But, you're not in your office,' he says. Brearley is standing inches from him, so close that Edward moves back against the wall and feels his shoulder blades graze the rough exterior. Brearley brings his face close to Edward's own, and hisses; 'Don't take that supercilious tone with me, young man.' He steps back, and coughs - ahem - and jerks his head to the side, in the direction of the main building. Edward lets his face go blank.

Doesn't move. Again, the head jerk, a grimace, as if in spasm. Edward steps uncertainly to the side. 'You want me to go to your office?'

'Now!'

'Oh.' He does what Brearley seems to want. Brearley hesitates for a moment, then follows the boy, strides past him as they make the entrance and takes the stairs two at a time, so he can be sitting at his desk when the boy walks in.

'So,' he says, steepled fingers, slightly out of breath from the jog to his office. 'Theft. Trespass. Failure to comply with expectations. Failure,' he leans forward at his desk, the better to fix Edward with a steely glare, 'to represent Henge School in an appropriate manner.' He lets it sink in, then leans back in his leather chair. 'What do you have to say for yourself?' Edward has nothing to say. He doesn't understand why he's here, in this room, with this man. 'Where's Skylark?' he asks, 'I mean, Miss Riley.'

Brearley smiles, revealing neat, white teeth. 'Miss Riley is not in school at the moment, and nor are you, Edward. I'm placing you in internal exclusion.'

Edward takes this in, frowning. 'How can you have internal exclusion,' he asks? 'If you're inside, you're not excluded are you?'

Brearley is filling in a pink paper slip with Edward's name and details; he writes the words 'three days' with an expansive flourish and hands it to Edward, who doesn't take it.

'And you said, 'nor are you,' which implies I shouldn't be in school at all, but if it's internal then I have to be.' Brearley rattles the pink slip at him. 'You're excluded from the company of other students, and your teachers,' he says.

'Oh,' says Edward, taking the slip and reading it. 'So there won't be any other students or teachers in the special room...what's it called?'

'Exclusion unit,' says Brearley, 'and there are just a handful of people in there today. And a supervisor.'

'Not inclusion unit?'

'No. Or...maybe it is. I can't remember.'

Edward narrows his eyes at Brearley, who narrows them back.

'Go,' says Brearley.

Edward does as he is told.

The exclusion unit, or inclusion unit, is a separate building; a prefabricated hut with plastic cladding and a flat roof, which is located on the other side of one of the playing fields. It has been raining, and the route takes him along the perimeter of the field on which a rugby match is taking place between some Year 11 boys, so that the wet ground is rapidly becoming a quagmire. The grass at the edges has not been mown, and as Edward walks, he sees his leather shoes darken as they absorb the damp, while his socks rapidly become water-logged by the thick bladed, rain dropped grass. Beyond the perimeter, a high hedge separates the field from the privately owned land beyond, and it's from this hedge, that Edward hears the noise. A high pitched hiss, like air being released from a bicycle tyre - *psssssssst*. He stops, and looks around. In the distance, he hears the shouts and clamour of the older boys clashing through mud and each other, and he hears the shrill screech of the teacher's whistle to halt play. But then, again, closer this time - *psssssssst*. He peers into the hedge, but it's an impenetrable thicket of criss crossed branches and shiny green leaves. A lone magpie perches on a high twig, its head sunk into a ruff of damp feathers. 'Edward,' he hears and he finds himself staring curiously at the bird for a moment, before hearing his name again. 'Edward, over here,' accompanied this time by a rattling of twigs, which send a deluge of drops onto his already damp shoes and socks. He peers again, and sees this time, in a space between the leaves, an eye. It's pale and watery, but curiously bright, as though a spark has lodged itself deep inside. Then he sees more; a mass of grey curls, a pair of pursed lips. 'Miss Pilcher?' he says.

Shhhhhh, she admonishes, rather loudly. Edward glances warily back at where the rugby match is in full but distant swing, then back to his old tutor. 'Edward,' she says, and he detects the urgency in her tone. 'You need to get away. You need to get away now.'

CHAPTER 9

Skylark

By the time I've showered and slept the vodka off, it's early evening. I come downstairs to find Xav has boiled up a pan of plain rice. He hands me a bowl of it and orders me to eat, which I do, despite the fact that it's tasteless and has formed into sticky clumps. 'I'm sorry,' I say, 'for being such a mess.' He shrugs. 'And for ruining the evening,' I add.

'If we're going to make this work,' he says, 'make us work, then we need to get to the bottom of things.' He spoons a clump of the rice into his mouth, and grimaces. 'This is disgusting,' he says.

'I thought we were doing that,' I say. 'Last night,' but he shakes his head, and holds his spoon up to stop me.

'That was recent history,' he says, 'about us. I mean really get to the bottom of stuff - further back.'

'Right,' I say, though I'm unsure of where he's going with this. He takes another mouthful of rice and swallows it down.

'Your dad,' he says. 'We're going to find out what happened, and why he's in Edward's sketch book.' He puts the bowl to one side, and stands up. 'C'mon,' he says, 'let's go visit that tutor of his to see what she can tell us.'

Pauline Pilcher's house is a prim little bungalow in the middle of a cul-de-sac. Pink bricks and tidy plastic porch. Nets at the window, well tended patch of garden at the front. Identical to the others, which curve away from it on either side. Retirement land. 'This one?' asks Xav, peering at the house number on the crumpled brown envelope in his hand. 'This one,' I agree. A white front door with a frosted window, a small coach lamp casting its feeble glow onto the tiled path. We ring the bell, and hear its playful tune resounding through the house, but no one comes to the door. We press the bell again, and wait. Nothing. 'Well, we can come again tomorrow,' I say, but Xav is leaning in, peering through the frosted window. 'There's someone moving in there,' he says, and then I see it too - the shadowy outline of someone's head popping up at the window, then ducking beneath it again. Xav taps on the window, 'Miss Pilcher?' he calls. Silence. 'Could we talk to you please, Miss Pilcher?' We wait. 'Maybe we should just go,' I say, but then we hear the rattle of a chain being bolted into place, and slowly, ever so slowly, the door opens.

'Yes?' she says, a hoarse whisper. The gold chain across the door twinkles in the yellow shine from the coach lamp, and behind it, in the six inch gap allowed, a ruddy faced woman with a square jaw and slate grey hair is dressed for bed, in a long pink quilted gown buttoned to the neck. I glance at my watch. It's only 5 o'clock. 'Miss Pilcher,' I say, realising too late that I should've rehearsed what to say. Her hand creeps to her neck, pulling the collar of her gown even further closed, 'I...I mean, we, we've come to talk to you about...well, my name is Skylark Riley, and I work at Henge School, and...' The gap in the door closes slightly, so only half of the face is visible - one wild eye staring. '...and, the thing is, I want to, we want to, we'd like to talk to you...'

'About Edward,' says Xav, 'you used to tutor him.'

The woman's lips press together to form a thin line before they part again to emit her clipped tones. 'I don't know anyone called Edward,' she says. 'Good night.' And she closes the door.

Xav and I are left staring at each other. 'Well,' I say, eventually, 'that's that then.' But Xav isn't so easily deterred. He crouches down, and pushes open the letter box. I expect him to call her name again, but instead he says, 'Oh, hello there.' He glances up at me, his face cocked into a bemused half smile, and then turns his attention back to the letter box in the solid section of the door, behind which, I gather, Miss Pilcher is attempting to hide. She's clearly as mad as a bat, but Xav persists. 'Please, Miss Pilcher,' he says gently, 'we just want to talk to you for a few minutes.'

'Who are you?' she snaps. I crouch beside Xav. 'I'm Edward's mentor,' I say. 'At his school. Actually,' I add, 'I'm more of his friend, really.'

There's silence. The letter box is spring loaded and when Xav removes his fingers it bites shut. He turns to me and shrugs, but then we see the pink clad form rise up at the window, and we hear the slide and jangle of the door chain. The door opens, slowly, but fully. 'Come in then,' says Miss Pilcher, 'quickly.'

We're shown into a square living room with a busy patterned carpet and flowered wallpaper. The curtains are closed and the overhead lightbulb is too bright; it glares at us from its covering of a thickly patterned light shade. There's a single armchair pulled close to the electric fire, which is turned up full despite the warmth of the summer evening, so the whole room feels cloying and claustrophobic. Miss Pilcher busies herself at a desk in the corner of the room, gathering loose papers together and closing them into a plain shoebox before turning to where me and Xav awkwardly stand, in the middle of the room. 'Sit,' says Miss Pilcher suddenly, 'Sit down.' I attempt to perch on the armchair, but it's made of some soft, squashy material, and I find myself sinking into it against my will. The only other chair is tucked neatly beneath the desk. Xav saunters over to it, and rests his hand on the curved back of it, but remains standing. Pauline Pilcher stands in the centre of the room, glancing from me to him. 'Well, what is it you want?' she says.

I try to prop myself up in the armchair, which is swallowing me whole. I have no idea what to say really. Once again, it's Xav to the rescue. 'We were wondering if you knew about any connection Edward may have had to Skylark's father,' he says. 'His name was Joseph Riley, and he died about ten years ago.'

Pauline blinks, tortoise-like, her mouth hanging a little open as she considers the question. 'But, Edward is only 11 years old,' she says. What connection could he possibly have?'

'Drawings,' I blurt. 'Sketches he made. Of my father.'

Miss Pilcher's eyes stray for a moment, as though the answer could be floating on the air around her, like sunbeams or strands of cobweb. Then she gives a tiny shake of her head and her features snap back into shape - hard stare, pale lips in a narrow line. 'I first met Edward when he was 5 years old and I'm sorry Miss Riley, but I've never heard of Joseph Riley,' she says his name with some distaste. 'So perhaps you have been mistaken in assuming the sketches are of your father. They could be of someone else.'

'I'm very sure,' I begin, but she closes me down. 'If you'll excuse me,' she says, heading to the living room door, it's late. Would you mind?'

Xav is already following her out into the hallway, while I struggle to my feet from the suffocating embrace of the armchair. 'Good night,' says Miss Pilcher. I hesitate. This can't be all, can it? But Xav is already out on the path. I look at Miss Pilcher before I step outside. She won't make eye contact, but stares at a spot above my head. 'Will you take my phone number?' I ask, 'in case you think of anything?'

'That won't be necessary,' she says.

'I care for him, you know,' I say. 'For Edward.'

Her eyes meet mine for the most fleeting of moments, and the thin line of her mouth twists slightly before she pulls it back. 'Good night, Miss Riley,' she says, and I think I detect a catch in her throat before Xav calls me from the pavement. Miss Pilcher closes the door softly behind me, and I hear the latch chain being slid back into position. I'm dithering on the doorstep - should I ring the bell again? Force the issue? Xav grabs my wrist and pulls me with him down the path and on to the pavement. He's striding quickly, so I almost stumble. Xav, what the hell? But he shushes me. 'We need to get out of sight of the house,' he says, 'Skylark, I've got something to show you, come on.'

Edward

He runs. The Judas spoon bounces in his pocket, beside the envelope she gave him, pushed through the hedge as she whispered what he must do. Her voice rings in his head - *take the bus to Exeter, and go straight to the police station there. Give them this, but don't mention who gave it to you*. And so he had backtracked alongside the hedge and ducked out of sight of the school buildings by cutting along a path to the main exit. And then he had started to run, along the pavement and across the road to where houses begin at the edge of the village. He doesn't know where he can catch the bus. Whenever Miss Pilcher took him to Exeter or Plymouth, they only had to walk a short distance from his house to a bus stop, but she has told him to stay away from the house - *you mustn't go home Edward - trust me*. Trust her? Does he trust her?

He slows to a halt. He's out of breath; the air, like a mobius strip, twists in and out of his lungs and he needs to get his bearings. He can feel his heart hammering in his chest with quick, rhythmic thuds. There's a low wall beside him, the one he often walks along on his usual walk home, but now he sits down on it, and pulls the envelope from his pocket.

It's plain white and damp from being slotted through the criss crossed twigs of the hedge. It's crumpled too, from being balled into his pocket and he smoothes it over his knee, smudging the blue ink of Miss Pilcher's rounded script, but it's still legible - FAO Police - though he doesn't know what FAO means? Code? He turns the envelope over and studies the back. She has sealed it with a broad strip of sellotape. He holds it aloft, against the light and squints at what must be a piece of folded paper inside. He can't make out any writing. He puts it back into his pocket and withdraws the Judas spoon to fiddle with as he thinks. He must think.

'What is it?' he'd asked, but she'd shook her head. 'You'll find out soon enough, the police will tell you. Edward, do you have money? For the bus?' He'd shook his head, and watched her burrow into her purse. Obscured by the leaves and twigs, but still her, his Miss Pilcher. He wanted to tell her things; about the school and Skylark's necklace, about the spoon in his pocket, though he knows she'd tell him off for stealing it - *Goodness Edward, you stole something? Whatever next!*

Her hand came through the hedge again, this time bearing a £10 note. 'Take it, Edward, take it,' and he did, but as he did, the hand took hold of his, awkwardly, gripping his fingers tightly for a moment. 'Edward,' she said, 'I'm sorry, but really, do as I say. It's for the best. There are people who, I can't explain now, but you'll understand. Do as I say.' And then she had gone, leaving him staring at the £10 note and the envelope, before looking around himself - at the players engrossed in their match, at the school

205

buildings rising up beyond the field, at the exclusion hut, so neat and quiet at the other end of the field, at the quiet sky, clouds shifting silently across the blue. And he had left.

But now, sitting on the wall, the Judas spoon in his hand, what should he do? *There are people —* that's what she said. But who? He doesn't know any people other than his mother and Miss Pilcher, Skylark and the children from the trip, and he didn't really get to know them apart from Melissa. He searches further, and it comes to him. The only other person he knows.

His father.

A woman with a pushchair passes on the other side of the street and looks at him with curiosity for a moment. He should be in school. It's better if he moves away from the main road. He stands and begins to walk, quickly, but not so quickly that he'll draw attention to himself. He thinks about his father.

Why did he leave that day?

He realises now that it was nothing to do with the spoons clattering down and spilling over the floor, though at the time, the two events had connected in his mind. His mother has rarely spoken of him since he left, and he knows that money has become an issue, or the lack of it. He recalls his father's voice, uncharacteristically soft in the dim light of his study, showing him the spoons - *find the missing one and I've got myself a fortune.* But even if he were to find it, how would he let his father know? His hands close around the false Judas spoon; his spontaneous act of theft forever contained in its dented bowl, its tarnished metal. *There are people who* - what? Wish to harm him? Want something from him? Did his father do something wrong? Like him, stealing the spoon. Did his father run away too?

He has reached the safety of the woods and the path that will eventually take him home to his mother. *You mustn't go home Edward - trust me.* But how can he trust the words of a woman who left, with his father's old typewriter in her hands, and has never returned, not once until today. No card or letter to say goodbye. Through the trees, he sees the house built by the old man. Smoke curls from its chimney in a drift of grey and on a fencepost, a magpie perches. The path curls up from here towards his own home, and Edward takes it.

Skylark

'So what is it?'

We've reached the edge of the cul-de-sac, but Xav is determined to walk further. 'I'll show you in a minute?' He cuts down through a side street, pulling ahead of me to weave through a further narrow lane until he reaches the main road that runs through the village. I watch his straight back marching ahead, slim in his scruffy leather jacket, hands thrust into the pockets. There's something different about him, a purposefulness to his stride that I first observed as he marched away from me in Exeter to search for Edward. Generally, he's a man who saunters with an air of lazy calm, but these last two days, he has taken command of almost every situation - from finding Edward, to cleaning his own shirt while I slept off the vodka, and now this. I'm finding him quite sexy to tell the truth. 'Let's go home?' I call as he turns around, impatient for me to catch up. 'In a minute,' he says, 'but first, look at this.'

He has something in his hand, a piece of paper, which he unfolds as I approach. It's a photocopy of a newspaper cutting, grey and thin with age. The lines of the fold are virtually worn through and it's difficult to see properly in the burgeoning darkness of the street. He sidesteps towards a street light and holds the paper out to me. 'What do you think of this?' he says. I take it in my hand and peer at it; there's a small picture in the top right hand corner, and a headline; *Tiny Tomas Case may be Connected to Antique Jewellery Theft.* 'It was lying on the desk,' explains Xav. There was an old shoebox, and she stuffed some things into it as we came in - I saw her - but she must have missed this.'

I read the article - something about a theft from a London Museum, in which a valuable artifact was taken. Police believe the artifact may have been taken on the same night that Tomas Kovaleski disappeared from the museum, although the item was not reported as missing until several weeks later.

'Okay,' I say. 'So what?'

'What do you mean, so what?' I glance at Xav's face; his eyes are glittering and he's grinning the same toothy grin I associate with him as a boy, or as a teenager curled asleep on my bedroom floor. 'The picture, Skylark, have you looked at it?'

I turn my attention to the small picture at the top of the article. The paper has been folded and unfolded so many times that whatever is in the picture is marred by a vertical line. Also, as a photocopy, the picture has come out darker than the original might have been, and in the orange warmth of the street light, all I can really see is a mist of black on grey. Xav steps beside me, and turns the paper slightly so that it's more fully illuminated, and I see it - vague and shadowy, but unmistakeable. My hand reaches to clutch the original that nestles in the hollow at my own throat, and I run my fingers over the familiar edges. My necklace, given to me by my father all those years ago, hidden in a cigarette packet and the only birthday gift I'd ever received from him. In the photograph, it is mounted on a piece of board and a label runs beneath it, though I can't distinguish the words. 'It makes sense,' says Xav. 'Your dad did have a history for that sort of thing.' I nod. Deep down, I suppose I've always known it could've been stolen. I fold the photocopy into my coat pocket and begin to walk home with Xav in step beside me. I'm so caught up in the memory of that last night I saw him, I don't even think of anything else; it's Xav who raises the question of what the photocopy is doing in Miss Pilcher's house. 'And who is Tomas Kovaleski?' he asks.

'I don't know,' I reply. I suddenly feel exhausted. 'Look, Xav,' I say, 'let's sleep on it for tonight. We can look up this Tomas whatever-his-name-is tomorrow. We walk along in silence for a while. Xav links an arm with mine and I lean into him as we walk, breathing in the leather smell of his jacket, feeling the warmth of him beneath it. 'The thing I'm wondering about though,' says Xav eventually, 'is the thing he said as he left that night. Do you remember?'

'Keep safe,' I say. 'He told me to keep safe.'

'No, that's not what I heard,' he insists. 'Keep *it* safe, is what he said, I'm sure of it. Keep it, the necklace, safe. Skylark, what if the necklace wasn't a birthday present at all? What if he needed to hide it? And you were the safest place.'

We've arrived at the house and I'm fumbling through my pockets for the key. 'Well, I guess if it was stolen, he would need to hide it,' I say, 'but we've got no proof of that. There are any number of reasons why Miss Pilcher had a photograph.'

'Oh c'mon Skylark,' he says as I slide the key into the Yale lock and twist it. 'Edward's sketches of your father? And him being convinced he used to own the necklace? There's got to be a connection to that night, and what happened to your dad.'

The door swings open, and we shuffle into the unlit living room, which is still redolent of wallpaper paste and damp, and something else - a feeling that something isn't right - something that doesn't make itself clear until Xav snaps on a switch to flood the room with light. 'Jesus,' he says. The room has been ransacked; CDs and books have been tipped from the shelves beneath the window, my few items of furniture have been displaced, and in the kitchen, cupboards have been opened and rummaged through. The wooden frame of the kitchen window is splintered and the window itself hangs at a lopsided angle. Xav gives a low whistle as he inspects the damage. 'They've jemmied it open,' he reports, but I'm rooted to the spot, staring at the staircase and wondering if there's anyone hiding upstairs. Xav sees me, and resolutely marches up there, with a saucepan in one hand as a makeshift weapon. I hear him moving around, opening the wardrobe door and closing it again before he calls down to me, 'It's ok, all clear.'

I'm shaking. I pick my way between the wreckage of splayed books and broken CD cases and join Xav upstairs to see dressing table drawers yanked open and my clothes and underwear cast about the room and bed. The bathroom looks relatively untouched, 'Clearly, they were after more than toothpaste,' says Xav, before putting an arm around me and pulling me towards him. 'It's just kids, Skylark. Or addicts after some drug money. Don't let it upset you - we can sort out the mess.' But I'm looking at my bedside table, and the radio that sits on top of it, and I glance towards the dressing table, which has been rummaged through, but on which a jewellery box still stands. I pull away from Xav and flip the lid to see a familiar tangle of rings and bracelets, mostly solid silver, and a pair of gold earrings my mother gave me one Christmas. Still there. Untouched. 'Why didn't they steal anything?' I murmur. Xav takes a sharp intake of breath. 'Are you sure?' he asks, 'what about from downstairs? Anything missing?' I shake my head, knowing that I won't even have to look to find out all will be there. I reach for the necklace hanging from its leather string around my neck. 'I think it's this they must have wanted,' I say.

Edward

After slipping along the narrow track that rounds the house and brings him to the crumbling gate posts of his home, Edward stops. There's a car parked outside the gates. A long, sleek, black car with tinted windows. He has never seen it before. The only vehicle that ever parks outside his house is the delivery van that brings groceries each week, or the electric float that hums down the hill each morning with milk and bread. This car is thickly tired, and hunkers low to the ground like a muscled dog growling over a bone.

Edward steps back behind one of the gateposts and peers through the wrought iron gates towards the house. All is silent. A light breeze lifts his hair. He has a key to the front door, but finds himself scanning the building for another point of entry. No windows are open to climb through, and while there's a back door that opens onto the large, overgrown garden behind the house, he'd have to struggle through years of growth to reach it. The only other way into the house is through the dilapidated conservatory that clings to the far right hand side of the house. A long abandoned feature, which leaks rusted water through the windows every time it rains, and which serves as an area to store mundane items; a couple of worn out chairs, a rusting wheelbarrow, and his babyhood paraphernalia - a high chair, a dismantled cot, and an old fashioned coach built pram. Edward, looking all the time at the windows of the house, which stare back at him emptily, slips through the gate and skirts around the perimeter of the tarmac courtyard. He pauses at the entrance to the conservatory - is it open? He gingerly presses down on the slim door handle and feels it give, but the door doesn't open. He tries again, this time nudging the door with his shoulder, and the ancient wood yields with a slight squeak. He steps inside, and listens.

There are voices. A low murmuration, punctuated by long pauses as he listens, but the words can't be distinguished. Two voices, both low, and neither of them belong to his mother. Who are they? He recalls a visit his mother had once from two council officials, who came to enquire into Edward's 'Home Education Programme.' She had made them cups of tea, and had asked Edward to come downstairs from his room to explain what he was learning each day with Miss Pilcher. They had nodded and smiled and made notes on a lined pad of paper as he told them about the books he was reading, and the maths problems he was able to solve. They handed his mother a bundle of leaflets before they left, which contained colourful photographs of smiling children and their parents. The pamphlets had titles like, *Co-operative Home Learning* and *Home Education for Families*, and the two men had suggested his mother make contact with other families who had chosen to home educate their children. His mother had thrown the pamphlets in the bin as soon as they'd left, but until then, she had behaved almost normally. Answering their questions, smiling politely. If the men in the room are the same council officials, then he'd be able to hear her speaking too, wouldn't he? He considers further. He's at school now. It can't be them. He creeps closer to the door that adjoins the kitchen in the main house, and crouches down to listen.

'We could take the rest of the paintings, leave it there.'

A pause, before the second voice responds. It is more refined than the first - lighter, cooler, not quite English.

'It simply can't be left, as you say. A debt is a debt, and when the debt cannot be paid in full, then the item purchased must be returned.'

'And what will you do with it? The item?'

'Why Martin, you have no head for business. It will serve as security until payment is received.'

'And if it isn't? If he doesn't come scurrying back?'

A further pause

'Well then, it will be disposed of.'

'Does she know that?'

'Why worry the lady? And if she does know, well, I don't think we can expect any repercussions.'

'Why not?'

The second man laughs. A cold, humorless chuckle.

'Let's just say, Eleanor Parry has her secrets. Secrets she wouldn't want discovered.'

'Even at the expense of...'

'Even at that expense. Ah, Mrs Parry.'

Edward freezes as he hears his mother enter the room. 'I have them here,' she says. Her voice is high pitched and breathless and he aches to nudge the door and peer in, to see her with these men - *There are people who* - are these the ones Miss Pilcher spoke of? He recalls her frantic face behind the hedge, the way her square fingers gripped his own. His mother speaks again. 'There's one missing, but even so, John expected a high price for them.' Edward listens to the soft clatter of something metallic being placed on the table. There is quiet for a moment. The sounds of things being lifted and replaced.

'A fine collection. Your husband has an eye for such things, Mrs Parry. They'd fetch a small sum. But as you say, there's one missing, which makes our transaction of a different colour.'

'Then what?' she says, and Edward flinches at the timbre of her voice, at the thread of panic shooting through it. 'There are the paintings too, you can take all of them. I don't care.'

'Calm yourself, Mrs Parry, calm yourself.'

A chair is scraped back, and Edward hears the clip of shoes on the tiled floor before the calm, cool voice continues. 'Sit, won't you? There's no reason to upset yourself. We'll take the spoons, and the remaining paintings for now. But really, they'll barely cover our costs in this matter.'

'Then what will?'

'I've already informed you of that, Mrs Parry. Now, are you going to tell me how long we have to wait?'

Again, there's silence. Edward looks around the conservatory - there must be a way to see into the kitchen. Glancing upwards, he sees it. A row of small rectangular glass panes at the apex of the slanted conservatory roof. They're dusty and cobwebbed, designed to allow light into the kitchen, but high above him. He scans the glass room. There's a small wooden table in the conservatory, left over from the days when people must have breakfasted in this room. If he can slide it into place against the wall, and mount one of the old chairs on top of it, it might give him the height he needs to peer in through one of the windows.

He moves deftly, carefully lifting objects from the path of the table before nudging it an inch at a time into place. Between each tiny shove, he waits. Having moved from his listening position near the door, the words of the three gathered in the kitchen become once again remote and indistinct. He lifts a chair into place on the table, and carefully pulls himself up to stand beside it. The table wobbles under his feet, but only a fraction. He stands on the chair to find the top of his head in alignment with the bottom edge of the window frame. He steadies himself by grasping the thin wood of the frame between his fingertips, and stretches up, on tiptoe.

There isn't much to see; his mother is seated in full view, but the men have their backs to him and through the dirty windowpane he's unable to see clearly. His mother is pale, and she's pulling threads from the cuffs of her blouse. He listens - but the three sit in silence. One of the men is smoking a cigarette and blue-gray plumes rise from the glowing tip to spread and float over the room. What are they waiting for? The backs of his legs are beginning to tremble, but rather than rest he tries to shift his position slightly so he can get a better view of the man holding the cigarette. He edges to the left, then further, straining now at an awkward angle, but still he can't see, so he moves just a fraction further, gripping at the ledge with fingertips that are white from the pressure. He feels the chair tilt beneath him and tries to regain his balance, but the chair has tilted too far. He falls, sending the chair skittering, and he crashes painfully on the flat wood of the table, which gives way beneath him, sending him head first to the hard floor, where his head smacks the tiles. Prone, he sees the door yanked open, a confusion of legs and movement, and as he tries to push himself up he finds himself staring into the narrow barrel of a gun.

'Good to see you, Edward,' says a tall, thin man in a long black coat. Edward glances from the gun, to the man's pale blue eyes, and feels a wave of darkness and nausea wash over him. His eyes close, heavy as lead, and he's aware of nothing.

Downstairs, I begin to scoop my scattered belongings and shift the disarranged furniture back into place. 'You should probably leave it,' says Xav, 'the police might want to take fingerprints.' But I shake my head. 'I don't want to call them,' I tell him. 'This isn't a burglary Xav, this is something that runs deeper than that.' I stack things neatly into place, and the whole time I'm aware of two things; Xav standing watching me from the kitchen doorway, and the necklace, which seems to have gained weight around my neck. It knocks against me as I move, suddenly insistent for my attention. I stop what I'm doing to unclasp it, and stand for a moment with the crucifix cupped in the bowl of my hand. What the hell does it all mean?

'It's only half past nine,' says Xav. 'It's not too late to call on Mrs Parry and Edward.' I nod. 'We can take a look at those sketches,' he continues, 'I'm pretty sure I could recognize him, if it really is your Dad.'

'It is,' I say, shooting him a look that makes him raise his hands in defence.'

'Okay, okay,' he says. 'It's your dad, I believe you. Thing is, if Edward was, what? Only a year or so old when he saw him, then the only person who can explain things is his mother.'

219

'Hmmm,' I say, wrapping the crucifix into its leather cord and slipping it into my jacket pocket.'

'My theory,' he says, warming to his theme, 'is that perhaps the necklace belonged to her, and that's how Edward recognised it. Maybe your Dad stole it from the house, and Edward saw him.'

'But it was stolen from a London Museum,' I say, 'it said so in the newspaper article. And we lived in London back then. We moved here after Dad's death, remember?'

'Yeah,' says Xav, thoughtfully. 'Ever wondered why that was?'

'What?'

'I mean, why here? Or, this area, anyway? I know why I came here from London, but why did your mum choose this area? Have you ever asked her?'

I have no answer, and so don't reply as I return to dragging the sofa back into place. Xav walks over and lifts the other end of it. 'It's a bit of coincidence, isn't it? Your Dad gives you a necklace, which just happens to have once belonged to Edward, who has lived here his entire life. Has he ever even been to London?'

'I don't know,' I say, a little too snappily. There are so many things firing off in my head at once that I'm desperate for a minute's quiet. I flop on to the sofa, feeling mentally bruised, but Xav is like a terrier with a rat and won't let go.

'Fact one,' he says. 'Your father stole things for a living. Art, we know about, but possibly jewellery too, which explains the necklace. Fact two, Edward at some point must have seen your father, and the memory of his face has stuck with him. Combined with the fact that he recognizes the necklace, we must suppose he's telling the truth.' He begins to pace across the room, every inch Sherlock Holmes. 'Fact three, Pauline Pilcher has, or had, a picture of your necklace, which means she's mixed up in this as well.' He pauses. 'Does your mother know Miss Pilcher?' he asks. I feel tired.

'I don't know, Xav,' I reply wearily. There's something bugging me on top of the mystery of it all. A nagging voice in my head, Edward's voice, quiet in his bedroom, but casual and self certain, while my own head spun at the sight of those perfect pencil sketches. *That's the man who took me to be killed.* My father was no killer, just a common thief, who ended up being killed himself - and why? Because he knew something, and he had something - the necklace - which someone else wanted, and which they still want now. I glance warily around the room. From the sofa I can see the damaged window, which Xav has already secured with a few flimsy nails, but it could easily be wrenched open again. Whoever was here didn't find what they wanted, which means they'll be back.

'Xav,' I say, 'we need to get out of here.'

Edward

He's the bog boy again. Pressed in and unable to move, the dark weighing on his bones, the iron scent of mud, and the peace of it, deep underground. He doesn't want to wake, but he's being brought to the surface, excavated, he feels hands upon him, and a voice saying his name, Edward? His mother's face is the first he sees, swimming in and out of focus, but close to his own - closer than she usually gets to him. Her eyes are wide and frightened and he wants to comfort her, but there is someone else in the room. He sees a dark coat. The outline of its wearer is against the window and fading evening light seeps around him, making him fuzzy and indistinct. He recalls the gun, the pointed barrel like an empty eye, and the pain in his head from thumping against the floor in his descent. The dull throb of the bruise booms like a clock. He's lying on the small sofa in his father's study at the front of the house, and the man is looking at his watch. The gun is nowhere to be seen. 'It's going to be all right, Edward,' his mother whispers, 'they'll be gone soon. It'll be just you and me again. Just you and me.' She strokes his cheek with the back of her hand, and he feels the raised grazes where she has clawed them red.

He can't see the second man. The tall man leans calmly against the window frame, regarding Edward and his mother coolly, saying nothing until the dull buzz of a phone breaks the silence.

As the man reaches inside his overcoat for it, Edward sees the dimpled handle of the gun poking from his belt. He closes his eyes, he hasn't imagined it. The man answers the phone, and walks from the room to the hallway where his conversation can't be heard. 'I've been very clever, Edward,' his mother whispers. She brings her lips to his ear, so close that they brush against it. 'I've sent them off the trail,' she says, her voice light and twisting, 'I told them she had it. I told them she had the spoon.' and she giggles. A soft, girlish sound that he has never heard before. He pulls his face away to look at her and sees that her eyes are lit; they shine in the darkening room as the man's phone call drones on the other side of the living room door. 'They said if we had the last spoon, then they'd leave us alone, and I thought of something Edward, I thought of it all by myself.'

'What?' asks Edward, his new voice cracking in his throat. 'What did you tell them?'

'About her,' she says, insistent now, her voice a hiss. 'About the woman who was here. The mentor. Sparrow.'

'Skylark?' says Edward.

'Yes, her.' She nods vigorously. 'They think she has the thirteenth spoon, the Judas spoon. He's gone to get it. The other one, the other man who was here.'

The throb in his head pounds louder. There is no Judas spoon, and what is his mother trying to gain? And why Skylark? He opens his dry mouth to speak, but she presses a finger to his lips and then takes both his hands in hers to pull him to his feet. 'There's no time Edward, you must go, you must go now.'

The monotone of the stranger's voice continues beyond the door. 'Where?' he asks. 'How can I go anywhere?' He feels dizzy and sick and his mother is staring at him with glittering eyes. 'Why, Edward,' she says, 'through the tunnel, of course.'

Skylark

We drive to my mother's house. A light rain begins to fall as we turn off the main road and speed our way through narrow lanes, which wind like capillaries across the splayed body of the moor. We drive in silence for the most part; Xav beside me in the passenger seat, fidgeting with the stereo and occasionally extending his foot to press an imaginary brake pedal as we approach the more sudden turns. For a motorcyclist, he can be surprisingly timid of the way I drive, which at the moment, I admit, is fast and reckless. I want to get there - to my mother's cottage with its rambling roses breaking out from bud above the door. With its tidy rooms and tastefully arranged furniture. I want to get there and force an answer from her. It's impossible that she has nothing more to say, and that Dad's death simply closed the door on all those years of marriage, those shared confidences between husband and wife, or if not shared confidences, then at least suspicions. She snoops in on the details of my life so regularly that it's hard to believe she didn't know more about him; his friends, the people he worked for, the crimes he committed.

'Slow down,' says Xav. We're approaching a pedestrian crossing near the start of Mum's village, and I slam on the brakes as a young man blithely sets foot on it without looking. 'Fucking idiot,' I say. Xav casts me a sidelong glance, then thinks better of saying anything. We drive more sedately to Mum's small cottage and pull up on the street outside.

She's surprised to see me at this time of night, especially when she sees Xav behind me. Her feigned smile fades as she greets him with a simple but questioning, 'Xavier?' I'd forgotten that I haven't told her about him and me, and I still don't bother to, but explain about the burglary instead. 'Did you call the police?' she asks as she ushers us into her kitchen. 'They didn't take anything,' I say, and then, as confusion creases her features, I pull the necklace from my pocket and let it dangle from my fingers on its leather cord. 'They came for this,' I say, in a tone I'm hoping will strike a note of drama into proceedings, but she doesn't look at it as she has already turned away and is busying herself with filling a kettle for tea. She glances back over her shoulder from the sink, 'That ugly old thing?' she says, 'Why on earth would they want that?'

'It's not ugly,' I say, and I wince at the hint of teenage whine that creeps into my tone. 'Mum,' I say, more calmly, 'we need to talk about a few things,' but she's foraging in a cupboard for biscuits, 'I've got chocolate digestives or these plain ones,' she says, brandishing a packet in each hand. Exasperated, I throw the necklace on the round wooden table that occupies most of the available space. It lands with a light thump. 'Mum, sit down.'

'Let's have both,' she says, loosening biscuits from the packet onto a small china plate. 'Xavier, tea or coffee for you?' He's looking at me uncertainly, but then I see a flash of resolve cross his face, firming the line of his lips and narrowing his eyes. 'Jeannie,' he says, 'I'll have a beer if you have one, and then we need you to sit down.' He pulls out a chair and raises his eyebrows at her. 'I'll get the beer myself,' he says, when she doesn't move, and he walks past her towards the fridge. She's still hesitant, and fidgets with the biscuits on the plate, pushing them around with one finger until they're more perfectly arranged. 'What's this all about?' she says slowly, meeting my eyes with her own. I pick up the necklace from the table. 'I want you to tell me about this,' I say. She sits on the chair Xav has pulled out for her, and reaches out a hand to take the necklace from my own. Her reading glasses hang from a beaded chain about her neck and she puts them on to study the contours of the crucifix, turning it in her hand, appraising it, in the way a jeweller might. 'Xavier,' she says at last as she carefully places the necklace back in the centre of the table, 'there's a bottle of white in the fridge. You may as well open it.' She removes her reading glasses and pinches the top of her nose, a habitual action with her when tired or stressed. I wait. She lets out an exasperated breath of air. 'All right, the last night he came around, on your birthday,' she says, 'he phoned me later that night.' I wait, as Xav places two glasses on the table and quietly fills each with wine. 'He told me that I wasn't to worry, but that if anyone came calling, I was to say he hadn't been there and I hadn't seen him.'

'And you said?'

'Well, Skylark, what do you think I said? I hit the roof.' She sips the wine and I do the same, catching the full oaky scent of it - it's an expensive bottle, smooth on the tongue but caustic at the edges. 'Oh, I can't remember what I said exactly, it was years ago now, but you know how things were between me and your father at that time. I wanted distance. I wanted safety more than anything. To raise my daughter in something resembling normality, rather than prison visits and seedy underworld doings. I told him to get out of our lives, I told him he was no good, I think I threatened him with a solicitor and that I'd be getting an injunction against him. I said a lot of things.' She pauses to drink her wine, not a delicate sip this time but a long swallow, with her eyes closed. 'And then, two days later...' She stops speaking and reaches for the necklace, touches it gently with her fingertips. I finish the sentence for her; 'He was dead.'

'Yes,' she says, meeting my eyes briefly before averting them again. 'He was dead.'

A quiet ensues, broken only by the ticking of the kitchen clock and the minute sounds of the house; the hum of the fridge, the almost imperceptible creak of the floor as Xav shifts his weight from one foot to another. 'Were you sorry?' I ask, and she raises her head to look at me. 'Oh, Skylark, of course I was sorry. He was your father, and I loved him once.' I feel the oh so familiar rise of emotion in my chest; that wave gathering force towards the base of my throat. But I fight it down until it subsides, softly. A diminishing swell. 'I had no idea he'd brought you the necklace that night,' she continues, 'if I had, I would've handed it to the police. Then, when I saw you wearing it that first time, after we'd moved here from London, I didn't have the heart to say anything. I didn't see the harm in you having something from him, even if it was stolen. You needed to have something from him.'

'So you knew it was definitely stolen,' I say. 'Right from the start, you knew.' She shrugs. 'It's how he made his living,' she says, 'chances are it

228

was.' But there's something in the way she casually lifts her wineglass and looks away from me that tells me she still isn't entirely on the level. 'Why did we move?' I ask.

'Why? Well, wasn't it obvious? A fresh start. A new life. I needed out of London. I needed you out of London.'

'But I was happy enough to stay.'

'Oh C'mon, Skylark. You were grieving.'

'I didn't stop grieving when we came here,' I say. 'I just grieved in a new place, at a new school,' I glance at Xav, 'where I didn't know anyone.'

'Yes, well,' she says, her shoulders tightening as she sits more upright in her chair, 'I think enough time has passed to be over that now. And it's a good life we've had here, isn't it?'

Xav strolls over from his position near the fridge to refill our glasses like some scruffy Maitre D. He gently squeezes my shoulder as he stands beside me and I reach up and touch his hand for a moment. 'So, you two,' says Mum, jumping on the chance to change the subject, 'I take it things are back on? When did that happen?'

'Recently,' I say, but I'm determined not to be drawn. 'Why here?' I say. 'I mean this place rather than anywhere else?' But she has turned her attention to Xav. 'I know we don't always see eye to eye, Xav,' she's saying, 'but you've virtually been a part of this family since you were a boy, and no one could have been more delighted than me when you turned up in Exeter that time.' She takes a deep draft from her wine glass, and I notice that her cheeks are pinkening with an alcohol flush. 'If I've sometimes criticized you for not having a proper job, or for smoking too much...' she carefully pronounces the word, '...marijuana, or for going off with that other woman that time...'

'Oh Mum, just stop,' I say, but she's on a roll, '...bear in mind, it's because I care about my girl.' She turns her glassy amber eyes on me and reaches across the table to grip my hand in her own. 'My girl,' she says, her voice cracking into a hoarse whisper, 'my girl.'

'I know why I came here,' says Xav. 'Why I moved here from London, we just wondered why you did is all.' Mum looks puzzled for a moment, and withdraws her hand from mine. 'Well,' she says, gathering herself, 'it's no mystery really. We used to come here, your father and I, before you were born Skylark, and a few times when you were a baby. Just weekends away now and again. And I liked it here, so, when I had the choice, I chose here.'

'You came here with Dad?' I ask. She nods, reaching for one of the untouched biscuits she arranged on the plate earlier. 'I thought he was an art dealer, remember? And we'd come together with a few canvases in the back of a car for some contact he had down here.' She takes a dainty bite of the biscuit, and chews thoughtfully. 'He'd go off and deliver the paintings, then come back to whatever little cottage we'd rented for the weekend and we'd go for walks, or drive to the beach.' She looks at me. 'It wasn't all bad with your father, not in the early days.' I say nothing for a moment, picturing the two of them strolling across a white strand while breakers roll in the distance, my father with a camera, Mum with me in her arms. I see it unwind like one of those old home-cine movies – flickering and grainy, shy smiles and faded colours. 'Anyway, Skylark,' says Mum, reaching her arms above her head and stretching her mouth into an exaggerated yawn. 'I have to go to open the shop in the morning. You and Xav know where the spare room is.' She taps her palms on the table, before standing. 'If you'll excuse me, I'll say good night,' she says. But as she slides out from behind the table, Xav asks, 'Jeannie, have you ever heard of Tomas Kovaleski?'

'Who?' she says, and for a moment, just the tiniest moment, I see something cross her face. A shadow? The crease of a frown? Almost instantly, it is gone. 'No,' she says, 'never heard it. Who's he? Sounds like a Russian name or something, but really, you two, I must get to bed,' and she's off, leaving me and Xav alone. He raises his beer bottle and takes swig from it. 'Why *did* you come here from London?' I ask. He wipes his mouth with the back of his hand before answering. 'For you,' he says, and he shakes his head, 'I came here for you, Skylark. Didn't you know that?'

Edward

She has just closed the trapdoor. How can he have lived in this house all his life, and not known it was there? She pulled him from the sofa and, deftly, with one foot, slid the rug into rumpled waves, and there it was, a door in the floor. 'Quickly Edward,' she'd said, and so he had tugged at the sunken brass ring and the door had opened, a small trap door, barely large enough for him to slip through, and with no ladder or stairs, just a drop into earth smelling darkness. So he had fallen, stumbling to his knees as he hit the soft solidity of the bottom, a drop of about twice his own height, and the door and the darkness had closed over his head immediately. Complete blackness.

He pulls himself into a crouch and listens - movements from above - the quick shuffle of his mother's feet replacing the rug, the sharp crack of something - not a gunshot - a tinier noise, and a creak, and clatter - the window? She has opened the window and he hears voices now - hers and the man's - and here he is, alone and crouched and trembling. He steadies himself and reaches out to the sides, meets the resistance of damp walls, rough beneath the scrape of his fingernails. Ahead, a nothingness; bleak and empty and cold. Tentatively, he stands. He moves forward an inch, then another, and another. His arms stretch before him and his hands search, twisting and turning like blind tentacled things. The dark is blanket thick, layer upon layer surround him and he feels sick at the weight of it - the sodden weight of the dark and its black reek of mold and stone and rot. His hands touch a surface and pull back sharply - is he boxed in? Is this nothing but a pit beneath the house, a tiny storeroom? But his mother said tunnel, so he touches his palms to the surface and feels the wet flat of something - tiles? Worn brick? As his hands slide lower, again an opening, smaller, but a space through which a boy can easily pass. He stoops, and enters - narrower, lower, but ongoing. He must walk with his head bowed, leaning forward, like a half cocked pen knife, and he feels the roof brush the top of his head as he walks, and at intervals, fat beams under which he must duck, and all the time, dark. Nothing but the dark. The tunnel narrows as he walks until his shoulders almost touch the sides, and he's bent double now, pushing himself deeper and deeper into the black. He feels something brush his face, making him start back as though bitten. He stops. He's breathless, his heart juddering. He reaches, tentatively, for the thing that touched him - finds something dangling - a rope? Or a root, pushing through from above. He grasps it and feels the frayed texture, the tiny hairs furring the thick braid of it, and calculates. How far has he walked? He must be beneath the garden, and as he pushes further, more roots, creating a thicket, ever denser. He turns, as if to go back - blind eyes peering back the way he has come - blind eyes peering into the nothingness he has navigated. Go back to the man? The gun?

He thinks of his mother, the red ridges scratched into her hands, her eyes sparkling with that desperate gleam. He leans against the rough wall, feels the chill of it through his coat, and slides down it, his face wet and hot and his grief rising in knots from the bottom of his chest. He digs into his pocket for the comfort of the spoon, the Judas spoon, but he fumbles it, and it falls beside him somewhere. He feels for it and finds it, but something else too - a raised bump, smooth to the touch, but shaped like a dome, half submerged in the earth. He explores it with his hands - a stone? Something hard but smooth, with holes where he can dig his fingers. He tugs it loose, feeling the soft shale-like fall of dirt as it yields, and he cradles it in his hands, this small thing, strokes the smooth dome of it like a cat on his lap. He closes his eyes and feels the cool dark seep into his skin, staining like ink, filling each pore and flooding his mouth, his nostrils, his ears. He's the bog boy, sinking through the murk, and here he must rest.

Skylark

We don't stay at my mother's house. I let Xav drive us back to Stonemoor and sit in the passenger seat watching the dark of the moor roll out from the car headlamps, seemingly infinite, and defined only by the vaguest hint of paler sky pressing lightly on its contours. I feel headachy and fuzzed by wine. My mother's words chase their tails around my head; my father knew Stonemoor, and had been here often. He had told her not to let anyone know he'd been at the house that night, and she had kept the secret of the necklace, despite suspecting it was stolen. And that name, Tomas Kovaleski, the shadow that passed over her face. 'Penny for them?' says Xav, and I shrug. 'I don't know what to think,' I tell him, but I'm aware of the shape of a thought gathering in my mind, coming together the way droplets of water cool and coalesce into a cloud. 'We'll google Tomas Kovaleski as soon as we get back to yours,' Xav says, 'don't know why we didn't do that to begin with.'

'The small matter of the burglary?' I remind him. And I'm worried too, of being in the house - what if whoever it was comes back?'

'I'll protect you,' grins Xav, but I'm in no mood for mock chivalry. 'I think we should go to Eleanor Parry's house,' I say.

'What? Now?' Isn't it a bit late?'

'She doesn't sleep so well,' I say. 'Chances are she'll be wide awake, but Edward will be in bed and that's a good thing, because there's something I need to ask her.'

'And what's that?' asks Xav. We're on the main road, which is well lit, so the edges of the moor reveal themselves more clearly, and the outline of the Henge can be seen ahead of us as we rise up from a dip in the road. I take a deep breath before telling him the thought that has begun to crystallize and harden in the recesses of my brain. 'My father was a thief,' I say. 'He stole works of art, and jewellery. Precious things.' I pause before adding, 'What if he stole a child too?' I study Xav's face as I speak, watching for signs of surprise or disbelief, but he simply stares ahead at the road, unmoved, and I know he's been thinking the same thing. 'Tomas Kovaleski,' I say, and he nods. 'Edward,' he says simply. 'So Tiny Tom is Edward Parry. And what? You want to go to Eleanor Parry right now and confront her with that?'

We're approaching Stonemoor. Ahead of us, the village twinkles with tiny lights and as Xav slows to the speed limit, I'm aware of the wood on my right, dark and knotted, and heralding the turn that will lead us down to the Parry house. 'Yes,' I say. 'Yes, I do.'

'I hope you know what you're doing,' says Xav, as he peers through the windscreen, spots the turn, and swings into it. 'She'll never admit to it though, and even if she did, then what?'

'I don't know,' I murmur. We're approaching the house and there's something about it that unnerves me. There are lights yellowing each window, and the rusting gates, which I've only seen closed before, stand ajar. 'Nice place,' says Xav as he pulls up in front of the gates, 'pretty big - so she's rich then?'

'No, I don't think so,' I reply. I can feel a knot twisting into shape in my stomach as I get out of the car and gaze at the house. I'm thinking about the last time I came here; Edward opening the front door to reveal a darkened hallway and Eleanor Parry sitting in the candlelit kitchen while shadows danced on the walls behind her. Why would she have switched all the house lights on? 'Well,' says Xav, 'Are we going to ring the bell?' He has already stepped through the open gates and is waiting for me, his arms spread wide, askance. I glance at my watch - it has turned midnight and the air is chill and damp enough to make me shiver after the warmth of the car. The knot in my stomach has pulled itself tighter and I'm about to say we should forget it, that we've jumped to a conclusion too quickly and that we should think things through more carefully before making any rash decisions, but as I open my mouth to speak a movement from the house distracts me. The front door opens and there, standing uncertainly at the entrance to her home,

237

is Eleanor Parry. She extends one of those long, slender arms, and beckons us towards her. I find myself rooted to the spot but Xav, after glancing momentarily at me, heads towards her, breaking into a run up the wide steps to the entrance as Eleanor's body suddenly appears to waver and buckle. He reaches her at the point of collapse, catching her awkwardly about the waist as she crumples. I unfreeze and run to help him, but he manages to scoop her limp body into his arms and carries her into the house.

The faint is momentary. By the time Xav has laid her onto the small sofa in the room Edward told me was his father's old study, she is already coming around and sits up, her eyes wandering vaguely from Xav to me. 'I'll get you some water,' says Xav, hurrying from the room in search of the kitchen and leaving me standing there, staring at Eleanor and unsure what to say. 'Are you all right?' I manage eventually. 'You remember me, don't you? Skylark Riley.' She nods, closing her eyes as if gradually falling into a much needed sleep, and leaning back against the sofa cushions, her thin body seems to unravel and fold into their density. She is even paler than I remember her, but her cheeks are lit by two spots of livid red, and as Xav returns with a glass of water, her eyelids suddenly lift and she pinpoints me with a frantic stare. 'Edward,' she says, and her face contorts, her mouth twisting into the ugliness of grief. 'Edward,' she manages, 'If they find him, they'll take him. They'll take him.'

'Who'll take him?' I ask. 'Who are they?' She has taken the proffered water from Xav's hand and is gulping it down. I watch the workings of her slim neck as she swallows and I glance at Xav as some of the water trickles from the edges of her mouth to rivulet over her chin. 'Those two,' she says, gasping to recover her breath, then leaning forward and lowering her voice. 'I sent them to you,' she confides, 'I put them off the track,' and she laughs, an unnerving explosion - high pitched and tremulous. 'Yes, a wild goose chase, but they're looking for him now, and if they find him,' her face darkens, confused, and her body pitches forward from the sofa to vomit the water she has just drunk all over the floor. 'I'll find a towel or something,' Xav says as she leans back again, groaning. I perch beside her on the vacant side of the sofa and take one of her hands in mine. With the other, she mops at her mouth and face. 'Eleanor,' I say, 'can you tell me what has happened? Where is Edward? Can you tell me from the beginning?'

'From the beginning,' she echoes, almost dreamily. 'Sweet Edward, my sweet Edward.' Her eyes softly close once more, and I want to shake her, but I'm distracted by the unmistakeable sound of a car pulling up outside and the double slam of car doors. Eleanor hears it too, and she stiffens, pulling her hand free of my grasp and sitting bolt upright. 'Get out,' she hisses. 'You must get out.' And she's on her feet, pulling aside a striped rug that covers part of the floor to reveal a small trap door, which she lifts. 'They'll kill you,' she says urgently. 'You're a complication - they kill complications.' There's no sign of Xav, who has gone upstairs to find something to clean up the pool of regurgitated water on the floor. 'Go,' she says, and she shoves me with surprising solidity, so I stumble and fall on my knees beside the trap door, which yawns open to reveal an impenetrably dark space. I hear the twist of a key in the front door, and find myself scrambling for the open space, letting myself drop through the opening to land on a soft earth surface as the door closes over my head.

I'm blind, unable to see anything through the sheer black, and as I hear voices over my head, my heart begins to race and pound. I am, quite simply, terrified. I cock my head to listen. Male voices, indistinct but containing an air of...what? Authority? But without warning, a sharp rise in intonation and a sudden scuffle of feet on the floor over my head, and I hear his shout, Xav, his risen voice flooded with panic, 'Don't shoot,' he says. I freeze, barely daring to breathe as interminable seconds tick by. There's no shot - surely I'd hear a shot? More voices; lower, and movement now. With shaking hands I fumble my phone from my pocket, but there's no signal down here in the subterranean darkness. I need to get out and phone the police, but how? I stretch out my hands to feel damp walls on either side of me, crumbling to the scrape of my touch like damp plaster, but ahead of me, a nothingness; a space that may lead somewhere? I crouch almost on all fours and slowly shuffle forward, expecting at every moment to have my path blocked, but there's nothing. I'm in a tunnel; it's low and narrow, and before long I'm crawling like a baby on all fours, but I keep going because at the end of every tunnel, there's light. Isn't there?

Edward

He feels alone, but he has felt alone before. He has closed his eyes and slumps against the earth wall, his shoulders damp from the moisture contained within it, and his feet pressed flat against the opposite wall, so he forms a kind of human strut, his body curving between head and feet - foetal in this dank womb. He falls into a half sleep, one haunted by wispy dreams and remembered voices. His mother; *you're a good boy, Edward*, and his father, re-materialising in this darkness; *find that spoon, Edward, the Judas spoon, and your worries are over*. The false Judas spoon is safely back in his pocket, and though he feels like rubbing the nub of his thump into its worn bowl, his hand is occupied with the strange stone he picked up from the tunnel floor. It sits in his lap, and he strokes it, allowing his fingers to probe the almost perfectly round holes of its surface. He's the bog boy, sunk into darkness, and he feels calm and peaceful. He has no fear of the dark, of the cold, of the infinity of years that will leave him undisturbed here in the belly of the Earth.

He slumps further into sleep, his body relaxing, and he's walking again through the village; around cob walls and roofs thatched with straw, the mingled smells of dung and cooking pots, of unwashed bodies and wood-smoke. He's looking for someone, and peers at the barely lit faces of the men, who circle a low glowing fire of red embers. Then at a woman who squats beside a wide earthen wash bowl, and at two children who are scratching in the dirt nearby. Their voices are foreign to him; guttural shouts and low pitched chatter in a language he cannot understand. He is hungry, but has no food, so instead sucks on the metal of the cross that hangs about his neck. He enjoys the cool of it against his lip and the quiet clatter against his teeth when he softly bites on it. But then, without warning, he's there. The man.

Tall. Thin. Hands behind his back and eyes darting furtively before settling on his own. A smile creases the man's face and he takes a step towards him. 'You look lost,' the man says kindly. 'Do you want to come with me?' But Edward, frozen, doesn't reply. Doesn't know how to reply. 'C'mon, Sonny,' says the man, 'we'll find your mammy.' Another step. Edward could touch him if he were able to move. He can see the crisscross weave in the fabric of the man's trousers. He can hear the slight creak of leather from the man's jacket as he makes a sudden movement, and as something closes over his mouth, something sharp smelling and alien, he sees the deep sea green of the man's eyes, but something else too. As he kicks against the weight of unconsciousness that closes over him like a clamshell, he sees in the green eyes, a lost look - shimmering fear that mirrors his own. As Edward succumbs to the blackness that swallows him whole, his last conscious moment is not one of fear, but of startled recognition.

A noise awakens him.

He grips the strange stone in his lap and turns his head towards the sound, trying to place it. From the tunnel, a low sound. A breathing, but laboured and uneven. What is it? An animal? He pictures some subterranean creature, giant and mole-like and snuffling through the earth. He pushes against the tunnel wall behind him and lowers his feet so he's once again in a crouching position, but where can he go? The thick roots before him bar further movement, and the creature's getting nearer. He lets out a sound, a strangled whimper, and the creature stops. He's aware of its proximity, just feet away, perhaps only inches. He edges back against the fretwork of roots, and waits, his heart tight in his chest. And then, a rustling, and a fierce, blinding light that pierces the dark for just a second before being doused. Then again. And then again, but this time it steadies and resolves itself into a single flame and as his eyes adjust he sees behind it a cloud of unkempt hair and the reflected shine of known eyes peering past the flame towards him. 'Edward?' she says, before the cigarette lighter she holds aloft sputters and fails, plunging them into darkness once more. He feels a hot surge behind his eyes and the choke of sudden tears as Skylark reaches through the dark to grasp him in her arms.

Skylark

Fuck me but it's dark in here. I'm holding the shape of Edward, and he's shaking and crying. I wipe where I think his eyes are with the edge of my sleeve, and get the hot damp of upset and fear running down his cheek. I smooth his hair. Fine soft hair that has been allowed to grow too long, and wait until the juddering of his body stills a little against my own. I rub his back, feeling the ridge of his spine, knotty under my fingers. Never before has he seemed so small. But I need him calm and coherent so he can tell me what the hell is going on back at the house. I need to get out of here and call the police. Xav's in there with a gunman and I'm terrified he'll do something stupid enough to get himself shot, though what exactly, I don't know. I've never even seen a gun before, never mind a gunman. What if the guy's twitchy and nervous? What if Xav makes a grab for the gun and it goes off? I squeeze my eyes tight - we need to get out.

I release Edward and reach into my pocket for the cigarette lighter; it's almost out of gas but there's enough for me to spark a flame for a few moments and survey the problem. Tree roots, extending in through where the tunnel walls have broken down. Two large ones extend diagonally across each other to form an X shape, reminding me of one of the saints on Edward's damn spoons; 'St Andrew,' he tells me mournfully when I say this. 'Crucified.'

I hand the lighter and my phone to Edward. Although there's no signal on the phone, the screen emits a glow, and he holds both it and the lighter aloft to cast a pathetically dim duet of light on my attempt to bend the roots apart. They're thick and solid and immoveable and the crossed formation of them forbids entry; X - keep out.

I turn my attention instead to the smaller, peripheral growth in the top space of the cross, yanking and pulling at the more wiry, springier roots, and I have more success, eventually clearing a space wide enough to clamber through into the further growth beyond. And that's how we go on; wrenching, tearing and clambering through. More than a few of my fingernails are ripped off in the process, and though I can't see them clearly, I know my hands are wet and bloodied.

God knows how long we go on for. Perhaps it's only a few minutes, or maybe it's an hour. We twist and yank the roots apart, squeeze ourselves further into the root throttled darkness, using the phone and lighter only intermittently to illuminate the path of least resistance, until we reach a point where the roots seem to close in impenetrably and my hands can't seem to grip at anything. 'Hold up the lighter, Edward,' I say, the phone having died on us. The flame is a quivering mound produced by the mere fumes of what's left of the gas, but it's enough to show us that we've reached a dead end. In front of us is the ancient brick work of a closed tunnel, and as the cigarette lighter gasps its final fluttering breath and gives out on us, I realise that there never was any light at the end of this tunnel. We are underground, Edward and I, muddied and exhausted, and with nowhere to go but back the way we came.

I reach for him in the dark, and wrap an arm around his thin, bony shoulders. 'We should rest here a little,' I say, 'and go back. We'll figure out what to do on the way.' I feel his head rest against me and I brush the hair away from his forehead and kiss it gently - it's warm and gritty. 'It'll be all right,' I say, but it's hard to keep the shiver of uncertainty out of my voice. I'm so tired and disorientated by the interminable blackness of our surroundings that I want nothing more than to curl amongst the tree roots and cry myself to sleep. But then, a whisper. Above us, a sudden noise. A grinding, crunching sound, and we're struck by a fierce, piercing light that blinds us both and has us shrinking away, clutching at each other. Then, a voice. 'Climb up,' it says, and even through my terror, I recognise the distinctive, unusual tones. 'Quick now,' he says, 'I'll help you.' The beam of light flashes away from me from a moment and I see it for what it is - torch light - and reaching down through an aperture above, a hand, and an arm clad in a rolled up shirt sleeve. 'It's okay,' I say to Edward, who is clinging to me with his face pressed into my jacket. 'It's okay, Edward, it's Mr Lempel.'

'Take my hand,' my landlord says. And I do.

Edward

He has kept the strange stone next to his chest. It's tucked into the square, baggy pocket of his duffle coat and it only just fits. Skylark is tearing at the roots and passing them back to him. As she wrenches snarled holes through the maze, he can feel the stone pressing against him, digging into his hip as he squeezes through each tiny space.

When the old man pulls them out, Skylark goes first. Edward makes a cradle with his hands and cups her muddy boot to lift her towards the gap, where the old man has reached in to grab her hand. She's surprisingly light, or maybe the old man is stronger than he looks, because it's as though she's flying away from him, leaving him far below and alone in the dim root-bound space. There's a sudden quiet as she disappears from view, and he feels cold for the first time since climbing through the roots. He touches the stone through the fabric of his coat pocket, and reaches into his other pocket for the Judas spoon. But then the beam of torchlight returns, swinging crazily from a strap on Skylark's wrist, and the old man's hand, and Skylark's other hand, in its jangle of bracelets and bangles, are reaching for his. They pull him up between them and he lands on his back on the wet ground. He sees the face of the moon through the shadowy arms of trees, and he can smell the damp grass, sharp and green and cool against the nape of his neck. 'Come with me,' says the old man, and, 'quickly now,' and, 'Boy, time to get up.'

Edward does as he's told.

Skylark

We've come out on the edge of the wood, beyond the perimeter of the high wall that runs like a fortress around the back garden of Eleanor

Parry's house. From where we have emerged, through a space that could easily be mistaken for a foxhole, only the steep roof of the house is visible. 'I heard a noise,' explains Mr Lempel. 'I often take a walk at night, to settle my mind before sleep. I thought, at first, it was some animal, but then I heard voices. 'Mr Lempel,' I say, aware of an hysterical, gabbling edge to my voice, 'do you have a phone with you? The police...we need them. There are...there's...Xav's in danger, and Mrs Parry, and...' but my landlord has already begun to walk away, holding Edward's hand in his own as though guiding a wayward grandson along a tricky path. Edward submissively allows himself to be pulled along, tripping sometimes over his own feet, while the old man remains sure footed, the torch held steady in his hand to illuminate a narrow track that winds through the trees. 'Follow,' he says over his shoulder. 'Phone is at house. Then you can call. But quickly now.'

I'd noticed Lempel's house before on one of my walks to the Henge, a timber clad construction, tucked in amongst the trees beside a narrow part of the stream that roils through the woods. It's relatively new, the wood still pale and glowing, but built to look old, with sweeping gables and a small, arched front door like something straight out of The Brothers' Grimm - a dwarf's house, or a troll's. Tiny windows, and a door-knocker in the shape of a lion's head. Lempel opens the door and ushers us into a plain but cheerfully lit hallway. 'Come, come,' he says, bustling us into a small sitting room where a coal fire glows in the grate, casting red light between the bars of the fireplace. Lempel settles himself into an old, comfortable looking wingback chair and gestures towards a sagging leather sofa. 'Sit,' he says, 'sit.' Edward does as he's told but I'm looking around the room for the phone. 'Mr Lempel,' I say, 'the police. We have to phone the police.'

'The police,' Lempel echoes. He is filling a pipe with tobacco, tamping it carefully into the bowl with one thumb. 'Quite so, if you wish. But first, consider something.' He eyes Edward sitting nervously on the edge of the sofa, before turning his head to me. 'If you phone the police, and they come, with all their flashing blue lights and commotion and so on, what will happen to your friend? And to Mrs Parry? Do you think those men will simply raise their hands and surrender?' He fumbles in his pocket and retrieves a box of matches. 'No Skylark,' he says, shaking his head as he fishes for a match and strikes it, releasing the sharp stink of phosphorus as it flares against the side of the box. 'I know these men. I know their type.' He applies the flame to the bowl of his pipe and draws in the smoke, immediately puffing it out so it floats in a fragrant miasma about his head. 'They have a gun. And men with guns, they are killers. What if they shoot your friend? What if they shoot Mrs Parry too?' He nods, convinced of his own sagacity, but I'm incredulous.

'Are you mad?' I stare at him. 'There's a gunman in the house, and I'm going to call the police - where is your phone, Mr Lempel?'

He shrugs, and removes the pipe from his mouth to wave it in the direction of a small bureau that is piled with paperwork and newspapers. 'The phone is over there,' he says, 'somewhere, beneath the mess. Forgive me, I do not make many calls, or receive them. But if you must call the police Skylark, then think what it will mean for the boy. Even if they don't shoot, the police will find out more than they bargained for.' I'm already at the desk, clearing the newspapers to reveal a handset beneath them. I lift the receiver, and my finger is poised over the number 9. 'What do you mean?' I ask, and I glance at Edward, before freezing at what I see. Lempel must have seen it at the same moment, because he has risen to his feet, a look of astonishment arresting his features. 'Edward,' I say carefully, 'what is that?' Edward looks up at me from the sofa, frowning, as he holds the object he has been cradling in his lap aloft for me to see. 'I think it's from a child,' he says solemnly, 'it's too small for an adult.' I nod. 'You could be right,' I say, as I stare into the empty socket eyes of a tiny, jawless, human skull.

Mr Lempel pushes himself from his chair and walks over to sit beside Edward on the sofa. 'May I?' he asks gently, before taking the skull into his own hands and studying it, turning it carefully, tenderly even. 'Edward,' I say, 'where did you get that?'

'In the tunnel,' he says simply and he looks at me. 'Who do you think it is, Skylark?' I can't answer him, and I look to Mr Lempel, who has placed the skull carefully on the coffee table in front of him. 'Edward,' he says, before shaking his head and exhaling a low sigh, as though just apprised of a fact long known or suspected. 'Sometimes, the people we love, they do terrible things. Dreadful things.' He pauses, uncertainty now furrowing his brow, but he continues. 'I believe that this child,' he gestures at the skull, 'is the reason why those men are at your house.' He leans back against the sofa, drawing on the pipe again and saying nothing more until I say, 'Go on, Mr Lempel.' He turns his head to look at me for a moment, but then turns to Edward. 'I have seen them, over the years, many times. Always with your father, always wanting more.' He pauses, troubled by his own words and how to phrase them to Edward, who is still staring at the skull, his face customarily blank. Lempel continues uncertainly. 'But now your father has gone.' He hesitates again, thoughtfully drawing on the pipe for a moment, before turning his attention back to me. 'Do you still want to call the police?' he asks. I'm staring at him. What does he know? And how? I retract my poised finger from the phone dial and gently replace the receiver in the cradle.

'Who is he?' I ask, and the question comes out in a whisper, uncurls itself over our heads and hangs there, like dust motes in sunlight. Mr Lempel leans forward to lift the tiny skull from the table once more and he holds it in both hands, raising it to face him and speaking, as if not to us, but the dead boy himself. 'This,' he says, 'is Edward Parry.'

Edward

He says it. Edward's name. But not his name at all, The skull's name. Edward. Is he Edward? Or is the skull Edward? Edward is the bog boy - but what was the bog boy's name? Not Edward, not Edward Parry, and the skull isn't the bog boy, or him, so who is it?

It's Edward Parry.

Edward Parry is dead and his skull sits in the old man's hands, and the old man knows the truth. The truth. *The truth will out.* That was something Miss Pilcher used to say, one of the many things she used to say. Edward tries to focus on the skull, but it's swimming in and out of focus, and there's a buzzing in his head, a wasp in a jam jar. It's Edward Parry. But how can it be Edward Parry? That's what he asks, in a voice that doesn't seem to be his own; it could be anyone's voice - maybe it's Skylark's voice - maybe it's the boy talking - the skull - boney words slipping from

253

beneath tiny teeth - and Edward is spinning, or his head is spinning. There are black spots crowding in front of his eyes, and he feels himself sinking - sinking through murk with the clean stink of the bog cloying his nose, his mouth, his eyes - he sinks away, suddenly heavy and helpless and dead dead dead. *Edward?* he hears. Miss Pilcher's voice? Or Skylark's voice? Or his father's voice? Or his mother's voice all layered and floating like morning mist above the bog. *Edward*, he hears. But he's not Edward. He sinks further. Further, into the silence, into the comfort of noiselessness.

He's the bog boy. Safe. Listening. Waiting to return.

> *He'll be well again in a moment.*
> *Edward?*
> *Don't worry. He'll come around.*

He settles into the softness of the bog, and listens. He pricks his ears up - the truth will out. 'What do you know, Mr Lempel?' asks Skylark.

Mr Lempel doesn't reply straight away. Instead, he sighs. A deep, tired release. 'I have lived in this village a long time,' he says at last. 'I don't know all, but I know of the Parry family, and I see things.'

'Go on,' says Skylark.

'What can I say? Only that Eleanor and John Parry had a little boy. I used to see him with his mother - in his push chair at the local shop, or

254

walking in the woods. Oh, she went out then, in those days. Mrs Parry and little Edward. He looked just like his mother - blond hair. White blonde, like a halo about his head. And blue eyes, like cornflowers. Deep, deep blue. An angel boy.'

He pauses, and Edward waits, eyes closed. 'She used to bring him to the library,' continues the old man. 'That's where I'd see them together. When I first retired, I volunteered there for some time - as something to do, something to keep me busy. Anyway, once a week they would come together, Mrs Parry and Edward. She would sit with him on her lap, showing him picture books, spinning wonderful stories to go with them.'

'And?' says Skylark. There's an edge to the word, jagged and brittle.

'And,' says Lempel, 'one day she stopped coming. For quite some time she didn't appear but I thought little of it. In truth, I thought nothing of it. People come and go in the village. Then, one day, she came again, and she had a boy with her.'

'A boy?'

Mr Lempel's voice lowers, becomes quieter, and Edward strains his ears to listen. 'A different boy' he says, 'clearly a different boy. Dark haired, grey eyed. Yet, she called him Edward. She took out some books and I asked her, I said to her, 'Where's your little Edward today? I assumed the boy was a relation of some kind - a nephew perhaps.'

'And she said?'

'She looked me in the eye, and she said, 'This is Edward. This is Edward, my son.''

There's silence for a moment, and Edward feels a movement on his arm as Skylark's hand begins to gently stroke up and down, up and down. He remains still, but opens his eyes a little so he can see Mr Lempel. The old man is sucking on his pipe, fogging the room. 'I said nothing, and she wished me good day, and she left.'

Skylark doesn't speak. Edward wonders what's going through her head because in his own head there's a slow, high pitched sound, like air being released from the mouth of a balloon. He squints at the skull on the coffee table. Blue eyes - like cornflowers. Deep, deep blue. An angel boy. But Edward's eyes aren't blue. His hair is not a halo of blond. He's not the angel boy, he's the bog boy, streaked with filth, coated in the blood of his own death and reborn to become...what? A changeling for the angel boy? And what happened to the angel boy? *The truth will out, Edward, the truth will out.* He was killed. Edward knows it. The angel boy was killed - but who killed him?

'So you've known all this time?' says Skylark. That Edward replaced,' she gestures towards the skull, 'him. The Parry boy.'

Lempel sighs. 'I didn't know for sure', he says. 'Let's just say that I knew something was not right. And at the Parry house, many times from then on, a large black car and men coming and going. They would walk here through the woods, away from the house and past this spot - always the same man, smartly dressed, accompanied by some ruffian, for extra weight, I suppose, and John Parry with them, making promises. One day, when the house was half built, I was working in the upper storey. It was raining, and they came into the house, seeking shelter from the rain. They didn't know I was there, and I heard them talking. Oh, I didn't understand all I heard, but when you have been in the world as long as I have, and seen the things I have seen - well, you learn to spot trouble.'

Skylark is smoothing Edward's hair. She's brushing it from his forehead and he is dimly aware that she has put her arm right around his shoulders - he's caught in the crook of her arm and it's warm. Safe. But there's a crackling tension in the room - a silence pocked by the steady ticking of a clock, by the words which he knows are clinging to the inside of Skylark's throat - questions like the ones Edward has - who am I? What happened to the first Edward Parry, the real Edward Parry? And then she speaks, but she doesn't say what Edward is expecting her to say. Instead she says, 'I'm going to call the police, Mr Lempel.'

'As you wish,' he says, a shrug in his voice. Skylark retracts her arm from around Edward's shoulders, settles his inert form back against the sofa cushions, and stands, leaving him suddenly cold and alone. He opens his eyes and watches her as she walks towards the phone on Lempel's desk. She walks slowly, as though wading through water, and as she lifts the receiver, she looks back at him on the sofa, hesitant for a moment.

And Edward acts.

As her finger pulls back the dial he leaps from the sofa and races towards her. 'Edward, no,' she says, but he ignores her, and throws himself to the floor to slide in beneath the desk. He frantically scans the walls, the plug sockets, the cable stretching in a curly tangle from the phone in Skylark's hands. 'No, no, Edward,' she says, but he does it anyway. Before she has chance to dial the second 9, he has ripped the cable from its socket and wrenched the jack from its wire.

CHAPTER 10

Peter

Stonemoor

My Dearest Anna,

I heard a cuckoo this morning, the first of the year. I saw it too - its fat little body took flight from a tree branch at the edge of the wood and I followed its wobbling path until it flew out of my sight. I have a fondness for them, cuckoos, though I suppose they have a dark reputation amongst the bird population - interlopers, greedy oaths, who steal the food from the mouths of more worthy deservers. Still, all must find a way to live, and their call is charming to hear on a bright Spring morning.

Anna, you and I were cuckoos once.

How far we walked for on that painfully bright day, I do not know. I stumbled in the tracks of your older, more sure-footed steps; that's how I thought of them at the time. You were my big sister after all, and I trusted that you knew where we were going, though at twelve years old, it's probable that you knew no more than I. My nine year old stomach grumbled with hunger, and I complained and whined - you were harsh with me. Irritable. You told me to shut my mouth, that I was nothing but a cry-baby. As afternoon chilled into evening, I felt like shoving you, or kicking your shins, but I was too exhausted from our march through the fields. The memory is a dim one of wide landscapes and tall, stiff-leaved crops, and of crickets chirping in the lonely grass. Perhaps anger took root in the pit of my belly that day, the fury of a small boy sent he knows not where with his crabby older sister. Walking, walking, walking so far from home; why had we run? Why hadn't we travelled with our parents on the steam train that morning? You had no answers for me, so when we came upon a small outbuilding at the edge of some farm buildings and crept inside to settle for the night, all I knew was that I wanted my mother, but had only you.

The farmer found us. I awoke to the tall shadow of him, blocking the early morning light from the doorway as he called for his wife. She joined him just as he was urging us to stand on our feet - two children rubbing sleep from our eyes and picking loose straw from our dusty clothes. 'Gott im Himmell,' she whispered, glancing wide eyed from us to the grim line of her husband's mouth. But then, after staring at us for what must have been minutes, "Kommt, Kinder, in das Haus zu kommen. Sie müssen hungrig sein."

We sat in their dark kitchen and the woman served us a bowl of watery porridge, while her husband watched us sternly, rubbing his grizzled chin from time to time and scratching his bald head. I remember, as I shoveled the food into my mouth with a wide wooden spoon, that you spoke to them, answering their questions carefully and shooting me warning glances that told me clearly that I must not speak, I must not interrupt.

Later that day we found ourselves in the back of a hay cart. I huddled against you as the cart jolted over rutted farm tracks. "Try to sleep," you said to me, the first gentle words you'd spoken since we had run from the train station. I recall your hands, catching at the knots in my hair as I fell into a troubled slumber.

We arrived at the place that was to become our home for a while, in the hours of darkness. I remember the sky - cavernous and sprinkled with stars, which seemed seemed to burn with cold intensity as we stepped from the cart to be shepherded towards a tall, dark building with small, dimly lit windows. A convent, I know now, but at the time I had no concept of what such a place was. I have little memory of the conversation that took place on the doorstep between the farmer and the darkly clothed figures of the holy sisters. I was mesmerised by their faces, as pale and round as little moons, lit by a flickering candle stub that one of them held in a simple sconce. We were received inside, and led along a corridor hung with plain wooden crucifixes, and paintings of men in various states of torture, it seemed, the candle stub catching the gilded surrounds of their heads as they bent in supplication of whatever fate they were being subjected to. We climbed some stone steps, which curved around the inner wall of a stone tower at the far edge of the building, and from there, along another flagged corridor until we arrived a thick wooden door. And this marked our separation. I was ushered through into a dark room that smelled faintly of urine, and was shown to a simple wood framed bed topped with a thin, striped mattress and a rough woollen blanket. 'Take off your shoes, but sleep in your clothes, for now,' whispered the nun who had accompanied me into the room. I did as she told me, untying my shoelaces and obediently pulling the blanket to my chin. In the thin light cast by the candle, I could see an identical bed beside my own, and I fully expected this to be assigned to you until I saw the blanket shift slightly, to reveal the turning figure of a young boy, and beyond him, another bed, and another, all occupied by sleeping boys. 'Go to sleep now,' whispered the nun, as she turned from me, shielding the candle flame and pitching me into utter darkness. Where you were taken to that night, I had no idea. I lay quietly for a while, listening to the quiet breathing that pervaded the dark and listening to the occasional squeaks of bed springs as boys shifted in their sleep. From time to time, some would mutter gently through their dreams, until at one point I distinctly heard the word 'mother' spoken softly into the cool darkness. Her face came to me then; our sweet mother's face, lined with worry and framed with *greying hair, and I felt a tightness gripping my chest before I gave in to the bitter tears that must have been welling inside me all through the last days. I buried my face into the dank scented pillow and smothered my own sobs until I sank into an exhausted, dreamless sleep.*

Anna, I am too weary to write more.

With love always,
Your brother,
Peter

Skylark

He stands there, the ripped cable in his hands. 'Jesus, Edward,' I say, and when he looks at me it's with a face I've never seen before. His eyes have darkened beneath lowered brows and his features are set in defiance. 'You heard what he said,' he tells me, 'They'll shoot my mother.'

'Edward, that won't happen,' I say. 'They'll hear the sirens and they'll run, or if not, then the police will catch them.' I try and lighten my tone, 'People don't just shoot other people.'

'Don't they?' he asks, and I swear there's a sneer curling his lip. 'My father ran. What was he scared of? He knew that man - the man with the gun.' I stare back at Edward with his new-made face and I remember Eleanor Parry's words before she shoved me into the tunnel; *you're a complication - they kill complications*. And there's Xav - he's a complication too. What do they want, these men? What the hell do they want?

Edward answers the question without me even asking it. 'They want me,' he says simply, his face reverting to its customary blankness. 'They took me from somewhere, and my father paid them to get me, to replace,' he uses the torn cable to indicate the skull on the coffee table, 'him. Edward Parry.' I'm aware of a movement behind me, of Lempel rising from his seat and cautiously treading towards Edward. 'He died,' Edward continues, 'and he needed to be replaced. So she buried him in the tunnel and they got me instead - a boy the same age.' Tomas Kovaleski, I'm thinking, his name playing over and over in my head, Tomas Kovaleski, Tomas Kovaleski.

Lempel passes me and moves slowly towards Edward. I shake myself, trying to grasp control of the situation, trying to make sense of it. 'But when children die,' I say, 'they're not simply replaced. They get sick and die, but there are hospitals and doctors - you can't simply bury your child yourself and find a new one. I mean, it's...'

'She killed him,' says Edward bluntly. 'My mother killed him.' And I see Mr Lempel reaching Edward's side and gently taking him in his arms. 'I believe so too,' Lempel says as Edward buries his head into the folds of the old man's jacket. 'I think so too.'

I stand, numbed by the enormity of it - the truth. I think of Eleanor Parry and her child, her true son, his small body interred in a shallow grave in that dank tunnel. What on Earth did she do to him? And Edward's father, desperate to cover up the truth; so desperate, that he paid for another boy to be abducted. Of course, it makes perfect sense. He knew the thieves my father worked for, and how different can it be? They paid my father to take a break from stealing artwork and steal a toddler instead, little Tomas Kovaleski, who was unattended in the museum that night as his mother mopped the floors and polished the glass display cases. I'm suddenly aware that I have reached for the crucifix in my pocket - Edward's crucifix, the one he held that day. The one he was playing with as he wandered the dimly lit halls, looking up at the exhibits, his childish brain unable to differentiate between real people and wax models. I think back to what Xav remembered about that night my father broke into my room - *keep it safe, Skylark* - not 'keep safe.' Keep *it* safe - the necklace, the link between the boy he had just stolen and the place he'd been taken from. And then he was dead - for knowing

266

too much, no doubt. For being a complication. And Tomas' mother? The cleaner who lost her only child that night - what of her? Is she dead too? Is that why the police gave up on the case? With no one to search for him, with no one to plead and remind them that her child had been taken, they simply shelved the case.

'So he was paying them,' I say. 'Edward's father was paying them. But then, the money ran out.' Lempel has ushered Edward back to the sofa, where they sit now, side by side. Edward rubs his eyes with his sleeve while Lempel pats him gently on the shoulder. 'I only know what I've seen,' he tells me. 'Edward here became son to the Parrys; it must have been a simple matter - already a birth certificate with his name on, educated at home so no questions asked by school authorities, no need for them to collect medical records or any such thing,' he waves his hand dismissively. 'How could anyone ever know? Eleanor Parry has no relatives that I know of, no one that I've seen coming or going, and she's a recluse, you know? She simply continued to raise her son in that big house. Perhaps,' he glances at Edward, 'perhaps she believed in it herself, eventually.' He turns to Edward. 'She loves you, I think, Edward. I believe she loves you.'

Edward doesn't respond. He has taken a spoon from his pocket and is fidgeting with it, rubbing the bowl with his thumb. 'They want the

Judas spoon,' he says. 'If we bring it to them, they might go away.'

I'm stunned for a moment, before realising that, although I've made connections in my head, Edward is still very much in the dark. He doesn't know about Tomas Kovaleski; he hasn't even asked about who he, himself, may be. He knows nothing about my father, and nothing about the connections my father had to Stonemoor, the weekend visits that my mother told me about. He must have delivered stolen artwork to John Parry himself, must have stood in that darkened hallway, perhaps even speaking to Eleanor. Did he go there to hand over the child? I feel my body grow chill at the thought, but now isn't the time to tell Edward what I know. 'Edward,' I say, 'you know that isn't the Judas spoon, not the real one.'

'Judas spoon?' says Lempel, 'What is that, this Judas spoon?'

Edward glances at me, so I tell Lempel. 'Edward owns a valuable collection of apostle spoons,' I say. 'but one of them is missing - the last spoon - the Judas spoon.'

'And my mother told them that Skylark had it,' Edward says, 'so they went to find it, but when they couldn't, they came back.'

'Edward thinks that if they have the full collection, it will be enough to satisfy them. But Edward,' I turn to him, 'that's not the missing spoon in your hand.'

'But it looks a bit like it,' he pleads, 'we could fool them and then escape somewhere. Somewhere they won't find us.'

Lempel takes the spoon and examines it. 'If these men are experts in art and such things, they won't be fooled easily, Edward. To a trained eye, this spoon is worthless. He lets out a low, mirthless chuckle. 'You want to see a Judas spoon, Edward? A real one?' He stands, and shuffles over to the bureau, where he begins to open and close small drawers until he finds what he's looking for and comes back to the sofa. 'Here,' he says to Edward, handing him a small, metal object. 'Here is a real Judas spoon.'

I peer at what he has handed over. A spoon, yes, but one which is rusted and dented. The handle has serrations down one side, no longer sharp, and with several of the teeth bent inwards. Edward studies it before turning his bewildered eyes to Mr Lempel. 'What do you mean?' he asks, 'this isn't an apostle spoon, it's just an old spoon.'

'I made it in the camp, during the war,' says Lempel. 'Oh yes,' he adds, reading the astonishment on my face, 'I was in a concentration camp during the war, Skylark. A long time ago now, and I was just a boy. One of the lucky ones. One of the survivors, you might say. My mother, my father, my sister – they did not survive. Only I survived.' He takes the spoon from Edward's hands. 'This spoon helped me to survive,' he says. I made it in the metal workshop there, secretly of course, and I smuggled it out.' He turns to Edward. 'They gave us soup each day,' he explains, 'and a little bread.' The soup was watery, with just a few vegetables at the bottom, but with a spoon, you could scoop them out.' He enacts the action. 'You could scoop them out and fill your empty belly more the quicker. And with the handle,' he turns the spoon to show how the toothed handle becomes a knife, 'with the handle you can cut a slice from your bread and swap it with another hungry soul. Swap it for a little extra soup, or a bar of soap, or a warmer blanket.' He hands the spoon back to Edward. 'You can keep it, Edward. Keep it, as I have kept it all these years. Keep it. It helped me to survive. As you will too, Edward. You will survive.

Well, what the hell can one say? We're silent. Edward examines the spoon while Mr Lempel shifts forward a little in his seat to bow his head and stare at the grained wood of the floor, his hands loosely clasped between his knees. And me? I remain standing, my head feeling ready to burst from the weight of new thought. What to do? What to do? I think of the people in the house. Xav and Eleanor Parry at the mercy of two homicidal gunmen - they could already be dead. And there's something else too, something buzzing at the edge of my overfilled mind, like a trapped fly batting uselessly against a window pane; there's something else, something else.

'We have to go back,' I say.

CHAPTER 11

Peter

Stonemoor

Dear Anna,

        We fell into a routine at the orphanage. In the morning, we were woken, the other boys and I, and after prayers we were permitted to wash and dress ourselves before tending to our various chores. My job was to weed the vegetable gardens behind the chapel, to drag a hoe and loosen the soil around the beets and cabbages that would eventually find their way into the kitchens. After an hour or so, the bell would ring for breakfast and we'd all gather at the long refectory tables in the dining hall to wolf down a simple repast of bread and milk. Sometimes, there was butter, or best of all, jam. But usually, it was simply bread. While I sat with the other boys of my age, you were seated with the Holy Sisters, your hair veiled like a novice nun and your eyes demurely downcast. You rarely looked at me, never mind spoke to me.

After breakfast, more prayers, and then we boys would gather in the schoolroom to learn Mathematics or Geography. We were given long lists of spellings to learn, and sometimes we had to read aloud from a bible, though it wasn't the bible you and I had read from to our parents. At the time, I had little idea of what this new view of God was - much talk of Jesus and sin and eternal penitence. One day, I asked the teacher, a kind eyed nun called Sister Benedicta, if she truly believed in the Hell we learned about; a place of fires and pitchforks and relentless torments. She did not answer me, only told me that those who sin must repent if they are to enter God's kingdom, and that God would forgive those who were sorry for their sins. 'You are a good child, Peter' she said to me, 'your soul is clean yet - keep it so.' She thought me a good child, Anna. How could she know the truth? That each day a slow anger burned within me, anger at you seated at the high table with the sisters, never looking my way or speaking to me. Your hands and nails remained clean, for you never had to hoe the gardens or carry food scraps out to the piggery as we boys did. I was jealous, Anna, of what I saw as your special position, and I was confused by your quietness, your reserve. That's why I did what I did on that terrible day, the day when the peaceful routines of the orphanage were shattered. The day the Nazi soldiers came.

Anna. Not a day has passed when I haven't begged for forgiveness. For redemption. For an opportunity to make things right.

Your brother,

Peter

A History of Stonemoor
by **Pauline Pilcher**

It was easy enough for Tom Watkins - once life got too tough on the farmstead he simply packed up his meagre belongings, probably in a spotted kerchief, and took his scrawny body out of there; swapped his life in the muddy fields for one on the ocean waves - I wonder what ship would take on a stupid old woman like me? Perhaps a cruise ship in need of a cleaner? Or some

273

rusting hulk of a fishing trawler in
need of a cook? Not that I can cook.

Pauline Pilcher shakes her head. The rhythmic hammering of typing usually calms her, but not tonight. She is being melodramatic, of course. She has no intention of escaping to sea, and she doesn't think the men will return - she told them that Edward was at a boarding school to throw them off the scent, and they seemed to believe her. That was all they required of her, and as long as Edward followed her instruction to go to the police station in Exeter and show them her letter, then by now he must be safe - probably cosy in the spare bed of an emergency foster carer or some such thing. Yes, she has done her duty and all she has to do now is await a call from the police. 'Oh, I only recently put two and two together,' she'll say, 'I always knew there was something fishy about the Parry family,' she'll say, 'I'm so glad to have solved the mystery,' she'll say. For a moment, she allows herself to imagine celebrity. An appearance on The Good Morning Show, perhaps, smiling benignly from the sofa with Edward beside her. An interview on Radio Devon too. Or even Radio 4? A shudder of excitement thrills through her. Would Eleanor listen in? And it's the sudden picture of Eleanor Parry that strips her of her reverie and punches her firmly in the stomach. Eleanor.

She has blocked her, until now. Too fraught from the visitations of the suited man and his sidekick, and then the quickly scrawled note to the police before returning home from her mission to Edward and curling in a ball in her bed. And then those other two. The quiet man, and that Skylark woman, with her wild hair and deep green eyes. She has not permitted herself to think of Eleanor at all, has closed the image of her down, scrawling through it like a crazed child with a black crayon. But now, here she is again. Eleanor Parry in her delicate silk scarves. Eleanor Parry sipping green tea from a thin lipped china cup. Eleanor Parry, listless and tearful, perched on the side of the bed while she, Pauline Pilcher, gently touches the meltwater soft of her hands.

Can she really allow her to be thrown to the wolves?

Pauline Pilcher throws off her pink flannel dressing gown and rushes into her bedroom to don her familiar tweed skirt and a thick wool sweater. She pulls on a pair of brogues and fumbles the laces into sturdy double knots. She will go to Eleanor. She will confront her with as much of the truth as she knows - essentially, that Edward is not her true son. That Edward is an abducted child, stolen from his own mother and given a new identity. And Eleanor? Eleanor will fall to her knees and weep at what Pauline knows; she will admit everything, and fill in the missing pieces of the puzzle before begging for forgiveness, for redemption. And Pauline Pilcher will raise her to her feet and take her in her arms, and rescue her. Yes.

Resolutely, Pauline Pilcher puts on her coat and buttons it to the neck (it's a cold night, after all) and strides out of the front door. Slamming it shut behind her, she sets off at a march towards the Parry house.

But she hasn't gone far before doubts begin to creep in, doubts as insidious as the cold night air that trickles into the upturned collar of her coat. Suppose she's wrong about Edward? Suppose he isn't the stolen Kovaleski boy at all and is, just as John Parry explained all those years ago, an unusually timid little boy. Just like his mother, too sensitive to undergo the brutish cut and thrust of a typical school environment. And is it really credible, she has wondered before now, in these modern times, to steal a child rather than simply adopt one? She pauses for a moment, trying to order her thoughts. The day has been tumultuous - terrifying - yet, she considers now, exhilarating? It has brought her to this moment, one she has barely dared to fully imagine before this night. To lay her cards before Eleanor Parry, to spread them out before her - she imagines them whimsically as actual cards; John Parry, the King of Clubs; Eleanor, Queen of Hearts, naturally; and Edward, the Knave - Janus headed - two boys in one, looking ever backward into the dark past of his own invention.

She shakes her head and walks on, trying to think clearly. How will she approach Eleanor? Would it have been a good idea to bring the shoebox of her collected evidence? The newspaper stories about Tomas Kovaleski's abduction and the translation she had made of a small obituary in a Polish gazette - the untimely but convenient death of Edward's poor mother just a month after his disappearance. She considers turning back to retrieve it, but she has almost reached the turning for the Parry house and it is as she approaches it, that she perceives something strange, something different. She has walked this path many times, and at first, it isn't clear to her why her senses have become suddenly alert. There is the turning for the Parry house, leading steeply down, away from the main road and curving out of sight as it disappears through the wooded banks of the slope. It looks no different from usual, but if she looks up, to where the stark ebony of the trees meets the lesser black of the clouded night sky, there's a lightening - an orange glow, which hangs in the air like the faint scent of smoke that reaches her too. Not the usual wood smoke smell that filtrates the village throughout the winter, but a more bitter, acrid miasma. She starts, suddenly aware of what it may be, and all at once she is running, her brogues slapping the tarmac and sending sharp shocks up through her brittle ankles and shins. She follows the curve, aware of the increasing intensity of the smell and even over the gasping rattle of her own throat she can hear the dreadful crack and splinter of the conflagration awaiting her. As she rounds the final bend of the twisting road, she sees it - the Parry house is ablaze; black smoke billows from the heat smashed windows and the whole left side is a roaring inferno of gold and crimson, of vicious reds and sulphuric yellows. Pauline Pilcher stands before it, a tiny silhouette against the furious rage. She stares, her face already reddening and her eyes watering from the heat. She stares, and has not the faintest idea what to do.

CHAPTER 12

Edward

He's running. Skylark stumbles behind, calling out to *slow down, Edward*. But he won't, because he's not Edward - he's the bog boy, the skull on the table, the other boy. And so he runs and he runs. Twigs and branches grasp at his coat, his shoes slide on the piney track and send up flurries of needles behind him, and as he glances up through the bare branches, he sees the underbelly of the clouds are lit with a strange light, a shifting of faint orange, and he slows, and stops, and lets Skylark catch up with him. 'Jesus,' she says, catching her breath, 'fire.' And he pulls free of her and starts to run again. Faster. Faster than ever, because despite not being Edward, he needs to get her out and he has nothing to lose because he's the bog boy, nameless, and if he can rise from the bog, then he can rise from the fire too. Eleanor Parry is his mother, the only mother he knows, and he will pull her from the flames.

When he reaches the garden wall he leaps at it, scrambling for a foothold in the mossy brick, but Skylark grabs his duffle coat and pulls him back. 'It's too dangerous, Edward,' she says. He tries to twist loose, but she takes hold of his coat sleeve with her free hand. 'Edward,' she says, and for the first time ever he's grateful for his too big coat, because he simply slips out of it, letting the shiny lining slide over his arms, and he takes off - leaving Skylark with the coat in her hands, while he speeds off around the garden wall to reach the front driveway.

When he gets there, he sees Miss Pilcher is standing there too, but he doesn't say anything to her, and he doesn't have time to wonder why she's there either, because the whole left side of the house is a bonfire, and he can see that the blaze is making its way into the rest of the house too. Flames are leaping from the roof and spreading out as far as the right chimney. Skylark catches up behind him so he makes a dash for the conservatory. The fire hasn't yet reached it, and he knows he can get in that way and through the kitchen to the main part of the building.

When he reaches it, the door is still slightly ajar from when he had nudged it open earlier in the day, but the interior is already a swirl of smoke which has threaded through the house and is coiling around the old furniture and gathered junk. Edward plunges through, tiny eddies forming around him, and breathless from his run, he gasps too deeply and coughs violently as his eyes fill with water. He can barely see as he covers his mouth with his arm and makes his way towards the internal door that will lead through into the kitchen, but from beneath it the smoke creeps thickly and softly. He can hear Skylark behind him, herself choking on the fumes, and he reaches the door and grasps the handle. It's hot, but not hot enough yet to burn him, so he tugs at it and the door swings open. A wall of black heaves itself at him and beyond it, through streaming eyes, in the fraction of a moment before he's forced to double over with coughing, he sees a figure. A tall man, his face masked with some ragged cloth, is striding towards him. Edward's lungs fill with smoke and as his small body bends in two, the man lunges forward and catches him around the middle, lifting him off his feet.

Skylark

I'd love to say I was too caught up in the drama of it all to think of the danger, but the truth is, when Edward made a dash for the conservatory, the only thought in my head was, *that fucking kid*. I could already hear the fire engine sirens wailing from way up on the main road; should I wait? I could send them directly in after him. The Pilcher woman is there, and has turned her back on the blaze to study the narrow road that leads steeply down to the house. 'They won't get around the curve,' she says, her voice thin and anxious. 'And it's too steep for big vehicles.'

That fucking kid.

I take the deepest breath I can and run after him. Why I still haven't already thrown down Edward's coat, I don't know. It's still in my hands as I step into the conservatory, so I lift it to my mouth to block the acrid smoke. It does little good, I find myself coughing anyway, and I can barely see where Edward is until he opens the far door and obliterates us with a wave of warm, bilious smoke. I'm forced to squeeze my eyes shut and I press the coat firmly into my face and count to five, to let the smoke clear a little, before I go on. I can hear Edward's cough from the doorway, and beyond it the vicious crackle and roar of the blaze as it eats its way further through the house. I open my eyes, determined to grab Edward and pull him out with me, back outside and as far from the house as possible, but when I open my eyes, I see I won't have to. Xav is there, blackened and coughing through some kind of towel he has wrapped over his mouth and nose, and he has scooped Edward up into his arms. 'Xav, this way,' I call, and though it comes out as a strangled croak, he hears me. We stumble outside; the man, the boy, and me, and we fall onto a patch of damp grass. I reach over to Xav, but he winces and releases Edward to hold out his wrists to me; they are raw and blistered. 'They tied us up,' he explains in a hoarse voice, 'with tape - I managed to get loose as the fire reached us, but Eleanor,' he nods towards the house, where we can see the red heart of the fire glowing beyond the veil of smoke, 'she wouldn't leave. I couldn't get her to come with me.'

'The fire brigade is on its way,' I say, 'it'll be okay.' But in that split second, I see it won't be okay, because Edward has recovered himself enough to jump to his feet, and is charging full tilt back into the fire. 'That fucking kid,' says Xav as he struggles to get up, but I'm on him, pinning him to the ground. 'Please Xav, you'll get him and yourself killed.' The wail of the fire engines is closer than ever, surely they must make it down the hill soon? And then a familiar figure corners the building and stands above us, looking down on us for a moment, before turning his gaze to the conservatory. 'The boy?' says Mr Lempel, 'He has gone into there?' I nod, and Xav takes advantage of this momentary distraction to shove me away from him. 'I'm going after him, Skylark,' he says as he pushes himself off the ground, so I do the only thing I can think of under the circumstances. I grab his burned, blistered wrist. He screams, so I squeeze harder and he falls to his knees, his face a mask of agony. And that's when I notice what Mr Lempel is doing. While I've been forcing Xav to the ground, the old man has calmly, and deliberately, walked into the conservatory. His short, rotund frame is almost invisible as he hesitates just inside the doorway - just a pale, man-shaped patch against the vicious backdrop. I scream his name but he doesn't respond. Instead, he steps forward, and as I call his name a second time, he vanishes into the swirling obscenity of the inferno.

What happens next is that all hell breaks loose. We hear the sudden screech of tyres on the driveway and within seconds firefighters in full gear are swarming around us. I point wildly at the conservatory and gabble incoherently as two paramedics gently usher Xav and I back towards the front of the house, which is awash with blue light from the gathered engines, ambulances and police cars. We're forced to sit down in the brightly lit interior of an ambulance, where Xav proffers his injured wrists for treatment, and I stare at the chaotic scene unfolding before me. Thick, yellow hoses are being unreeled, and firefighters in breathing apparatus are smashing the front door of the house with an axe. It splinters into charcoal with each blow, but they're not quite through before a sudden explosion from the house sends glass flying from a wide window pane, and that's when I see him. A man on fire. Lempel. His hair a flaming torch, he is stepping on to the low windowsill and preparing to jump to the ground, and he is carrying something, or someone, in his arms.

The fire brigade see him too, of course, and my view is blocked as a team dash towards him. I leap out of the ambulance and run to the scene in time to see that Lempel has handed his precious cargo to one of the crew. Edward, dead or unconscious, is being scurried to the second ambulance, but Lempel has vanished back into the smoke and flames, only to reappear moments later with the thin figure of Eleanor Parry clutching his arm. The fire crew are all over them. Lempel has had some kind of blanket thrown over him to douse the flames that have spread from his hair and beard to ignite his shirt, and is being carefully lifted onto a stretcher, while Eleanor Parry is walked to a second ambulance. The old man is still conscious, his eyes rolling in his head as he endures the pain, but something happens in that moment - that split fraction of a moment before I race back to the first ambulance, which is preparing to take Edward to hospital. To this day, that tiny second replays in my head when I'm least expecting it. I am standing at the edge of the circle of fire and ambulance crew, about to turn away from the terrible sight of the old man's excruciating pain, when his eyes suddenly lock on to mine with a focus as lucid as the first day he showed me around the rented cottage. His eyes meet mine, and despite the agony he is undoubtedly enduring, despite the raw blackened skin that has replaced his beard and hair, Mr Lempel looks at me. And I swear to God - he smiles.

I'm in the ambulance within moments and before I know it we're careering back up towards the main road that will take us to the hospital. Edward begins to come round in the ambulance, moaning and coughing and retching, as a paramedic stretches an oxygen mask onto his face and talks to him calmly, and soothingly. 'Are you a relative?' I'm asked. I hesitate before replying; the words taste strange on my tongue, but they tell a truth that I have become convinced of in the last 24 hours. The thing that has been knocking around at the back of my mind has come to the fore, clean and right, as though purified into being by the flames of the fire itself. 'Are you a relative?' asks the paramedic. 'Yes,' I say. 'Yes, he's my brother,' I say.

Peter

Stonemoor

Dear Anna,

They came early, the officers. We were breakfasting in the long hall when we heard a commotion and there was much nervous excitement as a group of soldiers entered and demanded that all children should gather in the courtyard outside for inspection. Most of the boys at my table were more concerned with grabbing at the last of the bread and stuffing it into their mouths, but I felt sickened. I tried to catch your eye as we filed out of the building, but you were not looking at me, as usual.

Outside, we boys formed two orderly lines on one side of the courtyard, while the sisters, you included, made up a small group on the opposite side. There were eight soldiers, and four ferocious looking dogs with dark thick fur. They strained at their leashes as we passed them. When one boy unthinkingly reached a hand out to touch one of them, it growled viciously at him.

In charge, was a tall officer in a long leather coat and black leather gloves. He held a clipboard, which held several sheets of paper and he was running a finger down the top sheet and consulting with the Mother Superior about what it said there; a list of names, I was to discover.

Once we were all silent and waiting, the officer stepped forward and began to call each name one by one. He began with Jurgen Gruber, a small red-haired boy who slept two beds along from me in the dormitory. 'Where are you from?' the officer asked, and Jurgen answered him directly. 'From Munich, Sir,' he said. 'My mother is dead and my father is fighting in the war.' The officer nodded, and looked at the boy's face closely; at his eyes, and at his shock of red hair. 'Good,' he said, simply, before moving to the next boy in the line.

I was, to an extent, prepared. I had been told that while at the orphanage I was to tell no one my real name. I was not Peter Lempel, but Peter Grunwald, of Dusseldorf. My parents had both died when a bomb hit our house. I rehearsed the line in my head as the officer moved down the line. I felt hot and faint, and my palms were sweating. At last, the officer stood before me. I stared straight ahead as he studied me closely, peering into my eyes, and grasping my chin to tilt my head upwards, and to the side. When he spoke, it was calmly. 'Name?' he asked. I offered the name I'd been given and he referred to the list of names on his clipboard before asking, 'Your parents?'

'They are dead,' I explained. 'A bomb hit our house.'

'Indeed? And where were you when the bomb hit your house?'

I stared blankly at him. No one else had been asked for more than basic details. 'Well?' he asked, as I hesitated. He leaned in to me, as though to confide a secret. 'How did you escape this bomb?'

'I was staying with my grandmother,' I said. 'When it happened, I wasn't there.'

'Ah so,' he replied. 'And now you are here. Tell me, why are you not still with your grandmother?'

The Mother Superior, who had stood beside the officer throughout his inquisition of her charges, chipped in here. 'Peter's grandmother became very ill,' she said, 'too ill to care for him, so we took him in.' The officer nodded, but continued to stare at me for some moments before saying, 'very well,' and turning his attention to the boy beside me, but before speaking to him, he turned to me once more. 'What is her name? Your grandmother's name?' I faltered. 'Her name?' I said. I desperately cast around for a name, any name, for this imagined woman, but the officer, his tone now snappish and abrupt asked, 'And her address? What street does she live on?' Again, I faltered, my mind a blank of panic. Then, 'Turn around.' I did as I was asked, facing away from the officer as he grabbed the back of my head and pushed it forward so my chin grazed my neck. 'Here,' I heard him call, and I heard footsteps as one of the soldiers strode forward to join him. 'See here,' said the officer, 'see the shape of the ears?' My head was released, but was followed by a sharp knock that sent me staggering forward as the officer slapped his hand across the back of my neck. 'Juden,' he said, as the soldier grasped my by the arm and began to pull me towards one of the trucks that stood waiting at the courtyard entrance.

And then it happened. The moment that has haunted me ever since. That hung above me like a dark cloud in the journey we were to take in the army truck to the train station, and then onto the camp where we would be separated, never to see each other again. It has haunted me from that day to this, Anna. It haunts me as I write these words.

The soldier had me tightly by the arm, and he was roughly dragging me to the truck when I saw your face, there amongst the gaggle of helplessly watching sisters. You were looking at me with terror upon your face, looking at me for the first time in weeks. And I raised my free arm and extended my index finger in your direction. I pointed directly at you and shouted it out. 'Her,' I cried. 'She is my sister. She must come too.'

And in the heavy silence that followed, you carefully removed the veil from your head, and walked to the truck.

Anna. I am so very sorry.

Your brother,

Peter

CHAPTER 13

Skylark

At the hospital, I was treated for smoke inhalation and sat with Xav as his burns were salved and bandaged. Then, together, we sat beside Edward's bed until he came round. Like me, he'd breathed in a lot of smoke, but otherwise, he was fine. Eleanor Parry's skin was blistered and peeling from the heat of the fire, but we were able to tell Edward that the doctor's were content she'd make a full recovery. 'I cut her free,' Edward told us. 'There was tape around her ankles and her wrists, but I cut her free.'

'How?' asked Xav. 'When I burned the tape off my own wrists, I tried to find something to cut the tape on hers, but I couldn't find anything, and she was screaming at me to leave her, so...' he bowed his head. 'I should have just carried her out, but she was kicking me away, I couldn't even get close to her.' I pat his wrist gently, and watch him wince. 'You'd have done it if she'd let you,' I say. 'I used the spoon,' Edward tells us. 'It was in my pocket.'

'You cut through tape with a spoon?' I ask.

'With Mr Lempel's spoon,' he says. 'He was right. He said it would help me, and it did. He reaches for his soot blackened shorts, which hang over the back of Xav's chair, and pulls Lempel's gift from one of the pockets - the crude metal spoon with its jagged, rusted handle.

'You're a hero, Edward,' smiles Xav. If you hadn't done that, she'd never have made it out. But without Mr Lempel, you wouldn't have made it out either.'

'I know,' says Edward. 'When can we go and see him. I'd like to tell him about the spoon.' I exchange glances with Xav, who sighs. 'Mr Lempel didn't make it,' he tells Edward, as gently as he can. 'He passed out and never regained consciousness. He died in the ambulance.'

Edward silently turns the spoon in his hands, while Xav and me watch him, unable to find words to say. What is there to say? I think of the letters I found in the old tin box, addressed but never sent to his sister, and make a mental note to read the last few. 'He was sad,' says Edward, suddenly. 'He was sad about his life, and alone.'

'Not necessarily,' says Xav. 'Lots of elderly people like to live alone; he never struck me as a sad man, though I suppose I didn't really know him.'

'No one knew him,' says Edward. 'He told Skylark and me that he was in a concentration camp, but I don't think that was something he told everyone. It was his secret, and that's why he

293

respected other people's secrets, like my mother's. He knew I wasn't really her son, but he kept her secret all the same.'

Xav raises his eyebrows at me, but I shake my head. 'We'll talk later,' I mumble. A nurse arrives to tell us Edward should sleep, and that we can come back in the morning to visit him, but when we step outside the ward, we find a couple of policemen waiting for us, and I realise that with all the things I have to tell, it's going to be a hell of a long night.

And I'm right. My statement to the police takes until the small hours of the morning. I tell them everything I know. That I believe Edward to be Tomas Kovaleski, the illegitimate son of my father. That my own father abducted him and gave him to Eleanor and John Parry in exchange for a large sum money, as a replacement for their own son, who died from causes unknown. That my father was subsequently murdered, as was Edward's natural mother, and that the man who co-ordinated the whole thing went on to blackmail the Parrys until John Parry disappeared. Once his payments dried up, the men returned to the Parry house and threatened to take Edward, which led to his escape, and their arson of the house, with Mrs Parry and Xav inside it. I tell them about Pauline Pilcher, and her collection of newspaper cuttings. I show them the necklace I'm wearing, and how my father gave it to me on the same night Edward was abducted, telling me to 'keep it safe.' I tell them I suspect Edward was playing with the necklace at the museum where his mother worked as a cleaner, and that my father gave it to me either because he suspected it may be valuable, or possibly to safeguard it as a link between 'Edward' as he was to become, and Tomas. I'll never know, I suppose, but I prefer to think it was the latter because that might mean that my father intended to reveal the truth at some point, and restore Tomas to his mother. What I do know, is that my father committed a terrible crime, and died because of it. And even though I report this to the police with a stoney face, keeping my voice level and emotionless, the sense of betrayal is so overwhelming that as soon as Xav arrives to drive me home, I collapse against him and weep into his shirt until it's drenched through. 'It's okay,' he tells me over and over again, rubbing my back and stroking my hair. I cry for a long time. Not just for my father, but for Edward and the little boy he replaced, and for Mr Lempel, and for myself. And when I'm calmer, and once Xav has placed a glass of wine in my hands, I tell him the thing I should have told him a long time ago, those words that, unspoken, came between us and broke us apart.

I tell him that I love him. That I have always loved him. That I love him still.

Life became pretty chaotic for a while after that. I can't even begin to tell you how many people I had to speak to; the police, social workers, the press, various counsellors and public officials, but the upshot was that Edward was allowed to live with me as his main carer. The cottage I'd rented from Mr Lempel was way too small, so we moved in with my mother for a while, before finding a house in the village she lives in. Me, Xav and Edward live together as an unorthodox little family, and things haven't exactly been plain sailing, but it seems to work. My mother is a regular visitor, and she's kind to Edward, treating him like a favourite nephew or grandson and bringing him homemade biscuits or a new sweater.

She came clean about my father too. Yes, she knew he'd had a brief affair with a Polish woman called Kovaleski, not long after being released from prison, and that they'd had a child. 'It's why he didn't come to see you for a couple of years after being released,' she told me. 'He was busy with his new girlfriend, and was only interested in seeing you after she left him. I was angry with him about that.'

'Didn't you think I had a right to know I had a brother?' I asked. She shrugged. 'I didn't know how to tell you,' she said. 'He'd already let you down so much, and I didn't want to tell you he had a whole other family. I didn't know it hadn't worked out, and that she'd already left him by the time the baby was born. Skylark, I'm sorry. I wanted to protect you.' And when she said that, her eyes earnest, I accepted that, yes, protecting me is all she has ever tried to do, and I can't really feel angry at her for that.

I told Edward the whole truth one day soon after he was released from hospital. I took him to the museum in Exeter, and we sat together looking at the bog boy curled on his bed of soil. He took it all in very quietly, only asking questions now and again; mainly about my father and what he was like. 'I loved him,' I told him. 'He did a terrible thing, taking you from your mother, and it's difficult for me to accept the truth about that, but I loved him, and I have to remember that he loved me too, in his own way. Maybe he believed that giving you to the Parry's would give you a good life - I don't know, but that's what I'm telling myself, because I don't want to hate him.'

Edward nods at that. 'Like I don't hate my mother,' he says. To him, Eleanor Parry is the only mother he knows, and I have to respect that, which is why we visit her regularly. She was admitted to a psychiatric hospital after the fire, and is still there, awaiting a decision by the police on whether she'll be charged with anything. What will happen to her, we don't really know, but she's not alone. Each time we visit, we find Pauline Pilcher by her side. The word stalwart always springs to mind when I see her there in her sensible skirts and shoes, bustling about with bowls of carefully arranged fruit, or reading aloud from magazines and books. One day, I asked her why she was always there, didn't she have other things to do? 'No,' was her simple answer, accompanied by a look of surprise - why on earth would I ask such a question? 'As long as she needs me, then I'll be here,' she explained in her school teacher voice, as if to a half-wit, and she gave me a curious Mona Lisa smile.

Once, we arrived to see her reading from a manuscript of loosely bound, closely typed pages. 'It's my own book,' said Pauline proudly. 'An historical novel I've been working on. It began as a history of the village, but I got a little stuck and decided to make things up instead. It's much more fun.' I don't know if Eleanor is glad of her friendship, or simply resigned to it, but it's there all the same.

Another time, Pauline told me what had happened to the baby as revealed to her by Eleanor herself from her hospital bed. The baby was crying, and unable to cope, Eleanor shook him; gently she thought, but then the child's head lolled back and she saw he was no longer breathing. She tried to revive him, but failed. Her husband was away, and when she realised the boy was dead, she simply didn't know what to do, so she buried him in the underground passageway.

When John Parry came home some days later, his solution was to contact his dodgy contacts and organise a replacement child, thus circumventing any nasty police business. As luck would have it, my father knew just where to locate a child - his own, estranged child by Tomas Kovaleski's mother. When Tomas arrived at the Parry house, too young to comprehend what the hell was going on, his identity was already in place; a birth certificate, medical records - all he had to do was grow up and be Edward Parry.

'Do you think I'll ever see my father again?' Edward asked me one day. Of John Parry, there is no trace. The police suspect he may be somewhere in the world, but no doubt with a different identity. 'His name wasn't Parry to begin with,' the police tell me. 'He took Eleanor Parry's name when he married her, and before that he was married to another woman, much older than him, who died and left him quite a substantial sum. With that track record I wouldn't be at all surprised if he's living it up in South America with a wealthy widow or some such thing.' I don't tell Edward that, of course. I tell him that he may see John Parry again, or he may not. I tell him that his mother may get well, or she may not. I tell him that the one thing he can be sure of is that he is loved, by me, and that I'm going to do my absolute best to care for him. And I mean that. I really do.

We go to family counseling sessions regularly. Xav comes too. He has introduced Edward to the world of video games, and they share an interest in cars and bikes, often spending hours together in the little garage that adjoins our house. Edward likes to take things apart and under Xav's guidance, he learns how to put them together again. He still likes to collect things, but has lost interest in the apostle spoons, preferring instead to collect old coins and fossils. He reads a lot, especially history, and he has got me back into history too. I've enrolled myself back at university and am completing my abandoned History degree. I may train to be a teacher once I've completed it. Xav tells me I'd be good at that, and rather surprisingly, so does Mr Brearley, who comes to see me when I pop into school to clear out my office. The investigation into the school trip came to nothing, by the way. The school governors felt I'd done everything that could be expected of me under the circumstances and I was reinstated, but resigned anyway; after all, I had Edward to take care of, and he still attends the school. His skill at computer games and burgeoning knowledge of motorbikes has earned him some much needed street cred with his peers, and he's not seen as quite such an oddity now. Dare I say it, he's even considered to be a bit cool, and often he'll arrive home from school with a few friends in tow, to shoot up spaceships on his computer console or lurk in the garage with Xav, talking about whatever teenage boys (and I'd include Xav as one of them) like to talk about.

'You have a way with the youngsters,' Brearley tells me in his usual, clipped tones, 'a natural rapport.' He shows me a letter, written and signed by all who came on the trip, demanding my immediate reinstatement, and despite a whole plethora of spelling errors and weird grammatical constructions, it's heartfelt and touching. 'I daresay they'll miss you,' says Brearley, and then, his guard falling at the way my eyes have filled with tears, 'there's always a job for you here, Skylark. You did good work.' He reaches a hand out tentatively, to give me an awkward pat on the back, and I find myself suddenly grabbing him into a hug, which I regret immediately as his entire body stiffens into something like a plank of wood, so I release him to see his face red and his glasses askew. 'No need for that, Miss Riley,' he says, but he smiles, before making an excuse to hurry out the door.

I no longer wear the necklace given to me by my father - it had to be handed back to the museum it was stolen from, albeit accidentally, by Edward. We went there together to return it, and the chief curator was kind enough to show us around. 'The necklace would have been on display in the Elizabethan area over here,' he told us. 'And right though these doors, was the iron age settlement – a reconstruction of one, anyway.' He showed us old photographs of the set up; mannikins in their sack-robes, tending livestock or crouched around glowing coals. Edward thumbed through the album dreamily, pausing now and again to study some half remembered face or object. Afterwards, he told me that the pictures had seemed both familiar and unfamiliar. 'It's like I built my own memory from it rather than an exact replica of it all,' he tells me. 'In my head, it was so real. It's hard to look at those pictures and see how static it all was.'

'But really, all memory is like that,' I tell him. 'You add the missing details, place meaning where there probably wasn't any.' I think about the night I woke to see my father perched on the windowsill - was he really so shadowy and strange? Did I really detect an air of regret in his manner, as though this was his final goodbye, or did that feeling come later, when I heard of his death? Did I place it there because I wanted it to be there? Or was he already lost to me as a father. I tell Edward this. 'I don't think there's any harm in remembering him as someone you loved and miss,' Edward tells me, his face creased into that wise old man expression he carries off so well. And if the boy my father stole from his own mother and effectively sold can be so forgiving, I decide I can be too.

And that's where we are. Things aren't uncomplicated. The family of Edward's natural mother have been informed of everything and they want to meet him. They never knew their daughter gave birth to a son in England, and a new murder investigation has been launched to find her killer. The blue-eyed man figures large as the chief suspect, but where he vanished to after the fire is a mystery. Edward is nervous to meet his Polish grandparents. They speak no English, but have written to him with the help of a translator and he sent them a photograph of himself. He has his mother's eyes, they wrote back to tell him, he has his mother's smile.

Together, we drew a family tree. I filled in the English side - my father and the names of his parents, and branching off, my mother's name, and mine and Xav's names, and Eleanor Parry too. On the Polish side, the complicated spellings and relationships of his mother's family - there are aunts and uncles, and cousins, yet to be met, but aware of him and his story. We have pinned the tree to a notice board in the kitchen and sometimes I see Edward studying it carefully, silently mouthing the names he reads there, each one a building brick of himself, a link to who he is. Not Edward Parry, though he retains the name, and not the bog boy either. He is Tomas Kovaleski, and he has led a fascinating life. For now, that feels like enough.

The Magpie

What is there to see this day, this sunlit day? I perch upon the tallest stone, my talons gripping rock older and more weathered than each of my tucked in wings. I watch. I see the white clouds shaping and reshaping as they drift across the blue, I see the breeze ruffle the long grasses, I see the tiniest creatures beetling between its blades, each locked in its own life of eat and shit and sleep, over and over until death takes it. Ah me, Maggoty-pie is tired, but there's something still to see.

They crest the hill hand in hand - the woman and the man. Before them, the boy; a little taller now, his hair a little longer, and he finds a spot amongst the stones and calls back - here will do. They join him there. The man lays a rough blanket on the ground and unpacks the things they have brought; a loaf of bread, hard dead eggs, lifeless bird bones still encased in flesh. I shiver as they eat, as they talk, as they laugh. The meaningless twitterings of human birds. When their bellies are full, the boy wanders off to explore, to peer into the empty tombs beyond the stones. The man lays flat on his back, one hand behind his head. The woman rests her head upon his chest, and with his free hand, the man strokes her hair.

They cease their twitterings.

I cock my head to one side, ogle them closely, to see what lies in their hearts.

Dishonesty, of course. Betrayal. Pain. Better to be a magpie - to flit from here to there and feel nothing at all. I have hunger, I eat. I am tired, I sleep. Life on the wing needs lightness, but human birds carry such stones in their hearts. Guilt and sorrow, desire and yearning. They build nests that fragment and crumble to the ground.

And yet, there's love.

I watch them, the man and the woman. As he preens her feathers with his beak fingers, there's such tenderness in his touch that her eyes close and she sleeps.

That's when they come. The ghosts who wander these moors. They step silently from the shadows and watch with me. The bog boy, and the men who killed him. Their wives and their children. They perch upon the stones, or sit upon the grass, their faces to the sun.

You're not so different, Magpie, they say. You can live forever, and watch. Or you can simply live.

And so it is.

I watch until the boy returns. He wakes them gently, to show them a pebble he has found. A pretty thing, striped and rain-washed, smooth as silk. The three sit together, surrounded by the stones, by the ghosts of the dead, cocooned in love. Smooth as silk.

Maggoty-pie has been alone a long time. Perhaps it's time to find a mate. Perhaps its time to build a nest and line it with the things I find. Perhaps with another, I can rest.

Before I take flight, I look my last at the human birds - the man, the woman, the boy. Each their own, each with a heart full of stones, yet, like the pebble the boy holds in his hand, each stone is becoming rounded, smoother at the edges.

I chatter my farewell, but they do not hear. They are lying side by side on the grass, bodies warming in the sun, seeing shapes in the clouds. As quiet, and as comfortable, as spoons.

The Tale of Tom Watkins

by

Pauline Pilcher

The Broxhill Literary Agency
London

Dear Sirs, or Madams (as the case may be),

        Please find enclosed the opening chapters of my debut novel, The Tale of Tom Watkins. My name is Pauline Pilcher, and I am a writer of fictions, as you will no doubt see as you peruse the enclosed pages.

        I began my writing career as an historian, and indeed, the eponymous hero of my novel is a bona fide historical personage – Thomas Watkins is a well known figure from the past in my home village of Stonemoor, famed for his exploits on the high seas as captain of The Magpie, one of a piratical fleet under the command of none other than Sir Francis Drake himself.

        In researching the history of Captain Watkins, I found

plenty to inform me of his privateering career, but little on his early life beyond simple dates of birth and marriage in old church records – and into these intriguing gaps crept the desire to create a fictitious history for him.

The story you shall read is one of love and murder, of yearning and betrayal, of morality and immorality, played out against the backdrop of rural Elizabethan England. I also found myself taking the liberty of including a somewhat fantastical character. In short, a bird, whose contributions to the narrative may seem a little whimsical. My only explanation is that he simply popped into my head and had something to say. I beg that you indulge this inclusion and I hope you shall find the novel interesting. I await your expeditious response.

Yours most faithfully,

Pauline Pilcher (Author)

Stonemoor

1570

CHAPTER I

In which Tom is sent on an errand

He has been sent to gather mushrooms. Prodded into wakefulness by Farley's boney finger, in the bed he shares with one of the dogs; not so much a bed as a muddle of blankets and straw in a dim corner of the kitchen. 'Mistress mun have sustenance Tom,' says Farley, 'but she'll none o' salt beef, nor pullet neither.' She has lit a fire and is boiling the birthing sheets in a wide, blackened pot. The stink of them belches into the air as she shifts them about with a stout length of wood. Queasy, Tom buries his head into the dog's warm flank and steadies himself with familiar scents of musk and earth, before pulling on his jerkin and rising to his feet. 'There are penny buns and puffballs enough if you look about ye,' says Farley. A pinkish scum has gathered on the seething water. Tom wraps a blanket about him for a cloak, and calls to the dog. It thumps its tail at his voice, but yawns, and rests its massive head on its paws. 'Stay there then,' says Tom, as he pulls open the door and steps out into the cold.

He has slept late and the dark is already streaked with day, even at this time of year. He walks briskly, cuts across frozen fields like a man of purpose rather than a skinny farm boy, as though the woods might offer warmth and companionship, other than a cold and fruitless search beneath leafless limbs. Too late in the year for mushrooms, he thinks. It's long past Michaelmas and all's dead in the ground. But he relishes the walk, and an excuse to be alone with his thoughts. He's hungover, and the cold numbs his feet, but clears his head. He reaches the first trees and slots between them; the forest dark plucks him in, as though he were a berry.

How long does he search? An hour or more? Kicking up the frost rimed leaves and peering between cleft roots. Nothing. It's women's work, this foraging. He cuts a strip of young oak and turns it in his hands. He has a mind to carve a spoon for Marianne, but fears Farley will guess what he's about and go hen cackling to the village. She has a gossip's tongue. 'Young Tom fancies a maid,' she'll leer. He recalls her face from the morning, heat blotched and time worn. The tiny veins wriggling beneath her skin like threadworms.

He has come near the stream and scents woodsmoke seeping through the chill air. He tucks the strip of wood beside the knife in his belt and makes his way to the water, following a track pocked by hoof prints; the deer know of shallow places where he can drink. The stream has frozen into a thin sheet at the edge, and he snaps it loose before scooping a mouthful of liquid. The water is so cold it shocks his teeth and he gasps. On the opposite bank of the stream he senses a movement and glances across to see the pale eyes of an old woman gazing back at him. He knows her, and raises his hand in greeting. She nods and moves back through the trees, a pail of water sloshing at her side. Widow Creeley. Tom ponders crossing the stream to pay her a visit. The aroma of woodsmoke promises a warm fire in her tiny hovel, and though she keeps herself to herself, she's never been known to turn anyone from her door. She might even know where he can find a few mushrooms. He considers, decides against, retreats.

It's full morning now, and sunlight is tickling the upper limbs of trees, though it doesn't yet penetrate to the forest floor. Tom's tired. He can no longer feel his feet and his fingers prickle with cold. How long can he reasonably stay away? Farley'll have him chopping wood, or worse, out scraping horse shit from the yard. He climbs a little way into an oak and pulls himself up onto a thick branch that abuts the trunk almost at right angles. He leans against the rough bark and feels the sun on his face. Though weak, it touches him gently and he smiles. He pulls out his knife and the length of wood, and begins to whittle a spoon.

'A boy, Tom, a boy,' the master had cried, clapping him on the shoulder and laughing the kind of big, free laugh that usually only comes to him with drink. A strong boy too. A squalling, red faced infant, who bawled as the priest packed salt about his tender gums. Anointed, plunged into water, and named for his father; Matthew.

Marianne brought the crysom, a gift from Lady Eleanor, along with good wishes. The women admired the quality of the linen, touched the tiny seed pearls with their coarse fingers. 'Was it made for her own child?' they asked. 'The one born dead?' Marianne didn't know.

There'd been feasting at the house. A hog killed and spit roast, skin blackened and crackling, dripping globs of fat that flared in the fire pit. Farley handed out slabs of it on hunks of bread. The hot grease ran between Tom's fingers as he bit into it. There were kegs of ale and cider, and dancing. He hung back at first, embarrassed, for he had never learned to dance. 'Fie on you, Tom,' said Farley, 'if you trip o'er you feet then who's to see, and who's to care?' So emboldened with cider he'd taken his place in the ring, and when he stumbled he learned who was to see, and who to care, for Marianne laughed and said, 'Why Tom, your legs have grown long since last I saw you?' and he felt the blood rise to his cheeks. She'd grown uncommon tall and slim. Her wild hair tamed into a smooth plait and the freckles gone from her nose. Her eyes were green. Had he never noticed them before? When she lifted her arm in the roundel, the skin of it was white as milk, and soft. He turned his face away.

'The lad'll knock you from your perch, eh?'

'What?'

'The lad. The babe.'

The speaker was Harry Alcock, a thick-set luggard of a man, ten years Tom's senior and with a reputation for fighting and drinking. He had a pugilist's flattened nose, and a missing eye from where a spurred cock had flown at him in a fury the year before, clawing at his face. He'd beaten the bird to death against a barrel, but not before the spur had gouged his eyeball and sliced it beyond rescue. The eyelid flapped over the terrible hole of it. Tom didn't know what he was talking about, and said as much. 'Well, stands to reason, when the lad's of age, there'll be no place for you.'

Was there ever a place? Tom has lived with Master Hart since the age of 8. Taken in on the death of his family when the fever struck. Sir John's orders; 'I'll not have the boy starve, Hart. See to it he's fed and clothed, and send him to the priest to learn his letters.' Matthew Hart had bowed and said he would, for what choice did he have? Wasn't it Sir John who trusted him with the running of his lands? Hadn't he given him a house, and a generous stretch of ground to call his own? So he'd obeyed. And then Marianne had come, his sister's child and an orphan like Tom, and Hart with no time nor wife to tend them. They ran wild.

Tom looks up from his carving and basks in the winter sun. A siskin flitters about him. A lone magpie eyes him from the next tree. To the South, trees peter out into pasture that rises toward Hart's farmhouse. Beyond that, the scattered smallholdings of Sir John's tenants, and the manor

317

house, where Marianne has been the last year or so, tending to the whims of Lady Eleanor.

Westward, Tom can make out the steep ascent of Edge Hill, topped with its crown of standing stones. He climbed the hill with Marianne once, though he's never liked the stones. 'The dead lie beneath em,' he'd explained to her, for Father Skerrin, who taught him his letters had said so, and they were heathen dead, unsanctified, their souls burning in Hell. She'd dared him run up and touch the tallest stone, and he had, for even as a boy he was wont to please her. There'd been a sharp wind that day, and it roiled the grasses as he ran, and as he touched the stone he heard a keening, like that of a child wailing. How Marianne had laughed as he stumbled back down the hill, his eyes wide as ladles. 'It's only the wind o'er the stones, Tom, there are no ghosts.' And though he'd begged her not to, she'd marched up the hill and stood among the stones, grinning back at where he cowered in the bushes.

Master Hart had been away courting that day. A woman he'd found in the neighbouring village. Clean and kind hearted, past her prime at five and twenty, but soft voiced and possessed of a shy smile. Her presence caused barely a ripple in the workings of the house, for she was content to let Farley continue in her dominance of the kitchen, interfering only mildly to suggest Tom have a scrap of extra bread with his soup, as he'd been working in the fields all day, and to teach

Marianne a little needlework. 'Where is it you walk to Mistress Hart?' Tom asked her one evening. She had lived at the house a little over a year. Master Hart had been called away to solve a dispute between two tenants who'd come to blows over some stolen sheep, and she had come to sit by the fire in the kitchen and was combing tangles from Marianne's hair. He had seen her, a few times, crossing the fields away from the farm and passing into the green dark of the woods. She paused before answering. 'Simply to walk, Tom,' she said, 'to breathe the air.'

'I'd like to breathe the air,' said Marianne, who had spent much of the day scrubbing soot from the blackened chimney breast, 'this house chokes me.' When Sir John's wife expressed her desire for a new maid a few months later, Marianne was pleased to go.

There's a sharp breeze, and Tom gathers his blanket about him and rests from his carving to watch clouds scudding above. He likes the whiteness of them against the blue. Master Hart took him to Plymouth one day to tend to some business of Sir John's. He was in good humour, and had tossed Tom a penny and bid him find himself some dinner. Tom had wandered to the harbour to look at the ships docked there. He'd never seen one before, and marvelled at the size and majesty of them. He watched sailors high up the masts, breathed in the brine, saw mackerel slithering on the quay beside great barrels of tar. It seemed a great thing that men could set sail toward new worlds over waves that danced in the sun. He imagined himself in the rigging, calling to shipmates, seeing the world as a gull does.

'Were it not for the boy, Hart'd ha' learned you his trade,' said Alcock maliciously. 'Daresay you'll be kicked out now.' Tom studies the spoon. The bowl has taken shape, and he has cut a simple daisy in the haft, for he knows Marianne is fond of them. He considers other shapes. A heart? An anchor? He closes his eyes.

They say the new world prowls with strange beasts. Great forests echo with the chatter of rainbow plumed birds and there are savages, hideous to look on, and vicious. Tom sees himself in the rigging, sails billowing about him and waves glittering at the prow. Green and sparkling, like Marianne's eyes. He takes her in his arms, feels the soft white flesh of her beneath her skirts, 'you'd not leave me for a sailor's life, would you Tom?' Her breath is sweetly spiced, warm on his cheek. Farley's toothless face looms over him. 'A sweetheart, Tom?' she sniggers, and he's tumbling, down through the billowing sails, down through Marianne's skirts, landing with a thump and a curse and the snort and jangle of a horse somewhere, and before he can spit the cold rot of leaves from his mouth and look about him, he feels the sharp heel of a boot on the back of his neck, and the flat of a cool blade against his cheek.

He stifles a cry, and the blade tilts and presses. It's fine edged and poised to slice open his skin in what Tom imagines will be a riotous burst of blood. Twisting an eyeball as far as he can, he sees the length of it stretching away to a black gloved and tremorless hand. He swallows.

'What are you? A brigand?' The voice is low, controlled.

'No sir, I swear it,' he says. The sword lifts a little, but the point of it nips at him, prompts him further. 'My name is Tom Watkins, sir, as lives with Master Hart.' There's a moment, before the boot is lifted away, and Tom hears the slither of the sword being sheathed, but it isn't enough to reassure him. He still feels the cold sting of it on his skin.

'Stand. Don't you know me?'

Tom does as he's bid, slowly. He touches his fingers to the raw nick on his cheek and allows his fearful gaze to travel the length of the man's boots, the brocade of his good cloak, to his face, tired and bearded. 'Sir John,' says Tom, and he bows deeply, but Sir John has turned from him already to catch up the reins of his horse. 'Lucky I didn't kill you,' he mutters.

Tom stares stupidly at the ground. 'Yes sir. I thank you, that you didn't.'

Sir John grunts. 'Take the reins, boy. I'm weary of the saddle. I'll walk with you as far as Hart's and call in on your master.'

'He'll be glad on't sir.'

'Will he?'

It's not a matter Tom has thought on. As Sir John turns to face him again, he bows, again.

'Pick yourself up, boy. Will he be glad to know you're throwing yourself from trees, armed with a knife?' He nods to where Tom's knife has fallen into the leaves. Tom retrieves it, and tucks it into his belt. He leaves the half carved spoon where it lays and his face is red as he tugs at the horse's reins.

They walk in silence awhile.

'You've grown, Tom,' says Sir John, presently. Tom mumbles assent, and glancing sideways, is surprised to note he's only a half head shorter than Sir John himself, though skinnier. He feels tongue tied in his presence. Sir John has been away on the Queen's business these last seven months, and has rarely spoken to him before, though he has had occasion to pass through Master Hart's kitchen before now. An event which once threw Farley into such paroxysms of clumsy curtsying that she fell backwards and almost into a cauldron of soup that hung over the fire, causing Tom and Marianne to dash outside for fear of bursting into uncontrolled hysterics.

'So, tell me Tom, what news? How fare your master and mistress?

'Very well, sir,' Tom replies, 'the mistress had a baby son this night before last, and both hearty, sir.'

'What mean you?' The sharpness of his voice takes Tom aback.

'Why, as I say sir,' he says, warily. 'The babe is strong, and was christened just yesterday.'

They have come to the edge of the wood, where the trees thin and allow a distant view of Hart's farmhouse. The pasture is dotted with sheep, grey with wool. Sir John pauses in his walking and looks silently ahead.

The boy was named for his father,' says Tom. 'Matthew,' he adds, pointlessly.

'And your mistress. Well, is she?'

'Still abed sir, but quite well.'

Sir John nods. The horse, restless, whinnies and tugs at the reins in Tom's hand.

A lone fox is ambling over the fields and though it is some distance away, it stops to stare at them with amber bright eyes. Sir John remarks on the animal, advising Tom ensures his master's hen-coop is secured tight. 'If it's a dog, chances are it'll give up at the first difficulty. But a vixen Tom, a vixen will find her way in.' They watch the fox backtrack the way it has come. Skirting the edge of the field and vanishing into a ditch. Sir John stares at the spot and follows the line with his eyes to where it meets the woods. Then lifts his gaze above the trees to where the Henge stones rise quietly from the winter green of the hilltop. The sun hangs above them, white against blue sky. 'I'll ride on to my house, Tom,' he says, taking the reins from Tom's hands and swinging himself into the saddle.

'Tell your master I'll send for him by and by. And to your mistress, greetings.' Tom nods his assent and watches as Sir John clicks his tongue and turns his horse's head back toward the wood. As the dark of his cloak merges into the trees, Tom remembers he was sent to gather mushrooms, and has found none.

CHAPTER II

In which Marianne is sent on an errand

She has risen early to lay out Lady Eleanor's clothes. The master returns today, and her ladyship has asked for the black silk. The embroidery of the bodice has loosened in places. Marianne has seen Lady Eleanor absentmindedly picking at the threads with her long fingernails, and has taken a needle so she can effect a quick repair before her mistress returns from offering devotions in the tiny chapel she keeps at the far reaches of the house. She spreads the garment across her knees and runs a hand down the silk, finding out the snags by touch rather than sight, for the embroidery is intricately wrought, and not easy to see in the dim winter light that seeps through the casement. The fabric is smooth to the touch, fragrant with holy water. Marianne breathes its cool bitterness as she threads the needle.

As she stitches, the house awakes. Doors open and shut, footsteps scurry through corridors, floors creak. From the kitchens far below, she hears the clatter of pots, the clink of pewter and glassware. All this fuss for one woman's breakfast, she thinks. Baskets of manchet and pats of salted butter. Cold fowl and mutton, and her Ladyship will barely nibble a morsel, barely sip at a cup of mead, before ordering all to be cleared. She holds the bodice to the window, examines her handiwork, before attaching the kirtle and pressing the dress to her own body. She gazes at the faint reflection the window offers. The waist is narrower than her own; the bust less fulsome, but the dress could be made to fit with a snip here, a patch of extra fabric there. Lady Eleanor has given her two dresses; one of a soft velveteen green, and the other pale yellow, sprigged with tiny golden roses, though there has been little occasion to wear them. Her Ladyship has worn black since the burial of a stillborn child three years ago, and Marianne must dress as befits the servant of a woman in mourning. Simply. Modestly. A ripple in the window glass makes the distant moor shiver. Marianne's own reflection trembles as she enacts a low curtsy. 'My Lord,' she whispers.

He arrives later that morning, his boots muddied and his cloak damp from the chill air. The servants fuss about him, laying out fresh linen and bringing him warmed ale spiced with cinnamon and cloves. He eats in the kitchen, famished. The cook, who has known the master from boyhood, prattles ceaselessly. What news from London? They say folk there'll cheat a man soon as look on him, that every second Londoner is a thief or cutthroat and she's heartily glad he's returned to his home with no hair on his head harmed, though looking at it, he's in need of a haircut. Sir John smiles at this, tolerant. He tells stories of the Queen, her infinite majesty. Of new laws and statutes wrought in the parliament. Simple tellings, sparing of detail, enough for these country dwellers to grasp. The servants nod and frown and comment that all is done for the best, they daresay, if the Queen would have it so. He's tired, and takes his leave of them, retiring to his private chambers for a few hours. It is past midday when he taps on the door to his wife's rooms.

Marianne is there, perched on a low stool beside the window. Lady Eleanor reads from the bible each day, sometimes aloud, but mostly in silence. At certain passages, her lips part in quiet utterance of the words. Marianne's role is to turn the pages when her Ladyship lifts a hand, and to mark the page when she has read enough. The bible is large, bound with thick, dark hide. The pages are translucently thin, barely thick enough to carry the weight of holy words, Marianne thinks. When Sir John knocks and enters, both women stand. 'Madam,' he says. Lady Eleanor moves toward him and curtsies. She kisses his lifted hand, and lets it drop. Marianne dips as he looks at her, though his eyes merely pass over her before settling on the black book on its stand. 'Shall I take the bible, Ma'am,' she asks. Lady Eleanor nods, and Marianne lifts the heavy tome and passes into the ante-chamber, closing the door quietly behind her. As she stows the bible in its chest, she hears the low murmur of voices. Calm exchanges. She listens, tries to make out words and tone, but can gather nothing.

A week passes. Perhaps more. Sir John rises early each morning and eats a hearty breakfast before saddling his horse and leaving for the day. He returns in darkness and eats dinner with his wife before retiring to his rooms. Marianne tends to her mistress. She prepares her clothes and helps her dress. Combs her hair. When it is not raining, she walks with her about the gardens. 'Where do you suppose my husband rides to each day?' Lady Eleanor asks her one afternoon. Marianne, accustomed to her Mistress's silences, is surprised at the question. 'To visit his tenants, my lady,' she replies, 'to see all is well.'

Lady Eleanor pauses in her sedate steps and gazes toward the distant stones on the moor. 'To Plymouth,' she says at last. 'Some days past, my husband rode to Plymouth.' She turns her gaze on Marianne, her blue eyes tinged grey in the light, as though the damp air has crept into them. 'To buy a gift for your uncle's child. Now, why would he do that?' Marianne says she does not know. 'But my uncle has always served Sir John well,' she offers. 'It's a great kindness of Sir John to bestow some trinket on the child.'

'A trinket?' says Lady Eleanor, and she presses her lips into a thin line. 'Thirteen trinkets,' she says. 'A full set of silver spoons. A generous gift to bestow on the son of a servant.' Marianne agrees that it is, and that her uncle and his wife will no doubt feel greatly honoured at such benevolence. Lady Eleanor continues to look at her, searchingly, it seems to Marianne. She bows her head respectfully. 'You will visit your aunt,' says Lady Eleanor, as she begins to walk again. 'You will bring her a letter, and you will mark how well such a gift is received by Mistress Hart.' A light rain has begun to fall, and Lady Eleanor draws her fur cape more closely about her. 'Tomorrow, you shall go,' she says.

CHAPTER III

In which Tom speaks with Marianne

He has seen the spoons. Sir John had already left when he came in from the fields in the early dark. 'Look at these, Tom?' Master Hart said. He had laid them out on the rough wood of the table, all in a row, where they glowed in the light from two tallow candles. The mistress, now strong enough to leave her room, nursed the babe on a low stool beside the fire, while Farley ogled the new treasures with eyes round as the spoon bowls themselves. 'Fit for a prince,' she kept saying, picking the spoons up one by one and rubbing them against her apron before setting them down again, 'and his initials pricked out in 'em too,' she said, 'made for the boy himself, as though he were son to some fine lord.' She shakes her head while Master Hart scratches his. The mistress brushes her son's head with her lips, and keeps her eyes on the fire. Tom sits at the table and studies the figures carved into the knops; their impassive faces. 'Which one's which?' he asks.

Marianne comes the following day, with a letter addressed to Mistress Hart. The master sends her upstairs to his wife's room. 'She'll be glad to let you dandle the babe awhile,' he calls after her. Sir John's gift has put him in good humour and he's allowed Tom a day of rest from his usual winter task of cutting back the hedgerows that divide the pasture. Tom's attempting to whittle a spoon again, but tucks it into his shirt when Marianne arrives. Once she's gone up to the mistress he wanders outside and across to the stable. He's irritated by his own awkwardness. He roughly shoves at the stable door so that Hart's placid mare startles and whinnies at him. When Marianne passed by him in the kitchen her dress moved with a faint swishing sound and he caught the scent of rosewater. He soothes the mare, and leans his head against her warm neck.

Beyond the stable is a storeroom, where fruit and vegetables are kept in cool darkness through the winter months. He checks for signs of rats or mice; droppings amongst the onions, or tell tale teethmarks on the turnips, but finds none. He sets about turning the apples in their beds of straw, and that's where Marianne finds him. She stands in the doorway, casting a shadow on the earthen floor, an uncertain smile on her lips until he nods a greeting and looks down at his feet. Then she laughs. 'You're shy of me? Tom, you used to yank my hair and tease me till I beat you with my fists. Come now, talk with me a little. Why won't you?'

He smiles. Meets her eyes. 'Promise you'll not beat me then,' he says. She moves into the room. 'Promise you'll not tease,' she replies. She stands beside him, and helps him turn the apples in the wooden crate. He watches how her hands move deftly. Her fingernails are clean and neatly trimmed, while his are black with dirt, jagged and split. He's not sure what to say to her. He steals sidelong glances at her. Her dress is simply cut, but of good cloth, and prettily sprigged with delicate yellow flowers. He remarks on it.

'Lady Eleanor gives me dresses,' she says, 'she wears only black herself, or grey. Since the child died. Tom, shall I tell you something?'

He shrugs, but turns to her and sees how her eyes gleam. 'Tell me,' he says. She stops turning the apples and leans against the stacked crates, drops her voice to a whisper. 'The spoons Sir John sent,' she says. 'Lady Eleanor disapproves. Here, look.' She tugs at a thin chain about her neck and reveals the pendant that has been hidden beneath the neckline of her dress. It's a small ring, crafted for slim fingers, and set with a chip of blue stone. Tom regards it blankly. Is aware only of how, as she leans towards him, the maddening scent of roses mingles with the sweet, sharp tang of apples. Marianne continues, her voice lifting in excitement. 'My Lady Eleanor puts the letter in my hand for Mistress Hart, and with it this ring. She says to me, 'Marianne, this is for you. Bring me news of Mistress Hart and the child and there'll be more for you.' Tom,' she hesitates, twisting the ring at the end of its chain, 'what can it mean?'

He hoists the apple crate to one side and thinks of the half carved spoon that's still tucked beneath his shirt. A crude object compared to the ring. 'There'll be advancement for you,' he says, 'she's pleased with you, it's plain to see.' He struggles to bar resentment from his voice.

'But what news can she want from me?' says Marianne. 'I'm to go to her now to say, Mistress Hart humbly thanks you for your kind wishes and for the generous gift. The boy is well, and Mistress Hart is well,' she raises her hands and lets them fall in exasperation, 'what's the import of it?'

Tom thinks of Lady Eleanor, a thin, ashen faced woman, who comes to the village church just twice a year, to stand beside her husband at Christmas and Easter time. It's well known that she keeps to the old religion and worships alone at home, in the tiny chapel built by Harry Alcock at the far edge of the house; a project supposedly completed in secrecy, but which he boasts of in the tavern as proof of his standing and craftsmanship. Father Skerrin conducts the Anglican mass in the village church, swears allegiance to his Queen as Defender of the Faith, and creeps off to Sir John's house with the sacred body of Christ concealed beneath his robes. 'I have a blind eye,' sneers Alcock, 'but not so blind as the one Sir John turns on his wife.'

'What was in the letter?' he asks, but Marianne has wandered along her own path of thought. 'Only good wishes,' she replies vaguely, 'Mistress Hart read it to me. Do you think, Tom, she envies her the child?' Tom shrugs, wary of such talk about his betters, and distracted by the way Marianne toys with the ring, which hangs prettily above the swell of her bosom. He averts his eyes. 'Her own babe dead in the ground three years,' Marianne is saying, 'and no sign yet of another.' A wintry breeze gusts through the open door of the store room. 'We'll go in to warm up a little before you go back,' he says.

Farley plies Marianne with spiced cakes and a cup of mulled ale in the kitchen, and the two chat of women's things; the baby, linen, marriage. 'Lady Eleanor is like to find you a fine husband when the time's right,' croons Farley, 'you've the air of a lady about you now, too grand for a village lad to bed,' and she laughs raucously at Marianne's blushes. Tom frowns into his ale. Though her cheeks redden, her eyes sparkle with mirth, not shame.

After she's taken her leave of the mistress, he walks her away from Hart's farm and along the frozen track that leads through the outlying tenanted strips of Sir John's lands. The meanest of these is rented by Harry Alcock; a rubble strewn patch of weeds, dotted here and there with meagre patches of cultivation. He grows beets and turnips, and raises scrawny chickens too ill nourished to lay. The hens end up in the pot, the cocks are trained to fight, and sold to pay for his bread and ale, or kept as champions so Alcock can supplement his drinking with winnings. He labours for others at harvest time, or carpenters if he can find the work.

He has a reputation for shoddiness, but has worked at Sir John's house enough to keep himself fed. Tom knows him for a drunkard and a brawler, but one clever enough to win the favour of his betters where money's involved; he'll bow to their contempt, but jam a fist through the teeth of his own sort should they offer their disdain. He's clearing a patch of ground as Tom and Marianne pass, and lifts his head to stare at them as they follow the footpath to where it dips below a shallow rise, before disappearing into a copse that marks the boundary to Sir John's private land. 'You'll make your way from here?' asks Tom. Having reached the edge of village habitation, it would be unseemly to step further along together, and Marianne bids him goodbye before slipping away between the trees. As he returns along the path, Alcock raises a hand in greeting, and calls him over. He's been tearing up brambles, and his hands are scratched and dotted with blood. There's a flagon of ale beside him on the ground, and he tilts it into his mouth as Tom approaches. His lips, cracked with cold, glisten when he lowers the flagon. 'You're courting,' he says, and he grins. 'But a whelp you are, to court such a maid as she.' He takes another swig from the flagon and wipes the dribble from his chin with his sleeve. 'Tell me pup,' he whispers, 'ha' you swiven the wench?' Tom's blush is red and hot. He shakes his head, and as he stumbles back to the path, Alcock's throaty laugh smacks at the air.

CHAPTER IV

In which a curious magpie watches events unfold

Who's in the copse? He calls out to her, his voice cracked and runnelled as ancient bark. He trip trip runs and catches at her sleeve. Air's metalled and I shrink into my plumes, watch at them through eyes like scales. He swivels about her, blocks the path and presses himself to her, the whole bulk of him pushing until she steps back, but he's cuffed her skinny wrists in his handlocks, and his courting call is nay nay nay pretty one, a smooching kind o' call. He spools her in and crushes his lips on hers, sniffs at her smooth skin, and all the time crooning as she skrarks and whimpers. His hands snout at her like dogs, lifting and prodding, snuffling beneath petticoats, tugging at strings. Nay, she whispers, and shuuush he soothes. Her eyes widen, sudden chasms of dark. I sidle along a branch and watch. I waggle and dip and chachacha, as she pushes him away. Not yet, she says.

He stands back a little. She reaches out a hand to touch his face. Fingers tiptoe about his stubbled chin, stroke the flat nose, step gingerly about the gaping hole of his eye, till he grabs them away and kisses her again, his lips nuzzling the soft nook of neck and shoulder bone. She looks up through the fretwork of branches to where I preen and shake out my tail, and she looses her call; a tumbling burble, like pebbles dropped through water; a free, full throated, babbling song.

Laughter.

CHAPTER V

In which Tom makes a promise to Mistress Hart

The house is alive. Master Hart croons over the child, tickles his chin, delights in his tiny gurgles, his miniature sneezes. 'What's Christmas without a child in the house?' he asks of no one in particular.

Grace wears her motherhood like a soft gown, shrugging it on when needed and lifting the child from her husband's arms at the first sign of squalling. She settles him in the crook of her arm as she walks upstairs to nurse him.

Farley is severing feet from chickens and trussing them to be baked in thick pastry coffins. Master Hart has invited two of the village dignitaries to dine; a pre-Christmas ensemble of the respected and the good. Men like himself, literate and godly, who've done well for themselves; Will Thornbury, owner of the abattoir and butchery, and Joseph Connett, timber merchant, in the process of extending his house to better accommodate his five children, and to show off the fine cabinets he's had made in Exeter to furnish the new rooms. Their wives are invited too, and Tom has been bid to don a clean holland shirt for the evening and to comb his hair, for Hart does not keep a manservant. Tom will have to do.

At the moment, he is polishing the silver christening spoons in readiness for the evening. The upstairs parlour has been swept and scrubbed and firewood stacked in the hearth. The spoons will be displayed upon the mantle, a centre piece and talking point for Master Hart's guests; evidence of his standing with Sir John, proof of his baby son's future patronage. Tom breathes on the concave bowl of the spoon he has been rubbing with a soft cloth, watches his own face vanish beneath a mist. He thinks of Marianne.

He hasn't seen her since the day she helped him turn apples in the storehouse, though according to Farley she has called at the house more than once since then. Both times on an errand from Lady Eleanor to Mistress Grace, and each time bringing some small gift; a square handkerchief to dab up the baby's possett, a tiny pot of sweet smelling oil to smooth into the creases of his skin. Tom was at work in the pasture when she called, and she didn't seek him out either time.

He studies the silver spoon in his hand, takes a moment to lay it across his palm and feel the heft of it, the balance of bowl and knop. He has been trying to carve a second spoon for Marianne, but each time he has shaved the bowl too shallow, or the shapes in the handle have come out clumsy and crooked. He has thrown one effort into the fire, snapped another in two. He will see her, he knows, on Christmas Day, when the tenant farmers and labourers are invited to gather at Sir John's house for the feast. There'll be a calf slaughtered, and all manner of pies and sweetmeats, along with barrels of ale and spiced wine. He takes up another spoon and rubs it, dreamily. He will take her aside from the feasting and give her the spoon he has carved, and she'll marvel at the delicacy of his craftsmanship. She'll lean towards him, and kiss his cheek, and a deal will be struck for the future, for when the time is right.

'Ha' you swiven the wench?' The unbidden echo of Alcock's voice blasts loud in his head and he fumbles the spoon and drops it to the floor. 'Fool!' says Farley, cuffing him sharply as he stands up from retrieving it. 'Is it damaged?' asks Hart, grabbing the spoon from Tom's hand and inspecting it closely. 'It's only a spoon,' sighs Mistress Grace, who has put the infant down in his crib and is returning downstairs. She wears a thick wool cloak, and outdoor boots. She smiles at Tom. 'Will you come with me, Tom?' she asks. 'I want to gather ivy and holly leaves and such, to lay about the dinner table.' Hart blinks at her. 'And leave the babe?' he says.

'He'll sleep an hour or more,' says Grace, 'we'll be back before he wakes.'

They walk in silence across the yard and into the pasture. The ground's hard, and grey full bellied clouds hang thick and still in the sky. Tom has always felt at ease in the company of the mistress, but since her pregnancy she has been

340

possessed of an unnerving quietude. A self possession wrought, it seems to him, from the impenetrable secrecies of women and childbirth.

They walk towards a low dividing wall between strips of pasture, where ivy strains thickly upward and over the stone. He takes out his knife, thinking this is from where she means him to gather it, but she continues to walk, alongside the wall, towards the bottom end of the fields where the land peters out into woodland. He hesitates a moment, and she turns and smiles at him. 'Let's walk further, Tom,' she says, 'it's still light, and I've a mind to walk into the woods a little way.' He nods, and falls into step beside her, telling her he knows of a holly bush they can prune not far from the woodland path. 'Do you miss your walks, mistress?' he asks, and he reminds her of when she first came to the house and he used to see her crossing the pasture. Since her pregnancy, she hasn't strayed far from the farmhouse at all. Only to the church, each Sunday, or to call on some of the tenants when she has heard of them being taken ill. She's well liked by the villagers, and can be relied on to bring parcels of food or a few kind words to those in need. She seems wrapped in thought for a moment before asking, 'Did you ever see where I walked to, Tom?'

'No,' he replies, truthfully. 'Through the woods, I supposed.'

'Yes,' she says, 'There's peace in the woods.' He agrees, telling her he likes to walk there himself sometimes. 'No further, Tom?' she asks. They've reached the edge of the woodland, where the trees are still thin enough to allow, through their slim branches, a view towards the Henge high above them. She lifts her head, indicating the grey stones with her eyes and Tom shakes his head. 'No Mistress,' he says, 'not unless I have to. There's sometimes a sheep will stray up beyond the stones and I must find it out, but I don't like it up there.' They stand side by side, boy and woman, staring at the Henge. 'It's haunted,' adds Tom, but she chuckles softly. 'Ghosts, Tom? Do you believe in such things?' He doesn't answer, but hangs his head a little, feeling childish and ashamed before saying, a little sullenly, 'No one walks there Mistress. There's nothing but bog and marsh, and dead men's bones.'

'Yes,' she says, softly. 'No one walks there.'

They find the holly tree, and he cuts an armful of leaves and places them in a woven basket she has brought for the purpose. When they emerge from the woods, it's beginning to grow dark. He strips ivy from the pasture wall and they walk back to the farmhouse, guided by flickers of light that shine in the windows. A gibbous moon has risen. It hangs low and yellow beneath the cloud line and, before entering the house, Grace turns to look at it for a few moments. Tom waits, his hand on the door latch, until she turns her face to him again. 'Tom,' she says quietly. 'If you see me, some day soon, walking to the woods, promise me you'll tell no one.' He pauses, letting the questions crease his face, before shrugging under her steady gaze. 'Aye, Mistress,' he says, 'if it please you.' She smiles. 'You're a good boy, Tom,' she says, 'a kind boy.' He opens the door and they are greeted by the warm fug of heat from the fire, the scuffle of dogs, the scent of roasting meat, the broad bawl of the woken infant.

CHAPTER VI

In which Marianne considers her secret sins

She can feel Alcock's presence even though she has left him standing in the gloom of the chapel. The touch of his freezing fingers hangs on her skin like bruises. Stolen moments, before he sent her scurrying for Lady Eleanor.

They have some private business, Alcock and Lady Eleanor, and she knows its nature. He is building a secret entrance to the chapel. Hacking down through the ground it stands on and out a short distance to a spot screened by low bushes and sapling growth. Sir John has put his foot down, and has demanded there be an end to papist services in his own house. The law demands it. The queen herself has spoken. She desires not to make windows into men's souls, but the new religion must be enforced, by him on his own lands, and it doesn't do to have the Catholic mass spoken beneath his own roof. Father Skerrin is no longer welcome at the house, but must preach the gospel, the approved gospel, from his pulpit at the church. Lady Eleanor has acquiesced on the surface, but her windowless faith drives her to find a neat solution to the problem; Alcock, and his ingenuity with a pickaxe and wooden struts. The priest will come and go in secret, carrying the body of Christ along a tunnel just wide enough for one man and his God. Sir John need never know. So Alcock arrives, each day, after Sir John has left. Marianne's role is to ensure the way is clear before fetching him in and leading him to the chapel. Bound by such clandestine behaviour, they have come to an understanding.

She hasn't given herself to him yet. Not fully. Though she knows it's only a matter of time before he succeeds in coaxing her into his bed. 'We'll take a tumble soon,' he has told her, with a certainty she finds convincing even as she pushes him away. She has come to consider him handsome, in spite of the ruined eye, which he has taken to covering with a patch, at least when meeting with Lady Eleanor. He has a stone mason's build; broad backed and deep chested, with thick forearms. His hands are large and squat fingered, rough and capable. When he comes to the chapel to carry out his work, they have some privacy before she must return to her mistress, and she has allowed him to touch her in places she has never been touched. Once, before the simple wooden alter, she stood with her back to him and let him funnel his hands beneath the loosened front of her bodice. He weighed her naked breasts in his hands, let them sit there for a moment, like eggs in cups. He talks, Alcock, with words that make her face redden with shame and an uncertain pleasure. Last time he came to the chapel, he ran the tip of his tongue about the whorl of her ear and in a hot whisper breathed, 'next time, it'll be tha' pretty cunny I'll tongue.' Alone in her narrow cot at night, she recalls the warm rasp and wetness, grows hot until even the tips of ears seem to burn. She throws back the counterpane and kneels by her bed, prays for forgiveness, lets the cold night air wash her shivering and clean.

Lady Eleanor suspects, she thinks. Though she has neither asked nor hinted, she seems cautious that the girl does not attend to Alcock's needs for any length of time. While defiance of her husband's wishes regarding the chapel do not strike her as a dereliction of wifely obedience, her duty of protection toward her maidservant's virginity is not one she takes so lightly. 'Deliver food to him and return to me forthwith,' she commands. On the occasions Marianne has overstayed in the chapel, Lady Eleanor demands to know why and searches Marianne's face for signs of deception, for downcast eyes or reddened cheeks. Marianne knows to look her mistress in the eye as she lies; 'Why, he bid me stay and help him move some tools about,' she replies, artful in her artlessness. Lady Eleanor holds her gaze, nods, and turns away with some directive; 'Fetch my shawl, Marianne. I feel the cold today.'

There's talk amongst the servants, who for all the secrecy, are aware of Alcock's work in the chapel, even if not its precise nature. Entering the kitchens there's an abrupt cessation in the chatter; sly glances, concealed mutterings. She collects a loaf and a round of cheese; 'the mistress is hungry' she explains, though all know that her ladyship eats nothing between breakfast and evening. Whether they know of Marianne's dalliance with Alcock is not clear. Since her arrival at the house a year before, Marianne has remained an island amongst the servants. Elevated in her position as Lady Eleanor's maid, but too lowly to be considered an equal of Sir John and his wife. Sometimes, she misses her life at Hart's farm. The simple routine of chores, punctuated by those freedoms permitted by her uncle; lazing by the fire in the evenings, walking freely about the countryside with Tom beside her.

Tom.

Tom's about his work on the farm when she visits. Farley teases; 'He's sweet on you,' her voice honeyed; her grin, gap toothed. Marianne chides, 'Who? Tom?' Tom, her childhood playmate, more brother than would-be suitor. 'Aye,' sniggers Farley, reading her thoughts, 'for he's no kin to you, and he's like to grow a handsome man, he's on the cusp of it e'en now.' Marianne laughs it off, but knows she has avoided Tom. If the servants know about her and Alcock, she doesn't care. If her uncle were to admonish her, she'd brush away his disapproval with a turn of her head and a frank denial, but were Tom to know? She feels a pricking of shame behind her eyes. Who can she tell of her secrets, if not Tom?

Not only about Alcock, but her other knowings too.

It was late in the evening when Sir John sent for her the first time. A note, in his elegant hand, delivered by the cook's boy, who sleeps in a truckle bed downstairs. Marianne had not yet undressed for bed, preferring to sew in the yellow light cast by a rush lamp she keeps in her private room. Lady Eleanor had retired already; helped into her nightgown by Marianne herself, her greying hair plaited into thin ropes, her prayers offered to God. 'The master bid me give you this,' piped the boy when she opened her door to his soft tap. 'The master?' she asked, surprised at seeing her own name scrawled in ink. The letter was sealed, the wax still a little soft. 'Aye,' said the boy, disinterested, already turning from her to hurry away. She watched him go before closing the door, breaking the seal in the lamplight, and reading the note.

Tonight, another note arrives. By day, Sir John barely acknowledges her presence. Little more than a stiff nod in her direction when he visits his wife's rooms; a signal to absent herself rather than a greeting. But several times now, a formal summons to his study, at nightfall, while the house sleeps. Marianne quickly attends to her dress, her hair, and taking the lamp in one hand, slips along the darkened corridors to Sir John's study.

CHAPTER VII

In which Master Hart hosts a good dinner

The evening has gone well, the guests and their womenfolk impressed at the spread; baked chicken, goose in a sorrel sauce, fat oysters steeped in vinegar, pigs' livers stuffed with sage, and leverets smothered in mustard and sugar. All evening, Tom has hefted the wooden platters up and down the stairs between kitchen and parlour, has ensured a steady flow of rhenish and malmsey, has snatched his own dinner from the left over rinds and discarded skins, and now, as the men slide strips of green cheese between their greased lips, Tom sits on a low stool in a darkened corner, and listens. He wishes they'd leave so he could curl into his bed and sleep, but the talk shows no sign of abating just yet. The women have retired to the adjoining room to coo over the baby. From beyond the closed door he hears their soft, feminine sounds, their amiable laughter. The men talk business; profit and loss. Investments. He longs for sleep.

'There's more money in timber than ever,' says Connett. He should know, for he grows fat on the demand; ships being built, towns expanding ever outward. Two good harvests in a row and Englishmen's purses are bulging. Hart has a mind to negotiate a deal with Sir John and take a modest mortgage out on an area of woodland below his own pasture. Once the timber has been felled and sold, he'll pay off the mortgage and turn the land over to livestock; more sheep, the price of wool being buoyant, but Thornbury, the butcher, suggests beef; 'more value pound for pound,' he says, slaughter the bullocks and keep the heifers for milk and breeding; expand the dairy, Hart; cheese'll fetch a good price should the harvest fail next year.' Hart nods and smiles, eyes far away; Hart, the gentleman farmer, strolling his lands with his son beside him. Sir John's right hand; a good manager, firm, and with enough land and money of his own to bequeath his boy a good living when the time comes. P'raps there'll be more children by then, a daughter too. A sudden squall of laughter from the adjoining room makes the men turn their heads, before returning to their conversations with indulgent smiles and shaking heads; women. 'What's become of the girl you had?' asks Connett? 'Slip of a thing, Maria?'

'Marianne,' says Hart. 'Lady Eleanor took her for a maid a year back.'

'Maid?' says Thornbury, and he emits a sharp snort that makes Tom sit a little straighter on his stool, 'No maid, she,' he says, before knocking back his Rhenish and thumping the drained cup on the table. A silence edges into the room and Thornbury blinks stupidly at Hart for a moment, before slumping back into his chair with a sigh. 'O'course, she's your niece, Hart,' he says, 'I mean no slur on you, but,' he reaches for the empty cup, 'damn it, boy, it's empty.' Hart nods to Tom, who has risen already to lift the earthenware jug from the table so it can be replenished from a keg kept in the kitchen downstairs. Hart, ever the gracious host, smiles on his friend to ease his embarrassment. 'We're old friends,' he says, 'tell me, what news have you of Marianne? I take it as no slight.'

Tom half descends the staircase that leads to the kitchen and waits, out of sight, where the treads bend through a patch of shadow, and he listens as the men lean in towards Hart. Thornbury's voice thickens like pea soup to tell them what the gossips say of she, Marianne, and Alcock.

He listens, and when all has been said, he continues to the kitchen and places the jug beneath a tap hammered into the wine keg. He watches, as a thin stream drizzles from the spigot. Farley asks him some question about the gathered company and, when he doesn't reply, she prods him hard with the end of a wooden spoon so that he turns to stare at her. Her face swims before him, reddened and worn and miasmic in the kitchen's heat. Her lips move and her eyes bulge, and before he even knows it, he has pushed past her and seized the latch on the door, has wrenched it open and is standing outside, bent double, heaving his dinner up from his stomach so that it splashes onto the frozen cobbles and sullies his shoes. 'You've been at the wine,' scolds Farley, though he hasn't.

He stands straight, at last, and wipes his mouth on the sleeve of his good shirt. From the rooms above he hears Hart calling down for him to hurry along there and bring up the wine, but he stays where he is and lets Farley bustle upstairs with the heavy jug. He gulps at the air. It has an iron smell, and is filled with snow.

CHAPTER VIII

In which the magpie watches a deal being struck

Night dark's no time for Maggoty-pie to be up and about and flurrying. To and fro, hither and thither, and in this weather? No. Night time's for roosting in a huddle of twig and bone and feather and shut-eye; but there are footsteps below, and a magpie can't help but pry.

Things move shadowy. Dusk is time for secrets and quiet voices. I grip a branch slippy with rime, and cock my head to hearing. A woman. A man. She, pale grey. He, thick set and glowing like a coal, his breath hot with drink, while hers shivers wispy through thin lips. Magpie don't know the meaning of voices, only sees them rise and shift into flight; but these voices creep along the ground, stalk about each other, wary, not like any birdsong I know. She, a heron, stalking. Voice, a sharp beak, same shape as cruelty, same shape as spite. And he puffs out his chest, prances a little and fans his tail. Cockerel. Too stupid for fear. Sharp clawed too, like the one that sliced his eye so the sight in it bilged out like sticky yolk. Had he two eyes, he'd perhaps see sense, but the one eyed man is transfixed by glitter, by the promise of riches. They have made a deal, these too. They have made a deal, and there'll be pickings for Maggoty pie too.

All around, secrets.

I scatter off to the window and there again. A man, a woman. He tall and bearded, she slim as a sapling, bending before him as if in a breeze. Firelight smears their faces as he asks her something, extracts a promise, and grants her a smile. She basks.

Fickle, these human birds. Their wings nettangled in secrets and promises; they can never hope to fly, but dream of it all the same. Dream a bird life of rich pickings and a mate for life, of a feathered nest fat full with eggs.

I soar through the dark, stopping once where a lovesick boy has gobbetted in easy reach. I feast, then home to roost, where I sleep, wake, fly, eat, and drop my shittings. Each simple day, for me, the same. But below, things unfold and stretch and gather like the broadest wings on the most terrible of birds.

Watch.

CHAPTER IX

In which Tom has words with Marianne

The days pass and he moves through them. Snow tumbles from thick cloud and muffles his footfall as he spreads fodder for the sheep, as he hacks dead limbs from the hedges. He is numbed by cold and barely registers the days falling away to Christmas. The sun brings only a fleeting grey, like a man, who turning fitfully in slumber, pulls the blanket after him; like so, the sun drags the dark. Of Marianne, he cannot bear to think. Of Marianne, he cannot stop thinking.

He has glimpsed her, Sundays at the church, where she takes her place amongst the servants of Sir John's household for the prayer service. Once, returning from the fields at dusk, he thought he saw her walking along the ridge of high ground above the woods, where the Henge stones stood in a veil of lowering cloud, but she disappeared from his sight and he had to shake his head and cross himself for fear he'd seen a spirit instead. He has taken to closing his eyes and muttering a prayer to purge his thoughts, not only of her, but the words he heard that night while standing in the darkened stairwell with an empty wine flagon clutched to his chest. Thornbury's words; 'Talk at the tavern is that Alcock has tupped her. Or plans to - he has the scent of her in his snout it seems.' And Master Hart's diffident response; 'Well, should he come asking for the marrying of her, I'll say aye, for goods can't be easily rid once they're soiled.'

Soiled. That's the word that tolled in his head as nausea surged up through his gut. Out in the fields each day since, where the purity of new fallen snow is quickly smirched by sheep piss, he hears it. Soiled. And as the snow thaws a little and hardens, develops a thin sheen of ice that cracks beneath each step he takes, so his nausea solidifies into something colder; a brittle anger. He has stopped carving love spoons. He has ceased to imagine her hand in his own. He no longer rubs his own fingertips against his lips and pretends them to be hers. She is soiled, and he's well rid of her, so he hoists bales of hay on his back and flings them into the fields. He takes a pick and smashes the ice on the drinking troughs. He sets rat traps in the barn and listens, satisfied, for their cruel snap. He kicks loose stones back into their places in the boundary walls and he splits firewood, swinging the axe like an executioner - good riddance - and then, one day, she comes to him, and his anger contracts into a fist, before melting away into an empty space. It's her, and she is standing before him in the place he splits logs out in the courtyard.

Despite the cold, he has worked himself into a sweat, and has discarded his jerkin and rolled up his shirt sleeves. She is there, and he can't take her in all at once. He stops his work and wipes his brow and is aware only of the impression of her - a long cloak of some soft, dark stuff. A face, changed somehow, thinner and paler, and eyes that have lost something of their light. She says to him, 'Tom, won't you put on something warm? It's bitter.' And her voice seems to be not the voice he remembers, but a quieter one, worn at the edges, the teasing cadences smoothed away. He puts down the axe and leans it against the chopping block. 'Aye,' he says, 'it's bitter.'

They walk to the stable together. Hart's mare whinnies at their arrival and Tom watches as Marianne smoothes the white blaze of the horse's nose and gently pats its neck. It's warmer there, amongst the hay bales and the pungency of dung. 'Why have you come?' he asks her.

'I brought a letter,' she says, 'for Mistress Grace.' She has produced a wizened apple from beneath the folds of her cloak and holds it, flat on her palm, as an offering to the mare. 'Lady Eleanor shows interest in the babe,' he observes flatly, and she shakes her head as the mare nuzzles the apple. 'Not from her,' she says, 'from him. From Sir John.' She stands back from the horse, watching as it crunches the apple to pieces. 'Are we friends, Tom?' she asks. The question unguards him, and he stands silently, staring at the horse. 'Are we?' she asks again, turning to him now, tilting her head a little, searching his face for an answer. He shrugs. 'We were always friends,' he says, but she won't take it as an answer. 'Aye, but are we now?' she asks. 'At the church, you would one time always have a smile for me, and a few words, but I've seen you the last few weeks marching away without a look at me, or hanging back until you see I've gone. What ails you, Tom?' She reaches out a hand to touch his sleeve and he pulls back from her, looks desperately around for something he can do with his hands and, finding nothing, places them on his head. 'You and Alcock,' he says, his tone anguished. 'You and he.' He can utter no more, and he will not look at her. He lowers his hands and pulls a handful of hay from one of the bales stacked behind him, then steps past her to thrust it into the horse's feeding rack.

There's a quiet, broken only by the shifting of hooves. Then she says, 'Alcock courts me Tom, but no more than that.' He grunts, disbelieving her, and hears the echo of Thornbury's thick voice - Alcock has tupped her. He watches the horse pulling wisps of hay from the feeder. 'Whatever you've heard,' Marianne is saying, 'isn't the truth. On my faith Tom, he courts me only. He's working up at the house and I'm charged to bring food and drink to him, and,' she hesitates, 'we walk together, sometimes.'

'And you fancy him?' says Tom, 'you would have him, should he ask?'

'What if I would?' she says, and there's a sharpness in her voice that makes him flinch. 'What if I would, Tom? What is it to you? You're

358

not my Uncle Hart, nor my brother. What care you? What? Am I to stay a servant to the whims of Lady Eleanor and die a spinster?'

'I've work to do,' he says, and he pushes past her towards the half open door, but she grabs his arm and holds him. 'I asked you, are you my friend, Tom? I came to speak with you as such, but,' she loosens her grip on his arm, but her hand remains there, 'if you'll not listen, then what am I to do?'

'Try speaking with Alcock,' he says as he strides towards the door.

Back out in the courtyard he balances a log on to the chopping block and resumes his work, swinging the axe out and behind and up, so its edge falls vertical on the wood, cracking it apart in one blow. He doesn't bid her goodbye or watch her depart along the track that has been worn through the snow until he knows she is far enough away not to hear him pause in his exertions. When he does, finally, look in the direction she has walked, she has already receded from view. He touches his arm in the place her hand gripped it, touching the flesh where her fingers pressed.

CHAPTER X

In which Marianne regrets her indiscretions

The trodden snow is slippy underfoot, but she doesn't slow her pace. On either side of her, the intermittent snowfall of the last few weeks has built into layers that reach almost to her waist. She holds her head high, refusing to look back, and it is only when she reaches a bend in the track, where she knows Tom cannot see her from the house, that she stops and releases the sob that has risen like a bubble in her throat. She steadies herself by placing a hand on the crusted snow bank, but it breaks through, so her fingers close around the delicate pins of snow beneath to form a compact ball of ice, which she throws, ineffectually, at a nearby tree. It misses the target and lands with a soft pock. Damn him.

She had wanted to share things. To tell of the secret works Alcock carries out in the chapel, and of the letter she has only now carried to Mistress Grace, but Tom's words about herself and Alcock - indignation rises in her chest - how can he know? Has Alcock boasted about her in the tavern? Or has one or other of Sir John's servants spied in at a gap in the chapel door to see him touching her in the way he does; each time, a little more intimately; each time, received by herself, she knows, a little more brazenly. A hot shudder passes through her as she continues to walk. She has given herself to Alcock. Several times now. Quick couplings in the dark of the chapel. Has someone seen? No, no, she has always taken care to slide the bolt across the chapel door, and surely Alcock wouldn't tell of his exploits. The tunnel from the chapel is being built discretely, he'd exercise as much discretion about herself, wouldn't he?

She has reached the part of the track that passes Alcock's small cottage and his scrap of land. She knows he is not there. The secret passage he's building from Lady Eleanor's chapel is nearing completion and with just three days remaining until Christmas, Sir John is sure to take some rest from his daily excursions and remain at home awhile, making continued work on the project impossible. She knows Alcock is in the tunnel at this moment, lying on his back in the dark of it, shoring the sides with brick and timber. It's a slim channel, just wide and tall enough for a man to crawl through. She imagines Father Skerrin on his knees, grappling through the dark with the host and the wine, while Lady Eleanor awaits him in the chapel, yearning for the Latin mass to be delivered by a priest with muddied knees and earthworms in his hair. The image makes her smile, yet her own smile troubles her. Is God watching her now? Is he present in the chapel when Alcock fumbles with her clothes, when he whispers his longings in her ear? She looks around herself, at the white landscape, at trees hung heavy with snow, at Alcock's meagre spread. She has never been inside his cottage. She lifts the latch on the gate and pushes it open a little, making a gap just large enough to pass through, then hesitates, turning over her decision before telling herself she is only going to check on the hen coop, to see the birds have not frozen in their nests. With a final glance over her shoulder, she walks lightly towards the cottage door, pushes it open, and steps inside.

It's dark. Too dark to see, and the sudden scuffle and scuttle of a rat startles her. She hovers just inside the door. The only window, glassless, has been boarded up against the cold and as her eyes adjust to the dim, she breathes in the scent of him. She is reminded of the hot sweat stink of him, the salt tang that lines the creases of his skin, but here, in the cottage, that familiar scent lies thicker and cooler than it does on his body, and combines with further smells; the rankness of rotting food, the dank cold rising from the dirt floor. There's something else too, something sharp and fetid, which seems to seethe beneath everything else; the stink of cold piss, which turns her stomach even as she walks further into the room.

One large, square room is all the accommodation offers. There is a plain wooden table at the centre of it, upon which lies an assortment of knives and an oiled whetstone. There is an empty ale flagon, and a basket of bread covered with a stained cloth. The scattering of rat droppings around it shows they have been feasting on it, and there is a metal pail beside the bread, also covered with a cloth. When she lifts the corner of it the stink of rotten meat and vegetables rises solidly and makes her step back, away from it. She knows it is waste, or perhaps a forgotten collection of carcasses and roots for the stock pot, but a sudden image of Alcock flashes through her mind, his head in the pail, a hog gorging on swill, and she is sickened, momentarily, before dismissing the image and turning her attention to the rest of the room.

The fireplace is cold and blackened with a thick fur of soot. A round-bottomed pot hangs above the ashes and she peers beneath the lid to observe Alcock's dinner; a brown murk smelling of turnips. There is little else to see. A shelf runs along the wall above the fireplace, but seems only to be a storage place for flagons and jars. A sack of chicken feed, almost empty, sits beside the door. Where does he sleep? Her eyes, now atoned to the gloom, scan the room and see that a corner of it is hidden behind a curtain. She walks towards it and touches the coarse fabric. He has told her of his bed. How he'll lead her to it one day soon. In the quiet of the chapel, he has painted a picture of smooth linen and feather pillows. 'I'll cradle you in my arms upon that bed,' he has said, in his softer moments. She pulls back the curtain.

The rat leaps for her face, squealing. She screams, raises her arms, and it hits her arm before falling with a squalid thump and skittering crazily out of sight beneath the bed. Her heart pounds in her chest and she's trembling, her panicked mind full of yellow teeth and scaly tail and the tilt of the room as she backs away from the bed, a rumple of woollen blankets on a straw mattress. She runs for the door and yanks it open - escapes outside to catch her breath, but it's the bed she takes with her. The rough wooden frame, the old mattress, torn open so stuffing spills out where the rats have entered to nest, to breed, to squirm over each others' blind bodies. She has heard that rats, deprived of food, will eat their own young, and disgust floods her. We'll take a tumble in my bed, he'd said, and she cannot dissolve the thought; the grotesquery of herself and Alcock in that muddle of rough blankets, the stinking room alive with rats. She breaks into a run towards the gate and slips through it into the channel trodden through the stacked snow. She stumbles along the path, her feet slipping and sliding, until she reaches the leafless copse and stops to gather herself, to calm her own breath and quiet her thoughts beneath the dark limbed trees.

It must end, she decides. She must end things with Alcock.

CHAPTER XI

In which Tom reluctantly attends the Christmas festivities

Evening falls, and his body aches. He eats his bowl of stew at the table and listens in silence to Farley's account of the day; mundane details she habitually shares with him for no other reason than to talk. He learns that the linen is only half washed and dried, but must be done afore Christmas Eve for the Master and Mistress to awaken in clean linen on Christmas morn. The house has been swept and dusted, foodstuffs prepared, new candles made. The Christmas feast at Sir John's house will go ahead as usual, after the church service. The Hart household will attend, as will all the village, all the tenants. He scrapes a last mouthful from his bowl and swallows it down. 'I'll not go this year,' he says. Farley looks at him sharply. 'You'll not?' she says, before a sly smile crawls over her lips, 'You're fearful of seeing her,' she says, 'Marianne,' she says. She takes the bowl and spoon from his hands, 'You've heard it then? She and Alcock? At it like rabbits in springtime.' He glowers at her, but she carries on, witless to his discomfort. 'He'll be stuffing a fat little bun inside her oven 'fore too long. Then Hart'll force a wedding if Alcock don't do the decent thing, and she'll be away from Sir John's in disgrace, dear me, to live in that filthsome hovel of his, a brood o' squalling brats to feed, and how shall she do that when there's him turning money into ale like good Christ Jesus himself turning water to wine?'

'That's blasphemy,' mutters Tom, though he cares not the slightest if Farley damns herself to Hell; she ignores him, shaking her head at the profligacy, but unable to hide a reveling grin. 'And anyway,' he says, surprising himself, even now, at his impulse to jump to Marianne's defence, 'she's not done anything with Alcock.' He recalls her words, and feebly utters them; 'he courts her only.'

Farley laughs, 'Ah boy.' She ruffles his hair and he bats her hand away just as Master Hart descends the stairs from the upper rooms and enters the kitchen, rubbing his hands and making for the fireplace, where he stands, his back to the flames, allowing the warmth to heat his rump. He's in convivial mood; 'Well, do you look forward to the Christmas feast?' he asks.

'Aye,' replies Farley, 'but he'll not go.'

'You'll not, Tom? And why?'

He shrugs, but Farley, for once, comes to his assistance. 'He complains of aches, Master Hart. He'll spend his Christmas abed lest a fever catch him.'

'You look well enough to me, Tom,' says Hart, 'but do as you will. P'raps tomorrow will see you well enough to change your mind. And if not, you'll have company Christmas day at least.'

'He will?' asks Farley

Hart nods. 'The babe's too young for feasting,' he says. 'When Marianne called in earlier, she offered to come tend him an hour or two, so as the Mistress can join the revels.' He turns to stoke the fire, while Farley winks at Tom's darkening scowl. 'Now there, Tom,' she says, 'you shall keep Christmas merrily after all, in the company of your old friend.'

He glares at her. 'I may go, as it is,' he mutters.

He does go. After the services on Christmas morning, he follows the stream of villagers as they make their way to sample Sir John's hospitality. Trestles have been erected in the courtyard that leads down to the snow encrusted gardens, and they are laden with steaming joints of meat from the house kitchens, baskets of fresh bread and bowls of apples. There are platters of cold cuts, and mince pies fashioned to look like tiny cribs. Mulled ale, enriched with cinnamon and spices, is handed out in clay bowls. All eat their fill, and once the ale has warmed them, a few of the men strike up their instruments and begin to play, so that there may be dancing.

Tom moves among the throng. He eats and takes some ale and talks, with people he has known all his life, of inconsequential things. At times, he joins in with the general laughter at the tomfoolery of the dancers as they enact a bawdy tale, and he listens respectfully to an aged farmer as he sings a plaintive song of his youth. But mostly, he sits on the wide stone steps that lead down from the front of the great house, and surveys the scene. The gaggles of girls, clustering in little groups, their hair tied in ribbons and turned out in their cleanest smocks, while the young men look on, coaxing each other to beg a dance. Children run about, tumbling and shrieking and getting beneath the feet of the villagers until their mothers scold them and threaten to cuff them lest they behave more respectfully. Sir John and Lady Eleanor, hosts of the feast, have not appeared, which is usual for them at this annual event and goes unremarked by those in attendance; it's an unspoken truth that it's better for all that they can enjoy their revels from without the watchful eye of their betters. The ale flows, and when the food is almost eaten, more appears. Say what you will about Sir John and his rents, about his long absences, about the delegation of his duties to the priest and to Matthew Hart. Say what you will about the pale severity of his wife, he knows how to keep Christmas with a generous spirit, and so God bless him and let's raise a glass to his name.

'Now Tom,' says Farley, sitting herself heavily beside him. She's wheezing from her exertions in the jig and her breath reeks of meat and ale. 'Won't you choose one of the maids yonder and walk them o'er to the kissing bower rather than sit here alone with a face fit to start drizzling.' He glances over to where she points, but sees only Alcock strutting amongst the females like the cockerel he is, bending to whisper in their ears and grinning at their foolish giggling.

Hart and his wife arrive late, as Mistress Grace had insisted on returning home after the mass to settle her son to sleep before leaving him in the care of Marianne. Hart is filled with bonhomie and cheer, and strides amongst the guests, shaking hands and slapping the broad backs of the menfolk. Tom watches Mistress Grace as she moves beside him, nodding her greetings, but remaining still and reserved. She wears a hooded cloak against the cold, and he's struck by the quiet elegance she displays beside her noisy husband. He has never thought of the mistress as anything other than the mistress, but he sees now, that she's a beauty. Slimly built and dark eyed, with a tumble of curls framing her face beneath the hood. As if in response to his gaze, she turns to look at him where he perches on the steps, and smiles as she makes her way towards him. As she does, Tom's attention is caught by the figure of Alcock, who is watching her from a position he has taken up near the ale casks. His one good eye stares at her intently, his mouth set in a grim line. As Mistress Grace greets Tom and asks if she can sit beside him awhile, Alcock knocks back the ale in his bowl.

'Well, Tom,' says Grace, 'a good spot you've found.' He shifts himself so she can be seated, and asks her how she does. When he glances back at the spot where Alcock stood, he sees it's empty, and that the clay bowl he drank from lies abandoned on the ground.

CHAPTER XII

In which Marianne has an unwelcome visitor

It's as well she's not at the feast. She's glad of it. She has spoken her mind to Alcock, has broken with him, and is grateful for the escape these next few hours bring. The baby sleeps, and Mistress Grace has assured her it's the child's custom this time of day to slumber on for two hours or more. She need only stoke the fire and sit beside the cradle, perhaps sew a little, but she's restless and must walk about the house, through the rooms of her childhood.

The baby sleeps in a woven basket in Grace's private sitting room, off the room she shares with Hart. Marianne looks in and recalls when the carpenter came to build the square bed frame for her uncle's marriage years before. Tom was beside her, and asked, 'What need has the master for such a big bed?' at which the carpenter chuckled. 'He needs a big bed for to fill it with his children,' he told Tom And to Marianne, 'P'raps brothers and sisters for you.' For though all in the village knew Marianne's relationship to Master Hart, most had come to consider her more a daughter to him than a niece. Her status in the house lay above Tom's, that much she knew. While he had nothing but a pallet in the kitchen, she had her own little room, and that's where she stands now. A tiny room, only large enough for a narrow bed and a low cupboard. It will be the boy's room when he's older, but for now it still feels like the room she slept in as a girl. She sits on the edge of the bed, then stretches out upon it.

She remembers almost nothing of the time before she came to live with her uncle Hart. She has tried, before now, to reconstruct her mother's face, but finds it impossible to place the components together. A softness of skin, a red lip, the sense of her own fingers entangled in a tress of hair. Matthew Hart doesn't speak of his younger sister, except to say that she died too young, leaving Marianne as his inconvenient ward. Of her father, she knows nothing at all, and nor does she bear his name. She is Marianne Hart, servant of Lady Eleanor Parry, and entitled to nothing. Though it has never been spoken of in her memory, she knows she was born outside Christian wedlock, probably fathered by a travelling labourer taking his advantage with the wayward Hart girl in a hayfield.

Before coming to live with her uncle she lived with her ailing mother in a tiny cottage at the very outskirts of the village. How they lived, she cannot remember, though there was a tiny garden with vegetables and herbs, and her uncle must have sent them a little money now and then. If she closes her eyes, she can see her mother's thin hands pricking seedlings into the soil, but the memory is disturbed by a noise from somewhere else in the house. The click of a latch being raised and a door swinging upon its hinges before falling shut. She imagines it to be Grace, but on slipping downstairs and entering the kitchen she stops short, frozen by the sight of Alcock standing alone, the bulk of him taking up all the space and a hot scent of sweat and spiced ale emanating from him.

He wipes the sheen from his forehead with the sleeve of his coat. 'Now then, Marianne,' he says, 'I've come to take my due.' She takes a step away but he surges forward and grabs her wrist, twisting it above her head and forcing her against the wall. He pins her there with his body and brings his face so close to hers that his breath feels thick as fur on her cheek. This is her punishment, she thinks, for giving herself to him. For letting him touch her, for listening to his crude imaginings in Lady Eleanor's makeshift chapel, where surely God heard and saw. And here is God's subtle retribution; to turn her from Alcock, to wait until she finds him loathsome, and then to send him to her now, evil intentioned and reckless with drink.

Alcock pushes his body more firmly to hers, grips her more tightly, and emits a dry laugh. 'Oh, I'm not come to force myself on thee,' he says, 'but you'll aid me in something.' His grip loosens a little and she lets herself look on him, at the ruined eye and the rough jut of jaw. 'Aye,' he nods, 'you'll aid me.' He releases her and steps back to observe her gulping at the air for a moment before he turns his head in the way of a half blind man, to look about the room; searching it seems, though for what she cannot guess until he asks it of her directly.

'Where's the child?' he says.

CHAPTER XIII

In which Tom discovers a most terrible happening

They watch the dancing awhile, he and the mistress. Companionably silent save for shared chuckling as an old wife heaves her graceless bulk into the jig, only for her husband, drunk and tottering, to fall flat on his face before her. She says to him at last, 'Tom, I shall leave you awhile,' and he nods and turns to smile; no doubt she wishes to mingle with the guests, but he's arrested by her face, pale and earnest, her eyes dark in their hollows and, it seems to him, seeking him out, searching his own face as one might scan the horizon. 'Mistress,' he says, 'are you well?'

'I must go awhile,' she says, 'and if Master Hart asks for me, you must tell him I'm tired of the revels and am home to the babe and he mustn't come.' She leans close to him and reiterates, her voice gathering itself into a fist of certainty. 'He mustn't come to me, but shall stay and keep Christmas with his friends. You'll say that for me, Tom? You'll do that, won't you?'

'I will,' he promises, 'but,' he wants to ask her again, is she well? Should he fetch Master Hart, or bring her a morsel to eat, but she has stood and is brushing her skirts as she trips lightly up the steps and onto the galleried deck that runs in front of the house. Confused, he glances at the crowds throning the courtyard and spilling into the gardens beyond, and by the time he glances back, Mistress Grace has gone from sight.

It troubles him, but suddenly Farley is before him, grasping at his shirt with her skinny hands and pulling him up and into the crowd, where the younger men are arranging themselves into a shambolic line, opposite an equal number of older women, to dance a roundel. There's much laughing and jesting and ribald cries from the onlookers as the grinning young men fall into step, each taking the hand of a woman old enough to be a mother or grandmother, to lead them skipping down the line. By the end, Tom is red faced and laughing, and he welcomes a flagon of ale pushed into his hand, just as he welcomes the easy chat with boys his own age. Together, they flirt with a crowd of village girls, safe in company, and for once, Tom's glad that Marianne isn't there to leave him tongue-tied and clumsy.

Overhead, the winter sky hardens to lead and darkness creeps upon the revellers, who, thinning in numbers now, build a fire to stave off the encroaching cold. Only once, when he sees Master Hart standing alone, is Tom beset again by the gnawing doubt that clutched at his gut when Mistress Grace peered deep into his eyes. He must tell him, he supposes, that Mistress Hart has gone home. But, if that's the truth of it, then why has Marianne not arrived in her stead? Released from

376

her duty of care for the child, then surely she'd come here. But he recalls that Alcock is not here either, and with a sickening lurch of his stomach he knows the truth of it; that Marianne is together with her lover in that tiny hovel, and Tom has drunk enough ale this night to know he must seek them out. He'll find them, together, and rid himself of his lovesickness once and for all.

Before he knows it, he is stumbling away from the fire-lit revels, and is jogging to the path that will take him past Alcock's mean hut. He'll walk in on them, he thinks, and his head fills with the images of flesh he will see when he yanks the door open to find them there. As the hut hoves into view, he is running, and he doesn't stop until he has stormed through the gate and kicked the door so that it flies open and slams into the wall to reveal nothing. An empty, dark, cheerless room. No Alcock. No Marianne. Just Tom, out of breath, and gulping back shards of cold air just as he gulps back the sudden hot rise of tears.

He walks more evenly on to Hart's farm and even feels gladdened at the flicker of light from a window. Marianne must have stayed with Mistress Grace when she returned. He imagines them seated either side of the fire, cooing over the baby, but on opening the door he finds the large kitchen just as empty of life as Alcock's cottage. A candle is lit on the window sill, and embers glow in the hearth, and there, a rush chair is overturned and lies, broken legged, on the floor. And from somewhere, there's a weird sound, like the keening he remembers hearing near the stones that time, and the hair rises on his neck as he makes his way up the stairs towards it.

He finds them crumpled on the floor of Mistress Grace's bedroom. Two women. The first, Marianne, prone and unmoving. And the second, Mistress Grace, her shuddering sobs rising to a wail as she sees him, runs at him, grasps at his shirt and pulls him further into the room. He falls by Marianne, sees the stickiness of blood through the strands of her hair and connects it at once with the stump of wood, a snapped chair leg, lying beside her.

A knot of grief gathers at his throat as he touches the wound and says her name – is she dead? But then, a soft moan, and a flutter of movement. He stares in disbelief - she is not dead - she is coming back to herself, but he does not see her open her eyes for Grace is tugging at him once again, her face glazed with tears as she drags him to his feet and points, inchoate, to the baby's crib beside her bed. At first he does not understand and looks at his mistress blankly, wanting only to tend Marianne that he might soothe her to wakefulness. Grace stares back at him, and opens her mouth to speak, but once again a sob is all she can utter. He again eyes the crib, letting the dark realization creep up on him.

The baby is not there.

CHAPTER XIV

In which Marianne awakes

First, the shock of it; a twist of pain at the very centre of her head, and a dull thumping that radiates from it and reverberates against the wall of her skull. But that's just the first layer of it - beyond the pain and the ache, a choking, hiccupping chaos of noise; of things being shifted and lifted and knocked aside. She keeps her eyes shut, concentrating fiercely on making it go away; the pain in her head, the sensation that she is shifting and slipping, while points of light flash and sparkle inside her eyelids. She wonders if she's dead and has the sudden sensation that she is in her coffin, that clods of earth are being shoveled upon the wooden lid of it. She swallows, and bile scorches her throat. She should move. She should push the coffin lid up and away from her. She imagines blue sky for a moment before something causes the pain in her head to bulge and throb, and all goes so black again that she feels afraid. Her name. From far above, her name is said. Little more than a whisper, but they are known to her, these syllables, and she knows, too, the voice. She parts her lips to say his name, but her tongue won't shape it and her eyes, weighted with lead, will not open. Still, there's a coming to herself. She must see him, the whisperer - what is his name? He is saying something, a repeated phrase, but it's all underwater, all bubbles and murmurs and she wants to sleep again, to sleep again, but oh, the pain, the pain in her head, and it's louder now, sharper. She recalls his name. 'Tom?' she says, and her eyes flicker open to let the knife of daylight strike at them. Tom stands above her, dear Tom, what's he asking? She tries hard to hear. 'What happened?' Is that what he's asking? 'What happened, Marianne? What happened?'

How should she know?

CHAPTER XV

In which Tom goes in search of the missing infant

He runs. In the fading light he's more shadow than boy. All about him is grey, but in his head, colour; the green of Mistress Grace's dress, the blood mat of Marianne's hair; the silver spoons cast about on the floor and the terrible white of the crib's linen, a crease in the sheet, the slight indentation where the boy's head lay - where is he? Tom runs, though his chest aches and he feels his heart may burst, he runs to find his master, Hart. Hart will know what to do.

At the house the revellers' clamour rises toward the fading sky; they cluster about the braziers, their faces glowing red, their throats oiled with so much drink, and he cannot find Hart, cannot pick him out from the dancers and the drinkers, cannot distinguish his loud laugh from that of other men. He sees what could be the master's good coat there and darts towards it, only for it to be some other coat. Then, Hart's voice from somewhere, ale slurred and pontificating, and he spins around to face it, but it's not Hart - it's Thornbury, or Connett, he cannot tell for in spinning he has set the world off its axis and it's all spinning now; faces and bodies and the sky above him and the ground at his feet - he cries out. 'Hart,' he cries, and again, 'Hart,' though his voice cracks on the name like an egg cracked in a bowl. He feels faint, and as he falls, arms reach out to catch him, to steady him, and the cry goes up for Hart, who pushes his way through to the boy to hear of what has befallen his house, his wife, his son, himself.

And Tom will never make sense of that night. More than a decade later, he will still awaken himself with a stifled cry and sit upright in whatever bed he is in to blink furiously into the darkness; for his dreams have taken that night and made it misshapen, uncertain. He will recall a tumult of noise, of men holding torches, striding out into the snowy fields to search for whoever, or whatever, had come to Hart's house to snatch a child away. He'll recall the greying of the day, and Sir John, arriving on horseback, calling orders to search every path and ditch, every lane and ginnel. And Alcock, a suddenly sober voice, appointing himself as deputy; rallying the men, organising and assigning, sending them outwards from himself like the spokes of a wheel, while Tom stands beside his master, shivering with cold and feeling himself caught on thorns.

He must join the search, he must go back to the farm, he must comfort his master, comfort his mistress, tend to Marianne, but the child - he must find the child. And of a sudden he's running. Running back along the snow bound lane, thronged now with men drunk on ale and excitement, their eyes gleaming in the torchlight, Alcock at their head shouting, 'we'll find him Master Hart, we'll find this villain in our midst.'

Himself, running back down to the house and into the barn where the dogs have set up a howling and a whining. He lets them out, and they circle him, yapping and senseless and no more use than the chickens huddled clucking in the henhouse. But one, the sandy hound, who most often shares his bed, whimpers by the gate that leads out into the pasture and Tom follows his lead, opens the gate and strikes out into the field, where even in the gathering dim, he sees a thin trail, a dimpling in the snow that leads away to the wood. The dog follows it, and Tom follows the dog.

CHAPTER XVI

In which the magpie witnesses the most awful truth

Woods blacken at night. Branches merge with the thick air and while it's winter, and leafless, there's no moon this night, this Christmas night, to help a magpie peer through the twigs and limbs.

The boy runs, knows his path, calls to the hound who trots and snuffles while I hop hop hop along; branches like hands passing me one to another.

They make for the river, and if it were day I'd have made it before him - day gives magpies jewels for eyes, sharp diamond chips seeing every wink, but night-time's clouded black, so I follow the boy and his dog to see what I'll see.

River flows sluggish, in places ice chokes it, but where the dog stops you can hear the gush of it over rocks, you can smell the metal cold of it. The hound whines, cowers at the bank as the boy stares sightlessly; he knows where he is, can smell the cold stink of woodsmoke from the widow's hovel on the far side, but can see nothing. He crouches, listening for some clue, wishes he'd brought a lantern or a brand, and then the clouds part to show the face of the moon, full and white over the cage of branches and all is illuminated, all clear and glistening and he gasps at the wonder - the silvered branches and river reeds, the splash of water, tumbling like coins over rocks obsidian, and there, in a cleft root submerged at the river bank, the shine of something gold, a tiny sun winking back at the moon.

He grasps for it, Magpie-boy, at the thing that shines there, the wet treasure, rounded like a scoop. He grabs it and pulls, but it sticks, and the clouds efface the moon once more so he cannot see, he cannot see the golden thing in his hand, but must trace it's outline, a slim rod, widening out into a bowl - a spoon he understands, tied with string to a sodden weight which he loosens, blind, from the thick root, while the dog whines behind him and the river water numbs his fingers. The men from the village close on him, having followed his tracks in the snow - their torches are wavering yellow tongues, bringing him light and vision as he stumbles back from the river carrying a weight wrapped in sack cloth and tied with string. He walks to them, the offering in his arms, and the moon once more floats free as he lifts a flap of cloth to reveal the babe's face; river swollen, and pale as the moon herself. He falls to his knees in the snow, as the men come with their torches to peer at the child in his arms.

Dead, of course.

I stretch my wings, throw back my head, open my throat, and scream at the sky.

CHAPTER XVII

In which Tom questions Marianne

Christmas day comes and goes. Tom watches as Farley pushes a coin between the child's tender gums and wraps him in the winding sheet. Her tears, heavy and round, drop onto the baby's pale skin as she works. Tom watches them quiver and drip, and he turns his face to the wall.

Mistress Grace will not leave her room to watch her tiny son being laid into the plain wooden box that serves him as a coffin, but when the day of the funeral arrives she comes downstairs, dressed all in black, and she walks beside her husband at the head of the procession. She is blank eyed, while Master Hart, his wind-blown face glazed with tears, carries his only son's coffin in his arms to the churchyard. The whole village follows, heads bowed, sprigs of rosemary in their hatbands. Sir John and Lady Eleanor do not attend the funeral, though they send a man to the farm with a message of condolence and apology - Lady Eleanor is indisposed, he explains, and Sir John feels it better he stay beside his wife.

At the funeral, though, as the parishioners respectfully take steps forward to cast handfuls of earth into the yawning grave, Tom finds himself feeling sick to the stomach, and turning from the crowd he sees a lone figure standing some way off beneath the shadow of some trees. He feels sure it's Sir John, but when he looks a second time, the figure is gone.

Marianne doesn't attend the funeral either, as she's still dizzy from the blow to the head she received that terrible day and she is fuzzled in her thoughts and memories. For the time being, she has taken up residence at the Hart's, in her old, narrow room again. Farley bustles up and down the stairs with jugs of watered ale and soft bread, and each day she applies a poultice of her own concoction to the wound on Marianne's head; gummy boiled roots of comfrey, mashed with yarrow and scabwort.

Marianne falls in and out of sleep, and from time to time, Tom climbs the stairs to sit with her awhile. He stares at her face, peacefully dreaming, and tries to forget the other face that haunts his own dreams and has him waking in the night, sweating and trembling - that of the murdered child, clammy and cold and expressionless in death.

It is on one such evening, as he watches over Marianne by the pale light of a candle, that she wakes. 'Are you well?' he asks, and she smiles gently. 'It hurts sometimes,' she replies, 'and when I've tried to stand, I come over dizzy and like to faint away.'

'Well, best to stay abed,' he says, 'I'll fetch Farley.' He stands to leave but she extends an arm as though she would catch hold of his shirt. 'Nay

Tom, stay awhile with me,' she says. He sits and they are both silent for a while. 'The candlelight is pretty,' says Marianne, 'the shadows it casts.'

'Aye,' says Tom, as they both look at the little, dancing flame. He wants to speak. To ask her about that day and what befell her, and at whose hands. But there's a part of him also that doesn't want to know. A part of him that only wants to sit here beside her, for as long as he can, watching shadows skitter across the walls, across the plain wooden dresser, across her face. Eventually, it's Marianne that speaks. 'Tom,' she says, 'Farley tells that Sir John looks to appoint a constable, to discover the murderer.'

'Aye,' he says. The village has been agog with gossip upon the whole matter, and Farley has apprised him of every development she's gleaned from the market. That Sir John himself has posted notices in the tavern and the church, to the effect that he wishes to recruit an honest man. One who'll aid in revisiting the events of that day to uncover the serpent in their midst. A man who'll lead the investigation, solve the crime, and bring the felon to quick justice. 'It's tomorrow morning it'll be decided,' he tells her. He swallows, his throat drying as he tells her the likely outcome. 'Farley says Harry Alcock has put his name forward, and that Lady Eleanor favours him, and counsels her husband that it must be a man such as he, with the common touch, is best suited to be constable.' Marianne doesn't respond, but continues to stare at the candle flame, her face unreadable. 'Well, I'm sure Sir John will choose the best man,' she says.

'Most like, whomsoever is Constable will want to talk to you first,' says Tom, 'being that he who hurt you is the one they seek as the murderer.'

'Aye,' says Marianne. She pauses before adding, 'though I've no memory of it, Tom. None at all, no matter how many times I'm asked.

'You must recall something,' says Tom. 'Some moment or voice perhaps?' But Marianne doesn't answer. 'I'm tired, Tom,' she says at last. 'You'll leave me now, won't you? It tires me to talk.' He nods. 'I'll bid you good night,' he says, standing, but she has already closed her eyes. It's only when as he leaves the room and turns to close the door softly behind him, that he sees her eyes have opened again to stare at the candle flame, and in its dim light, he sees the sparkle of tears on her cheek.

CHAPTER XVIII

In which Marianne recalls events

She recalls it. Fragmented at first, as ragged as a shredded tapestry in her aching head; the click of the latch as it lifted, the beer scented breath in her face, and him reaching for the chair when she'd blocked his way to the stairway, snapping it like kindling before her eyes. He had thrust the broken leg at her and, when she dodged it, he had pushed past her to make his way upstairs. She had followed him and the sight of his huge, work roughened hands reaching into the cradle made her act. 'Nay, you shan't take him,' she'd cried, and she had rushed at him to snatch at his arm, but the arm had flicked her away like a fly, sending her crashing back against the Harts' bed. Still, she had recovered herself and run at him again to grasp the child from where it lay now, in his broad arm. But he had taken up the chair leg with his free hand and as she came at him, he had brought it crashing down upon her; a crushing blow to the crown of her head, leaving her dizzy and stunned but still conscious, because she recalls the sight of him tucking a spoon into the swaddling before she again stood and reached for the child, now bawling and red-faced. 'Hush now', she had said, 'hush now.' And then?

All blackens.

It was Tom's voice she woke to. 'What happened, Marianne? What happened?' His face a blurred but merciful block against the needles of light. And all around, confusion. The wailing of Mistress Grace, the empty cradle, the fact of Tom's arms around her, propping her into a sitting position, and the heave of sickness rising in her gullet at each bludgeoning throb from the wound on her head. She had closed her eyes again and allowed herself to sink back into the welcoming dark.

Since then, she has curled into the cocoon of her own recovery; the comfort of her childhood bed, and the rough tenderness of Farley as she changes the dressing on her head wound, or brings her bowls of broth and slices of buttered bread. It is easy, amid the dreadful sorrow of little Matthew's death, to pretend a fecklessness of mind. What other response could there be to such terrible violence? And she tells herself, in those hours of feigned sleep, that her amnesia was at first real. On waking, she really couldn't recall what had happened. Just suppose, she considers, that her gradual awakening of memory is just invention? Perhaps it wasn't Alcock at all. Perhaps it was a stranger, over whose murderous face she has simply placed the mask of her former lover. Maybe Alcock is a true innocent after all - an upright, decent man - soon to be the constable, and a worthy father for her child.

Her child.

It is past the time for her bleeding, and she knows it to be true. Her tiredness doesn't come from the healing head wound, and nor does her nausea. A child is quickening in her womb and there is nothing she can do against it. How soon, she wonders, before someone notices the inevitable swell of her belly? She thinks back to Mistress Grace's pregnancy - was it a month or two months before Farley had to begin letting out dresses to accommodate the burgeoning child? She rubs a hand over her, for the time being, flat stomach, and shivers. How shall she tell it? Her uncle, bereaved and desolate, will not stand a child other than his own in the house, and she cannot return to Lady Eleanor in this state of shame. There is only Alcock who can aid her - but can she bear to look on him, knowing what she knows? She buries her face in her pillow and holds her breath, imagines herself dead. How much easier if the blow to her head had simply killed her.

Alcock arrives at the house three days later. He wears a black hat, and a clean shirt with an armband encircling the bulge of his upper left arm. He has been appointed as constable, and is here, he says, to discover the truth. Hart himself leads him about the house and shows him the scene of the crime, while Alcock makes a show of inspecting the door latches, the window frames, the still empty crib, and the broken chair. 'You'll leave us, Master Hart,' he says, when Hart at last opens the door to

Marianne's room. Hart hesitates, but Marianne nods as she pushes herself upright against the bed head, and he reluctantly withdraws. Alcock stands silent for a while, looking around the room and seems, Marianne notes with some surprise, uncertain of himself. 'Won't you sit?' she says, and he looks at her for the first time, his solitary eye glowing fierce beneath its brow. 'Aye,' he says as he looks away and pulls a chair up beside the bed.

They remain in silence for some minutes, broken only by Alcock clearing his throat and fussing over his new attire; straightening the armband and removing the hat, then replacing it when he can find no place to put it down. 'What would you have me tell you?' asks Marianne. She stares ahead, unwilling to look at him. 'Why, whatever you can recall,' he says. 'Your uncle tells that your memory is lost. Is that so?' She turns her head then, sharply, and studies his face. The eye glares back at her, stubborn and indifferent, but edged, she sees, with wariness. He's fearful of her, and of what she knows, and she too is fearful. Of the child in her womb and the future it will bring. Of Alcock himself, and the memory of his powerful right arm bearing down upon her.

She swallows, her throat has become as dry as sand. Her words, when she speaks them, are frost thin. 'I remember it all,' she says. 'I recall it all, Alcock. But the question remains - what am I to do about it?' She doesn't allow her stare to lift from his own - she will battle him, this man who has murdered - she will force him to look away, and when he does just that, as he shifts in his seat and bows his head to stare at the floor between his feet, she says, 'I'm with child, so whatever you must conjure about the boy's death, I will recall it for you. And then you must make a wife of me, for I'll not raise your child alone, Alcock.'

He is, possibly for the first time in his life, without words. 'You're sure of it?' he says at last, and she nods. She hears the guttural slump of his swallow, but still some moments pass before he leans in towards her and his voice comes, suppressed and urgent now. 'There were no intent to harm him, Marianne. I were only to take him and hide him some place, where he'd be discovered with the spoon, but then you came at me and...' She raises her hand to stop him, and he does so, but when he clumsily tries to take her hand into his own, she snatches it back. They stare at one another. 'Why?' she says, at last. 'Why did you try to take him?'

'It were Lady Eleanor's bidding,' he says quietly. 'T'weren't Hart's child at all, but Sir John's. A bastard child, and his mother no more than a whore.'

'Peace,' whispers Marianne, and again, they sink into silence. Can it really be? And of course, she knows the answer. The prying questions Lady Eleanor asked of her about her Uncle's wife, and the letter Sir John bade her carry to Mistress Grace. 'See to it Marianne, that my wife does not

394

learn of this letter,' he had said. 'It is merely a request that Mistress Grace bring the child to visit from time to time, that my wife may see the boy grow.' And a pause then, as he turned his back to her and stared into the fire. 'We lost our own child - it would comfort my wife to know the boy a little, but her pride doesn't permit her to build such a friendship of her own accord.' And of course, she, Marianne, had believed him, and basked in the warmth of his smile as she promised her silence on the matter. While Lady Eleanor must have known all along that the boy was her husband's son, and bade Alcock take him and hide him; a dramatic sign of her knowledge. 'And the spoon?' she asks, 'what's the import of the spoon?'

'It were the Judas spoon I were to leave with him,' Alcock answers, 'she thought Sir John would know her meaning. That he's the Judas, so to speak.'

'Aye,' she says simply. 'But you killed the boy instead of hiding him.'

'What?' says Alcock, with such genuine astonishment that she turns her head sharply to stare at him. He has risen to his feet and glares down on her. 'But, you said you recalled all. Marianne - I didn't kill the child.' She regards him speechlessly, while her thoughts crash about her aching head. Alcock's solitary eye is a fury of horror and disbelief and his face is reddening as he quiets his voice back into a gruff whisper. 'You killed him, Marianne. You killed him.'

CHAPTER XIX

In which the magpie listens to a plan being hatched

Maggoty-pie doesn't need love, doesn't know love, doesn't want love. Maggoty-pie flies alone, finds comfort in the brush of leaf against wing, in the grip of talon on branch, in the soft yolky slither of a sparrow's egg cracked and guzzled; I watch the human birds love, and my bead-eye sees the blue sheen of pain all around them, the dirty yellow of guilt and the dark indigo of despair. Maggoty-pie is black and white. All's simple to me, all's certain in the steady drum of a magpie's tiny heart.

The girl could be a magpie too, for she's a-listening to the one-eyed man, taking in his words and ordering them in her magpie head. He's a schemer, a hatcher of plans, a getter-out-of-trouble kind of bird, and he's cocking his tail feathers and building a nest - all ramshackle lies, all woven with untruths, all stuck with the spit of deceit. He's building her a nest and if she'll sit in it, if she'll settle and brood within it, then it'll hold, this nest. It'll hold against the worst rains and storms, against the fiercest gusts. He'll bring her dainty morsels - the best bits of guts, the wriggliest worms, all shall be hers, if she hold faith with him. But love? No. The girl knows love isn't part of the bargain; the girl knows that the one-eyed man has that one-eye focused fully on what she may one day bring him - her uncle's position, and the land he owns - for the old man has no heir but she, not now his only nestling has fallen featherless to the ground. What choice does she have? The one-eyed man has planted a scheme in her head as sure as he planted an egg in her belly

And she must hatch it.

CHAPTER XX

In which Tom meets Sir John

He studies the spoon. In the aftermath of
the boy's death, it has not been asked for by Hart
or Mistress Grace, and though he knows he must
eventually slot it back into place beside its brothers,
for the moment, it has all but been forgotten. He
has taken to carrying it about with him, tucked into
the pocket of his leather jerkin as he goes about his
daily work. From time to time he reaches for it,
and feels its outline through the rough leather - it
grants him a little comfort to know it is there, as
though the innocence of the dead child is
contained within it. It has become a talisman of
sorts, a harbinger of goodness against the bitter
coldness of truths he yearns to uncover, yet feels
afraid to face. A stolen spoon, dropped with the
child in the burglar's haste to escape? Or perhaps
left intentionally with the body, as an apology for a
hideous crime gone wrong.

Hart has said he cannot believe anyone
would come to his home to kill an innocent for no
reason. The crime, Hart has suggested, is a thief's
work. The killer thought the house empty and was
in the process of stealing the apostle spoons when
he was surprised by the presence of Marianne and
struck her into oblivion. But why take the child
then? Has Hart himself, in his role as Sir John's

manager, made an enemy? A disgruntled tenant displeased with however he has been dealt? Tom watches his master as he sits beside the fire pondering these possibilities; his aging face darkening with anger as much as it whitens with pain. Who would do this to him? Who?

Tom feels sure it is Alcock, but cannot fathom why he would have done it. He recalls the empty drinking bowl at the Christmas feast - where did Alcock go if not to the house to see Marianne? But why would Alcock kill a child? A braggart and a bully he may be, but a murderer? And the spoon - Tom twists it in his hands and examines the tiny figure of the apostle at its hilt. The craftsmanship is detailed and delicate; Judas, perfectly delineated. The figure wears a long robe, and a twist of rope hangs about his neck. 'What did you see?' whispers Tom, but the apostle, eyes downcast, gives no reply.

It is the day after Alcock's visit, that Tom sees Sir John. The snow has begun to melt, and he has herded some goats into the lower field, where they graze on sparse meadow grass now revealing itself in patches beneath the snow. He is studying the rise of the hill beyond the woods, still frozen white, and wondering how soon it will be before he can release the herd to range freely on the moor, when he hears the jangle of a bridle and snaps his head sharply down to see a familiar cloaked figure. He is on horseback, and standing quite still at the edge of the wood beyond the field boundary. Though the man neither waves nor nods a greeting, Tom feels he is being bid, and so walks towards him.

He has aged, Sir John. His beard is untrimmed and flecked with grey. His eyes are lined, the creases tinged red from lack of sleep, or worry. The horse bridles a little at his approach, and Tom reaches out to it, clicking his tongue and letting the horse nuzzle his open palm. 'How do you, Sir John,' he says.

Sir John inclines his head in silent response, but when he speaks, it is to ask after the Harts. How does his master cope with the loss? And the mistress? Mistress Grace? How fares she? Tom answers as best he can, but what is there to say? That his master sits brooding by the fire while the mistress keeps to her room. She is, each day, a little thinner and paler than ever she was before, but will eat little and speaks to no one. 'And Marianne?' asks Sir John, 'Alcock says she remembers nothing.'

'Nothing at all,' says Tom, 'though her head wound is healed, she's sickly yet.'

'Indeed. Well, these things take time,' says Sir John. Tom nods, but he has worried at Marianne's recent descent into illness. Since Alcock's visit, she has become increasingly withdrawn, and speaks sparingly, if at all. She complains of nausea, and prefers to be left alone in her tiny room to read or draw. Alcock has been back once again since his first visit, and he and Marianne spoke behind a closed door in muffled whispers, which even Farley, despite her best efforts, was unable to overhear.

'Give my greetings to your master, Tom,' says Sir John, as he tugs at the horses reins to ride on, but then he pauses a moment, and stills the creature once more. 'You found him, didn't you, Tom? The child?'

'Aye,' says Tom. 'In the stream yonder, near the widow's place.' Sir John nods. 'And, there was no mark on him that you saw, Tom? No wound or bruise or anything to suggest...you know,' he pauses, setting his mouth in a grim line, a struggle to maintain his composure, 'violence on him of any kind?' Tom shakes his head. 'No sir, nothing like that.'

He reaches into his pocket then, for he's a mind to pull out the spoon and proffer it to Sir John, but Sir John is speaking again, and Tom hesitates, uncertain of himself. Days have passed since the murder, and he fears Sir John's anger that he hasn't revealed the spoon to anyone earlier. Besides, he has become used to its presence, the comfort that comes from touching it in his pocket, from running the ball of his thumb against the smooth metal of it. 'And you say you found the lad near the widow's place?' Sir John is asking. Tom nods, and Sir John again tugs at the horse's reins and readies himself to ride on. 'Well, we'll discover who did this,' he says. Now, go about your business, Tom. Good day to you.' Tom steps back from the horse, now skittish and restless to be off, and bows as Sir John takes his leave and canters back the way he came, towards the manor. He watches him until he has disappeared from sight, leaving behind only hoof prints in the thawed mud, and a silence filled only with the soft clatter of goat bells from the field and the melancholy calls of winter rooks from the naked trees.

CHAPTER XXI

In which Marianne considers her position

You killed him, Marianne. You killed him.

She has woken in the night again, all breath caught in her gullet and the heave of sickness in her stomach. She's hot with sweat and bewildered by the darkness closing in on her. The thickness of it seems to push against the walls of her narrow room, seems to crawl over her skin - did she call out again? Last night, she woke to Farley standing over her bed, her face lit yellow in the light cast by a candle stump and her eyes hollow blanks. 'Hush, child,' Farley had said with unaccustomed tenderness, 'what is there to moan and cry over so?'

You killed him, Marianne. You killed him.

In sleep, it has returned to her. Torn into strips and ragged with noise, the moment has returned. Alcock, thrusting the broken chair leg at her, his face contorted and ugly, and then savagely smashing it down upon her. But she had recovered. She had recovered herself and stumbled to grasp the baby from where he lay on the broad stretch of Alcock's arm. She had pulled him close to her, screaming and bawling in his panic, and when Alcock made a grab for him she had tightened her grip, pushing his face into her body and turning away. 'Hush now,' she had said, 'hush now,' and when Alcock grabbed her shoulder to pull her back to him she had wrenched herself free, conscious only of the child and the piercing screams she must quiet - she held him tighter, tighter against herself - until he did quiet and fell limp in her arms. And then. And then...this is the moment that wakes her each night. She loosed her grip on the child, and his head lolled back away from her to reveal his tender face - his innocent, still face. Already dead. Smothered by the crush of her body. A mere soft weight in her arms. She had turned then, horror-struck, to Alcock, and as she turned, he had once more brought the chair leg down upon her, and she had fallen. Fallen deep into blackness with the dead child in her arms.

This is what Alcock told her when he came again to see her. How he had taken the boy and tried to revive him, filling the tiny lungs with air from his own, again and again he had tried, but all for nought. And so what choice did Alcock have? He had taken the child, but rather than hide him where he could easily be found - out in the barn had been his intention, somewhere warm and safe - he had wrapped his body and taken him to the river where he'd be washed away downstream. How was Alcock to know he'd get caught up in a tangle of tree roots? His only thought was to protect Marianne. And now, with his child in her belly, he has all the more reason to protect her, has he not? What would she be? A murderess? Or a blameless wife and mother? 'If you be hanged, Marianne, then there are two dead babes staining your soul.'

What choice does she have?

Alcock has a plan. He has surveyed the place where the child was found. He has discovered footprints in the mud of the river bank, on the opposite side. Who's to say the child wasn't cast into the water there? The old widow - Widow Creeley. She knows the ways of witchcraft. She, with her herbs and medicines, she with her secret ways. Wasn't she seen, a year since, passing through Nathan Manley's pasture and not a week later his best heifer birthed a dead calf? Is it not possible the child was ta'en for some dark practice? A sacrifice for the devil himself? Alcock speaks with such genuine horror, it is as if he believes his own thoughts. Perhaps he does.

And if Alcock can believe it, thinks Marianne, then so can she.

CHAPTER XXII

In which Tom finds something belonging to Mistress Hart

He doesn't return to the farm. He secures the paddock and takes a walk through the woods, following the thaw swollen river until he comes to the crossing place; a simple footbridge made with a slab of stone taken long ago from where the Henge stands. From here, he walks up through the woods and breaks free of them on to the wide, white hillside of the moor. He follows a cattle track until he is in sight of the Henge, and then he cuts off from the track and strikes out toward it, finding a route between the cold tussocks of grass. The ascent steepens, and he feels his muscles ache with each step, his lungs labouring with each deep intake of freezing air.

He recalls his boyhood fear of the Henge and wants to scorn it, yet as he approaches the stones, he can feel it still - more an echo of the fear he once had than a real belief in all those tales of hauntings. He reaches out a hand and rests it on the mottled surface of the nearest stone, rubs his thumb on a patch of verdigris lichen that clings to its rugged face. There's a comfort to be had from standing amongst them, the stones. From allowing a stillness to fill him, a knowledge of silence broken only by the air shifting through the grasses, broken only by the sound of his own breath, his own beating heart. Is this why Mistress Grace came here, he wonders. He thinks of her before the way she is now, before she became broken and childless. He remembers the sight of her figure cutting into the woods as she took her solitary walks; her head covered by the hood of her green cloak, her purposeful step.

He should head back to the farm, he'll be missed by Farley if no one else and she'll chide him for his tardiness and the mud on his shoes, but he has a mind to walk on beyond the Henge a while. From the stones, he can see the gathered hovels of the farm tenants, the low roof of Hart's farm, and the tall chimneys rising from the Parry manor. He turns his back on them and traverses the circle of stones to step out again onto open moorland, where the ground falls slowly away to the dips and mounds of the old burial places. It is the very place he has always feared, where the bones of ancients lie, where no one walks; yet he feels compelled to stand amongst them, the long dead - out of sight of the village and the farm, and with only land and sky about him.

The ground is more difficult to walk on as he nears the mounds, the grass is longer and thicker, and where shadow is cast into the dips between the mounds, the crusted snow remains in wide white patches that crack softly as he steps on to them. He wades through them, the snow reaching his knees in places and coating his gaiters.

It's while he struggles through one of the deeper stretches, that something catches his eye, or rather, a nothing catches his eye; a blankness in the earth, an opening to one of the larger mounds.

He stops to look at it. He is aware, of course, that the burial mounds are long empty of treasures, long ago broken open and disemboweled of anything of worth. It's for that very reason that people believe the dead are unsettled and walk the moor at night, bemoaning their lost riches. The openings to the mounds are long overgrown or filled in, but this one has been cleared a little, and perhaps widened, for it's easily big enough for a man to pass through. Tom swallows, his throat suddenly dry. He has no idea why he doesn't simply walk away, why he doesn't avert his eyes and continue on beyond the burial places and up on to higher ground once more. But he doesn't walk on; he instead makes his way to the mound, studies the entrance for a few moments, and then crawls inside.

It's dark inside, and the ground is wet, but there's enough light from the entrance to see that the interior of the mound widens a few feet ahead, giving him enough room to stand upright. He does so, and finds himself in a long, narrow chamber - wide enough for him to stretch out his arms, but when he does, his fingers brush some small object, making him start and pull back his hand. He peers through the dark, before reaching again and touching it. A candle, almost burned to the stub, is standing in a small alcove that has been cut into the earthen wall, and as his fingers explore further, he finds a small wooden box. He opens it, and inside he finds tinder. He grapples amongst it for the flint and fire-steel, and within a few moments the candle is lit. Tom holds it aloft and surveys the chamber.

There are other candles, and at his feet a brass lantern, which he lights from the candle stub to provide a warm, steady glow. He supposes a vagrant has used the barrow, for a mound of blankets lie at the far end of the chamber and there is an empty wine flagon on the ground, with two cups beside it. He studies these, which are of good quality and decorated with fine paintwork - stolen no doubt, no vagrant would own these. The blankets too, when he looks at them, are brightly coloured and woven with soft wool. On the ground, rush matting has been laid and over it are some small rugs, again of good quality.

He ponders the space around him - a thieves den perhaps? But what thief would hoard only blankets and rugs? A tinker's storehouse? Yet the only tinkers who pass through the village sell cheap linens and cambrics from their old wooden carts, along with pots and pans, and worthless trinkets for a man to buy his sweetheart if he so desires. And so it strikes him - what a man does for his sweetheart. Wouldn't a man in love build a nest for his girl? A private den, softened with rugs and candlelight. He allows himself to imagine what Marianne would make of this place, the delight she would take in it - this place of bones and death become one of romantic prattle and love's deep sighs. He feels suddenly awkward, as though he has walked in on an intimate moment. He should leave, at once, before the lovers arrive and find him here, and it is as he turns to leave, that he sees it, and is shocked into stillness.

There, curled by the entrance to the barrow and unseen by him when he entered, is a soft green cloak. He lifts it, and studies the cut and the cloth of it. It is hooded, and trimmed with soft white fur. At its neck, is a clasp shaped like a hummingbird.

Mistress Grace's cloak.

Chapter XXIII

In which Marianne tells a terrifying tale

If Alcock can believe it, then so can she. The next morning she rises and dresses and goes downstairs to find Farley coddling eggs for Master Hart's breakfast. He is still in his nightshirt, and sits beside the new made fire, idly stoking it. The words are out of her mouth before she has even thought how to form them. 'T'was the widow,' she blurts, 'It came to me in the night, my memory.' She stares at Farley and Master Hart, and they stare back. 'T'was the widow - old Creeley - she came to the house and cast a spell on me - then I know not how to say it, but she took the boy, she took Matthew.'

She feels dizzy, and her vision blurs for a moment as she staggers backward, but Hart is on his feet and catches her roughly by the arm to steady her. 'What's it you say?' he's demanding, 'Say it again, Marianne, what is it you said?' She takes a deep breath, and tries to calm her own breathing, which is fast and ragged. Her face burns, but Hart guides her to a chair and makes her sit. Farley is still staring at her, mouth agape. 'Tell it again,' says Hart, 'slowly now.' And Marianne takes a deep breath and does tell it again, her eyes demurely downcast and her hands folded carefully on her lap.

In the night she woke, and it came to her; she remembers every detail. How the Widow Creeley, with her basket of herbs and dried flowers, tapped on the door and asked for a cup of water. So Marianne invited her inside to sit and rest awhile - she thought her a harmless old woman, after all - anyone would do the same, especially on Christmas Day. So the widow thanked her and sat down at the table, and Marianne poured two cups of water and sat with her to talk of this and that. How did the Widow keep Christmas that day? And what did she have in her basket? At which, the widow pulled a bunch of some unfamiliar herb and plucked some leaves from it. Marianne pauses - she must get this part just right - the widow plucked some leaves and told Marianne that this herb was good for use as a restorative, that when sprinkled into water and drunk, it alleviated tiredness and reduced aches and pains, and then she had crumbled the dried leaves over Marianne's own water cup and bid her drink it, which Marianne, believing no harm could come from the draught, had done.

'And then?' asks Farley, wide eyed.

'And then,' Marianne says, 'I heard sweet Matthew's cry from upstairs, and I stood to go to him, but when I did I felt a great dizziness and I must have fallen, for when I came to I lay upon the floor and I could hear the widow's voice crooning a lullaby to the boy.' She glances from Farley's aghast face to that of Master Hart, and continues her story. 'I raced upstairs, but I still felt dizzy and uncertain in my steps. I entered Mistress Hart's room to see the widow standing o'er the cradle, and her face had changed. I saw she was no longer a sweet old woman, but a very devil, with dark eyes and a wicked grin upon her face.'

Farley cannot contain herself. 'God's truth,' she exclaims, 'I've always known it. She's a witch, that one, versed in the gospel of Satan.'

'Peace,' spits Hart, 'let her speak. How came you to be injured, Marianne?'

'I was coming to that,' says Marianne. 'I saw her reach into the cradle, and I knew not what to do, so I came downstairs again and grasped the first thing I could see - the chair. And I smashed it over the table, here see,' she points at the table as though some mark can be seen there, and though there isn't one, Hart and Farley nod as though they see it clearly. 'I smashed it as hard as I could, and it broke. Then I took the chair leg as a weapon and away upstairs I sped again, for I'd a mind to bar her way and challenge her, but when I got to the room she couldn't be seen.'

'What mean you, she couldn't be seen?' demands Hart. Marianne closes her eyes, and raises a hand to her forehead. 'She couldn't be seen,' she says slowly, 'because the room was black as pitch. As though night had come in the day and blotted out the sun.' She hears Hart's sharp intake of breath, and the rustle of Farley's wide sleeves as she crosses herself. She continues. 'I raised my hand with the chair leg, and when I did so, I saw it weren't in my hand at all. It had been taken from me, by some mysterious means. And then I heard a noise behind me, a low, slithering sound, and I span on my heels to face it, but when I did, I felt the blow land on my head and I fell. Next thing I knew, I was being awoken, and I could not remember how I came to be there.'

'God a mercy,' whispers Hart.

CHAPTER XXIV

In which Tom discovers a secret

He lifts the cloak and studies it. The soft folds of it are damp from the ground and the chill air. A musty scent rises from it. How long has it lain there? He tries to think back - when did he last see Mistress Grace wearing it? He touches the clasp, rubs it with his thumb, and the coloured glass fragments that ornament the hummingbird's wings glitter at him in the winking light. Christmas Day, he thinks. At the feast. She wore the cloak at the feast. He recalls her elegant figure sitting beside him on the wide steps of the house, the way she had gathered the cloak about her against the cold, and the things she said to him. That she was tired of the revels and was away home - home to the babe - isn't that what she'd said? And what's more, that the master should not come, that he must stay and keep Christmas with his friends. And then? And then?

He squeezes his eyes shut and recalls the feast. He had danced, and drunk of the ale, and eaten until darkness had begun to fall - only then had he made his way to Alcock's hovel. And from there to Hart's farm and the terrible sights it contained; Mistress Grace, wailing the absence of her son, and Marianne on the floor, blood spilling from her head.

The truth reveals itself as he handles the cloak, as he shakes it out. Mistress Grace did not go directly home - she arrived at the farm just minutes before he himself had - that's why he entered to find her in such shock and distress. Had she arrived home to find Matthew gone any earlier, then the alarm would have already been raised. She would've run back to the feast. But of course, she was here, in the barrow. As her son was lifted from his cradle, she lay here, in the candlelit dark, with another. With the man who truly fathered her child - he understands it now.

She lay here with Sir John.

He leaves the cloak where he found it, but detaches the clasp to return to Mistress Grace. As he walks back to towards the Henge, he pushes the pieces into place in his head. Sir John's long stay in London - she must have already been with child when he left. He recalls the day of his return, when he'd fallen from the tree and felt the prick of a sword at his cheek. And the walk towards the village, when he had told Sir John of the child's birth just days before - the sudden pause in his steps, and his words when they saw the fox - *a vixen will find her way in* - did he mean Mistress Grace? Is she the vixen? Finding her way to him despite his long absence, mother to his child, does she love him? And he her? And is this why they have continued to meet in secret in the dark barrow of the dead, a place where no one walks.

He ponders the matter. Each day, Mistress Grace donned her cloak and went walking, out beyond the Henge to where her lover had spread rugs upon the ground and lit candles. Where he awaited her with a jug of wine and open arms. Meanwhile, Hart tended to his master's business, and later, rocked the child he believed to be his own son in his arms. And at the Parry Manor, Lady Eleanor had Alcock build her a secret chapel entrance, that the priest may enter to absolve her of her sins as fast as she committed them. He remembers her interest in the baby, and the letters she bid Marianne to carry. She came to know, he realises, that her husband had fathered a living child, so seeking revenge, she hired Alcock to do her bidding, bade him leave the Judas spoon with the child as a secret message to her husband. 'This is the price you must pay,' the spoon will tell him, 'this is the cost of betrayal.' But Sir John has not seen the spoon. No one has seen it but he.

He has arrived at the crest of the hill where the ground descends towards the wood and the throbbing river. He stops to survey the familiar scene - the only vista he has ever known; the tiny cottages and hovels, smoke rising and twisting from their chimneys in grey threads; Hart's farm, squat and snug in its surrounding pasture and beyond, the rooftop of Parry's manor. All so quiet. All so still and at peace. Yet within the walls of those houses, the melancholy of a child's death, the pain of a mother, the cold fury of a woman betrayed.

He pulls the hummingbird clasp from his pocket. If he returns it to Mistress Grace, she'll know, immediately, where he has found it, but no more than that. How can he tell her that he knows the whole truth? That the killer of her son is not only at large, but even acting as constable. He makes his way down through the wood until he can hear the torrent of the river. No, he decides. He shan't go to her straight away. He'll go instead to Sir John - he must show him the spoon and tell him where he found it, so that the truth can be known.

He crosses the river at the stone bridge, and cuts back beyond Hart's pasture. From there, he can circumnavigate the farm entirely without being seen by Hart or Farley, and cut up through the village towards the manor. When he arrives at the village edge, he sees he has come upon a gathering of sorts. A few of the village men are milling about outside the tavern, and are engaged in a discussion, for one of them is gesticulating widely while the others listen and nod their assent. He makes to pass them by, when one of them calls to him - a man named Porritt, who tenants a small strip of land that borders Hart's own. 'Were you there, Tom?' he calls. 'Were you there when she said all?' Tom stops and turns to see the men are gazing at him hopefully. 'No,' he says, 'for I've no notion of what you speak. There when who said all?'

'Why, Marianne,' says Porritt, 'you bide in the same house. Weren't you there when she named the murderer?' Tom feels his skin prickle with sudden cold, and as he cannot think what to speak, he simply shakes his head. 'Out in the fields, were you?' says Porritt, his voice edged with disappointment, 'then you're no clearer than we.'

'Go you home?' one of the other men asks, 'If you do, then you'll find it out quicker than we, for Hart will allow no one past his door until Alcock has spoken with Sir John.' Tongue-tied, Tom simply nods and takes his leave of them, but he doesn't head back to the farm. Instead, he quickens his pace until he is on the path to the Parry manor. If Alcock is already there, then he must tell Sir John all he knows while Alcock stands before him. Then Sir John can take action, there and then, without hesitation.

Tom breaks into a run.

CHAPTER XXV

In which Marianne dreams of Tom

And so it is done. Hart, his baffled face wet with tears, had run to find Alcock asleep on his seamy bed and had shaken him awake to tell him all, and so Alcock has gone to Sir John to report the news, but not before he'd knocked on the tavern door and bid word be spread - the murderer is known, and he seeks a band of worthy men to help him roust the criminal - justice shall be served before the day is out, as sure as he is the constable, to this he swears his oath.

Marianne lies upon her narrow bed, one arm stretched lazily behind her head, the other stroking a hand over the smooth swell of her belly. It will burgeon further, soon, with child, and she is fearful. Of the soft stirring of its limbs within her, of the lie she has told, of Alcock's feigned self-righteousness, and of what the day shall bring. She thinks of the widow - alone in her mean hut beside the river, unaware of the fate that is gathering like dark clouds over the village. Since Alcock left the house, neighbours have rapped upon the door, fawning like beggarly dogs for scraps of news, but Hart has turned them all away. 'You'll know it soon enough,' he tells them. 'Give us peace, I beg of you - you'll know all by day's end. Let Alcock do his work in the proper way, let Sir John make his judgement, and let justice be served beneath the eyes of God.' And so they leave, grumbling impatiently, yet quivering with the excitement of it. In the clatter of kitchens, in the still frozen fields, in the hot of the tavern, the villagers talk and chatter and surmise; the winter air is shot through with a fever and no work will be done that day - they await Alcock. What the devil is keeping him?

Farley comforts the mistress. Marianne can hear her from the room across the hall, her incessant voice like the babbling of doves while the mistress remains silent. She had been expecting to be sent for, to retell her story to Grace herself, but Grace has asked for no one and endures Farley only because it is simpler to let her chatter on than to send her away. Marianne recognises the mistress's listlessness - the emptiness of loss. She has felt it herself since making her pact with Alcock and entwining her future with his own. She stretches her limbs out on the bed, enjoys momentarily the slow ache of sinew and muscle, before closing her eyes and descending into sleep.

She dreams of Tom. She is awakening in Mistress Grace's room again, the crib beside her, and her head is cradled in Tom's arms. No one else is there - the house is quiet and empty, and Tom is smiling down on her. He smells of cut grass and fresh apples, and he strokes her hair and laughs as it tangles in his fingers. From the crib, she hears the soft sigh of a baby as it turns in sleep, and Tom is saying her name and lowering his head to her own. 'Marianne,' he says, and he kisses her - full and bold on the lips, and she kisses him back - deep and soft and warm.

She wakes up, with the kiss still on her lips, and she knows what she must do.

CHAPTER XXVI

In which Tom tries to see Sir John

The manservant won't let him in. Sir John is busy with an important matter and Tom must come back tomorrow. Tom remonstrates - he has a message, he says, from Master Hart. Sir John won't be pleased if he doesn't get the message. 'Then tell it,' says the manservant, a tall, balding man with crooked teeth and a hooked nose. 'I cannot,' says Tom. 'Master Hart bade me let no ear hear it but that of Sir John.' Hook Nose scrutinizes him, but Tom holds his gaze until he sighs and nods. 'Stay there,' he is told. And so he is left alone to wait, for what seems an hour, before Hook Nose returns to say that Sir John cannot see him for he is engaged in important business with Constable Alcock, so Tom must return later with his message. 'But I must speak with him,' insists Tom, feeling ashamed that his voice sounds high and plaintive. Hook Nose shakes his head, and the heavy oaken door is shut in his face.

What now? He could rap again at the door, and have Hook Nose come to box him about the head and throw him off the grounds. He steps back and looks about the house - one of the galleried windows must reveal Sir John's private rooms - he could tap at the glass. But peering in he sees the kitchen staff at their work, and he fears they'll see him creeping about. He drops back, and scuttles the length of the house to find safety in the far reaches of the gardens.

Screened a little by the leafless bushes and trees, he pauses to think. He could skirt the house altogether and find another entrance - perhaps the stableman would allow him access? Or should he simply wait until he sees Alcock leave the house? Sir John may accompany him and he could beg to speak with him then. He feels impotent and tearful, unable to think straight. Would Sir John even listen to him? Would he believe what he has to tell?

He pulls the Judas spoon from his pocket and gazes at it for a while. Telling Sir John what he knows would mean that he, Tom - a scruffy farm boy with no family of his own, with nothing to his name but the shirt on his back - would be facing the Lord of the Manor with an accusation of his own infidelity. Sir John, a man who has looked the Queen of England herself in the eyes. The hopelessness of it all overwhelms him. He has no place here, and really, what proof does he have that Mistress Grace met with Sir John in the funeral mound? Only her discarded cloak. Perhaps she went there alone, simply craving the peace of a lonely place rather than the bustle of the farm, filled always with the noise of Farley's gossiping tongue and the whining of Hart's dogs.

Sir John is a good man, Tom knows. Severe and solemn in his duties. God fearing and respected by all. And he, Tom, has allowed himself to believe that such a man would engage in an infidelity with his manager's wife. He feels suddenly foolish, creeping about Sir John's garden - if he's found he'll be whipped as a trespasser. He ought to go home. Yet, there is still the matter of the child's death. The murderer has been named, Porritt said. What has Marianne recalled? What name has she given?

He's cold, and he slaps his arms about himself and stamps his feet to warm himself - walks a little further back through the bushes where a small area has been cleared - and stamps his feet again to find...what? He looks down at his feet, and tentatively taps a foot again. Beneath it, the ground is solid. Not yielding, as it is elsewhere beneath the thick squelch of dead leaves. He crouches, and scrabbles with his fingers, pushing leaf litter aside to reveal the source of that soft, hollow sound. A square of wood. A trap door in the ground, easily hoisted open with an iron ring that serves as a handle. He looks around, and without thinking too hard about what he's doing, lifts it to reveal a set of crude wooden steps descending into the dark below. A storage chamber, he thinks, for it's not uncommon for people to dig them out - but here? In the gardens to the house?

A noise distracts his attention, and he glances up through the tangled lattice of naked branches to see one of Sir John's servants leaving the house. He doesn't want to be found here, so he slips through the trap door and pulls it closed over his head, before feeling his way down the steps.

He's in a darkness so utter and complete that he's struck with a dread far greater than the fear he felt when crawling into the funeral barrow. At least in there, there was some light from the entrance, and the candles he'd found had diminished his terror, if not the wavering shadows. But here, the darkness is thick and disorientating, it presses in on him, making him nauseous.

His instinct is to scramble back up the steps and throw open the trap door so he can gulp the cold air and be dazzled by the pale winter light, but the darkness somehow paralyses him. What is more, he feels compelled to venture further into it, as though the emptiness before him is inviting him in, softly beseeching that he allow himself be embraced by it, swallowed by it. Stupid, he thinks. If he just walks a few paces he'll come up against the wall of the storage chamber, and wanting to prove this to himself, he takes those few steps, one arm stretched out before him so he can touch the cold earth. But there is no wall, and as he continues to walk, he's aware that the smell of the place isn't just of damp earth, but tinged with the freshness of new wood, recently cut and still exuding it's resinous scent. He's in the tunnel, he realises. Alcock's secret tunnel, newly built and fortified with timbers, and which will lead him into the chapel Marianne has spoken about. And if he can get into the chapel, he thinks, then he can get to Sir John's rooms.

CHAPTER XXVII

In which Marianne is left alone

By noon, Master Hart has been to his wife's room and explained all that Marianne has told him, and Mistress Grace has dressed herself in a soft dove grey dress and is going with her husband to church. 'To pray for Matthew's soul,' says Hart. Mistress Grace, pale and thin, asks Marianne if she would like to come with them, but Marianne shakes her head. 'It's for you and my uncle to pray alone together,' she says, and Grace takes her hand and squeezes it. 'Thank you, Marianne,' she whispers. 'Thank you for remembering,' and Marianne averts her eyes from Grace's tear stained face.

Once they have left together, Farley announces her intention to take a walk. To wander near the tavern, perhaps. She can't conceal the brightness in her eyes, her eagerness to be amongst the villagers on this day of all days, knowing something that they do not - the guilt of Widow Creeley - how shall she contain herself? Marianne hands her her shawl and watches as Farley wraps it about herself. She'll be gone until Alcock returns from Sir John's, until whatever is to be decided is decided. She bids Marianne farewell, and Marianne finds herself alone in her uncle's house. The relief of it almost overwhelms her.

She walks upstairs and dresses, for she is still in her nightgown. She puts on one of the dresses given to her by Lady Eleanor, the one of green velvet, and she unbraids her hair and brushes it smooth, arranging it carefully over her shoulders. Then she sits by the window in her little room and gazes out over the courtyard and the pasture beyond. She does not think too deeply about her intentions, only that the deed must be carried out, and soon.

CHAPTER XXVIII

In which Tom speaks with Lady Eleanor

It doesn't take him long to walk the length of the tunnel, stooping in places where the ceiling brushes his head. At its end, it widens and he can stand at full height. A wooden ladder is tied to the wall, and above it, another trap door is visible, for its edges are softly illuminated by the room into which it opens. The chapel. He takes a deep breath and steadies himself, before ascending the ladder and pushing the door open.

The chapel is empty. He peers around the small space from the trap door, allowing his eyes to adjust to the thin yellow light that creeps timidly from a small window set in the thick stone wall. He takes in the alter, spread with a plain linen cloth; the small but ornate tabernacle elevated on a plinth behind it; a single pew and kneeling mat; a wooden crucifix hanging on the wall; a painted statue of the virgin gazing beatifically at the ceiling, which is cross-beamed and whitewashed. He climbs out from the trap door and closes it softly behind him.

What now? He can feel the rapid pulse of his own heart, and he stands still, breathing deeply to calm himself. At each exhalation, he watches dust motes swirl and eddy in the air. The silence of the chapel is thick and complete, sharply fragranced with the woody musk of holy water and incense. His eyes fall on the door at the far end of the chapel, which will take him into the corridors of the house and to Sir John. It's only a few steps away, but he is too afraid to move - afraid of one of the servants finding him before he can find Sir John, afraid that Sir John will have already left, afraid that he will find Sir John, and that his words will not be believed.

The trap door is just behind him, he can easily scuttle back beneath it and make his way out of the house, out of the gardens, and home. He closes his eyes. He is in a chapel of God. He bows his head, and he prays, allowing the comforting patterns of the Pater Noster to fall in a mumble from his lips. And it is as he prays, eyes squeezed shut, that he hears the latch on the chapel door click. He looks up, startled, to see Lady Eleanor standing before him.

Neither of them move, or speak. His hands are still clasped in prayer, and he lowers them to wipe his sweating palms on his legs. He casts his eyes down at his feet, and tries to stammer a pardon, but his throat has closed over and he feels faint before this tall, slender woman, dressed all in black and as silent as the night, as silent as the dark. He doesn't know what to do with his hands, and holds them awkwardly clenched at his sides. He has never been so close to Lady Eleanor, has only ever spied her from a distance when she has appeared with her husband at the Sunday mass, kneeling at the front pew, her face veiled, as aloof and distant as the moon. He glances up at her; sees the disdain in her cool, blue eyes, and lowers his head again, afraid.

'Who are you?' she says, at last. Her voice is chilly and thin. 'What is your name?' He attempts to speak it, but it comes from his throat as a croak, so he coughs and says it again. 'Tom, Milady. Tom Watkins, as lives with Master Hart.'

'Indeed,' she replies. 'And may I ask how you come to be here, in my private chapel?' Her tone is calm, and measured. If she is angry, or afraid to find a ruffian in her home, she does not show it. Tom thinks fast, in spite of his fear. 'I'm here to speak with Sir John, Milady, he knows me, you see. And I was to wait for him outside but I found a trapdoor, milady, and I was curious to see where it led, and it led me here. Please, I meant no harm by it.'

'It led you here and, what? You felt compelled to pray?

Tom swallows. 'Aye, my ladyship. I beg your pardon, but I felt the need of God's guidance.' He raises his head, and looks her in the eye for a moment, and in that moment, something happens to him. Perhaps it is the coldness of her blue eyes, perhaps it is the faint reflection of himself that he sees in them, but he's aware of a gathering inside himself. A sudden lurch and recovery, as though he has stumbled and found his

432

footing in the same moment and so pauses to take stock before finding his way again, this time with care, with certainty. He meets her gaze again and speaks, more slowly, more coherently than he has before now. 'My master lost his son but a short time ago,' he says. 'You'll know of it, I suppose, milady, and I've something I must show to Sir John. Something as might solve the matter of who took him.' She merely blinks, leisurely, cat-like. He continues. 'I was he that found him, the boy. Matthew. I found him in the river, and he had something about him. Something I put in my pocket and forgot about until now.' He reaches into his jerkin, and pulls out the spoon. 'This, milady,' he says. 'I found this. The Judas spoon.'

She looks at it, expressionless, then looks at Tom. 'And?' she says simply. He takes a deep breath. 'I believe Alcock put it there. I believe Alcock put it there, at your bidding, milady, when he killed the boy.' As he says the words, the gathering in his stomach clenches into a knot, and he feels suddenly winded and sick, but he doesn't let his gaze fall from Lady Eleanor's own.

And then, she smiles. It's almost imperceptible, a mere movement of the lips, just the breeze of a smile over her pale features, without warmth, and gone as soon as it arrives. 'Boy,' she says, 'do you imagine for one moment that it matters?' And that is when he falters, and can no longer look at her. 'Go to my husband if you will,' she says. 'Show him your spoon.' She steps to the side, unblocking his path to the chapel door. 'I came here to pray,' she says, 'you'll leave me now.'

As he opens the chapel door, he turns to look at her once more, but she already kneels at the alter, head bent in prayer.

The corridor from the chapel is long and thin, its walls hung with paintings, but he spares no time to look at them. He walks until the corridor opens out into a wide hallway, with doors leading off from it, and a further corridor that sinks downwards and out of sight. It is as he stands in the hallway, deliberating where to go next, that a door is thrown open - Sir John, trailed by Alcock in a clean white shirt and his constable's armband, strides over the threshold. The sight of Tom halts him, but he says nothing. It is Alcock who questions him, approaching him like a terrier to bark and growl at his presence. What does he there? How did he come to be there? The temerity of him to stand here, in the very hallway of Sir John's home. Alcock grabs him roughly by the arm and twists it behind Tom's back, but Sir John raises his hand. 'Leave him, let the boy speak,' he commands.

'I beg to speak with you a few moments, Sir,' says Tom, as Alcock reluctantly releases his arm. 'Alone,' he adds, glancing at Alcock's reddened face. Over the eyepatch he wears, Alcock's brow lowers and bristles. Sir John stares at him levelly for a few moments, before he allows a slight incline of the head. 'But Sir,' tries Alcock. Sir John silences him with a cold glance. 'I'll meet you at the stables, Alcock,' he says, 'bid my man to ready my horse.' He steps back towards the door of his study and gestures to Tom to walk in ahead of him, and Tom does, his head bowed, his stomach churning.

'Well?' says Sir John. He has closed the door and stands before Tom with his arms folded, his expression a mixture of confusion and annoyance. Tom takes in his surroundings; the softness of a rug beneath his feet, the bright reds and deep blues of an arras hanging on the wall, the crackle of logs in the fire grate. 'I'm sorry, Sir, I meant to give this to you this morning.' He produces the spoon and proffers it. Sir John takes it, and turns it in his hand. When he speaks, it is with puzzlement, 'And?' he says, simply. Tom feels his stomach plummet. The spoon means nothing to Sir John, he realises, and all the meaning Tom has attached to it, the jigsaw of truth he has built around it, fractures in the face of Sir John's incomprehension. Doesn't he see? Can't he see?

When Tom speaks, it is gabble. 'T'was with the babe, Sir - with Matthew when I found him. And I kept it. I forgot it, and then I didn't give it to Master Hart for I found some comfort in it, and I supposed it had just been dropped there, by the thief, but then I was walking - walking up beyond the Henge, this morning - and there's a burial place there - and I found her cloak - Mistress Grace's cloak, and I think, I think that...'

'You think what, boy?' Sir John's question is sharp, as cold as steel, and Tom's breath has run dry, his nerve has failed him. He shrugs, and casts his eyes down to stare ashamedly at his feet. Beneath them, the patterns of the woven rug, the same as the rugs in the burial mound, twist and turn. 'I think that it may have been left there on purpose,' he says quietly. 'As a message, Sir.'

Silence.

When Tom dares to lift his eyes, he sees Sir John staring dumbly at the spoon that lies across his palm. His face is as white as ash. 'It's the Judas spoon,' says Tom, and it's then that Sir John closes his fist about the spoon, and strikes Tom hard across his face, knocking him to the floor.

'You'll leave, Tom,' says Sir John. 'You'll get up and go back to Master Hart's house, and you'll say nothing of this. Nothing at all.' Tom is dizzy from the blow, his eyes wet from the shock of it and his cheekbone bruised and throbbing. He is too afraid to speak. 'You're wrong,' says Sir John. 'Whatever you think is true, is not. The murderer has been named and justice will be served today. This very day, d'you hear me?'

Tom nods, for what choice does he have? Sir John strides from the room, slamming the door behind him, and in his head, Tom hears the echo of Lady Eleanor's words; *do you imagine for one moment that it matters?* He rests his head into the

436

soft wool of the rug. Of course not. Of course it doesn't matter. The truth has no place here, and neither it, nor he, matter one piece.

CHAPTER XXIX

In which Marianne awaits Tom and tells him the truth

She awaits him at the narrow casement window of her room. She will see him from here as he approaches the house along the track that skirts the pasture. She sits with her hands folded upon her lap, the fingers dovetailing until she parts them to smooth her dress, or to tuck stray tendrils of hair back into place. She hums soft catches of a song to herself as she watches. As she waits.

The daylight has almost passed. The fields, the woods beyond, are veiled in a pall of winter twilight that drains the landscape of colour. There is quiet, broken only by the occasional muffled croaks of rooks as they wing to their roosts. He must come soon. She'll watch him as he approaches along the track to where it widens before the gated entrance to the yard, and then she'll slip downstairs and greet him as he enters the kitchen. He'll be cold, and tired from his work, and she will take his hand and lead him here, to this little room in the empty house. She won't need words.

She doesn't allow herself to think of what may be happening in the village. Her uncle and Mistress Grace, she feels certain, will go there after paying their devotions at church, to join Farley and the womenfolk, wrapped in their winter shawls. Hart will stand apart, perhaps with the men, or perhaps even beside Sir John as the sentence is read. They will watch justice being served as Father Skerrin leads all in prayer, and then it will be done. It will be over, and she, Marianne, will have other news to tell of herself.

She smiles as she sees the slim figure of Tom cresting the horizon. 'My love,' she whispers, as he walks ever closer to her, becoming more distinct, more real, with each slow step he takes. 'My love,' she says again, louder this time, to fill the quiet, to give the words meaning. His head is bowed. He's tired, she believes, for he has been at his work in the fields since morning. He knows nothing yet of what has transpired this day. She shall tell him all - of her memory returning, of Widow Creeley's spell on her and how she broke it through prayer. She shall tell him all once he lies in her arms on the narrow bed, once their love has been declared and consummated. For love her, he must. Has he not always loved her?

He is lifting the latch on the gate. She must go to him.

The kitchen is warm as he enters, for Marianne banked the fire with logs before taking up her vigil, and they glow red and hot now against the bars of the grate. She enters to see him caressing the ears of the biggest of Hart's dogs as it pads around him, and he doesn't notice her as he stands up straight to remove his jerkin. She says his name, softly, and he only glances at her before turning his attention again to the dog. 'Where's Farley?' he asks only, but she has seen the raised blue of his cheekbone where Sir John struck him, and doesn't answer his question. 'Why Tom, what did you here?' she asks as she steps toward him and gently reaches a hand to his face. He jerks back from her touch, for the bruise stings. 'I fell,' he says, 'I hit it upon a tree stump.' And he turns away from her, for he feels ashamed and broken and sad, and must stop his eyes from filling with tears. He steadies his voice. 'Where's Farley?' he asks again, 'And Master Hart?'

This isn't how she had imagined it. She had imagined that she would wordlessly take him by the hand and lead him upstairs - that he would simply know, and follow her. But he seems agitated, and is avoiding looking at her by instead petting the damned dog. 'They're at the tavern,' she says, 'or will be by now. Tom, I've recalled that day, I know who took Matthew and I have told all.'

He meets her gaze, but only stares at her.

It was Widow Creeley,' she says earnestly. 'She came here and cast a spell on me, and beat me, and she took Matthew.'

There's a pocket of noiselessness. Tom stands perfectly still, staring uncomprehendingly, directly into her eyes. She gazes back, perplexed, unable to read him. She extends a hand and takes his own in hers, lifting it to her lips to kiss the knuckles, but he snatches it away, as though burned. 'Is that true, Marianne?' he says at last, and his voice seems deeper than usual, firmer and more solid, as though the words are carved from rock. 'Is that really true?' he says, 'or are you protecting him?'

'No,' she responds, too quickly, 'no, I...' and she falters and turns her face away.

'The widow's no witch,' Tom continues. 'Alcock took the child. You know that, don't you Marianne? Lady Eleanor bid him take Matthew, for he's Sir John's son, and she couldn't countenance his bastard on her lands.'

Marianne is shaking her head but Tom steps forward and grips her by the arm, roughly turning her to face him, but she won't meet his eyes. 'She bid Alcock take him, and kill him, as a sign to her husband that she knew all, isn't that right, Marianne? Isn't that so? Didn't you tell me yourself that you carried letters between Mistress Grace and Sir John?' He has her by both arms now, and shakes her, but she will not look at him. 'And you invent this tale to protect Alcock because he's your lover. A child killer, Marianne! You'd accuse an old woman to protect a man such as he?'

'Leave go of me,' she cries, for his grip is crushing her, but he will not. 'How can you Marianne? How can you do this?'

She breaks.

'He didn't kill Matthew,' she says. 'I killed him, Tom. I killed him.'

441

CHAPTER XXX

In which Tom makes a decision

As she talks, he can barely hear her voice over the buzzing of his own head. She sits on a chair at the table, rubbing one of her arms where he took hold of her. She talks, her eyes brimming with tears, her voice trembling. She tells all as it happened, and she tells him of the child in her womb, and she begs him to say nothing, but to be her friend still, her truest friend, her only friend. 'As God is my witness, Tom,' she says, 'there was no intent to harm him. It just happened. It happened, and what would you have me do?'

He doesn't reply, for what can he say? That she should take the fall instead of an old woman near the end of her life? And as he thinks it, he sees the old widow; stooped and weathered, collecting water from the stream, solitary and harmless. 'But if you explain,' he tries, 'that it was an accident, and that Alcock only tried to help. Hart won't see you hang. What, his own niece?'

Marianne shakes her head. 'It's too late, Tom. Why, the widow may already be dead. Isn't it better if Hart believes Matthew's murderer has already been punished than to have her death on his conscience.'

'What do you mean she may already be dead?' he asks. 'If she's accused then there'll be a trial. Marianne, you can stop this if you tell the truth.' But even as he says the words, he recalls what Lady Eleanor said to him in the shadowed chapel; *do you imagine for one moment that it matters?* No. The Parry reputation has more value than the life of a tired old woman. Of course the truth won't matter, and yet, and yet... surely it must be known? Even if refuted, it must have a place.

Marianne is speaking. 'Let her be taken, Tom - she's near the end of her life anyway, and I have another, growing inside of me. She pauses. 'If you love me, Tom, then you'll let things be.' She moves towards him. 'As I love you, Tom. As I have always loved you.' She takes another step, and stands, perfectly still, before him, so close that he catches a faint scent of her - clean linen with that faint redolence of apples, and beneath it, the dizzying fragrance of her skin. 'I've no wish to marry Alcock,' she says. 'It was always you, Tom. Always.' And she leans towards him and gently presses her lips to his. He feels their touch; soft, warm and yielding against his own, and he kisses her back, tentatively, afraid of this long imagined newness. He kisses her and he feels her arms encircling him, her hands upon his back as her lips part, surprising him into opening his eyes and seeing her face, her own eyes closed, the lashes long and delicate. He kisses her as a drowning man might gulp in the air, he kisses her with all of his being, as a man in love might kiss. Her breath is sweet and hot as she murmurs in his ear. 'Come with me, Tom,' she whispers, as she steps back from him, takes his hand in her own, and leads him to the stairs.

But he stops, and pulls his hand from hers.

'I cannot, Marianne,' he says. 'I cannot.' And he walks to the door, lifts the latch, and steps out into the cold.

CHAPTER XXXI

In which the magpie wins, and loses, his prize

Dusk, and the one-eyed man lifts a flagon to slake his dry throat, wipes froth from his lip, and calls to those gathered there. I perch on the tavern sign and watch them flock about him. These menfolk, they crane their necks and honk like geese at his words; their breaths reek of ale and there's anger in their eyes, but not at the one-eyed man - no, it is his words that plump their plumes, his words that have them squawking. I watch them unfurl into the grey air, these words - they are pronged and talon sharp, they have the scimitar curve of a hawk's bill, and they goad the men into flapping their feathers and flexing their wings - they will strike, these men, they will strike.

They light torches, and arm themselves - with rope, and axes, and knives, before taking flight through the waning light and finding their prey. With a raucous cry they are off, the one-eyed man at the fore of this vicious skein. Where will they alight? I take off from my perch, leaving it creaking softly in the breeze, and flap flap flap high above. From here the men seem ants; mere specks of wavering light, and meaningless in the vast darks of wood and moor. I turn into the wind and glide, circling this hotch-potch of huts and houses - there are other things to see beyond such craven ferocity.

I slide down the smooth air to the biggest nest of all, many windowed and curtained and lined with soft things. My claws clutch the window frame and I peer inside.

He is speaking to her. She sits by the fire, head bowed, while he shows her the spoon, while he throws it at her feet and screams his rage. But she, calm as a swan, merely lifts it and gazes upon the figure carved there. A little man. They are all little men, thinks Maggoty-pie, as the woman hands the spoon to her husband and stands, proud and disdainful, before him. And then there's a clash and a clatter, because he hurls it aside, at me, though not at me, but through the window-pane, which shatters and has me flap-flapping to a tree branch. There it lies, a-twinkling on the grass, good pickings for a magpie, so I flutter down and hop-hop between the sparkling glass shards to grip it tight in my beak. Little man-spoon is heavy but bright, and I clamber back into the air with my prize.

Beneath, the goose-men circle more like buzzards than geese - they have found their prey. Old, grey, withered as tree limbs, and they have tied her hands and pull her like a dog to the pyre they have built. There's a sorrowing in her call, so plaintive that even Maggoty-pie must stop to listen, my prize clamped in my bill. I stop to listen, and to see, and had I tears in these cold bead eyes, they

446

would catch the rising moon and sparkle same as the spoon at the woman's calling. They tie her to a post, and about her feet they build a nest of twigs and branches. And I see him then - the boy - running toward them, and shouting out a word, but they can't hear, the goose-men, for they're squawking and a-flapping and there's such a clamour, such a goose-stink, that they'll pay no heed even if they do hear. They've nested the old woman and with a cry the one-eyed man lifts a fire brand and strides toward her. The boy is running still, and he calls out his words, but he stumbles and falls face flat in the mud, and by the time he lifts his eyes and himself, the fire has been lit and is catching fast. He runs at the flock and they push him back, honking and squawking and mad with fire. He can only watch, his face wet with tears, as the old woman sinks into the flames, melts sure as wax in the heat and smoke of it. He can only watch, but chooses not to.

Poor boy.

He walks away into the wood, choking on his sobs and blind with impotence and rage and sadness. I spy him from my perch, watch him walk beneath the limb on which I cling. He leans his head against the rough of the tree trunk. Sad boy. I sidle along the branch, peering down upon him, and thoughtless for a moment, I open my throat to soothe him. I part my beak to let soft sounds bubble, and I drop the spoon, so the soft sound becomes a *skrawk* as I watch my prize tumble to the ground beside him. How foolish to sorrow for these human birds. I curse, and chuckle my rage as the boy stares at the spoon beside him, looks up at me, and back to the spoon. P'raps he'll leave be?

But he doesn't. He plucks it up with his finger beak and tucks it into his dull plumage, and Maggoty-pie loses his prize.

Damn these human birds.

CHAPTER XXXII

In which Tom proffers a gift to Marianne

He has walked to Plymouth. He left early the previous morning, with a handshake from Master Hart, and tears from Farley. Mistress Grace stayed abed, as she always does these days. Even now, some months after the death of the widow and with Spring budding the trees, he does not know if she understands why her son died, and he has chosen not to speak of what he knows with anyone. Let Lady Eleanor offer up her cold prayers, let Marianne raise a brood of Alcock's children, let Sir John seek out another mistress to warm his bed; Tom has no place amongst them anymore.

After the burning, he continued for a while. Working the farm each day from before light until the fall of evening drove him home to eat and fall into his bed. He tries not to see the tiny moon of the child's dead face in his arms, he tries not to hear the widow's cries as the flames engulf her, he tries not to feel anything at all.

Sir John came to him in the fields one day after the thaw; one of those days when the weak sunlight would occasionally thread its way through the scudding clouds for long enough that he could turn his face toward it and feel its apricity, like a blessing, upon his face. The ground was not dry, and churned from the hooves of goats milling about and tearing at the first shoots of grass. It was Sir John's boots that Tom noticed first, mudded and worn. He nodded a greeting, and continued with repairing the goat pen that had rotted through the winter. Sir John waited, his arms folded, as Tom nailed fresh wood across the posts. 'I know what you think of me, Tom,' he said, at last. Tom didn't reply, and took a fresh length of timber from the pile at his feet. 'A man has a duty to his wife,' said Sir John. 'One day, when you're married, you'll understand that.'

Tom took a nail from his pocket, and began to hammer it home. 'As you say, Sir,' he said. Sir John continued to watch him at his work, and Tom methodically took fresh timber and nailed it into place, until the pen was repaired. A few goats ambled over to stare at Sir John. One of them, playfully, butted his leg.

'I'd like to do something for you, Tom,' said Sir John. 'I have written a letter for you, a recommendation - you can do with it as you will.' From beneath his cloak he pulled out a rolled piece of parchment tied with a plain black ribbon. Tom looked at Sir John, and the letter held out toward him in the gloved hand. He wiped his own hands on his shirt. 'And what would you have me give you in return?' he asked. Sir John shook his head. 'Nothing, Tom.' But they both know that the letter is a bargaining chip. As long as Tom remains on Hart's farm, Sir John must be reminded of his sins. He has lain with another man's wife and fathered a bastard child. He has allowed a woman to burn on a false charge of murder. He has placed his name and reputation above that of the truth, and he has forgiven his wife for her part in a child's death; his own child's death.

Tom reached into his pocket, where the Judas spoon nestled amongst spare nails, and drew it out, proffering it to Sir John. 'I came across this again,' he said, 'it fell at my feet from the beak of a magpie.' Sir John stared at the spoon as though Tom had drawn a knife against him. 'Keep it,' he said at last. 'And take this letter, whether you use it or not.' Tom nodded, and took the rolled parchment. Sir John turned, and walked back the way he had come.

Now, four weeks later, Tom wanders the narrow, twisting lanes of the Barbican where they writhe higgledy-piggledy beyond the wide harbour of the city. Gin soaked beggar woman, clutching babes disguised as mere bundles of rags, reach out to him pleading alms. Sailors on leave from their ships laugh uproariously in the taverns. Cheap women wink at him from corners. The cobbles beneath his feet are slick with fish guts and piss, and everywhere, there is the stink of the sea. He is wearing a good cloak, given to him by Master Hart as a parting gift, and in his pocket, a handful of coppers and the letter from Sir John. He no longer has the spoon.

The spoon no longer exists.

Two weeks before leaving, he had travelled, for the last time, to Exeter with Master Hart, who had tipped him a penny and bid him find some dinner while he negotiated some purchases with a merchant there. Tom sought out a silversmith in a tiny shop and handed him the spoon. 'I've no money to pay for it,' he explained, 'but you can clip away some of the silver as payment. The silversmith, bemused by this scruffy farm boy in his workshop, and having had a quiet day, agreed to his request, and allowed Tom to sit and watch as he melted the spoon in a crucible, and poured the molten silver into a mould to cool. Once solid enough, he plunged it into water, which fizzed and bubbled around the shape, then set about filing off the rough edges until it was complete. 'Not the finest workmanship,' the silversmith admitted. 'If you'd give me a day or two I could polish it to perfection.' But Tom had to get back, he couldn't wait that long, and the silversmith shrugged and placed it into his waiting hand. Tom smoothed his thumb against the metal, feeling the tiny imperfections and fissures, feeling the tiny heft of it in his hand. A crucifix. He thanked the silversmith, and left.

When he at last plucked up the courage to visit Marianne, he was glad to find her alone at Alcock's cottage. She had married him soon after the widow's death, and her belly was full and rounded now. 'I hope you're well,' he'd said to her, when she had invited him inside to sit at the now scrubbed table. 'I'm as you see,' she said. Tom saw tired eyes, dulled in the dim room, and hands reddened with housework. He told her his plan, to use Sir John's letter to find a place on a ship, and to learn the ways of the sea. 'I hope to see something of the world,' he told her. 'I know how to work hard, and I'll save my wages and put them to good use one day.'

'I wish you well, Tom,' was all she said. As he rose to leave, he placed the crucifix in her hand and turned away before he could see her response. He would never see her again.

Drake's ship is in the harbour and though he has to wait an hour or more before the captain will speak with him, his letter is successful. 'You'll start at the bottom,' he's told. 'You'll scrub decks and empty shit pots until you're ready to learn more.' Tom doesn't care; he'll do anything he's asked. 'Nursing a broken heart, are you boy?' says one of the men, 'that's the only reason any lad signs up as cabin boy,' and he laughs at Tom's blush and slaps him hard on the shoulder. 'C'mon boy,' he says, not unkindly, 'give a hand rolling these barrels below decks - we set sail with the evening tide. Let's go on an adventure.'

The End

Acknowledgements

My thanks to Lytton Smith for his guidance and advice in the early stages of completing the manuscript, and to Carmen Henderson, Jamie Edgecumbe and Alexandra Stopford for their feedback and encouragement. Thanks also to William Telford, Kenny Knight, Ben Serpell and all at the Athenaeum Writers' Group for their feedback and support. Especial thanks go to my family and friends for their invaluable encouragement and enthusiasm, particularly Jean Robinson, Rebecca Cohen, Rachel Smith, Tor Kelly and Jess Holloway.

Printed in Great Britain
by Amazon